JAKE: BOOK ONE

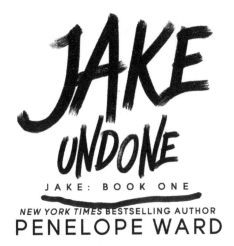

JAKE: BOOK ONE

NEW YORK TIMES BESTSELLING AUTHOR
PENELOPE WARD

Formatting by Elaine York, Allusion Publishing
www.allusionpublishing.com
Cover by RBA Designs
Cover Photography by PaperbackModel (PBM)

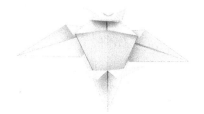

PROLOGUE

JAKE

She loved to pull on my lip ring. It was her favorite thing to do.

"Ow...that's a little too hard, baby," I said. "You're nothin' but trouble, you know that?"

She apparently didn't like that comment because then she scratched me in the face.

"Damn it, girl! Those nails are like claws."

She pulled my lip again and started laughing this time.

I loved her laugh.

I smiled and shook my head. "That's it. I'm done with you."

She laughed even harder, and it was infectious because now I was laughing too.

"You're so cute. You know I could never be done with you, right?"

I hugged her hard and then lifted her up as the smell of shit wafted through the air.

"Aw, hell, girl. What did your mother feed you this morning?"

My niece started giggling again, as if she understood me. That belly laugh was music to my ears. Holly was only six months, but I swore she understood everything I said. I reached over for a diaper and some wipes and began to unwrap the load.

"Oooh, so whatever you had, it was green. Nice."

Just then, the phone rang, and I could see from the caller i.d. that it was Alex, one of my engineering study partners. Why the hell was he calling?

I held up my hands. "Stay there, Holly. Don't move," I said, grabbing the cordless phone. "Yo."

"Jake, dude, where the hell are you?"

"I'm home watching my sister's kid. What's up?"

"Did you forget Professor Sarma moved the exam to this morning?"

I scratched my head. "No, he didn't. He moved it to Tuesday."

"Today *is* Tuesday."

The realization that he was right set in. "Oh, crap!"

My sister, Allison, had switched the babysitting day on me this week, and it screwed me all up.

"Fuck!" I yelled into the phone.

"You can still make it here in time if you hurry," Alex said.

Before I had a chance to respond, I looked over at Holly on the couch and saw that she had managed to touch her ass and get poop all over her fingers.

"Code brown, Alex. I gotta go." I hung up the phone and rushed over to the baby who was still smiling at me, happier than a pig in shit.

"Okay, sweet pea. That was Uncle Jake's fault. We are gonna get you clean and then hightail it outta here. I can still make the last half hour of the exam if we hurry."

Holly squealed in delight amidst the chaos.

I took her over to the sink, holding her with one hand as I used the other to spray her hands and bottom vigorously with the nozzle, adding some dishwashing liquid. That mess was too far gone for baby wipes.

Once cleaned and smelling like Palmolive, I bundled her up and propped her on my chest in the carrier my sister left me, grabbed the diaper bag and ran out the door.

Holly bounced up and down, as I ran down the street to the train station.

We boarded the train, and the looks and reactions I got from the yuppie passengers were typical. I could imagine what they were thinking: *Who is this tattooed, pierced bastard wearing all black carrying a little innocent peanut in a baby carrier?*

I envisioned Amber Alerts being called into the Boston police. They looked at me as if I was going to friggin' jump them with this baby on my chest. Those judgmental people always made me laugh, though.

The train suddenly stopped. The conductor announced that there was a small mechanical issue being worked on and that we would be moving in a few minutes.

Ten minutes and one bottle of formula later, the train started moving again.

I had totally screwed today up. If I were lucky, I would catch the professor at the end of the exam and play the sympathy card with Holly in tow.

When we got to Ruggles station, it was pouring out. I grabbed a plastic Walmart bag out of the black tote and put it on top of Holly's head like a hat, careful not to cover her face.

Running through puddles, we finally made it to the building. When I entered the classroom, it was a ghost town. Professor Sarma was gone. I had missed the entire exam and couldn't even plead my case.

Fuck.

We made our way back outside, and it was now raining cats and dogs.

Holly was giggling again and started to hiccup.

I adjusted the plastic bag away from her face. "What are you laughing at? Huh?"

I looked up and saw that Holly was staring straight ahead at a girl who was spinning around and dancing in the rain. Everyone else around us was running for cover, but this girl was staring up at the sky, letting the water pour down on her and relishing every moment of it. She certainly didn't seem to care who was looking at her.

After a few minutes of watching this in amazement, we walked slowly toward her. The closer we got, the more excited Holly became, flailing her arms and legs in the carrier.

She was probably a Northeastern student and looked about seventeen or eighteen, around my age. She was wearing a long flowing skirt that spun around with her and had red curly hair cascading down her back. She was pretty damn cute.

Her eyes were closed now as she lifted her head and opened her mouth to drink some of the falling rain. She didn't notice me as I stood there taking in the sight of her. She twirled around again reaching her arms out to slap the raindrops.

"Hey," I finally said.

The girl stopped short, looking startled, opened her eyes and smiled. "Oh...Hey."

"Do you always dance in the rain like that?"

She glanced down at Holly. "Do you always pick up babies at Walmart?"

I laughed and shook my head. "I'm Jake," I said holding out my hand.

She didn't extend hers, but smiled. "Jake, is that your baby?"

"Nah, it's my niece. She has a twin sister who's with their grandmother, but this one prefers me, so I take her a couple of mornings a week. We hang so my sister can get stuff done."

Holly was reaching her fat little hand out, and the girl took it. She smelled like patchouli and whispered something to Holly then stared back at me, but said nothing.

I wasn't entirely sure *why* I was still standing there, but there was something very intriguing about her. A guitar case was lying on the ground a few feet away, and it made me wonder if she played or studied music. I was just enjoying living in the moment with her under the falling rain.

Finally, she looked down at my arms and said, "I like your tattoos. They're hot."

"Thanks. You're pretty hot yourself," I said.

"You don't strike me as the babysitting type, Jake."

"Yeah, well, things aren't always what they seem on the surface."

I had no idea back then how prophetic that statement would become...when it came to *her*.

There was a rumble of thunder in the distance, and she finally cracked a smile. Then, came the three words that would change my life. "Hi, I'm Ivy."

ONE

NINA

SIX YEARS LATER

"**W**elcome to Brooklyn," my driver, Reza, said as he helped me out of the yellow cab. He took my bags out of the trunk, and I handed him a tip.

"Thanks. It was nice chatting," I said before watching him drive away, leaving me alone to face my new life.

I wasn't quite ready for it to begin, so I stood on the sidewalk staring up at the aging building that was now home as cars on the busy street sped by.

The apartment I'd be living in with three roommates sat atop a Greek restaurant called Eleni's, and the smell of lemon, garlic and grilling chicken saturated the air outside.

This neighborhood was nothing like the small rural town where I was from, upstate in the Hudson Valley. Seriously, this could be an episode of MTV's *The Real World*: *Country bumpkin afraid of trains and crowds moves to New York. Let's chronicle her trials and tribulations and watch in amusement as the big city swallows her up whole and spits her out.*

The vibe was different here, and I could immediately tell there would be loads of culture. The area seemed cosmopolitan and small townish at the same time and reminded me of movies like *Goodfellas*. I got chills because even though it scared the daylights out of me, it had always been my dream to live near Manhattan. Brooklyn was as close as I was gonna get.

It was the middle of the afternoon, so I was pretty sure my roommates, whom I hadn't even met yet, would be working. I wanted to take the time to get acclimated to the apartment alone, maybe take a bath.

I'd be living with my childhood friend Ryan and two other people: a guy and a girl whose names I didn't even know. When I was accepted into Long Island University's nursing program at the Brooklyn campus, I immediately contacted Ryan to see if he could help me find an apartment. It just so happened that one of his roommates had recently moved out, so the timing was perfect.

The steps creaked as I made my way upstairs. The faint sound of a woman swearing when I passed by the second floor made me wonder about the neighbors.

Our apartment was on the third floor, and I struggled with the key before slowly opening the door, which lead right into the main living area.

It was nicer than I had expected. There was a small kitchen off to the left, and everything was open concept. I looked around and noticed how homey the living room was, with a brown suede sectional and a multi-colored, knitted throw on top that looked like someone's grandmother had made it. There was a brick wall that added character and built-in bookshelves on the other side of the room next to a large window with a reading nook that let in generous sunlight. The apartment smelled like coffee, and there was some leftover in a pot on the kitchen counter. It felt like I was invading someone else's house. I had to remind myself that this was my home now.

Past the living room, there were two bedrooms on each side of the hallway and a bathroom straight ahead at the end. Ryan told me he would leave my room door open and there was a sticky note on the first door on the left that said "Nina's Room." A smiley face was drawn next to my name, which immediately gave me some comfort in an otherwise nerve-wracking situation.

I wheeled my suitcase inside and plopped the duffel bag on the full size bed. The walls were a pale gray, and there were no windows. This room was definitely going to need some sprucing up, and I couldn't wait to go shopping tomorrow. I was too tired today to deal with redecorating.

I unzipped my suitcase and started to unpack when I suddenly noticed that there seemed to be low music coming from one of the bedrooms. The doors were closed, so I had initially assumed no one was home. I cracked my bedroom door open to listen in and suspected it was coming from the room diagonally across at the far end of the hallway.

Then, I heard a girl's laugher over the music. *Crap.* I wasn't ready to meet anyone. I stayed still, wondering whether I should just hide in my room and pretend I wasn't here or go across the hall to say hello.

Before I could think it over, I heard a male voice moaning. Then, the girl moaned too.

Shit. They were having sex.

I stayed still, pondering whether I should just quietly sneak out of the house and go shopping now instead of tomorrow. It would be awkward running into them, if they knew I had heard them.

After ten minutes of trying to ignore the bed squeaking amidst "oh yeahs" and "aaahs" from the very vocal female participant, I decided to hightail it out of there.

I was lingering behind the entrance to my room, about to make my exit, when the door across the hall abruptly burst open releasing the sound of metal music and laughter. I froze behind the door, unable to open or close it completely, for fear of being found out. So I stayed still, peeking through the slightly open crack.

All I could see were feet pass by my room, but couldn't make out faces. The male was tall with dark clothing and the female had a large purple rose tattoo on her ankle.

They were talking and laughing in the living room for a few minutes, and then I heard some keys and a door slam.

The apartment then turned eerily silent. Relieved, I concluded that they had left together.

Thank goodness that was over.

I spent the rest of the afternoon alone in my room unpacking. After my clothes were put away, I meandered out to the kitchen to make some chamomile tea and relax while I got accustomed to my surroundings. As I was pouring the boiling water, I heard the front door latch.

"Neeners!" Ryan shouted as he noticed me in the kitchen.

I placed my tea on the counter and ran over to my old friend, hugging him tightly. "Hey! I made it."

"You did. How was the ride?" he asked.

"Not bad, just a couple of hours by bus and I took a cab here."

"A cab? Must have been expensive. You didn't want to take the subway from the bus station, huh? I figured."

I looked down at my feet. "No, I'm not there yet. I have to work on that."

Ryan had known me since I was ten and was best friends with my older brother, Jimmy. As a result, he was like a brother to me too and knew way more than he should about me, not all of it good.

Ryan sighed. "So, we're still not taking subways, not riding in elevators, not flying. What else are we afraid of these days? Our own shadow?"

"*We* are working on it, Ry...I told you."

He shook his head and tapped my shoulder lightly. "It's only gonna get worse, Nina."

The truth was, as of the past few years, irrational fears had started to rule my life. I avoided certain situations like the plague and would go to great lengths and inconveniences to do so, like taking a bus instead of flying from New York to Texas to visit my friend in Houston, or taking the stairs instead of the elevator.

Over the years, the situation had gotten progressively worse and was quite paralyzing. It kept me from doing things that I would have loved, like traveling the world. A couple of years ago, at its worst, I had started to develop a full-blown fear of leaving the house. Through cognitive behavioral therapy, I was able to overcome my agoraphobia. So, I had come a long way, but there were still a lot of phobias that remained.

This all started one day with a panic attack in high school. We were on a field trip to the New York Public Library, and a few classmates and I got stuck in a dark elevator. I had begun to hyperventilate and thought I was going to die. Fifteen minutes later, the elevator moved, but the post-traumatic stress from that moment stuck. I have gone out of my way ever since to avoid crowds, subways, planes, heights, enclosed spaces or anything else that made me feel trapped.

"How are you going to work in a hospital someday if you can't ride in an elevator, Nina? Are you gonna tell your dying patients to press five and fend for themselves while you take the stairs?"

"Ry, I'll have it under control by then, okay? I appreciate your concern, but I have to do things in my own time. For now, I just need to focus on school starting Monday."

"Okay, I'll lay off your case...for now."

I rolled my eyes and smiled. "Much appreciated."

Ryan looked around and gestured with open arms. "So, how do you like the place?"

The truth was, I was feeling a little anxious about living away from home for the first time, but I put on a brave face. "I like it. My room is a little drab but that's nothing that can't be fixed."

He started walking down the hall and waved for me to follow him. "Come on, let me show you around."

"As you know, this first room on the left here is now yours," he said, pointing to my room.

I nodded and followed him as he entered the next room on the left at the end of the hall, which was just past mine.

"This is my room," he said.

Ryan's room was immaculate with neutral colors and no clutter. On his chest of drawers, there was a picture of him and my brother Jimmy boating on the Hudson River. It made me smile to see that he had it displayed. I picked up the picture and looked around the room. "Wow, ever the neat freak, as always, Ry."

"Indeed, Troll."

"I was wondering how long it would take before that old nickname came out."

Ryan and Jimmy always teased me growing up, because of my resemblance to the Olsen twins from that old show *Full House*. They called me the missing triplet. The name started out as "'Trolsen," which stood for "Triplet" and "Olsen," then evolved over time into "Troll." Even though it was meant to be a term of endearment, it bugged me sometimes. Admittedly, with my petite build, long dirty blond hair and very large blue eyes, I did look somewhat like those celebrity twins.

Ryan stepped out of his room, and I followed him.

"Okay, you may need to put on some sunglasses for this one," he said as he opened the door across the hall.

"This...is Jake's room."

Jake. The sex room.

If this room had a theme song, it would be *Welcome to the Jungle* by Guns N' Roses. It was a complete contrast to Ryan's bedroom. It was smoky, musky and mysterious. Now, I knew what he meant about the sunglasses. The walls were a neon orange. Everything else in the room was black: black furniture, black bedding and a black window shade to keep out the light, since this room actually had a window.

It was like every component of the room contradicted another part: neon orange and black, bright window with a dark shade. On top of that, there was a large collection of gargoyle figurines atop the dresser, but right next to them was a black and white picture of two adorable little girls who looked identical. Whoever this guy was, he was an enigma.

"What's Jake's deal?" I asked.

Ryan ran his hand over his short blonde hair and laughed. "Jake...how could I possibly sum up Jake? He's... different."

I laughed. "What do you mean *different*?"

"I mean, he's cool...he's just a lot of things. You'll have to meet him to know what I am talking about. He's from

Boston. He pretty much takes off and goes back there every weekend. I don't know what he does there or if he has some side business or something. He's kind of secretive. I know his family lives there. He's close to his nieces apparently," he said gesturing to the photo.

"What does he do for a living?"

"Actually, it's sick how smart he is. He's an engineer for a company in the city, and he pretty much can fix anything that breaks in the house. But when you see him, you're gonna be like, 'he's an engineer?'"

"What do you mean, when I see him?"

Ryan grinned. "He's interesting."

"Okay. Whatever you say."

I didn't mention to Ryan that I had already kind of gotten a preview of my own regarding Jake's interests. I could never admit that I was hiding behind a door listening in while Jake "entertained" his guest.

Ryan led me back down the hall, opening the door right across from mine.

"This...is Tarah's room."

This was the best bedroom in the house. Like Jake's, it had a window, but was painted a delicate lavender. There was a built-in white bookshelf, neatly organized with books and pictures and the room smelled like fresh laundry. It looked like a page out of a Pottery Barn catalog. The sun was streaming in, and I was so wishing this was my room.

"So, what's Tarah like?"

Ryan blushed. "She's really cool."

"She is not with Jake, by any chance, is she?" I asked, thinking about the rendezvous I overheard earlier.

"Hell no! Why would you ask that?" he snapped.

"I was just wondering."

"Trust me, there is nothing going on between Tarah and Jake."

"And that's because...?"

Ryan's face turned red again, and he gave me a look that answered my question.

"Tarah...and *you*?" I asked.

He smiled. "Yup."

"Really..."

"Yeah, it's new...six weeks now. Wait 'til you meet her. She's awesome."

"Nice, Ryan. I am so happy for you. But what if it doesn't work out? I mean, you're living together. Wouldn't that be weird?"

"Probably. But I can't worry about that right now."

"Well, I can't wait to meet her."

"I think you two will get along really well. She's a hair colorist for a salon in the city. She's working until close tonight, but she should be home around nine."

I suddenly yawned, and then my stomach growled. "I am starving, but I haven't had a chance to food shop."

"No need. Let's go downstairs to Eleni's. My treat. Phenomenal Greek food."

"I know. I smelled it on the way in here."

As Ryan and I headed downstairs, I heard the same swearing from the apartment below us. The woman seemed to have a Jamaican accent.

"What is up with the lady on the second floor?" I asked.

"Oh, you just wait. That is just another benefit of living here, Troll. If I tell you, it will ruin it," he said laughing.

"Okay, I am not even going to ask."

After a fantastic dinner of Greek salad and chicken skewers, we returned to the apartment to have the baklava pastry the owner, Telly, gave us to welcome me to the neighborhood. After just one meal, I already knew I would need to limit my Eleni's intake, or I was going to go broke and get fat.

I brewed a pot of coffee as Ryan got out the plates, and we reminisced about high school.

"So, Troll, no boyfriend at the moment?"

I sighed. "No. I was seeing someone at home for a few weeks, but I just wasn't feeling it. Then, knowing I was about to move away, I decided to break it off. It wasn't worth the effort."

"Well, they can't all be like Stuart, can they?"

Stuart was my first boyfriend in high school. He was sensitive and sweet and the constant butt of Jimmy and Ryan's jokes.

"Ugh...did you have to bring him up? Poor Stuart. He was awesome, though."

Ryan snickered. "He was a friggin' *girl*. Stuart and his paper birds! What was it he used to do?"

I giggled recalling the memory. "Aw, Stuart was the sweetest thing. He knew the combination to my locker, and he would create these little ornate origami birds out of construction paper. Then, I would unfold them, and there would be these little poems that rhymed inside each one. It was romantic."

Just then, footsteps crept up behind us, and a deep raspy voice that cut through me said, "That is...the STUPIDEST fucking thing I have ever heard."

When I turned around, the immediate but unwanted reaction my insides felt at the sight of him told me I was in trouble.

Reality Show Scene Three, enter stage left: hot womanizing roommate.

Then, came the three words that would change my life. "Hi, I'm Jake."

TWO

Jake stuck out his tattooed-covered arm prompting me to take his hand and flashing a smile that could only be described as devilish. "You must be Neenee," he said.

I coughed nervously, and a weird sound came out of my mouth that I couldn't quite identify. It might have been my body saying, *Well lookey here, she isn't dead from the waist down after all.*

He was freaking beautiful.

"It's Nina, actually," I said shaking his calloused hand, noticing a silver thumb ring. The warmth of his skin in the brief contact didn't escape me, nor did the fact that my hand lingered longer than it should have. It might have trembled.

"I know your name. I'm just fucking with you." He flashed a wicked grin and winked. My body's reaction to that made me question my own sanity.

He smelled like a mixture of cigarettes and cologne, which was oddly arousing. He had a brow ring and a bottom lip ring, and his incisors were very pointed and sharp.

His eyes were green with gold speckles, brought out even further by his contrasting short dark hair.

Come to think of it, Jake was like a black cat – gorgeous, but very likely bad luck if it crossed your path.

"Nice to meet you, Jake."

He leaned against the kitchen counter, crossing his arms and gave me a once-over that sent a shiver down my spine. "So, who is Stuart, why is he making you origami bird poems, and who cut off his balls?"

I laughed. "Stuart was my boyfriend freshman year of high school. Ryan decided to bring him up now for no good reason."

"What brings you to Brooklyn?"

"I start nursing school on Monday. Long Island University."

Jake scratched his chin, sarcastically pensive. "Isn't that in Long Island?"

"No, there's a Brooklyn campus. It's actually not far from the apartment."

Ryan interjected. "With your fear of subways, that's a good thing."

I shot Ryan a death glare.

Great. He was going to embarrass me in front of Jake.

"What's this, now?" Jake asked, lifting his brow.

"Thanks, a lot, Ryan," I said, seriously pissed.

He gave me an apologetic look. "Sorry. It just came out."

"It's nothing," I said looking at Jake, waving my hand, hoping he'd drop the subject.

Jake continued to stare at me quizzically. "Are you seriously afraid of the subway or something?"

"She's afraid of everything: planes, elevators, heights..." Ryan let out a frustrated sigh.

I widened my eyes at him again, then looked at Jake and shrugged my shoulders trying to downplay it. "I just get a little nervous in crowded, contained places. That's all."

Jake nodded slowly in understanding. "It's like a phobia. So, places that make you feel trapped?"

"Yeah, basically," I said.

Jake squinted at me and seemed to be examining my face for the truth. His expression darkened like he somehow saw through my trying to pass my phobias off as nothing. Our eyes locked, and I felt an inexplicable connection to him in that moment that went beyond just physical attraction.

He scratched his chin. "Hmn."

Suddenly uncomfortable, I changed the subject immediately. "So where do you work?"

"I'm an electrical engineer for a company in the city. We design stadium lighting. And at night, I dance...at a male strip club."

I couldn't tell, but I was pretty sure the color must have drained from my face.

"Seriously?"

"Yup."

"Wow," I said.

He looked over at Ryan. "You didn't tell her she was living with Magic Fuckin' Mike?"

Ryan just laughed, gauging my reaction.

Jake looked amused and bit his bottom lip, his teeth clicking against his lip ring. Then, he let out a guttural laugh. "I'm just fucking with you again."

"You're *not* a stripper?"

He laughed and shook his head. "I like you. You're an easy target. It's gonna be fun to have you around. By the way, I really am an engineer. My cubicle mate Raj gets pretty pissed when I try to take off my clothes and give him a lap dance, so I stopped stripping a long time ago," he joked.

That's a damn shame.

Jeez, where was this coming from?

I couldn't believe how gullible I was sometimes, but then again, why wouldn't I have believed him? With his overall stature and the way his black hoodie hugged his clearly defined chest, his body could certainly pass for that of a stripper. Plus, I didn't know him from Adam. What I did know was that Jake was a ball-buster and did not appear to be the type of guy I *should* be attracted to. Or at least, that was my first impression of him.

I looked down again at the various colored tattoos on his right forearm. On his left, there was just a lone dragon. I wondered what else was underneath his clothing.

He walked over to the other side of the kitchen, picked up a banana out of a pile of about twenty, peeled it and ate the entire first half in one bite whilst looking right at me, grinning.

Ryan laughed. "I forgot to mention, that's Jake's bushel of bananas over there. We think he is part human, part monkey."

I looked at Jake. "You like bananas, huh?"

Still chewing, Jake said, "Damn straight, I do. I fuckin' love 'em. Mmm." He took the other half of the banana and stuffed the whole thing into his mouth, gesturing to me with the peel, his mouth full. "Wa-wan?"

"Huh?"

"Want one?" he said more clearly.

I held my hand out. "No, thanks. I'm good."

Still chewing, he continued looking at me, and my heart fluttered.

Ryan broke the uncomfortable silence. "I told you Jake was interesting."

I watched as Jake slowly licked his lips after finishing the banana. *He is interesting alright.*

The front door then opened, and in walked a cute girl with short black hair in a pixie cut.

Reality Show Scene Four, enter stage right: instant best friend.

She was wearing an adorable blue shift dress and immediately dropped her purse that was practically larger than she was, walked over to Ryan and planted a kiss on his lips.

"Hey, babe," Ryan said and then turned to me. "This is Nina. Nina meet Tarah."

She startled me when she immediately pulled me into a hug. "I have heard so much about you, Nina. I have been waiting for you! I am outnumbered here. You didn't tell me how pretty she was, Ryan."

"Aw, thanks...likewise," I said. "It's really nice to know I won't be the only female in the house."

Tarah had almond-shaped light brown eyes, defined, thick eyebrows and full lips. She was petite with smooth olive skin, and I could totally see what Ryan saw in her. I was curious about her nationality, so I asked her.

"Can I ask...are you Italian...Spanish?"

"No, actually, I'm Persian. My family is from Iran."

"Ah, I knew it was something like that. You have a very exotic look."

Tarah smiled and Ryan said. "Yeah, where Nina and I come from, there are two ethnicities: white and pasty white."

We all laughed, and then I noticed Jake walking back down the hall to his room. I was oddly disappointed by his sudden retreat.

Tarah immediately started playing with my hair.

"Who does your highlights?"

"No one. This is my natural color."

"Seriously? You are so lucky, girl. Do you know how much money people have to pay me to get highlights that look like this?"

"Well, it's a good thing I don't have to pay for it. I'm gonna be pretty broke this year since I am going to try to not work and just focus on school full-time."

"Nursing, right? That's probably a pretty tough curriculum."

"It is. So, the more focus on school the better. I have enough money saved to just about pay my rent and food for the year."

"Well, if you ever need anything, you let me know, okay?" Tarah said.

"That's really sweet of you. Thanks."

She had kind eyes, and I could tell we were going to be good friends.

Ryan nudged Tarah, kissed her forehead and looked at me. "I told you she was awesome."

It was obvious that Ryan had it bad. Feeling like a third wheel all of a sudden, I excused myself to go finish unpacking, even though I had already put most of my stuff away earlier.

"I'll come say goodnight later," Tarah said as I waved to her.

When I got to my room, I turned on the only light, a small lamp, and lay down on the bed, staring at the ceiling. It had been a long day, and even though I should have been resting, my mind kept racing.

I decided to take a shower. Gathering all of my toiletries and placing them in a caddy, I grabbed my robe and walked down the hall to the bathroom.

The sound of some kind of alternative music was coming from Jake's room, but the door was closed. It occurred to me that from now on, every time I used the bathroom or showered, I'd have to do it next door to Jake, since his room was right outside of the bathroom.

As the hot water poured down on me, I tried to relax. I had a lot on my mind, from anxiety about classes starting Monday to my unwanted attraction to my tattooed, pierced, smoking hot roommate, who based on first impressions, was quite likely a man-whore.

I wrapped my wet hair in a towel, securely tightened my robe and grabbed my dirty clothes off the floor. Cautiously peeking out into the hallway before I escaped the safety of the steamy bathroom, I tiptoed back to my room and closed the door.

After I brushed the tangles out of my wet hair, I slipped into a pink camisole and shorts and grabbed my Kindle to do some light reading before bed.

About twenty minutes into the book, there was a knock at the door. Assuming it was Tarah, I didn't think twice before opening it with no bra.

The sight of Jake standing there completely shirtless and fresh out of the shower with his hair wet nearly knocked the wind out of me. He smelled like the men's body wash that I had sniffed in the bathroom. *The one I would be bathing in from now on.*

Trickles of water dripped down his defined chest onto his six-pack. His chest had no tattoos, but I now saw that he had tribal ink on his side torso and upper arms. I knew he was attractive, but it truly stunned me how beautiful he was bare.

I swallowed, hardly getting the words out. "Ha...hi... what's up?"

Jake's heated stare burned through me as he quickly glanced down to my braless chest and back up to my eyes. He licked his lips, and I swear, I felt it. I could describe it as electric, but it was more like a dragon breathing fire down my throat, igniting a wet explosion at the site of my vagina.

Then, he reached into his pocket and handed me...a pair of underwear. "I found these on the bathroom floor... thought you might want them."

I reached for them, mortified. They were the dirty underwear I had been wearing all day and must have fallen out of the clothes pile I carried out of the bathroom.

Covering my chest with my arms, I clutched the panties and was pretty much speechless as he stood there in my doorway. "Thanks."

He stared at me for a few seconds, grinned impishly but said nothing else as he turned around. I watched him walk away and noticed that his back was just as defined as the front as he sauntered down the hall, his black pants hanging low on his waist, almost but not quite low enough to display the top of his tight, round ass.

Shaking my head, I took a deep breath and slowly closed my door.

This wasn't the type of guy you lived with every day. This was the type of guy who came out to play only at night in your deepest, darkest fantasies.

Stay. Away. Nina.

I was sweating, even though I had just showered. After a few minutes, when my hormones finally stopped doing the Macarena, I went back to bed and tried to focus on something other than my new roommate. Just when I had finally gotten my mind off of him, I looked over to my right and noticed something on my nightstand that I must have missed earlier.

Oh my God.

Someone must have put it there when I was in the shower.

Someone. I knew exactly who it was.

It was an origami bird made out of black construction paper, just like the ones Stuart used to make. But wait...it wasn't a bird.

It was a bat.

I held it in my hand and covered my mouth to contain the stupefied laughter. I looked around as if someone was in the room watching me, but of course, I was alone.

I unfolded the bat and noticed a message written underneath the left wing in silver gel ink.

Welcome to the "House." —Jake
How's Uncle Jesse?

THREE

It was Saturday morning and Jake was already gone before I could thank him for my little gift. Like Ryan explained, he took off for Boston every weekend and generally came back on Sunday nights in time to work on Monday.

The first thing on my mind when I woke up was the bat, how intricate it was and how Jake had now joined the bandwagon of people teasing me about my resemblance to the Olsen twins. At least I thought they were pretty and took it as a compliment.

Ryan and Tarah were in the kitchen eating pancakes when I walked in.

"Sit down and join us, Troll," Ryan said.

Tarah looked at me excitedly. "Nina, you and I should go shopping today. I took the day off."

"Really? Cool...I need to dress up my room badly."

She clapped giddily. "Perfect. We'll have so much fun." She handed me the syrup. "So, are you nervous about starting school?"

"I am...mostly about the math requirement. I have never done well in math. I failed it in high school, actually."

Ryan pointed his fork at me. "You should get Jake to help you. He is a whiz when it comes to stuff like math and science.

"I'll pass. Jake seems a little busy for tutoring."

Tarah placed a steaming cup of coffee in front of me and said, "Seriously. You should ask him if you're stuck."

"Okay," I said, mostly to shut them up. I knew full well I would never ask Jake for help.

That afternoon, Tarah and I went shopping at King's Plaza. She helped me pick out a pink and gray comforter, a couple of canvas floral wall prints, a gray shag rug, and a pink accent lamp. My father had given me permission to use his credit card for some apartment items, but I knew this spending spree would be the last hurrah for a while.

We stopped for frozen yogurt on the way home, and Tarah insisted on paying for me. We sat down at one of the tables to talk.

"So, you and Ryan. How did that come about?" I asked.

She closed her eyes briefly and sighed. "He is such a sweetie, isn't he? We were friends for a while first, you know. We had been roommates for like three months before anything ever happened. One night, we had the house to ourselves and just stayed up 'til all hours talking about anything and everything. All of a sudden, I looked at him and thought...huh."

"Huh," I imitated her, laughing.

Tarah took a spoonful of yogurt and continued talking with her mouth full. "I had always thought he was cute, but it was a gradual thing seeing him as something more."

Then, I stopped beating around the bush and asked the question I really wanted the answer to.

I wiped my mouth and asked, "What do you make of Jake?"

She rolled her eyes. "Jake. Hmmm. Where do I start?"

I started eating my yogurt unusually fast. "What's his deal?" I asked with my mouth full.

Tarah picked a raspberry out of her cup, ate it and said, "Well, first of all, the obvious...he's friggin' smokin' hot, right?"

I was a little taken aback at her blunt comment and felt a twinge of jealousy but reminded myself that she was with Ryan and would have to be blind not to think Jake was extremely good looking.

"He's alright," I said nonchalantly.

"Jake is...cool. I mean, he likes to bust balls. We don't spend a lot of time with him. He's obviously got his own stuff going on, traveling back and forth to Boston on weekends and what not. He keeps to himself for the most part when he is home."

"Do you think he has a girlfriend in Boston?"

"He hasn't mentioned one, and I have never asked him point blank, but there is definitely something going on there. He has mentioned a sister and nieces that he's really close to, but he goes back every single weekend, so it can't just be for them. Jake doesn't really open up, but that's okay. He's respectful, and we all get along. And boy, that dude can fix anything that breaks in the house. It's amazing how smart he is. He's got a rough exterior, but there is definitely somebody home upstairs," she said pointing to her skull.

"Yeah, he seems cool enough." I decided not to tell her about the bat. I kind of liked keeping that to myself.

Tarah leaned in. "Why were you wondering if he had a girlfriend? She paused and let out a huge smile. "You like him!"

Was it just me or was it getting in hot in here?

I laughed it off. "No, of course not! I mean, not in that way."

"Then, why did your face just turn as red as this raspberry?"

The weekend came and went as I busied myself stocking the refrigerator with my favorite foods and setting up my room. Tarah and I spent Sunday night hanging out in my newly decorated space, waxing our eyebrows and painting our nails.

That night, I tossed and turned, stressed about starting classes the next day.

It was about midnight when I heard the front door open, followed by footsteps passing my room and heading down the hall. I knew it was Jake returning from Boston. Immediately, the butterflies that lay dormant all weekend in my stomach came to life and kept me up most of the night.

FOUR

I t was a rainy early September day in Brooklyn, but the five block walk from the apartment to the main university building on the corner of Flatbush and DeKalb was a breeze.

This semester I would be taking Psychology, Anatomy and Physiology, English Composition and Finite Math. I was fairly certain I would be able to handle the material in all of the courses with little difficulty, except for math, which had always been a nearly impossible subject for me. Unfortunately, the math class was a requirement for the nursing program, and if I didn't get at least a C average, I was screwed.

Math was the final class of the day, and I wanted to cry when I saw the syllabus and skimmed through the textbook. Professor Hernandez seemed like a jerk on top of that. Listening to him lecture as he wrote out problems on the dry-erase board, I started to sweat. *Select a number "n" multiply it by 4, add 10 to the product, divide the sum by 2, and subtract 5 from the quotient. Heh?*

I hated math, plain and simple. My brain just wasn't wired to understand numbers. But so much rode on this class, and I was determined to find a way to get through it. My parents were certainly not going to continue to pay for nursing school if I couldn't pass my classes. I owed it to them to try as hard as I could, despite the current lack of faith in myself.

Feeling defeated, I walked home from the university in the rain. I was already stressed about the small amount of homework I had received for tonight and a math test scheduled for Wednesday.

I was one block away from the apartment when a van drove right into a puddle next to me, causing what seemed like a tidal wave of water to hit me. I was now drenched and looking like a drowned rat.

Arriving at our front steps, I noticed the woman who lived on the second floor peeking out of her window watching me approach the building. She looked to be in her sixties.

Still standing on the sidewalk below, I waved. "Hi, I'm Nina Kennedy. I just moved upstairs."

The woman looked at me and said nothing. She wore a scarf wrapped around her head and didn't look happy at all.

It was awkward, but I gave it one more try. "You live on the second floor?"

The woman squinted her eyes and looked angrier by the second. Finally, she leaned a bit more out of the window and in a strong Jamaican accent said, "Go fuck yourself!"

My heart started beating fast. "Come again?"

"Go fuck yourself!" she repeated and then abruptly shut the window.

I stood there in the rain stunned, not knowing whether to run into the building or away from it. This was definitely not my day. I opened the door and was panting as I ran up the stairs past her apartment to the third floor.

What was wrong with her? Why did she say that to me? What did I do?

I entered our apartment and slammed the door behind me, leaning against it breathing in and out heavily. That encounter shocked me so much that it took me a few seconds to notice Jake standing in front of me eating a banana.

"What the hell happened to you?" he asked.

I kept panting and then said between breaths, "I was attacked...verbally...by the woman on the second floor."

He nearly choked as he began to double over. He was laughing so hard that no sound came out of his mouth.

He stopped just long enough to ask, "Did she try to drown you too?"

I rolled my eyes. "No, that was something else."

Jake continued to laugh uncontrollably. He gripped his abs as if in pain and smacked the counter, then said "Now, you are officially part of this household."

"What?"

"You've just been Ballsworthied."

"Balls, what? Excuse me?"

My reaction seemed to make him laugh even harder now. My body stiffened when he walked over and pulled me into a quick friendly hug then patted me on the back. It sounded the alarm to the butterflies in my stomach. "It's okay. You're good. She's harmless."

I shivered. "What the heck is wrong with her?"

"That's Mrs. Ballsworthy. No one knows why the fuck she is the way she is. Some days she'll tell us to go fuck ourselves, and other days, she's perfectly fine. One time, I shit you not, she baked us a chocolate cake. It said 'Fuck You All' on top. It was the most delicious fuckin' cake I have ever eaten. She could have put shit in it. I still would have taken another bite. That's how good it was."

That story broke my funk, and I started to laugh at the absurdity of it all. I wiped my eyes. "Are you pulling my leg again?"

"No, actually. Even *I* couldn't make that shit up if I tried."

He and I both cracked up simultaneously, and when our laughter dissipated, I stared into his emerald eyes for a few seconds. His eyes then moved from mine to my mouth and back up to my eyes again.

"Seriously, you look like you had a tough day," he said.

I shook my head. "You have no idea."

Jake walked over to the fridge, popped open a beer, took a swig and handed the bottle to me. "Enlighten me."

I took a long sip, and the fact that my mouth was now where his had just been was not lost on me. "Thanks."

He pulled up a chair, sat on it backwards and listened as I vented.

"I am just really up shit's creek in school. There is this finite math class I have to get at least a C in, since it's a requirement for the nursing program, and I have never been able to understand math. It's like a brain deficiency I have."

He squinted his eyes in disagreement. "Bullshit. No such thing. You just need the right teacher."

"Well, the teacher, Professor Hernandez, is not a happy person to begin with, and as far as his teaching style, he might as well be talking Chinese to me. He just reads out of the book and doesn't explain anything."

Jake grabbed the beer from my hand, took a sip, handed it back, and stared into my eyes. "Like I said, you need the right teacher."

"But my teacher sucks!"

He let out a slight burp. "No, he doesn't. He is awesome."

"What do you mean? Have you not heard anything I have said?"

"I mean...he is awesome. Because...*he*...is *me*."

"You?"

"Yeah. I'll be your teacher. I'll tutor you. Math is easy as balls for me."

"You...tutor *me*..."

His eyes widened, and he gave me a menacing look. "Yes. Unless you want to fail," he said firmly.

"No. No, I don't."

"Okay, then."

I scratched my head. "When is this gonna happen?"

"We'll do it a couple of nights a week, set up a schedule."

"Why would you want to do this for me? What's the catch?"

I was about to take a sip of the beer when he yanked it from my hands and downed the rest of it. My eyes fixated on his lips wrapped around the bottle before he slammed it down. "What...people can't do things for other people without there being an ulterior motive?"

"I guess. But seriously, you don't have to."

"I don't have to. You're right. I want to. I wouldn't have offered otherwise. I told you, math is easy for me. The hard part is gonna be getting you motivated."

"Motivated?"

"Yeah. See, people are capable of amazing things when they're motivated."

"Isn't not getting kicked out of nursing school motivation enough?"

He smirked and shook his head in disagreement. "No, it's not. I can tell that's not enough for you. You need something that will really make you want to pass, like your life depends on it.

I rubbed my temples. "I am not following you."

"I'll explain then. Okay, so...I'm gonna tutor you, right? If you get an A on every exam, fanfuckingtastic! I'm doing my job because you should be getting an A on every exam. If you get lower than an A, then there should be consequences."

"Consequences?"

He nodded slowly with a mischievous grin. "Consequences."

"Like?"

"Like...when I first met you, you said you were afraid of a lot of things. And from the look on your face, I could tell it was more than just a slight fear. You need to get over that, Nina."

I shuddered at the seriousness of his tone and the fact that for the first time, he said my name.

"I am not following you," I said.

"Let me explain. I tutor you. But for every exam grade lower than an A, you will have to face one of your fears."

I felt a rush of panic creeping in, and my heart started to pound. Without saying anything for several seconds, I just stared at him before asking, "Can you be more specific?"

"Don't get all freaked out on me. I'll be there with you. We'll do something that scares you, that you've been avoiding, but you won't know what it is until we get there. It's better that way, so that you are not building up anxiety anticipating it. We'll expose you to it, until it doesn't scare you anymore. See, from what I can tell from your body language, I am making you really fucking nervous right now. And that's a good thing, because it means you are going to work your ass off to ace those tests. But either way, you win. You just might not see it that way."

He had to be kidding me. I barely knew this guy, but he could read me like a book.

"What if I don't want to participate in this bet?"

Jake got up and threw the bottle in the recycle bin. "Then, you're on your own, chica."

I felt like throwing up, not because I was about to fail math but because I knew I was about to agree to his terms. It scared the living hell out of me, but at the same time, I felt a bittersweet excitement like never before.

He stuck out his hand. "Deal?"

I hesitated then shook his hand as he squeezed mine tightly. "Deal."

Gosh, if my body reacted like this to just the touch of his hand, I couldn't imagine what it would do if he were to—

"You want to start tomorrow night?" he asked.

"Okay."

"Give me your phone," he said.

I looked at him strangely.

"Give me your phone," he demanded again.

I didn't ask why and just handed it to him. To be honest, with the way I have been reacting to this guy, I probably would have done anything he asked me to at this point.

"Stay here," he said.

He walked away down the hall to his room with it, and that made me extremely nervous. I didn't want him looking at my browsing history or text messages, even though there was really nothing incriminating.

I shouted. "What are you doing with my phone?"

"Don't worry about it," I heard him yell from his room.

"Can I have it back please?" Why was I listening to him and staying here in the kitchen like an idiot?

A few minutes later, he came back down the hall and handed it back to me. "I programmed my number in. So, if for some reason, you have to reach me for anything, you have it. I'll also call you if I am running late from work tomorrow night before we study."

"Okay, thanks."

"Don't be scared. You're gonna do fine."

I nodded silently, wondering how I got myself into this.

Jake grabbed a banana, then his jacket and laptop from the couch. "I have to get back to work. I just came home because I forgot my laptop. I'll catch you later."

"Okay. Catch you later. Oh, wait...Jake?"

He turned around. "What's up?"

"I never thanked you for my bat."

He said nothing, just smiled, winked and stuck out his tongue in jest. For the first time, I noticed it was pierced too.

Damn.

When the door slammed shut, I closed my eyes and sighed.

Oh yeah, I was in deep doo doo...in more ways than one.

From the street, I could hear Jake in the distance. *"Fuck you too, Mrs. Ballsworthy!"*

I covered my mouth in laughter. My new home was a bizarre place, but there was nowhere else I wanted to be at that moment.

Then, I looked down at my phone and noticed he had changed the wallpaper on the screen. It was one of those "Keep Calm and Carry On" sayings that pretty much summed up my day, in honor of my encounter with our lovely neighbor:

Keep Calm and Go Fuck Yourself.

FIVE

Tuesday was my day off from classes, and I spent the day doing laundry and nervously anticipating my tutoring session with Jake that night. I was 22-years old, but the level of obsession I was experiencing made me feel like I was sixteen.

I still could not believe I had agreed to the terms of his bet. Truthfully, I knew I wasn't going to get A's on my tests no matter how hard I studied, so I could pretty much start mentally preparing myself for the worst. Even though what Jake proposed terrified me, I really didn't ever consider telling him no.

He was like no other guy I had ever known. It wasn't just that he looked different (in a very good way). He had a self-assurance and commanding way about him that was hard to resist, but that oddly, also made me feel safe.

Growing up in my small town, the guys I had met from the time I was a teenager up until I moved here were cookie cutter. I had yet to meet someone like Jake: dark and dangerous on the outside but smart and clever on the inside; someone who owned a room the second he stepped into it.

My last serious boyfriend, Spencer, could not have been more different from Jake. He was a clean-cut, church-going kind of guy, who my parents and everyone else just loved. He was a few years older and sold insurance for a living, but looking back, if you ask me, the only thing he was ever really good at selling was a false impression of himself. What my family didn't realize was that behind that squeaky-clean exterior, was a man that constantly tried to berate me with critiques and put-downs. And ultimately, he cheated on me. I felt like I wasted three years and got nothing out of it, except a certificate of completion in Asshole 101. He was the only guy I ever slept with. What a waste.

I shook my head to rid my mind from thoughts of Spencer as I continued to fold shirts in the basement laundry room. Then, my cell phone rang, and I saw it was my father.

"Hey, Dad."

"Hi, sweetie. I am just checking in. How are things going at the new place?"

I can't stop obsessing over my roommate.

"Pretty good so far."

"How's Ryan?"

Who?

"He's great. Turns out he's actually dating my other roommate, Tarah."

"Really? Good for him. Nice girl?" he asked.

"Yes, very."

"Well, you know Ryan is like family to us. So, I couldn't be happier that he is there to look out for you."

Actually, Ryan's head is so far up Tarah's ass, I am lucky if he even realizes I still live here.

"Me too," I said.

My father sighed. "What about the other roommate? A guy, right?"

Yes, a really hot guy, with tattoos and piercings on his face...and tongue...and God knows where else...and I sometimes want to lick him.

"Jake...his name is Jake. Good guy, kind of quiet...an engineer."

"Ah, good, he must be nice and nerdy. I won't have to worry." He laughed.

Dad, you should be so worried.

"That's exactly right. He is a bit of a nerd."

"How are classes so far?"

I am going to fail math.

"So far so good. Math is going to be a challenge."

"Well, I have confidence in you, honey. You made this big move to the city, and I know you won't let yourself fail."

I just wish I had confidence in myself.

"Thanks, Dad. I better get back to folding laundry. Tell Mom I love her."

"Ok, sweetie. Love you. Bye bye."

It was 4:30 in the afternoon, and since I had been up tossing and turning the previous night, I decided to try to take a nap since Jake wouldn't be home until after six o'clock.

I had set my alarm—or so I thought—for 5:30. So, you could imagine my surprise when I woke up and saw that it was 7:45. My heart was pounding, and I was beyond agitated when I realized I had overslept.

I got up and scratched my head, lifting the alarm clock and noticing that, while yes, I had set the alarm for 5:30, it was for am not pm, which did me absolutely no good.

Shit!

I rubbed my eyes and matted my hair down, unsure of what I would be met with when I emerged from the bedroom.

To make matters worse, I looked over at my nightstand and my pulse quickened as I discovered evidence that Jake had been in my room while I was asleep. There, next to my tissue box was another black origami bat. I shook my head in disbelief and began to unfold it.

Did you know that you drool?
That's so not cool.
Showing up is my number one rule.
Now, get up, fool. You're late for school.

Mortified did not even begin to describe how I felt. Even though I would have rather stayed put at that point, I knew I needed to go out and face the music. I took a stick of gum from my purse to mask my sleep breath and quickly inspected myself in the mirror. I grabbed my math books and syllabus and headed down the hall.

When I got to Jake's room, his door was cracked open, and I could see that he was sitting up in bed wearing headphones and writing on a laptop. He hadn't noticed me, so I stood there for a minute taking him in.

His hair was flattened, like he had just taken a shower, and there was a loose piece hanging over his forehead. He had beautiful, shiny dark hair that looked jet-black when it was wet. He was wearing black cargo pants and a navy blue t-shirt that hugged his muscles and showed off his tattooed arms. The room smelled like cinnamon candle, musk and cigarettes, even though I had yet to see him smoking in the house. His long legs were stretched out to the end of the length of the bed. He was tapping his foot fast and nervously as he typed, bobbing his head to the beat of the music.

I clutched my textbook and was nervous just looking at him, while anticipating the grief he was going to give me for sleeping through our tutoring session.

I finally coughed to let him know I was standing at the doorway.

Jake looked up and slowly removed his headphones. "Well, well, well, look who finally decided to wake up."

I stayed at the threshold. Waving the paper bat he made me, I said, "I am sorry, Jake, I really am. I set the alarm for am instead of pm."

He closed his laptop and sat up into a sitting position at the edge of the bed. He wasn't smiling. "You should be apologizing to yourself. You're the one who's gonna fail."

Okay, hard-ass.

"Why didn't you just wake me up?"

"I tried to nudge you, but you didn't even move. I had to check your pulse to make sure you were still alive. Then, you farted, so I figured all was well."

"I did not!" I laughed, but was dying inside.

"I'm kidding. Relax."

Dear God, thank you.

"When is your first exam?"

"Tomorrow."

He shook his head and sighed. "Tomorrow..." Rolling his eyes, he ran his hands through his hair in frustration.

"Yes. Professor Hernandez doesn't waste any time."

"Well, then, it's a good thing you napped because I hope you're ready to be up all night."

Shit. He was serious about this. There was no joking around in his tone, making this situation all the more intimidating.

I looked down at my feet and then back up at him. "I am *really* sorry."

Jake's green eyes seared into mine for a few seconds. "I don't bite, you know," he said in a low voice.

"Excuse me?"

"Why are you still standing in the doorway, using your textbook as a shield?"

I laughed nervously as I entered the room. He was right. I was hesitating. But it wasn't for the reason he probably thought.

I wished...he would bite...and that's what scared me.

Control yourself, Nina.

"Should we study in here or in the living room?" I asked.

"That's your decision. You're the one that needs to focus," he said.

"Okay. Here is fine. Tarah and Ryan will probably come home and want the living room."

Bad choice. Being in his bedroom was by far the most distracting place.

"Let's get started then." Jake reached out his hand. "Show me the assignment."

I handed him the book and syllabus, as he pulled up a wooden chair and sat down, kicking his legs up onto the foot of the bed. I sat on the ground with my legs crossed.

"You don't have to sit on the floor. I sat here, so you could have the bed."

"Okay, thanks," I said as I got up and planted myself on his bed. The mattress was firm and it was like lying in a sea of his masculine scent. The black comforter was surprisingly soft, and I ran the tips of my fingers across it as I watched him look over my syllabus.

"Okay, this shit isn't going to be easy for you," he said.

"Thanks for the vote of confidence. That is certainly an understatement."

He looked up at me. "Let's start with the linear programming problem."

I scratched my head and leaned in. "Okay."

"You have to create a problem like the one listed here, using the same model but your own variables, and then you need to solve it." He grinned. "We can make this interesting if we want."

"Oh?"

"Yes. All it says is that it has to involve transportation."

"Yes." I nodded.

I had no idea what he was talking about.

"Okay, so the example in the book uses a lumber dealer transporting wood to warehouses."

"Yes."

"So, you could use, for example...a pimp transporting whores across the country."

"Excuse me?"

"We need to keep you awake, so let's go with that. The problem is to find the most economical way to transport the prostitutes to various cities."

I rubbed my temples and chuckled. "Oh my God. Okay."

"First, you have to determine your variables. There are two variables, x and y. If x represents the number of whores to be driven from New York to L.A., then since L.A. needs 25 whores, the number of whores to be shipped from Philadelphia to L.A. is 25 minus x."

He looked up to see if I was paying attention and continued. "And if y represents the number of whores to be driven from New York to Las Vegas, then since Las Vegas needs 30 whores, the number of whores to be shipped from Philadelphia to Las Vegas is 30 minus y."

He then built a cost table showing the transportation routes, number of whores and various costs of each route. Eventually, he came up with a formula and made me run through the entire problem until I understood it. Even though it took over an hour, I finally did get it. I was amazed at how capable I could be when interested enough to apply myself.

And I was definitely interested.

There was also a nutrition problem where the object was to design a low-cost recipe that provided required levels of proteins, calories and vitamin B12. We had to choose variables again and assign different costs. Jake substituted the samples used in the book for things that would make me laugh. In this case, the recipe was for Mrs. Ballsworthy's "shit cake," and the ingredients were chocolate, shit and whole-wheat flour. Again, he built a table to organize the data, and after another hour, I was finally able to run through the formula myself.

He was so animated and never seemed to tire when I couldn't grasp what he was teaching. Instead, he would just find a new way of explaining the problem to me, like he enjoyed the challenge. His tables and graphs made things easy to understand, and after running through those two examples repeatedly, I was starting to think that maybe I *could* pass the exam tomorrow. If only I could just remember Jake's methodology and apply it to whatever problem Professor Hernandez came up with.

By the end of the night, we were both sitting on the floor, stretched out with white papers everywhere. I was so tired, but I wasn't ready for the study session to end.

I started to yawn. Jake bonked me on the forehead with a rolled up piece of paper. "What do you say...one more practice problem?"

I yawned again and nodded. "Sure, one more."

"No falling asleep on me," he said.

I wish I were falling asleep on you.

"Okay...let's try this," he said as he began writing out a new chart with different variables.

Sitting on the floor with my legs crossed next to him, I stared at his intense expression as he wrote in bold, hard strokes. He was so focused and was one of the smartest people I had ever met. His intelligence made him even sexier in my mind and made me feel even more inadequate. He was a badass.

My eyes were glued to the way his tongue moved back and forth over the bottom of his mouth as he concentrated, his tongue ring clanking against the metal of the ring on his lip. It was so erotic, and I was so out of line for thinking like that while he was trying to help me. As my gaze meandered down to his tattooed arms, I also concluded that his masculine scent mixed with cigarette smoke was just about the most arousing smell I had ever known.

His eyes suddenly darted to the side at me, as if he could feel me staring, and I looked away instinctively.

Even though I wasn't facing toward him anymore, my mind still went to places I knew it shouldn't, like what his tongue would feel like...on me. I knew the answer. I wasn't sure if it was because I was overtired or merely the fact that I hadn't been with a man in so long, but I was suddenly experiencing sensory overload when it came to him.

He stopped writing and looked toward me. "Okay...so two trains 150 miles apart travel toward each other along the same track..." He paused and waved his hand in front of my face. "Earth to Nina."

"Huh?" I then realized I had been staring at his mouth the entire time.

"You're not paying attention," he said firmly, his gravelly voice vibrating through me.

"I'm...I'm sorry," I said.

"You want to just stop?" He sounded frustrated with me.

Instead of providing a yes or no answer, my exhausted (and horny) mind decided to take a detour.

"Did it hurt?" I asked.

Jake squinted his eyes. "Did what hurt?" he asked abruptly, almost seeming annoyed at me.

"That," I said pointing to his lip ring. "The tongue ring, the lip ring, the brow ring...all of them. Was it painful?"

Shrugging his shoulders, he said, "I don't really remember. I got them when I was like sixteen. I had way more of them back then, too. I don't think it was that bad, though." He lifted his brow with a smirk. "Why...are you considering getting one?"

I giggled like a drunk schoolgirl. "Me? No. Uh-uh. I don't think I could withstand the pain."

Jake's eyes darkened and met mine. "Sometimes if you are willing to withstand a little pain in life, Nina, you might discover a pleasure that you never would have otherwise known existed."

I felt flushed. "Are we still talking about piercings?" My voice lowered to a whisper. "Are you talking about... piercings...down there?"

His eyes widened, and he slammed the textbook down. "*Down there?* No, actually. I was referring to your fear of everything, Nina, but now I believe *you* might be referring to whether or not my cock is pierced."

Mortified, I looked down at the ground and shook my head vigorously. "Oh my God. Forget I ever said anything! I think I am so tired that I am delirious. It's probably time for me to hit the hay."

I immediately started messily gathering papers, along with my textbook and stood up. Speed talking, I said, "Jake, thank you so much for this. I think I really get it now. I'll let you know how I make out tomorrow."

He got up but didn't say anything.

I walked backwards out of the room, dropping things and tripped over his wastebasket which made him chuckle.

I practically ran to my room, and as I opened my bedroom door, Jake's voice stopped me from down the hall.

"To answer your question, Nina, *that* pleasure is worth the pain too."

Speechless, I entered my room and shut the door behind me, gearing up for another night of restlessness.

SIX

As I sat in class thinking about last night's tutoring session, Professor Hernandez began to address the room and startled me out of my daydream.

"Please quiet down, folks. We have a lot to get to today. We're going to spend the first half of class running through some of the examples you turned in. Then, the last half will be the exam."

He paused for about a minute looking through the stack of homework submissions.

"Where is Ms. Kennedy?"

I raised my hand. "Here, sir."

Professor Hernandez put his glasses on and examined the paper in his hand a bit more closely before looking over at me. "Pimps and whores, Ms. Kennedy?"

My heart fell to my stomach, remembering that I had submitted the two examples Jake and I put together for the transportation and nutrition word problem assignment. Whoops.

Please don't mention Mrs. Ballsworthy's shit cake.

The class erupted in laughter at the pimp reference, and when it started to die down, I said, "Yes, sir."

He shook his head and examined the document again. "All I can say is, you're lucky the solution is correct, Ms. Kennedy."

I nodded silently, wanting to crawl into a hole.

When the attention of the class finally left me, my breathing settled. Just as the professor moved onto another student's assignment, my phone vibrated then began to play a song I didn't immediately recognize, loudly disrupting the lecture.

I then quickly realized it was *Everywhere You Look*, the theme song to the show *Full House*.

No. no. no. no.

I looked down at the screen: *Jake Calling*.

I immediately silenced the phone, and the noise from the song was replaced with the sounds of my classmates laughing and whispering.

He didn't.

He did. Damn it, Jake.

Apparently, when he took my phone away the other day, he must have programmed it as a "special" ringtone for his incoming calls.

I looked up at Professor Hernandez's stern expression. "Ms. Kennedy, I suggest you silence your phone during my class."

I swallowed and said, "I am very sorry."

As the professor continued with the lecture, the guy next to me said, "That was classic."

I turned to him and noticed that he had a really nice smile. He was actually *very* good looking, not in the darkly gorgeous way Jake was, but in a preppy with fine features sort of way. His short, light brown hair was neat, and he had big blue eyes and a small perfect nose with a dusting of freckles.

"I'm Alistair," he whispered, holding out his hand.

I took it and smiled. "Nina."

Professor Hernandez glared in my direction again. Alistair took notice, so we stopped talking, turning our attention back to the front of the room.

After a few minutes, I looked down at my phone to find a text from Jake.

> **Jake: How did the test go?**

> **Nina: Still in class. We haven't taken it yet. He is going over the assignments and called me out for the whore example. Thanks a lot for that ringtone. That was the icing on the cake.**

> **Jake: The shit cake? LOL. My pleasure. Let me know how the exam goes. I need to know if I have to start planning. (Insert evil laugh here.)**

I laughed even though the text made me very uneasy and reminded me what I was up against.

My phone vibrated again.

> **Jake: Stop freaking out, Nina.**

How did he know I was freaking out? I smiled to myself, put my phone back in my purse and glanced over at Alistair who grinned at me.

Professor Hernandez instructed the class to put all mobile devices away and began handing out the exams.

The problems presented were very similar to the homework assignment, and I began to make some tables and break down all of the information like Jake had showed me.

By the time I had finished, I knew I had gotten at least two out of the five problems correct but was unsure about the rest.

I could feel the doubt and anxiety building, and then the professor indicated our time was up. He walked around to collect the exams and let us know that he would correct them after class and post the results online tonight. He had setup a page on his website where we could log in for exam results.

The class was dismissed, and as I was walking out of the classroom, I heard Alistair behind me out of breath. "Nina, wait up."

"Hey." I smiled. "How did you do?"

"Pretty good. I think I got them all right, actually," he said.

"I wish I could say the same. I know I got at least two correct, but not sure about the other three."

"Well, if you're having trouble, I'd be happy to help you after class sometime."

"That's really sweet, but believe it or not, I actually have a really great tutor and still can't manage to do well... so..."

Alistair nodded and flashed me another big smile. "Well, maybe we could just hang out sometime?"

I hesitated. "Sure. That would be nice."

"Great. Um, let me get your number. I'll put it in my phone."

As I watched him enter the information, I suddenly felt uneasy and deep down, I knew it had something to do with my growing attraction to Jake. I was pretty sure I wasn't even Jake's type but still couldn't help the crush I had on him. I guess in a strange way, in agreeing to a date with Alistair, I felt disloyal to my own feelings. I was never the type that could focus on more than one guy at a time, even if the guy in focus had no clue how I felt. But I needed to move past that. I was pretty sure that it was unhealthy to think something would happen with Jake, especially after the little sexcapade I had overheard when I first moved in. Clearly, my roomie has his own "stuff" going on. That, coupled with the fact that he disappears to Boston every weekend...well, even if I was his type, which I'm not, it just wouldn't—

Alistair interrupted my thoughts. "Hey...are you still with me?"

I didn't realize I had zoned out. "Sorry, I was thinking about the exam." I lied.

He handed me back my phone as we walked toward the exit. "So, what was the deal with the Full House song?"

"Ugh. My friend changed my ringtone without my knowing. It's a running joke that I resemble the Olsen twins."

Was Jake my friend? I guess he was.

Stop. Thinking. About. Jake.

Alistair grinned. "Really? I wouldn't have picked up on that. I mean, they're cute and all, but you're much cuter."

"Why, thank you. You would be the first person to hold that sentiment."

"Well, it's true," he said. There was that thousand-watt smile of his again.

"Thanks."

"So…I better run. I have a Psych class that starts in a few minutes next door," he said.

"Okay. Enjoy that."

"Bye, Nina. I'll call you soon."

That afternoon, on the walk home, I came up with a plan to butter Jake up so that he would go easy on me with the whole fear-facing punishment. Maybe I could make a deal with him where I could at least have some say in what he chooses to have me do. For example, even though riding the subway was something I avoided, it gave me nowhere near the terror that elevators did. I was sure he didn't realize just how incapacitated I had become over the years and how hard it was going to be for me to face my fears.

Even though I hadn't gotten my grade yet, I was certain it wasn't an A, so I needed to put my plan into action. They say the way to get to a man is through his stomach. I knew just what I was going to make for him.

Tarah and Ryan arrived home together just as I was starting the fire on the stove.

"What are you doing, missy?" Tarah asked.

"Trying to save my ass."

She laughed. "What are you making?"

"Did Jake say anything about our bet?"

Tarah shook her head. "No. Jake doesn't really say anything to me about anything. Is this about the tutoring?"

"Yes. Basically, each time I don't get an A on one of my exams, he is going to make me face one of my phobias. It's a sick sort of punishment, really."

Ryan laughed. "No shit? I think that's brilliant!"

"I knew you would feel that way, Ryan."

Tarah rubbed my back. "I am sorry, sweetie. I agree with Ryan. You can't live like this, especially since you live in the city now. Imagine how much easier life would be if you could get past all of that shit."

"I just don't like to be forced into it."

Ryan raised his voice. "No one is forcing you to do anything, and you know it, Nina. You agreed to Jake's little bet because you know that you need to be pushed, or you'll never change. These things only get worse the longer you let them fester."

I knew he was right.

Ryan and Tarah left to have an early dinner downstairs at Eleni's. About twenty minutes later, I was just about finished with my masterpiece when I heard the door open.

Jake slammed the door shut and started sniffing. "What do I smell?"

His immediate reaction to the aroma made me chuckle. "What do you think you smell?

His stride toward the kitchen area became faster with each step. "I smell heaven. What did you do? That's not—"

I bit my bottom lip and nodded with a smile. "It is."

"Bananas Foster? Bananas fucking Foster?"

"Yup. I made it for you, as a thank you for helping me last night." I burst into laughter at his reaction as his eyes bugged out of his head.

Jake said nothing, just sat down, took a huge bite, dipping his head back in ecstasy and moaned.

I've heard that moan before. I shook my head to get the disturbing thought of Jake with another woman out of my mind.

His mouth was full. "Ugh. Mmmmmm. Oh my God. You know this is like my wet dream, right?"

There's an analogy: What Bananas Foster is to Jake... Jake is to Nina.

"I figured you'd like it."

"Like it...Nina...I fucking love it," he said before taking another huge bite. He ate in silence for a few minutes with his eyes closed half of the time. "Where did you learn to make this?"

"I actually took a dessert-making class back home once. It's actually not that hard to make. It's just butter, sugar, rum, vanilla, cinnamon, ice cream and of course, bananas."

He continued to devour the entire batch until the plate was bone dry. I sat across from the table with my chin in my hands just watching it happen like a spectator sport.

He ran his finger repeatedly across the plate licking the last remnants, which caused my insides to tingle.

I suddenly wished I were wearing the plate.

When there was nothing left, he closed his eyes one last time, slowly opened them wide, shook his head and said, "Mmm...mmm...mmm. Promise me you'll make that again for me."

I laughed at how serious he was actually being. "That can be arranged."

"I don't think you understand. That was the best thing I have ever tasted in my entire life. No one has ever made anything for me like that. My mother couldn't cook for shit growing up. She worked hard and all, especially after my father died but never cooked, never baked. That's why I started eating so many damn bananas in the first place."

That was the first moment Jake ever shared anything important about himself with me.

"How old were you when your father died?"

He seemed caught off guard by the question but answered looking down at the plate. "I was five, almost six."

My heart broke for him. "I'm sorry, Jake."

"Yeah, me too." He coughed and quickly changed the subject. "Anyway, you're making this again, okay?

"Well, I did make it as a thank you, but I have to admit...there may have been an ulterior motive."

He wiped his mouth with a napkin, crumpled it and threw it at me jokingly. "Oh?"

"Yes. I was actually hoping that maybe you would go easy on me if it turns out I didn't get an A...maybe let me have some say in how far I'm willing to go with this punishment thing."

He threw his head back in laughter, and I could see his tongue ring. He scratched his chin, pretending to think about it and then said, "Um...no."

"Jake..." I whined.

He mocked me in the same tone. "Nina..."

"I am so screwed."

"Oh, Ye of little faith. Did you even get your grade yet?"

"I am pretty sure they're up. I just have to go online and check if they're posted on Hernandez's website."

He walked down the hall and returned with his laptop, placing it on the counter. "Check it."

I nervously keyed in the web address as he leaned in over me. I could smell the bananas and rum on his breath and could feel him breathing on my shoulder, which made me fidgety as I typed in the password.

The first thing I noticed was Alistair's grade: Alistair York: 100.

Scrolling down, I looked for mine, and there it was: Nina Kennedy: 78.

My chest constricted with mixed emotions. I had gotten a C+, which was better than I could have ever hoped for but far from what I needed to avoid having to pass Jake's test.

Jake and I turned to each other at the same time, and the gleam in his eyes told me I was in for it.

SEVEN

Thursday afternoon, I was cleaning the kitchen when I received a text from Jake.

> *I am getting off of work early and should be home around 3:30. I'll meet you at the house. Then we'll leave together. Be ready.*

A few minutes later, he texted again.

> *Stop freaking out, Nina.*

And so, the ruminations began. I had no idea what he had in store for me, and he specifically gave me no hints, so that I wouldn't "freak out." Well, the not knowing made me freak out even more.

I took a shower to pass the time and could not for the life of me decide what to wear. What does one wear to a date with disaster? Regardless of where we ended up tonight, I was going to be one sweaty, panicky, white-knuckled mess.

I finally settled on a pair of jeans and a fitted black t-shirt. I might as well be comfortable and honestly, why would I need to dress up? It's not like Jake is going to notice how cute my ass is when I am keeled over on the ground hyperventilating.

At 3:15, I decided to sit and wait in the living area, attempting to distract myself by watching the *Katie* show. The topic was about close encounters with death. I shut it off because it was a trigger for my anxiety.

The door opened, and Jake walked in with a couple of paper shopping bags, grinning from ear to ear.

"Hey, little miss sunshine! Are you excited about our date?"

That suddenly made me nauseous, and I couldn't tell if it was because he called it a date or because I was about to make a fool of myself tonight. "I didn't realize it was a date."

"It's a date with destiny. Freedom awaits you once you can get past all of this shit you are doing to yourself."

Thanks for clarifying the date thing, jackass.

The fact that he looked scorching hot right now in a red plaid shirt that opened up to a fitted black t-shirt underneath wasn't helping my confused state.

I raised my neck to peek into the bags. "What did you buy?"

He shooed me away. "Just some supplies we'll need."

"Great," I said sarcastically.

Jake took the bags to his room while I waited on the couch. He reemerged with a large black backpack.

"Let's go, Nina. You ready?"

I got up and swallowed. "As ready as I'll ever be."

Another wave of nausea came when we hit the pavement of the sidewalk, and I knew there was no turning back.

To make matters worse, Mrs. Ballsworthy was at the window watching us, and when I looked up at her, she gave me the dirtiest look before shutting it. That was all I needed right now. Jake hadn't noticed, so I didn't mention it.

I could feel him looking at me as I stared down at the ground while we walked together, our steps in synch. At one point, he stopped walking, and I turned around to face him.

"Why did you stop? I asked.

He approached me and put both of his hands on my shoulders. I shivered at the unexpected contact, and as we stood on the street corner, he looked into my eyes intently.

"Nina, I can tell you're going through all these little scenarios in your head right now. It's not helping. The only thing that is ever happening to you is what is happening in the moment, not all of the disastrous possibilities in your mind. So, cut the shit, okay? I'm not going to let anything happen to you."

While I didn't like the tone of his voice, the last part gave me some comfort.

We continued walking until we came across what I believed was our destination: DeKalb Avenue subway station. I was honestly relieved that he had chosen the subway as my exercise, since it was the lesser of the evils. Nevertheless, I wanted to stall.

"Where are we going?" I asked.

He lifted his arms and smiled. "Manhattan, baby!"

"That's it? How long is the ride?"

"Not long, but I didn't calculate it." Jake walked a few steps down into the station as I stood on the sidewalk above. He turned around and stared up at me.

My pulse quickened, and I closed my eyes unsure of what to do next. My mind flashed images of being stuck like a sardine in that tin can. When I opened my eyes, he was still standing in the same spot. His large green eyes lit up from the darkness of the stairwell.

He was so beautiful. I just couldn't move, though.

He stood there patiently on the steps waiting for me to come down. I was frozen. Finally, he lifted his hand toward me and silently urged me with his steady gaze to walk down and take it.

"Nina, come on. I've got you," he finally said.

At that moment, something clicked, and I moved toward him. His warm hand enveloped mine, and our fingers intertwined. His thumb ring pressed against my skin as he held my hand tightly and led me down the stairwell, which smelled of urine.

If I weren't so terrified of acting like a complete lunatic on the train, this moment would have been epic. It was a mixed bag of emotions with fear and lust shining above all. My body was trembling in confusion.

I felt a sudden coldness as Jake let go of my hand to pay for our subway cards.

He thanked the subway worker and surprised me when he grabbed my hand again. The butterflies in my stomach were now doing somersaults as he led me through the turnstiles.

We sat down on a bench as we waited for the train to arrive. Disappointingly, he let go of my hand.

Then, he patted my back. "You're doing okay so far."

"Yeah," I managed to say as I continued to breathe heavily. I kept nodding for no reason and wished the train would just hurry up and get there.

The B train finally approached and grinded to a screeching halt. He took my hand again and led me onto the crowded train car, which was bustling with evening commuters.

There were no seats, which didn't matter to me. I preferred to stand, since that made for an easier exit if I ever had to leap out at the next stop.

When the train doors closed, the panic really began to set in. I felt completely trapped and began to shake uncontrollably.

Jake put both of his hands on my trembling arms causing my conflicting emotions to assault one another. Lust was winning by a thread. "It's okay to feel nervous, Nina. You're not supposed to be comfortable. Stop trying to fight it and just let those feelings be there."

When he let go of me, my body craved the return of his touch. I just wanted him to hold me until this disastrous feeling passed or until we got out of that train car. Trying to calm myself, I focused on a baby who was sitting on her mother. If she could do this, I could. She smiled at me, and I smiled back.

He was looking at me, but my shame kept me from making eye contact. I was still shivering while holding onto a pole. It was difficult to accept the uncomfortable feelings instead of fighting them. The train swayed, and I couldn't tell if it was the normal movement of the vessel or my skewed perception due to nerves.

I jumped when Jake grabbed my chin forcing my eyes on his. "How are you doing?"

"Fine. I just want this to be over."

"Our stop is next." He smiled.

Immediate relief washed over me upon hearing that, and the last few minutes of the ride were somewhat bearable because there was now a light at the end of the tunnel.

When the train stopped at the 8th Avenue station, I followed Jake out of the car. My breathing immediately slowed, and I felt on top of the world. I was free.

Turning to me on the platform, he smiled and said, "You're still with us. Was that so bad?"

I breathed a sigh of relief. "It was about what I expected, but I am glad it's over. Can we take a cab home now?"

He stared at me silently for several seconds before leading me through the turnstiles and up the stairs to the streets of Manhattan. The noise and smells of the city were a stark contrast to the dark subway station. I hoped, at least, he was taking me somewhere fun.

"Jake? Where are we going?"

He stopped short in front of a Chinese restaurant. The scent of roasting chickens and MSG was nauseating. He turned around to me as swarms of people rushing home from work brushed past us. "Nina..."

Then, I had a light bulb moment, looking at the large backpack he said contained supplies and my heart sank.

"The subway. That wasn't the exercise...it was just a means to get here. You're taking me somewhere now, aren't you?"

Jake nodded. "You need to trust me, okay?"

Panic started to build all over again. The sounds of car horns from the street seemed to get louder as my nerves became sensitized.

I licked my lips nervously as we walked side by side through the sidewalks of New York.

I turned my head to him as we continued walking at a fast pace. "Where are you taking me, Jake? Tell me!"

"If I tell you, you are gonna overreact. Just wait until we get there, and remember what I said. I wouldn't let anything bad happen to you."

"What if I can't do it?"

"You always have a choice. But if you choose to back away from this, our deal is off. In the end, you know you'd only be letting yourself down."

As we walked in silence for about three more blocks, he stopped in front of a high-rise apartment building. "Here we are."

I hesitated before following him into the front door. A friendly-looking heavyset man greeted us and smacked hands with Jake.

"Jake, my man, how goes it?" He smiled.

"Good, good, Vinny. This is my friend, Nina."

Vinny stuck out his hand. "Nina, it's a pleasure."

"Same here," I said.

Jake turned to Vinny. "We still good to go?"

"Yeah, man. No problem at all. Take as long as you need."

"Thanks, Vin. I'll owe you one." Jake turned to me. "Come on."

"Who is he?"

"An old friend. He manages the building."

Jake led me through the foyer and down a hallway. I knew where this was heading, and it was not good. We stopped in front of an elevator, and he pushed the up button.

This was my absolute worst nightmare. I pleaded with him. "Jake, listen, I don't know if Ryan ever said anything, but this whole thing...all of my problems...they started in an elevator. It was where my first panic attack happened. I was in high school and got stuck in one and—"

"All the more reason to get past that. If you get in one right now, you can help undo the damage created by your own mind."

I grabbed his arm and begged. "Please...I'll do anything else but this." My eyes were beginning to well up.

When the door opened, he stuck his hand inside to keep it from closing. When he looked back at me, he noticed I was starting to cry.

"Fuck. Nina, don't cry. Come on, I promise you that nothing will happen to you in there."

I shook my head and covered my face to mask my tears. I was disappointed in myself for reacting this way, but this was too big of a leap to take so soon. Just the sight of that death box made me want to run far away. I couldn't imagine having to set foot in it.

He threw his backpack into the elevator and continued to stand in the opening, holding the door open one with of his hands and reaching the other out for me to take.

I considered running. I considered pretending to pass out. I considered screaming for help. In the end though, I looked into Jake's eyes, deciding to trust him and took his hand, letting him pull me into the elevator. He tried to release me, but I grabbed onto his hand tighter.

"Leave the door open," I demanded.

"Okay. We can take this slow."

Jake kept his hand on the open door button. "You tell me when you are ready to take a ride."

"I won't ever be ready. Don't you understand? I won't ever be ready for that door to close."

"Then you need to let me decide when, okay? You trust me, Nina?"

I looked at his pleading eyes and squeezed his hand tighter.

Why did he care? Why did he want to do this for me?

"I probably shouldn't trust you, Jake, but the truth is, I do. I am just scared."

I knew I had to do this. If I couldn't do this today, with this crazy guy who was willing to help me through it, I would never be able to do it myself. It was only getting worse over time. Even if it killed me, I knew I had to let him close that door.

"Nina, I'm going to let the doors close now, okay?"

I nodded silently and watched as he took his finger off of the button. When the doors closed completely, I began to shake uncontrollably. Memories of the last time I was in an elevator flashed through my mind.

He pushed a button, and as the elevator began to rise up, I instinctively leaned into him, holding on for dear life. I could feel his chest tighten as my nails dug into him, and I closed my eyes, breathing in his scent to calm my nerves. I was terrified and didn't care how foolish I looked. I needed him to hold onto me, because it felt like I was going pass out.

"You're doing good," he whispered into my ear, which was right under his mouth. "Look. We're on fifty now."

I shook my head, which was buried in his armpit. "Don't tell me! I don't want to know how high we are."

My heart was pounding against him for at least a minute.

Jake tapped me. "Nina, you did it. We reached the eightieth floor." He released me from his grip, and I was still breathing heavily as the doors opened. "You want to walk around up here for a bit or do you wanna go right back down?"

"Go back down. Please," I urged. I just wanted to get this over with.

"You got it," he said as he pressed the down button, and the doors closed.

I started to calm down a bit. I just had to keep myself from hyperventilating or fainting on the way down, and I could make it out of this box alive. I clutched his shirt again, using him for support. I could feel his breath and smell the mint gum he was chewing.

I peeked at the numbers and saw sixty-five, sixty-four, sixty-three, sixty-two, and then it happened: a massive jolt as the elevator came to an abrupt halt.

The rush of panic that swept through me in that second was the most overpowering I had ever experienced, and my body burned up like a fire had started inside.

I screamed.

"Jake! Jake? We're stuck! What's happening? What's happening?"

"Shh." He was hushing me to calm me down, and it took me a few seconds to notice his relaxed expression... and that his hand was on the stop button.

"Please tell me...*you*...did not just stop this elevator?"

"Calm down, Nina. Calm dow—"

I smacked him in the chest with all of my might.

"The fuck, Nina. Stop!" he yelled as he grabbed my hands and locked them together in his palms. He was strong, and I stood no chance of freeing them. He blocked access to the buttons as he held my hands together.

I was panting. "You told me you wouldn't force me to do anything I wasn't comfortable with. I am begging you... to move this elevator...*now*!"

He squeezed my hands, securing them even more firmly in his grasp. "Nina, calm down. It's okay. Don't you see you have to stick this out? You have to pass through the moment of panic. If you can get past that and see that nothing happens, you can do anything."

"I don't want to. It's not worth it!"

"What's not worth it?"

"Experiencing this...these horrible feelings!" I felt like I was starting to hyperventilate as my breath became impossible to catch.

"Nothing is actually happening to you right now. It's you and me standing here. That's it. It's all in your mind." He let go of my hands and cupped my face. "Look at me." He looked into my eyes and I could only imagine the freak he saw looking back at him. He inched closer and despite my nerves, my legs tingled when I felt his breath on my mouth as he said, "If you make me push that button, the deal's off."

"Fine...deal's off...do it. Now!"

He released his hands from my face then stood in front of the buttons, crossing his arms. He shook his head vehemently. "No."

"Jake...push the button."

"No. You'd be back at square one. You have to get over this, and the only way is to experience it. I'm not letting you give up that easily."

I began screaming for help and tried to nudge him away from the panel, but he was too strong, so I punched the back wall in frustration.

I was shaking, felt defeated and said under my breath, "Fuck me! I can't believe this."

"Well, that's one way we could pass the time, but I don't make a habit of doing that with women in the midst of a hyperventilation episode. It's too confusing...hard to tell what's actually causing the heavy breathing."

I stifled a laugh but tried not to let him see it. "Very funny," I said.

"I was kidding, of course. Just trying to make you laugh, but apparently it's not working," he said as he continued to stand against the panel, his criss-crossed, tattooed arms not budging.

I walked over to the other side of the elevator and slid down to the floor. I hugged myself, rocking back and forth in an effort to calm my panic. With my eyes closed, I could hear the sound of Jake opening the zipper of his backpack and tried to imagine I was somewhere else, anywhere but stuck in this death trap.

Breathe in. Breathe out.

Several minutes passed in silence, as I kept my head down in a fetal position. I was beginning to calm down a tiny bit when it happened: what sounded like an explosion.

Sheer terror ensued as I jumped and screamed simultaneously. When I looked over at Jake, he was on the ground laughing hysterically, covered in foam, holding...a bottle of champagne.

Son of a bitch.

"Jake! What the hell? What THE hell?"

Champagne dripped down the bottle that he held above our heads. "We're celebrating!"

"You are sick!"

"We are celebrating your survival, Nina! It's been twelve minutes and thirty-three seconds since this elevator stopped, and you are still alive."

His antics only got worse when he produced two champagne flutes from the backpack, followed by a small blanket, which he fluffed dramatically before placing it down onto the middle of the floor.

"What are you doing?"

"What does it look like we're doing? We're having a picnic."

He then took out an iPod, speaker and a bunch of food from Trader Joe's: crackers, hummus and chocolate covered cherries.

"You are not serious!"

"Dead serious. We need to change your negative connotation of elevators. The last time you were in this situation, you associated it with darkness and misery. Now, the next time you get stuck in one, you'll think of the amazeballs picnic we're gonna have."

Jake poured the champagne into the two glasses and handed me one. I didn't extend my hand. "You're being a jackass."

He glared at me. "You can take it, or I can drink it all. Then, you'll just be stuck in this elevator with a *drunk* jackass."

I let out a sigh and reluctantly took the glass. He began opening the packages of food he brought and popped a chocolate covered cherry into his mouth. "These are awesome. Try one," he said as he handed me the container. I had no appetite but took one and ate it. He was right. It was delicious.

I shook my head as I realized that, for a few seconds, he had really distracted me, and I had stopped focusing on the potential for disaster. I had been living in the moment without even realizing it. While not gone entirely, the fear had somewhat subsided in the midst of this absurd setup.

I stayed quiet in my corner of the elevator and rolled my eyes as Jake spread some hummus onto a cracker and ate it. Just when I thought things couldn't get any more bizarre, he started fiddling with his iPod, connecting it to a speaker. It took me a few seconds to realize what song he had played: *Free Fallin'* by Tom Petty.

That jerk! I started to laugh and covered my mouth.

Jake, who had been serious for the most part, aside from the champagne popping, also started to crack up when he saw he had broken through my bitterness.

"Nina Kennedy. Is that a laugh I hear? Are you seriously making light of this dangerous and life-threatening situation we are in? Shame on you!"

I began to laugh even harder, and he threw a cherry at me as he flashed a wicked grin.

"Jake, you are nuts, you know that?"

"Oh! Speaking of nuts..." He lifted his finger and reached into his backpack. "You need to sample *my* nuts, Nina. Try these." He snickered knowing he had succeeded in embarrassing me. "Why are you blushing?"

Laughing, I said, "I don't want to taste your nuts, thanks." When he handed me the container anyway, I looked at it and said, "Chocolate covered brazil nuts? I have never had these." I took one and ate it. "Mmm. They are good."

His smile shone through the glass as he sipped more champagne. "See?"

Several minutes passed as we joked around while listening to the music, picking at the food and finishing off the champagne. My fear level had gone down even more significantly.

I shook my head again as I realized that the next song on Jake's "terrorize Nina" playlist was *Stuck in the Middle with You* by Stealer's Wheel.

"You like that, huh?" he laughed.

I shook my head, just staring at him in awe. "You're crazy...but you know what? I am not panicking anymore, so there is something to this."

He winked. "Good girl."

Something about the way he said that made me shiver. I knew I must be calming down because my body suddenly became hyperaware of him.

Lust was winning again.

More carefully selected songs played one after the other as we continued to eat, and since my nerves were desensitizing, I had begun taking notice of all the other things I had been missing, like, how incredible he smelled. This time, it was just the cologne without the cigarettes. His hair was perfectly styled and gelled. The fitted tee he wore under the plaid shirt hugged his chest. The sleeves were rolled up, showing off his strong forearms. I looked closely at the colored tats on his right arm, unable to decipher what they all meant. He was wearing black jeans and black Converse sneakers. His feet were laid out next to me, and they were large, maybe size eleven. That reminded me of his hand and how big and warm it felt when he held my hand on the subway trip.

He smelled good enough to eat.

Jake interrupted my thoughts. "Earth to Nina!"

I blinked. "Hi."

"Have you had your fill?

I shook my head. "Excuse me?"

"Should I put this stuff away?"

"Oh...yeah...um...yes."

I laid my head back on the elevator wall, exhausted from my earlier self-induced panic episode. I was not completely calm by any means but was surprised to know that sticking it out actually did work. I had been sure that if I couldn't escape a terrifying situation, I would faint or even die from the panic. The feelings really do subside eventually. And if you can reach that point, it's actually exhilarating. What goes up must come down, I guess.

Jake had just about finished putting the items back into his backpack when the music changed. He joined me in leaning his head against the back wall and closed his eyes. He was sitting far away from me and I ached for him to move closer. The tone of this new song was completely different from the other ones. It was mellow with very little instruments. The female singer had a soothing, folksy voice. It was unfamiliar, but the words were breathtaking. The song was about a woman who gets stuck in an elevator with a stranger she was wary of initially, but he really grows on her, and she starts to fall for him, realizing eventually that their getting stuck together was meant to be and magical.

I opened my eyes to look over at Jake, who still had his eyes closed. "Who sings this?" I asked.

"It's a song I found online called *Stuck in the Elevator* by Edie Brickell. You like it?"

"Yeah. I do."

"Good."

"You're still insane, though."

He opened his eyes, turned to me and smiled. His dimples completely did me in at that point. Then he closed his eyes again listening to the song, and once again, I got to look at his handsome face in peace, without his knowing. His nose was perfect, not too big and not too small. His lips were crimson and the lower one with the lip ring was slightly more prominent. I noticed that his dark lashes were much longer than mine.

I thought about how my father would react if he knew I was stuck in an elevator with a guy as "dangerous" looking as Jake. Dad likely wouldn't get the irony: that Jake had done more for me than all the other straight-laced guys I had ever known put together. My asshole ex only laughed at my phobias instead of helping me through them. He was too busy cheating on me.

I didn't really know much about Jake's life at all. What I did know for sure was that he was complex and closed off. For someone who had done so much for me in a short amount of time, he offered very little about himself. But he didn't have to say anything for me to know that what you saw was *not* what you got. His choosing this emotional song confirmed it.

There was so much I wanted to ask him, so much I wanted to know, but I was afraid to find out. I didn't really want to hear what I suspected...that he had a girlfriend in Boston. Was it his girlfriend that I overheard him with that first day I moved in? There hadn't been any girls in the house since. Truthfully, I also didn't really want to hear that I wasn't his type.

I wondered if he really understood how much what he had done for me today meant. I also wondered if he knew that I felt exactly like the woman singing this song. That if I had to be stuck in an elevator with anyone, I was glad it was with him.

I turned away when he abruptly opened his eyes and asked, "You want to get going?"

"You mean you are going to put me out of my misery?"

"Yeah, that was the deal. When you finally relaxed... oh, I would say somewhere in the middle of *It's A Small World After All*...the mission had been accomplished. You know, when you're not hyperventilating, you're actually kind of fun to be around." He smiled. "Ready to get moving?"

I thought about it. "In a minute. Let this song finish."

Jake winked at me again, and suddenly, I wasn't sure if I ever wanted to leave.

EIGHT

The next morning I woke up to another paper bat by my bedside that said:

You didn't run...you saw it through.
Mr. Bat is proud of you.

I wondered when he had put it there and if I was asleep and drooling when he did it. I clutched the bat to my chest closing my eyes, grinning from ear to ear. I had felt such a sense of accomplishment after yesterday. The subway ride home was a piece of cake, too, after surviving the elevator.

It was Friday, so Jake had already left the house. He usually took the Amtrak train to Boston for the weekend straight from work. I wouldn't see him until Sunday night or Monday, depending on how late he returned to Brooklyn.

The house was basically boring on weekends without him around. Tarah and Ryan would ask me to tag along with them to the city or to a movie, but I usually declined and opted to stay home and study or catch up on laundry.

Early Sunday evening, I had finished most of my homework and errands and found myself alone in the house again. The door to Jake's room was left cracked open, so I went inside, plopping down on top of his bed. His signature scent was all over the comforter. I buried my nose in it, imagining that it was him.

I sat up on his bed for a bit and looked around, bouncing ever so slightly on the firm mattress. There was a collection of pens on his bedside table as well as a cigarette lighter. Oddly, next to the pens were four of those pinwheels that kids might get at a carnival. I took one and blew on it, watching it spin. Jake was so puzzling.

I opened the bedside drawer and immediately shut it when I noticed a strip of condoms inside next to a pack of cigarettes. It reminded me of the upsetting fact that the guy I was infatuated with was having sex with someone or some *people* other than me. Cigarettes, condoms...*pinwheels*, you know, the usual stuff you found in 24-year-old guy's bedroom.

I got up and walked over to the picture on his chest of drawers of his twin nieces that sat next to the gargoyle figurine collection. Maybe the pinwheels were for them? The girls were beautiful and looked so much like him with the same dark hair, light eyes and dimples.

His closet was open, and it smelled even better than his comforter. I ran my finger across the hanging shirts that were mostly black and navy with a few plaids mixed in and looked down at the closet floor at the mess of shoes strewn about, mostly Converse and Doc Martens.

I sat back down on the bed and noticed a stack of large sketchpads left out on his desk. I grabbed the first one off of the stack and got chills as I flipped it open.

What my eyes were met with took my breath away. The first picture was an amazingly lifelike drawing of a man on a motorcycle. The man was drawn from behind, and only his face was turned around looking over his shoulder. His eyes seemed to be staring at me right off of the page. How you could make that happen with pencil was beyond me. The drawing, with its texture and shadowing, just seemed to come to life. *Jake drew this?* It was unbelievable.

I kept going through the book, and each drawing was better than the last. Another one was of the same man riding the motorcycle into the clouds in the sky. There were also a lot of drawings of the same woman or girl, with wild curly hair. In one of them, she was dancing in the rain and had a long skirt that seemed to move within the picture. They were all done solely in pencil with blends of charcoal and graphite.

There was another picture of a butterfly, but the center was a lifelike woman, instead of a thorax. The drawings were so intricate, and the attention to detail was impressive. I felt guilty for looking through the book, but Jake left it right on his desk, so it couldn't have been something he was trying to hide. *Right?* At least, I made myself believe that.

I finished going through the first sketchpad and became hungry for more. I grabbed the entire pile and devoured each one with my eyes. Some were of people and others were just nature scenes. Certain ones were so stunning, that I had to stop and stare at them for several minutes at a time, examining every last detail. Then, I would go back to some of the pictures again if I couldn't get the image out of my head.

I was frantically searching these photos for clues about Jake's life. With each drawing, I was more and more confused about the possible meanings. Were they based on real people or just characters he created from his imagination? Jake was even more complicated than I originally thought.

At one point, I rested my head on his black pillowcase, relishing the rustic masculine aroma that invaded my senses. Between the drawings and the intoxicating scent, I was super aroused.

Several minutes passed, and I gradually became drowsy, deciding to close my eyes. That was the last thing I remembered before I awoke to Jake standing over me with a death stare, as I lay on his bed amidst a pile of his private sketches.

Was I dreaming? I rubbed my eyes from the sudden brightness. The realization that this situation was not imagined caused my heart to explode out of my chest. It felt like I was also about to lose control of my bladder, so I clenched the muscles between my thighs and jumped up, scooting back against the headboard.

"Jake...I can explain."

"What the fuck, Nina?" he whispered hoarsely, his tone angry.

The sad and disappointed look in his eyes scared me, and I was even more terrified because I had put it there by violating his privacy.

His hair was dripping wet from the rain which I could now hear pounding against the window. Under different circumstances, being holed up in his room during a rainstorm would have been a dream, one that would not include him looking like he wanted to murder me.

He continued to stand over me speechless, and I knew I had to say something, but the words just wouldn't come out. I noticed his backpack was thrown clumsily in the middle of the floor.

After several seconds passed, I cleared my throat and started with a white lie about the reason for going into his room. "Um...a few hours ago, I was alone in the house, and your door was open. I had thought I left the math workbook in here, so I came inside. I noticed these sketchbooks. I only meant to peek in at the top one, but when I saw how amazing the first drawing was...I just couldn't stop looking."

He swallowed and continued to look at me with a burning stare, but said nothing. His chest was rising as he breathed in and out. *Shit.*

I continued. "I must have closed my eyes and fallen asleep."

Jake blinked repeatedly but was still silent. A trickle of rainwater ran down his forehead.

My voice was shaking. "I am really sorry. I should have never thought it was okay to look at your stuff. For the record, they are the most phenomenal drawings I have ever seen."

I sat there against the back headboard frozen with my knees to my chest. Jake said nothing as he moved closer and took the sketchpads, piling them on top of each other. Then, he returned them to their original spot on the desk.

"Again, I'm sorry," I said.

I started to get up planning to return to my room, humiliated. Just then, I felt a firm grip on my wrist, and the return of his voice shook me. "Where are you going?"

"Back to my room."

He pushed me back down gently and released his grasp. "Just stay."

Huh? My heart beat faster.

"Stay? What do you mean?"

"I mean...you were comfortable here. Just stay."

"You're not mad at me?"He shook his head. "I didn't say that. You shouldn't have been snooping."

"I know. I really am sorry."

Jake didn't respond to my apology. Instead, he walked over to the door, closed it and shut off the light. I looked at the digital clock, which said 11:30. It was later than I thought. Only the streetlights outside illuminated the room now, as he removed his wet jacket and threw it on the floor. Then, he pulled his t-shirt over his head and was completely shirtless.

Oh...wow...okay.

I bit down on my bottom lip hard, and my body trembled as he approached the bed.

Yeah, this was more like the dream I had imagined.

"Scoot over," he said in a low voice.

I turned to my side and moved to the right, tucking my arms under my chin.

An indescribable sensation came over me when I felt his warm rock hard chest up against my back. Then, he put his arm around my waist. He was...spooning me.

Holy shit.

I closed my eyes, breathing in the masculine smell of his body: sweat mixed with cologne and rain, and I hoped he couldn't sense my nerves. The room was completely silent aside from the sound of the rain pelting the window, but I felt like he would be able to hear my heart beating through my ears.

His breathing was heavy, and I could feel it on my neck. At one point, I inadvertently moved and brushed up against the metal of his lip ring and it caused me to flinch.

He spoke low against my back, his voice vibrating through me. "You're moving around a lot. You okay with this, Nina? Would you rather go back to your bed?"

"No. I want to stay."

He had no idea how much.

"Good." His body seemed to relax further into mine after I said that I wanted to stay. His nose was buried in my hair and I could feel him smelling me. He gripped my waist and the heat of his breath behind me continued to make me crazy. My underwear was completely soaked from the need developing between my legs.

I didn't understand what the spooning meant or really, how such an innocent thing could make my body respond this way. I just knew that it felt amazing to be so close to him and that my emotions were going haywire. Those butterflies in my stomach? They were forming a conga line right about now.

After getting a glimpse inside his mind through those drawings and after bonding with him in the elevator last week, lying next to him like this was the most intimate experience I had ever had.

"Jake?"

"Yeah."

"I really am sorry for invading your privacy."

After a long pause, he said into my hair, "It's okay, Nina."

"Thank you."

"Nina?"

"Yeah?"

"Your underwear drawer might get rearranged this week. That's all I'm sayin."

My back moved against his mouth as I giggled. I started to relax, and minutes later, I fell asleep in his arms.

NINE

Two weeks later, and things with Jake were stranger than ever. I hadn't slept in his bed ever again after that night, and we never spoke about the spooning or the drawings I discovered. The morning after I slept in his room, I woke to an empty bed because he had already left for work.

He tutored me a couple of more times and made no effort to take things any further with me those nights alone in his room. He was basically acting like nothing ever happened. As a protective mechanism, I had convinced myself that this was for the best. In reality, his indifference made me furious and unfortunately, even more physically attracted to him, if that was possible.

The only positive thing to come out of the anger I felt was that it made me focus harder on my studies. I was now in a secret mental competition with him, determined to get an A on my next math exam. I didn't want to give him the satisfaction of taking me on another expedition of fear and felt like I needed to prove myself. At least, it was a positive way to channel the sexual frustration.

That's not to say I didn't close my eyes at night and imagine him lying behind me. Knowing what that actually felt like now was a curse. Keeping my feelings in check was so much easier before that night. But I was also determined to move on from my infatuation with Jake.

So, one Monday afternoon after math class when Alistair asked me for a date the following Friday night, my response was, "Sure, why not?" Jake would be on his way to Boston by the time Alistair came to pick me up from the apartment, so there would be no awkwardness. Not that Jake would even care, but it made me feel better knowing that he wouldn't be there to scrutinize my date. Alistair was pretty much the polar opposite of Jake except for the fact that they were both really smart.

The Wednesday evening before the Friday of my date, I had come home late from school to find Ryan, Tarah and Jake sitting in the living room watching television. It was unusual for everyone to be home at once.

I silently waved hello to them without making eye contact and went straight to my room. I was in a pissy mood and had spent the greater part of the walk home angry at myself for obsessing over Jake again. And when Mrs. Ballsworthy told me to "fuck off" on the way in, for the first time, I loudly returned the sentiment; that's how bad of a mood I was in.

Once in my room, I tore off my clothes and changed into my favorite pink sweatpants and put on a comfortable t-shirt. I was about to start a new book on my Kindle when Jake appeared at the doorway.

He stretched his arms up and touched the top of the threshold. Why did he have to look like a tattooed trophy and smell so good? His shirt rode up, showcasing his washboard stomach as he stood there before me saying, "What...you don't say hello anymore?"

"Jake, I'm not in the mood."

He walked slowly toward me. "What's gotten into you?"

I didn't say anything in response, so he continued, "Or is the problem that... nothing...or no one...has gotten *into* you lately?"

I put down my Kindle in shock. *That bastard.* "What did you just say?"

He held up his hands. "Relax, Nina. It was just a joke! You know, you're being uptight. Uptight people need to get laid? Just a joke."

I threw a pillow at him. "Get out."

He threw it back at me. "Fuck. I was only kidding. You used to appreciate my sick sense of humor," he said, looking seriously pissed.

"Well, I didn't think that was funny."

"Why have you been so weird lately?" he yelled.

"*I'm* being weird?"

He glared at me. "Yes, Nina, you are."

I huffed. "Whatever."

Jake just shook his head before walking out and slamming his bedroom door.

I put my head in my hands regretting what just happened. *Was* it me? Was I being a bitch to him these past couple of weeks and treating him differently because I somehow felt rejected by him? Did I make the spooning thing out to be something that it wasn't?

Maybe I needed to control my feelings better, because losing him as a friend was not an option; There were so few people I could count on here in New York, and I needed him in my life.

I immediately got up and was going to walk down the hall to apologize when we knocked right into each other as he was passing my room.

"Ow," I said rubbing my nose.

He briefly held onto my shoulders. "Watch it there, Speedy."

"I was actually coming to apologize. I think I *have* been a little testy lately. I guess I am just stressed out about school and the math exam today."

He shook his head. "I shouldn't have said that to you, Nina." His eyes were sincere, and I could tell he meant it.

"It's okay. I know you were just joking."

Jake stuck out his hand. "Truce?"

"Truce," I said, relishing the warmth of his firm grip on my hand and wishing that his idea of a truce involved more than just a handshake, something like...oh...sucking on his bottom lip.

Yeah, I was a lost cause.

He let go of my hand, and we walked down the rest of the hallway to the kitchen together.

Ryan shut off the television that he and Tarah had been watching in the adjacent living room. "Tarah and I are going down to Eleni's for some grub. You guys wanna come?"

Jake was drinking straight out of an orange juice container when he stopped and looked over at me awaiting my response.

"No, thanks. I am not that hungry...gonna just stay here and read," I said.

Jake then waved his hand. "Nah, man, I'll pass too."

"Okay, ya'll. Suit yourselves!" Tarah said as she and Ryan left the apartment.

When the door slammed shut, Jake walked over to the sofa and turned on the television. It was a rare sight, since he spent most of his time holed up in his room listening to music. He was channel surfing, spreading his long legs out onto the coffee table and looked over toward the kitchen at me. "Isn't your test grade supposed to be in by now?"

"Yes." I smiled guiltily, knowing it was most definitely in. I had been putting off finding out what it was.

"Did you check?"

"No."

Without saying anything, Jake left and returned from down the hall with his laptop. "Come on, Nina...it's d-day. I can't wait to take you on this next one. Is it wrong I'm hoping for a suck-ass grade?"

"Yes...very wrong," I said as I opened the laptop.

He was rubbing his hands together, in taunting anticipation.

"Are you trying to start a fire with those hands of yours?"

"Just gearing up for the inevitable."

"Thanks for the confidence," I said as I typed in the password.

"It's gonna be a good one. You should be hoping for a C."

Jake's excitement about our next little adventure gave me mixed feelings to say the least.

As I scrolled down, once again, I noticed Alistair's name before mine.

Alistair York: 90. Well, whattya know, he's not perfect after all.

Jake leaned in. His breath hitched because he saw it before I did:

Nina Kennedy: 94.

Holy crap!

When I saw my name, I had to blink multiple times to make sure it was real. I was speechless as I turned to him.

Jake's dimpled smile was bigger than the Joker's, and he threw his head back. "Nina Kennedy...you fucking rock, girl," he said as he pulled me into him hard for a congratulatory hug.

I closed my eyes and relished the heat and familiarity of being in his arms again amidst the excitement I felt at having achieved what I thought was virtually impossible. It was euphoric. My heart was beating fast against his chest.

He pulled back with his arms still on mine, and his eyes sparkled as he shook me. "Nina...you did it! You fucking did it! We have to celebrate."

"Jake, you did this. I can't thank you enough for all your help."

I wanted to kiss him.

He kept smiling at me, then said, "Where do you wanna go? What do you want to do? Anything you want."

I want to feel you inside of me.

"Actually, I know just what I want to do right now," I said.

"What?"

"I wanna make you your favorite dessert."

"No...come on. You shouldn't have to cook tonight."

"I want to," I said. "I owe you big time for this, and I could really go for some myself. Plus, all the ingredients are still in the cabinet from last time."

"Well, if you insist. Your Bananas Foster is like crack, so you're not gonna hear any argument from me."

"I didn't think I would."

As I gathered the pan, rum, spices and bananas, Jake leaned over the counter following me with his eyes as I moved around the kitchen.

"I am a little bummed about the excursion you're gonna miss. It was going to be killer. But there's always next time," he said.

"Now you've got me curious about what was in store for me. Something tells me I dodged a massive bullet."

His grin said it all. "You have no idea."

"You're evil," I said, throwing a banana at him, which he caught. "You can peel. I'll cut."

"I can handle that. I'm good at stripping off layers slowly," he said winking.

"I thought we established you were not, in fact, an exotic dancer."

"Doesn't mean I don't give private shows."

I must have momentarily lost my mind. Even though I laughed at him, the mental images that emerged made my cutting of the bananas faster and harder. And just like that, the knife I was using slipped and plunged deeply right into my finger.

"Ow...shit!" I screamed. "Ow!"

Blood gushed out, and the pain was excruciating. Jake immediately got up grabbing my hand. "Shit. Nina!"

"Ooh, ow, ow," I cried.

What happened in rapid succession over the next ten seconds nearly undid me. He looked around for a towel and didn't find one. On instinct he wrapped my finger in the bottom of his shirt and squeezed it. When he lifted it out and saw that it was still bleeding badly, he took my finger into his mouth and held it there, sucking it hard to stop the bleeding.

Took.My.Finger.And.Sucked.It.

Remember that saying about experiencing pain to attain a pleasure you have never experienced before? Well, I think for the first time in my life, I actually got it.

He was completely serious, mind you, in those seconds of applying pressure to my wound. He was just trying to get the bleeding to stop. It wasn't meant to be a turn on, but of course, everything Jake did had that effect on me whether he knew it or not, and well, this just put me over the edge.

It was not an exaggeration to say those seconds of my finger being trapped in his hot mouth while he breathed rapidly over it, were more exciting than full-on sex with Spencer had ever been, ten fold. The competing sensations of pleasure and pain were something I had never experienced together at the same time.

His mouth made a popping sound as he released my finger to the cold air, and there was a tiny bit of my blood on his lip. He took off his now stained shirt and wrapped it firmly around my finger. I couldn't help staring at his body. It looked as if it were carved from stone.

The bleeding had slowed, but it had not stopped. "We'll wrap it in this for now," he said, holding my finger tightly in his shirt.

"You have some blood." I nervously lifted my fingertip to his bottom lip, grazing the ring and wiping it lightly. "Right here."

Instead of wiping it with his free hand, he slid his tongue back and forth slowly across his bottom lip, licking away the rest as he looked at me. My heart skipped a beat. It was so strangely erotic, and my body became fully aware. He stared into my eyes as he held my wrapped finger, and I felt something shift. I couldn't put my finger on it (no pun intended), but something felt different between us in that moment. It was a feeling I had definitely never experienced before.

The room was completely quiet as he broke the stare, looking down at my wrapped finger. He cleared his throat, his voice was thick, "I'm gonna see what we have in the bathroom for first aid."

Still in a state of bewilderment, I nodded but said nothing, as he ran down the hall, returning with gauze, peroxide and bandages. Removing the shirt from my finger, he carefully treated the area with some peroxide on a cotton ball. I tried to look down at the wound and not at his bare chest as he blew on the cut before wrapping it in gauze, followed by a bandage to hold it together.

"That should do it for now," he said before releasing my hand. "You may want to take a look at it tomorrow. If it looks worse, there is a walk-in down the street. Hopefully, you won't need stitches."

I felt like I lost more than blood in this process, like perhaps my ability to speak. "Okay," I muttered.

The look in Jake's eyes was sincere. "I am sorry you got hurt trying to do something nice for me."

Not knowing exactly how to respond, I smiled and said, "I am sorry you had to suck my blood like a vampire."

His gaze stayed on mine, and it made me uneasy only because he wasn't laughing at my joke. "I wouldn't do that for just anyone, Nina."

My lip twitched in response, and I laughed nervously, not really knowing what to make of that statement. What I did know was that tonight was not helping my vow to get over him one single bit. "Thanks."

Jake started clearing out what bananas I had managed to cut. "I'm gonna get a new shirt," he said. "Why don't you change, and we'll meet Tarah and Ryan downstairs."

"I don't know..."

"Come on, we're supposed to be celebrating your exam, and those bananas are toast. I've ate enough blood for one night."

I threw a piece of banana at him. "Very funny."

He was unphased. "What do you say?"

There was no way I could say no. "Okay, I'll change."

About ten minutes later, he came out of the bathroom with a fresh coating of cologne. His hair was wet, and he was wearing a maroon colored long sleeve shirt that hugged his chest and black pants that hugged his ass. He looked and smelled amazing.

I had put on a black button down shirt, dark colored jeans and the six-inch heels I usually wore whenever I was feeling inexplicably inadequate. Somehow adding height seemed to give me a false sense of power when I felt I needed it. I didn't know why I was nervous about going downstairs with Jake. Something just felt different tonight between us. Maybe it was the sucking of the blood thing. I dunno.

When we entered Eleni's, the lights were dimmed, and a live Greek band was playing at the corner of the restaurant. The owner, Telly, immediately rushed toward us and got some extra chairs to add to Tarah and Ryan's small table. It was packed for a weeknight.

Our roommates were sipping coffee and eating dessert when Jake and I sat down to join them.

"To what do we owe this honor?" Tarah joked as she gave me a hug.

Jake grabbed my arm and lifted my hand. "Nina got an A on her test and then to celebrate, she chopped her finger off and got a sudden craving for Greek."

Ryan grabbed my hand. "What the—"

"It's partially true. I didn't chop off my finger, but I nearly did, trying to make Bananas Foster."

Tarah cringed. "Damn! Are you okay?"

"I'll be fine. Nurse Jake took care of me."

Jake joked, "Who's the nurse now, bitches?"

Tarah looked over at Jake and then to me and said, "You two are so cute together."

Insert sound of record screeching here.

Jake said nothing, and I stared at her dumbfounded before glaring at her.

Why would she say that?

I could have killed her and immediately changed the subject. "So, what's good on the dinner menu?"

Before Tarah could respond, a sultry female voice came up from behind us. "Actually, the best thing on the menu is the moussaka, but Jake will stick to the same thing every time, avgolemono and spanakopita...right Jake?"

I turned around, and my heart sank when I noticed a very attractive girl with long black hair around my age wearing a low cut white blouse that left little to the imagination and a black apron wrapped tightly around her waist.

This might not have bothered me so much if she wasn't undressing Jake with her eyes. I knew that look; shit, I owned that look.

"Hey, Des." Jake nodded.

She batted her eyelashes. "Hi, Jake. Long time no see."

He just looked at her and didn't respond. Ryan broke the awkward pause that followed. "Desiree, this is our new roommate, Nina. She grew up with me." He turned to me. "Nina, this is Desiree, Telly's daughter.

"Nice to meet you, Nina," she said to me while looking straight at Jake.

"Likewise," I said as my stomach became tied up in knots.

There was an awkward pause, and then "Des" began listing the specials. I heard nothing because I was obsessing over the realization that Jake was a chick magnet and I was just one in a long line of women who wanted him. This wasn't news. It was just the first time I had witnessed it first-hand and out in public.

"So, the usual, Jakey?" She winked. He simply nodded yes, making little eye contact with her.

She looked at me signaling that it was my turn to order. I really had no desire to eat anymore and had no idea what most of the stuff on the menu even was, so I responded with, "Um...I'll have the same."

Desiree looked at Jake suggestively again and went to put in our order. Her ass wiggled as she walked away, and I felt more insecure by the second. For the record, the heels I was wearing were of absolutely no help in this situation.

Jake was looking down at a dessert menu, bobbing his head to the song the band was playing. Probably sensing the tension in the air, Ryan and Tarah just looked at each other.

I couldn't stand it any longer and chimed in with, "What the hell did I order anyway?"

Everyone started laughing in unison.

"Nina, hope you like egg lemon and rice soup and spinach pie," Ryan said.

Actually, given my recent loss of appetite, that actually sounded horrible.

"Yum," I said sarcastically.

Jake then kicked my leg playfully under the table, and I kicked him back. We kept taking turns doing this, and at one point, he locked my feet in with his so that I couldn't kick him anymore. It was a strange way of making contact, but I delighted in it.

My attention then turned to a family who had just been seated at the table across from ours. The little girl was rocking back and forth and seemed very agitated. I noticed Jake wave at them.

"Hey, Jake," the girl's mother called out.

He got up from our table to go over to them and knelt down by the girl's seat, getting in her face to garner her attention. "Hey, Marina."

The girl, who looked about eight or nine, didn't say anything and started to cry.

"She's having a bad night," Marina's father said.

Jake snapped his fingers and said, "Wait. I have something for her. I almost forgot." He then ran out of the restaurant to head upstairs to our apartment.

I turned to Ryan. "What's up with Jake and the little girl?"

"That's Telly's sister Georgette's daughter, Marina. They're in here a lot. She has autism, so she doesn't really talk."

"I see," I said, trying not to stare too much at the beautiful girl with short brown ringlets framing her face. She was starting to hum loudly, as her mother tried to console her.

Jake walked back into the restaurant holding the collection of pinwheels I had first noticed the night I snuck into his bedroom. I couldn't help but smile.

He knelt down next to the girl again and handed the whole bunch to her. "Marina...look. I remembered you had one of these the last time you were in here, and you really liked it. Every time I pass by someone selling them now, I have to get one for you," he said.

Marina took the four pinwheels and lined them up on the table. One by one, she lifted each and blew on it, laughing hysterically each time it spun around. The joy in her eyes made me forget about my earlier brooding and put a smile on my face.

"I figured that would put you in a better mood," he said to her as he stood up.

The girl's mother beamed at Jake. "Honey, you are so sweet. Thank you. We'll actually be able to have a peaceful dinner now."

"Don't worry about it. It was my pleasure," he said, before returning to our table.

Jake didn't seem to notice the look on my face of complete awe, as it dawned on me that he was really just as beautiful on the inside as he was gorgeous on the outside. "That was so sweet that you actually collected those for her. I had noticed them in your room," I said.

"And you thought I was just a fucking weirdo?"

"Well, you are still a weirdo, but..." I scrunched my nose at him jokingly.

Tarah echoed my earlier sentiment. "Yeah, man...seriously. Look at her. She is totally content now."

Jake looked over at the little girl as he spoke. "Cedric, my brother-in-law, has a sister who's autistic. When I first spotted Marina, her mannerisms reminded me so much of Callie. It was crazy, and I just knew. It's like they're locked inside their bodies, but there is so much in there waiting to come out. You just have to know which keys to use to unlock it."

The four of us continued to look over at Marina playing with the pinwheels until Desiree approached with a tray full of food. As she placed the hot plates onto the table, her eyes were placed firmly on Jake. God, I may have been obvious in my checking him out at times, but she was flirting relentlessly, and I immediately hated her for it. It didn't help that she was absolutely gorgeous. Jake, on the other hand, dug right into his food and didn't seem affected by her one way or the other. I suppose he was probably used to girls throwing themselves at him.

After we finished eating, a group of people in the corner started dancing in a circle to the Greek band's music. Desiree came by to clear our plates and glared at me. I wondered if it was because she was jealous. Jake and I had been joking around flirtatiously all night and she constantly looked in our direction, even when she was serving other customers.

Bring it on.

I didn't like the looks of her. Even if my relationship with Jake stayed platonic, I felt protective of him and certainly didn't want that cheap hussie to have him.

The four of us lingered until almost closing time and shared an entire platter of baklava. It was late by the time we went back upstairs to the apartment, so all of us retreated to our rooms.

Exhausted from the day's events, I went to the bathroom to wash my face but skipped a shower. I couldn't wait to bury myself under the covers. As my head hit the pillow, staring back at me on the nightstand was another origami bat. I chuckled and opened it.

**Congratulations again on making the grade.
Imagine the possibilities when
you finally get laid.
P.S. Kidding, Nina! Just retesting
your ability to take a joke.
P.P.S. Your blood tastes like bananas.**

He was certifiably nuts, but he never ceased to make me laugh.

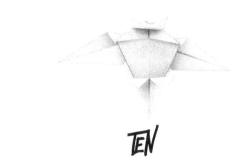

TEN

Friday morning, I awoke with the jitters, anxious about my date with Alistair that night. He was supposed to be picking me up at seven and taking me to a popular Italian restaurant down the street from the university.

It was bugging me that I was not looking forward to it as much as I had hoped and that I couldn't stop thinking about Jake. Thankfully, as usual, my roomie would be headed to Boston for the weekend straight from work and wouldn't be a distraction tonight. It wasn't healthy to be focusing on him so much, and I was convinced that going out with Alistair was a necessary step in the right direction.

I would have to get through a day of classes, though, before I could concentrate on things like what to wear and how to do my hair for tonight.

Alistair sat in his normal seat next to me in math and he immediately acknowledged our plans when he turned to me and whispered with a twinkle in his eye, "I can't wait to take you out tonight."

I just nodded, not wanting Professor Hernandez to overhear anything. It's a good thing I was paying attention to the lecture, because Hernandez called on me to come up to the dry erase board and work on a problem about Venn Diagrams. "Ms. Kennedy, shade in the parts of this diagram which correspond to the named set."

When I colored in the correct parts of the circles in red, he nodded in agreement. "Very good, Ms. Kennedy." Then, he whispered to me with a slight smile. "Most improved student, so far this year, it seems."

Maybe he wasn't such a jerk after all. Feeling a sense of achievement, I couldn't contain my smile. Alistair high-fived me when I returned to my seat.

After class, we walked down the hallway to the exit, and Alistair's blue eyes gleamed as he said, "I'll pick you up at seven." He truly was a handsome guy; maybe tonight, I would feel something stronger for him in a different setting.

"Yup, sounds good. See you later," I said.

That afternoon, Tarah was making an early dinner in the kitchen when I got home from school, and the apartment smelled like garlic and onions.

"Hey, girl," I said as I placed my backpack down on the couch.

"Hey! I am just making some rice and chicken. This gluten-free diet is a bitch. Want some?"

"No, I can't. Thanks. Actually, believe it or not, I have a date tonight."

Tarah dropped her spatula and picked it up, waving it at me. "Excuse me? How did I not know this?"

"It's no big deal. I'm not sure if I even like him like that. He's a guy in my math class. His name is Alistair."

"Interesting name."

"Yeah, tell me about it. He is really cute, though…and nice…and smart."

"As opposed to really hot…not so nice…and super smart, like Jake? You know, I thought that something was developing there, but I guess I was wrong?"

"Why would you think that?"

"I don't know. There is just this vibe between you two lately. I really sensed it when we were at Eleni's the other night. You guys are opposites, but you seem to fit together somehow."

I know.

I shrugged my shoulders in frustration. "Well, tell that to him."

"I knew it! I knew you liked him," she said pointing the spatula at me.

I held out my hands in protest. "Please don't go there right now, okay? I am supposed to be focusing on this date."

She rolled her eyes. "I wanted to slap that bitch Desiree the other night. She clearly wanted to get her paws into him."

My stomach knotted up when she mentioned Desiree. "Can we not talk about Jake right now?"

"Okay, okay…your date. First off, what are you wearing?"

"My black Donna Karan dress…"

"You mean your only dress? No. Boring. You are borrowing something from my closet. Next: what are you doing with your hair?"

"I was going to wear it up in a twist."

"No. I'll blow it out straight and do some loose sexy curls for you. What about makeup?"

"The usual. A little mascara and some lipgloss."

She closed her eyes and shook her head in disagreement. "Nah. Let's do a smoky eye on you. You are gonna look so hot for this date, Nina. What's his name again?"

"Alistair." I laughed.

"Alistair is not gonna know what hit him."

"Alright, whatever you say, T. I'm going to take a shower. Maybe we can do this thing after you're done eating."

A half-hour later, I emerged from the bathroom to find Tarah already in my room with a handful of dresses laid out on the bed. The small towel I was using was not quite big enough to cover my breasts, so I struggled to keep it closed over my chest to avoid giving her a private show.

"Nina...good God girl...you have the best rack! I don't know if I have ever really noticed before now. We are definitely showing those off tonight."

Letting Tarah dress me from head to toe might not have been a great idea after all.

"What do you mean show them off?"

"The girls—all three of you—will be hanging out with Alistair tonight." She winked. "Which of these four dresses do you want to try on first?"

"That one," I pointed to the dress that looked the least revealing.

"I figured you'd say that. Let's try this one," she said picking up a different dress, a strapless pink lace number. I couldn't get the top to fit over my boobs and nixed it as an option.

No luck either with the next two I tried on. The last wrap-style dress was fluorescent purple and low-cut but fit me like a glove. The color was a little bright for my taste, but it seemed this was *the one* out of the group. It was pretty revealing, but there was no denying how good it made my body look.

"You are curvy in all the right spots. I would kill for your body," she said.

I thought back to my ex-boyfriend and how he always told me I would look better if I lost weight to look more "athletic," even though I was already fairly thin except for my breasts and butt.

"Okay, this one is the winner. What's the next step in making me into a drag queen?"

"Let's get you into a zip-down jacket, then we'll do your hair and makeup and get dressed last." Tarah started taking out curling irons and makeup from a large black satchel.

After an hour and a half of blow-drying, curling, buffing and puffing, she handed me a mirror. My transformation into a glamour puss was staggering, actually. My light blue eyes appeared at least three times bigger with the gray shadow and mascara. She also applied a dark pink lipstick that made my lips look pleasantly plump. My hair was perfectly styled into big, soft curls that she sprayed to make sure they held. Her skills were amazing. Alistair wasn't going to believe his eyes.

It was 6:30 and Tarah helped me slip into the purple dress to avoid messing up my hair and makeup.

"Wait right here. I have the perfect shoes," she said as she ran to her room.

She returned with the most striking pair of purple stilettos.

"These are gorgeous." I looked at the inside. "Manolo Blahnik? Are you kidding me?"

"I used to have a shoe issue. Not anymore, but I have amassed quite a collection. What size are you?"

"Well, excuse me, Carrie Bradshaw. Apparently, I am the same size as you," I said as I slipped my foot into the shoes to discover they were a perfect fit. Several inches taller, I looked at myself in the mirror that hung on my closet door.

Not bad.

Actually, I couldn't have been more pleased with how I looked. "Wow. I can't thank you enough, T."

"Anytime, babe. You were like a clean slate. It was fun." She smiled.

Tarah packed up her hair and makeup accessories and left momentarily to return them to her room, leaving me standing in front of the mirror. The purple was a little bright for my liking, but it was kind of refreshing to wear something other than my usual black.

My body jerked suddenly when a male form appeared behind me in the mirror. Not just any male form. It was like that moment in a horror movie. Except, in my mind, this was worse.

"Nina, Barney the dinosaur called. He wants his skin back."

"Jake! What are you doing here? You're supposed to be on your way to Boston."

"Nice to see you too."

"Well, it's just that you usually leave from work and—"

"I missed the 5:15 Amtrak, so I might either catch the last train at 9:30 or just go in the morning."

"Oh." I licked my lips nervously, having forgotten about the lipstick on them.

Shit. Shit. Shit.

I turned around and faced him. His eyes immediately traveled slowly down the length of my body, coating me with his gaze. My heart was beating rapidly, and I got the

105

chills. This was exactly what I was trying to avoid. In fact, I probably wouldn't even have accepted the date if I knew Jake was going to be home to see me off.

He was never home on Fridays. Why today?

"Nina...you look—"

I interrupted him. "Interesting?"

He kept staring at my dress. "That's one way of putting it," he said as his eyes returned upward to meet mine.

Tarah walked in at that moment and seemed just as shocked as I was to see him. "Jake!"

"Tarah!" He mocked her tone, without taking his eyes off me. I would say he was undressing me with them, but truthfully, the dress left little to the imagination.

He finally moved from the doorway and sat on my bed, lightly bouncing up and down. "I didn't know we were going out tonight, Nina."

Tarah looked at me seeking permission with her eyes. "We...are not going anywhere. *She* is going on a date."

He turned to me and smiled, but it didn't look genuine. It was more taunting. "I see." He paused and then said, "I suppose he's taking you to the Vegas Strip in that outfit?"

"I think she looks awesome, actually," Tarah said.

I was beyond speechless and just shook my head.

Jake continued to stare at me with a look so intense, you'd think his beautiful green eyes could have burned a hole through my dress. "Have fun," he said like he didn't mean it. "And don't forget a jacket. You're bound to catch pneumonia dressed like that." Then, he turned around, walked down the hall to his room and slammed the door closed.

I'd rather be going out with you...you ass.

The time was now 6:55.

"It's almost seven. Your date will be here any minute," Tarah said.

"Do me a favor and let him in when he comes and then get me? I just wanna sit here for a bit and grab my bearings."

"No problem, sweetie. I understand." She left the room, closing my door behind her.

His cologne still lingered in my room, and I breathed it in. His surprise appearance had completely jarred me. I sat back on my bed, careful not to mess my hair too much and tried to inhale in and exhale out to relax. It wasn't working. I was still reeling from Jake's stare, from his words and from the fact that my body was craving him, minutes before I was supposed to be going out with another guy. If I were lucky, he would stay in his room until I left.

About ten minutes later, still lying on my bed in the same spot, I heard a knock on the front door in the distance. I sat up suddenly and heard Tarah open it and greet Alistair. "She's just in her room finishing up. Why don't you make yourself comfortable and I'll let her know you're here."

Tarah's footsteps got closer and closer until she entered my room shutting the door behind her.

"Are you okay?" she whispered.

"Honestly? No."

"Is it Jake?"

I took a deep breath and nodded silently.

"Well, come on, you don't want to keep your adorable date waiting. He's a cutie, and you look hot, babe. We'll chat about asshole later."

I got up and followed Tarah into the living room. Alistair was standing with his hands in his pockets, wearing khaki pants and a white linen shirt rolled up at the sleeves. His light brown hair was perfectly parted to the side and gelled. His smile was magnetic.

"Hey, Alistair."

"Hey, Nina. Wow. You look...awesome," he said as he approached me and kissed my cheek.

Tarah nudged me and said, "Why, thank you, Alistair."

"Thanks. It's all her doing," I said pointing to Tarah.

His head moved side to side slowly as he took in my appearance. "Well, you were beautiful before, but...man, I'm just...speechless."

Laughing, I said, "That was my reaction too."

The front door opened and Ryan walked in. Tarah immediately ran over to give him a hug. "Hey, baby."

"Hey," he said kissing her forehead before looking over at Alistair and me. "Troll...damn, you look nice."

Alistair turned to me. "Troll?"

"It's a long story."

Ryan walked over to Alistair holding out his hand. "I'm Ryan. Nina and I grew up together."

They shook hands, and there was an awkward silence among the four of us for a few seconds.

"Where are you guys headed?" Ryan asked.

I looked at Alistair for guidance, and he said, "That new Italian place near the university. It's called Porcello's. It's supposed to be really good." He turned to me. "If that's okay? I didn't even think to ask where you might like to go."

"She's always wanted to go to Top of the Rock," a raspy voice said from behind us.

Shit.

I turned around to see Jake standing there. He stared me down hard and continued, "Right, Nina? You love a good view from the top of a skyscraper. I hear the scenery is amazing, and the food is great."

"That's the one on top of the GE building in the city?" Alistair asked.

"We can save that for another time. I was really looking forward to that Italian place," I said glaring at Jake who had an intimidating look on his face and seemed to be sizing up Alistair.

Jake extended his tattooed arm toward Alistair. "We haven't met. I'm Jake." He was smiling, but it was angry and disingenuous.

They shook hands and I noted the stark contrast between Jake's defined marked arm and Alistair's, which was bare with light blonde hairs.

"I'm Alistair."

"Ass Hair?" Jake's expression was calculating.

Kill me now.

Looking none the bit amused, Alistair said, "No...Alistair."

"Ah...sorry, my bad," Jake said as he looked over at me.

Fuming was not harsh enough of a word to describe how I was feeling toward him.

I was still glaring at Jake when I said, "Alistair, I think we should get going."

"After you," he said, gesturing for me to walk in front of him. Ignoring Jake, he then looked over at Tarah and Ryan. "It was nice meeting you guys."

"Likewise. You kids have fun!" Tarah said.

Jake's eyes were piercing mine and the rims of his ears were red. When Alistair and I got to the doorway, I turned around one last time to find Jake's gaze still fixed on me. He wasn't saying anything, but in that moment, the look on his face was different. This time, there was no sarcasm, no anger. He just looked...hurt...like he didn't want me to leave. Then, he silently mouthed, "Bye," before turning away.

He had been a total bastard, but God help me, I would have dropped everything for him tonight if he had just asked me to.

The restaurant was several blocks away. On the walk, Alistair and I got to know each other, talking about school and our favorite types of music and hobbies. I discovered that we both really liked Radiohead, The Killers and Coldplay. He grew up in Connecticut, not far from the city and seemed to have had a privileged life, which was a direct contrast to my modest upbringing in the sticks of upstate New York.

Midway through our walk, he grabbed my hand. While I didn't mind, I couldn't help but notice that my body had little to no reaction upon touching his skin. I thought back to when Jake stood in the stairwell during our subway trip and reached out his arm for me to grab. I remembered how amazing it felt when I held his hand for the first time and when our fingers intertwined. There was no comparison and it was irking me right now.

Stop thinking about Jake.

We had a reservation, so they seated us as soon as we arrived at Porcello's. The restaurant was beautiful with dim lighting, candlelit tables and pictures on the walls of famous patrons. That song *Mambo Italiano* played in the background.

Maddie, our waitress, poured two glasses of water and read the specials at warp speed before we each ordered a glass of cabernet sauvignon.

"They're supposed to have the best Penne a la Vodka," Alistair said.

Vodka. That's all I took from that.

"Mmm. I was thinking of the Shrimp Scampi. I wonder if I can get that without the Scampi?"

Alistair put down his water and covered his face in laughter. "Nina...you don't get out to eat much do you?"

"What do you mean?"

"There is no such thing as Scampi. Shrimp Scampi is shrimp with pasta in like a garlic and olive oil sauce. So, Scampi is just the name of the dish. It's like—"

"Bananas Foster?"

There he was again.

"Yeah. Exactly." He paused looking at me like I was three. "You're adorable, Nina."

I felt like an idiot. "Well, then...I'll get the Shrimp Scampi. Sounds delicious."

Alistair flashed his signature thousand-watt smile. "How about we get an appetizer? What sounds good to you?"

"How about the Jerk Chicken skewers?"

"You got it." Alistair closed his menu then said, "Speaking of jerks, your roommate is a bit of a dick."

My stomach sank, and I wracked my brain for a response. "Jake? He's not that bad. He's a bit of a ball-buster, that's all," I said immediately downing my water.

"He seems like a loser."

Excuse me?

Hearing him call Jake a loser really pissed me off. There were many words I could use to describe my roommate: sarcastic, intimidating, wiseass, even dick fit the bill sometimes. But "loser" certainly wasn't one of them.

"Why do you say that?"

"I mean, look at him. His fucking eyebrow is pierced? He just seems like a loser."

Okay, now I was really getting angry.

"So, you are judging him because he has piercings and tattoos?"

"Yeah...among other things. I'm sure his mother is real proud."

"A lot of people don't view things like that as negative. Many find them quite interesting, even attractive, particularly women."

Particularly me.

"Well, I think he just looks dumb."

"He's actually an engineer, and he is really smart." I looked down at the napkin on my lap and sighed before saying, "Let's drop the subject."

I decided it was best to just end that conversation before I said something I would regret. I was expecting the fire alarm any minute because I was sure there was enough smoke coming out of my ears to set it off.

Alistair nodded. I think he could tell he had upset me. "Sounds good."

Maddie came back over to take our order. On the outside, I put on a cheerful front, but on the inside, I was disappointed at how close-minded and judgmental Alistair really was. There was no doubt that Jake was a total jerk to him. If he had just called him a dick and ended it, I might have been fine. But to attack someone based on looks, was just ignorant and unacceptable to me.

Our dinner conversation fell flat, as we sat there eating our meals amidst large pockets of silence. I was starting to think the highlight of the night was learning the true meaning of Shrimp Scampi.

Needing a breather, I excused myself to go the ladies room and lingered in the stall much longer than normal. My mind drifted again to thoughts of Jake and the disappointed look on his face when I left with Alistair.

When I exited the stall, I looked at myself in the mirror. I closed my eyes and thought about the way Jake stared me up and down when he first laid eyes on me dressed liked this. The look in his eyes gave me chills and I wanted so badly to just walk across the room and kiss him. But what else is new there? Then, he asked where "we" were going. If I hadn't gone on this date, would I have spent the evening with him? The truth was, I would have wanted to spend any amount of time with Jake, even if it were just for an hour before he had to catch his train. I would have loved to have just sat with him and talked or even studied. I looked forward to time spent with him more than anything because I never felt more alive. I wanted to be with him all of the time.

I just wanted...*him.*

I wanted him.

I couldn't deny my feelings or the fact that I was sure he was going to break my heart, even if he never so much as touched me. I started to get really emotional all of a sudden, so I concluded that it was the wine and tried to shake myself from thoughts of him for the moment.

Alistair was going to think I was doing drugs in here if I didn't hurry up, so I grabbed my bearings and reentered the dining room.

"Hey, I was about to send search and rescue in for you," he said smiling.

"Sorry about that."

Alistair placed a menu in front of me. "How about dessert?"

Why not? It's the one thing that sounded good all night.

Alistair pointed to the dessert list. "Didn't you say something earlier about Bananas Foster? They have that, if you like it."

Great.

"Actually, I think I'll have the chocolate cake," I said, which of course reminded me of Mrs. Ballsworthy's cake... which then reminded me of...yeah, this was a hopeless situation.

We placed our dessert order and Alistair excused himself to use the bathroom.

I took my phone out to check facebook, because this date was just too exciting for words, and my heart dropped. I had missed a text from Jake that came in about an hour ago.

> *Nina, I was a jerk to you and your little friend.*
> *I'm sorry.*
> *And the Barney joke was stupid.*
> *Actually, you looked stunning.*

Stunning. *Stunning*. He thought I looked stunning. This was the first verbal indication that he found me attractive and the butterflies in my stomach were now doing a Greek circle dance.

I read the text as many times as I could before Alistair returned to the table.

I put my phone away when our desserts arrived, and unfortunately, my brain and appetite must have run away together, because I was now just sitting there...well, *stunned.*

Alistair returned and sat down. "Are you feeling okay, Nina?"

"Yeah...I think my eyes are bigger than my stomach. I'll probably get the cake to go."

He nodded because his mouth was full of cheesecake. I just wanted to get home as fast as possible in case Jake hadn't left. He had said there was a possibility he would be leaving in the morning.

He held the door for me as we left the restaurant. The cold night air hit my face and blew my curls all over the place.

"What's so funny?" Alistair asked.

I must have been smiling to myself as we walked, thinking about the text. And even though Alistair was holding my hand, all I could think about was how much I wanted to sleep next to Jake tonight.

Alistair leaned in to kiss me as he left me at the door to the apartment and I kept my mouth closed, allowing it but not encouraging it to turn into the type of kiss I dreamt of with Jake.

Intentionally not inviting him in, I wished him a good weekend and let him know I'd see him in class next week. I would have to come up with an excuse as to why I wouldn't be able to accept another date with him if he asked.

The apartment was quiet, and all of the doors to the bedrooms were closed. My pulse raced as I approached Jake's room and knocked.

"Jake?"

Nothing.

I knocked again.

He was gone.

I felt a mixture of sadness, frustration, longing and relief, only because I was pretty sure I would have said or done something stupid tonight if he were here...like maybe jumped his bones.

Loneliness set in as I walked back to my room and kicked off Tarah's heels. I pulled the dress over my head, put on a long white t-shirt and brushed my hair back into a ponytail.

The water must have run for minutes on end in the bathroom as I washed the makeup off my face, lost in thought, without paying attention to the time.

I had really come to hate the weekends, when Jake was away. Even though we weren't together as a couple, I missed him and felt safe when he was around.

As I tried to fall asleep, the restlessness was overwhelming. I could not stop thinking about him and replaying the entire night in my head.

Insomnia was winning out, so I got up and made myself some tea instead of rolling around aimlessly in bed.

As I sat up sipping my chamomile and watching late night television in the living room, it dawned on me that Christmas and the end of the semester would be here before I knew it. That meant the tutoring sessions would end. Getting an A on the next exam suddenly seemed less important than getting to spend even more time with Jake, even though the thought of another "excursion" terrified me.

I shut off the television and started back toward my room when I impulsively passed it, heading over to Jake's instead. I opened the door and immediately jumped.

He was there. He was sleeping!

No way.

I approached the bed slowly to get a closer look and jumped again when I realized it was just a ton of bunched up blankets made to look like a body. And there was a baseball cap on the pillow.

What the heck?

I pulled back the covers. Underneath was an origami bat. I opened it:

Looking for someone?

I covered my face in a mix of embarrassment and disbelief that he somehow knew I was going to sneak into his room tonight. Determined to hide the fact that I took the bait, or in this case—the bat—I carefully folded it back together and placed it under the covers but not before I buried my face in his pillow, relishing the musky scent. The cigarette smell was almost completely gone, making me wonder if he was trying to quit.

Before I left, I noticed something else: three more bats crumbled in the wastebasket. I picked them out and saw that he had started to write something on each one before scrunching it up and tossing it out. It was as if he was struggling to find the right words and gave up.

The first one just said: **Hope your date was great...**

The second one: **How does Ass Hair compare...**

The third: **You looked...**

Wow...okay. I didn't realize that he actually thought so deeply about what to write on these things. This discovery both flattered and confused me. How he finally came to the conclusion that the best course of action would be to trick me into thinking he was sleeping was beyond me.

Back in my own bed, I stared at the ceiling and concluded that tonight proved Jake knew he had an effect on me. I just couldn't figure out what effect I really had on him and whether he thought about me the same way.

The same word replayed in my head until I eventually fell asleep: *stunning*.

ELEVEN

had received two more A's on the subsequent exams in November and now held a B average in math overall. Jake was happy for me but somewhat bummed each time, because apparently he was really looking forward to his next planned fear-facing exercise that kept getting put off by my stellar grades. Who knew this would become a problem?

With each A, I baked Jake something special to thank him for helping me. He didn't seem to enjoy the banana bread as much as the Bananas Foster but still ate the entire loaf in one sitting with his eyes closed. The second time, I made him a chocolate banana cream pie and his response to that was nothing short of orgasmic. Seriously, he was mumbling things I couldn't even understand. It was truly entertaining to watch.

During Thanksgiving break, I had bragged to my parents about my nerdy roommate who was helping me get through math, and they said they couldn't wait to meet him and thank him. I would deal with picking my mother's jaw up off of the ground when the time came.

There was only one exam left before the end of the semester. A couple of weeks prior, Jake and I were busy studying in his room early one Thursday night, and as usual, he was keeping things strictly business.

But that was the night that everything changed between us.

At one point, in preparation for a math problem, he went into his drawer and grabbed something, throwing it front of me. It was a pair of dice.

He looked at me intently then pointed to them. "You're going to tell me how many different outcomes are possible. Then we're going to have you figure out how many ways you can get a sum of five."

Looking down at the dice, something came over me as an old memory of playing Yahtzee with my brother Jimmy came to mind. The object of that game had been to score the most points by rolling five dice to make certain combinations. Even though it was based on pure luck, Jimmy would always beat me. I could hear my brother's voice, clear as day, *"Yahtzee!"* And that's what did it. *Yahtzee.* That was the word that made me burst into tears for literally the first time in years. Looking down at the dice, I cried while Jake watched, horrified.

"What...what the hell is going on, Nina?"

I covered my face to hide the tears that wouldn't stop falling.

Jake had been at the desk but moved over to where I was sitting on the bed and turned to me. "Nina?"

I wiped my eyes and looked over at him. "It's my brother. Those dice...for some reason, they triggered a memory for me. My brother and I used to play the game Yahtzee to pass the time, while he—"

"What?" He blinked in confusion.

"It was one of the few things we were able to do to-gether...before he died."

Jake looked at me silently, his eyes blinking rapidly in an attempt to absorb the bombshell I had just dropped.

"Nina...God...I am so sorry. This is the brother in that picture in Ryan's room?"

I nodded and sniffled. "Yeah. Jimmy was my only brother, my only sibling."

"What happened?"

"He had leukemia."

He looked down at the floor and sighed. "I had no idea. You never said anything. I just assumed—"

"I know. Ryan and I don't really talk about him any-more. It's just too painful sometimes for both of us. It sur-prised me that Ryan even had that picture displayed, be-cause I know he gets really broken up over it."

He closed his eyes briefly looking off to side then back at me again. I had stopped crying but was still shaken by the memories of my brother's last days. Those were im-ages I tried hard to fight on a daily basis, and two little dice managed to completely unravel everything I worked so hard to bury.

Jake startled me when he put his hand on my knee. "Why don't you want to think about him?"

It was hard to admit the true reason that it was so difficult to think about Jimmy, and I never talked about it. Never. But I wanted to tell him. I wanted to tell Jake because I trusted him, and he had always made me feel like he wouldn't judge me for my faults.

He kept his hand on my knee, and I used the dragon tattoo on his forearm as a focal point to gather my thoughts. "Toward the very end of my brother's life, I couldn't bear to watch him waste away. It was just too painful. He was only a year and a half older than me. We were so close. He was nineteen when he died. I was a senior in high school."

When I started to tear up again, he squeezed my leg harder and said, "It's okay. Take your time."

I moved my gaze from the dragon back up to Jake's eyes and could see my own reflection in them.

"We tried everything. They took my bone marrow because I was a match."

Jake shut his eyes as if it pained him to hear me say that.

"He had a stem cell transplant, but it wasn't successful. At first, we had so much hope. Then, it was destroyed and there was just nothing left. He was sick for about two full years before we lost him."

Silently willing me to continue, he squeezed my knee again.

"When he was in the hospital, we would play that game, Yahtzee. That was during the period about six months before he died. The last month or so, he had gotten so sick, so emaciated; I couldn't bear to watch it...couldn't handle seeing him like that." I paused to catch my breath. "I stopped seeing him, Jake. I just stopped visiting my brother. I wasn't even there when he died." The tears started to pour out again as I recalled the most painful time of my life, no longer able to speak coherently.

He wrapped his arm around me, pulling me into him. I closed my eyes and sunk my head into the heat of his chest as I cried.

He spoke softly into my ear. "He knows you loved him, Nina. You loved him so much that you couldn't bear to see him in pain. He knows. If he didn't know then, wherever he is—wherever it is that we go—he knows now."

I looked up at him. "You believe that?"

"Yes, I do. I wouldn't have said it if I didn't believe it."

"How can you be sure?"

"I can't be 100-percent sure, but you have to have blind faith. You have to believe it in your gut. The fact is, it's more likely than not that there is a purpose to this fucked up thing we call life. Your brother...he had a purpose. He just fulfilled it faster than you or me."

"I want to believe that," I said.

He let go of me suddenly and walked over to his closet, taking out the sketchpads I had looked through the night I snuck into his room. Flipping to one of the pictures of the man on the motorcycle, he sat back down on the bed next to me and stared at it for a bit before speaking.

"That's my Dad," he said with his eyes still focused on the drawing.

It blew me away that the haunting image that stuck out at me the most amongst his sketches was actually of his father. He had an impassioned look in his eyes as he continued to stare at the image without saying anything.

"That one was my favorite. The one of him looking back," I said.

After another long pause, he finally spoke. "This was the last memory I have of him. He died that night in a motorcycle accident. I was only five, but I remember this moment in the drawing very clearly. He was going out to meet some friends. He told me to be a good boy for my mother and that he would take me out to my favorite diner for breakfast the next morning. For some reason, he looked back at me one last time before he took off, and it always stuck with me."

This was breaking my heart.

"I don't know which is worse: never getting to say goodbye to someone or watching them suffer first," I said.

He put the sketch aside and turned to me. "Both scenarios suck. My point is, as painful as it was to lose my father that way, I never want to forget him. Ever. I do everything in my power to remember him, to remember the little things he taught me, even at that age."

I took a deep breath in and nodded, thinking about what he said as it related to Jimmy. I had been trying so hard to push away thoughts of my brother's illness, that all of the good memories were getting pushed away too, so there was nothing left of him.

Some random funny memories came to mind suddenly because I allowed them in. "My brother was such a jokester. Kind of like you."

He smiled. "Yeah?"

"Jimmy was shameless. Once, he brought a whoopee cushion to church and put it under this old lady in the pew in front of us. My parents grounded him for like three weeks after that." I shook my head remembering that day. "Whenever we got into fights, and I tried to stay mad at him, he would hold me down and tickle my feet until I begged his forgiveness. He knew that drove me crazy. Sometimes, he would get Ryan to grab the other foot. They would gang up on me."

Jake raised his brow. "Ticklish feet, huh? I'll have to remember that the next time you zone out on me during a math lesson."

"No, you don't!"

"But see, it makes you smile to think about those things. You need to just remember the good times with him. Your brother's last days don't define who he was. You can choose to remember him however you want, like I choose to remember my Dad on his bike...just going out for a ride. It's why I draw. It's therapy for me and helps me etch the things I want to remember in stone."

He folded up the sketchpad and returned it to the closet. I was kind of disappointed that he didn't go through some of the other drawings. They all had to be meaningful to him in some way. I would take what I could get, though. This was the most information that Jake had ever offered me about his life. I wasn't complaining, except for the fact that he returned to the chair by the desk, instead of sitting back down next to me.

As he logged off of his computer, he clapped his hands and said, "You know what you need tonight, Nina?"

Interesting question and you could guess where my mind was heading.

"What do I need, Jake?"

"You need to get shitfaced," he said getting up and putting on his black jacket. "Come on, enough studying for tonight."

I followed him out to the hallway before stopping in my room to freshen up and grab a coat.

"Where are we going?" I said as he stood in my doorway waiting.

"Don't worry about it. You'll like it. Trust me." The questionable smirk on his face told me that maybe I shouldn't.

After a seven-block walk to Brooklyn Avenue, we stopped at a building with a bright pink neon sign that flashed: *Kung Pao Karaoke.*

"We're doing karaoke?" I shouted through the sudden onslaught of noise as he held the door for me.

"Well, mostly we're having a scorpion bowl or two, but if you get drunk enough, yeah, maybe."

The place was crowded and the smell of grease and booze filled the air. A clearly drunk woman with curly dark hair and a butterfly tattoo was belting out Bon Jovi's *Living on a Prayer* while the patrons went wild. She couldn't sing to save her life, but clearly, that didn't matter here.

"So, whaddya think?" Jake asked as we were seated into a small booth in the corner, thankfully, furthest away from the stage.

"It's cool. I have never been to a Chinese karaoke bar. You've been here before?"

"Once, with the guys from work. I was too drunk to remember much."

"Ah. Do you usually eat or just drink here?"

"That depends on what you're hungry for."

Something about the way he looked at me and licked his lip ring when he said that seemed flirtatious.

"I am hungry."

"Okay. We'll get a Poo Poo platter of appetizers and a scorpion bowl. Sound good?"

"Great."

After the waiter came by and took our order, Jake startled me when he nudged my leg with his under the table. "No more talking about sad stuff tonight, okay? I want you to have fun."

"You're not going to make me get up there are you?"

His mouth turned slowly upwards. There were the dimples that had been hiding out up until now. "You know that I don't make you do anything you don't want to do."

"Good, because I would need a lot of alcohol in me to get up and do that."

A woman came by and set the humongous scorpion bowl down on the table. It looked more like a portable sink with two straws.

"Speaking of the devil," he said.

"I think *you're* the devil tonight, Jake. What are you trying to kill me? Look at the size of this thing."

"I have...heard that before," he said winking.

Lordy. I set myself up for that one.

I responded to the mental images that conjured up by taking a huge sip out of the bowl. This concoction was way stronger than it looked, and I coughed from the impact of it down my throat.

Oh, goodness. There were those images again.

Jake pulled the bowl toward him. "Whoa...slow down there, lush."

I coughed again. "That is some strong stuff. It's deceiving! It looks like fruit punch and tastes like rubbing alcohol."

"After a while, you won't notice."

"It's a good thing we're walking home," I said.

He lifted his brow. "You mean, I'm *carrying* you home."

"Possibly."

"In all seriousness, Nina, I can tell you're a lightweight, so you should pace yourself. I don't want you to get sick." He paused. "Oh, speaking of lightweight, what was your date's name again the other night? How did that go?"

"Haha, very funny. His name was Alistair. It was okay. I won't be going out with him again, though."

"Any particular reason why?"

You.

"He just turned out to be kind of a loser."

"Well, I could have told you that. He was wearing fucking boat shoes. What is he, seventy?" He laughed.

"Yeah, I don't really have the best luck with men. My last boyfriend, Spencer, was king of the losers, actually."

Jake sat back in his seat and crossed his arms. "*Spencer*...he just sounds like a pretentious prick."

"He was...a prick...and a cheater."

Jake nodded silently and looked around the room then his eyes met mine. "Well, I don't even know the guy, but if he cheated on *you*...he's a fucking idiot."

I didn't even know how to respond to that, but every nerve in my body immediately did. Thankfully, our Poo Poo platter came and I didn't have to say anything at all. We started digging into the chicken wings, eggrolls, spareribs and teriyaki beef sticks. It was one of those comfortable silences where neither of us felt like we had to talk. We just pigged out on the appetizers, taking turns sipping out of the bowl, enjoying each other's company.

When we finished eating, all that remained were the flames in the center of the platter. He moved it to the side, throwing a packet of hand wipes at me and caught me off guard when he continued where our previous conversation left off.

"So...Spencer...was he your last boyfriend?"

"Yeah. We broke up a little over a year ago. In retrospect, it was the best thing that ever happened to me. Besides the fact that I found out he cheated on me, he did nothing but criticize me."

He scrunched his eyebrows into an angry look. "What do you mean *criticize*? What kinds of things did he say to you?"

Was this conversation really going there?

I shrugged. "Let's see...what *didn't* he say? For one, he had no tolerance at all for my anxiety issues. He would just make fun of me instead of trying to understand the condition. And he criticized my body any chance he got."

"He criticized *your* body," Jake said, more like a statement than a question.

"Yeah...all the time."

"Really..."

"Yes. He told me I wasn't athletic-looking enough, that I could stand to lose ten pounds and that my ass was too big."

Why did I just tell him all of this? I must be drunk.

"Nina...I hope you don't mind me being blunt."

"I don't mind."

"This...*Spencer*...needs his eyes checked and his ass kicked. There is nothing wrong with your body...not one thing. I hope you didn't listen to him."

Gulp.

"That's the sad part. For a while, I did believe it. I realize in retrospect that he just got off on bringing me down. At the time, though, I really did think I was fat and I was even thinner than I am now."

"Nina—" He started to say something then stopped. "Never mind. Just know...that he was wrong, okay?"

"Say what you were gonna say," I said, downing more of the drink.

He slid his tongue ring between his teeth and looked away from me toward the stage when he said, "I am not sure that I should."

"Since when have you become tactful?"

He took a sip and replied while playing with his straw. "Since this conversation moved to tits and ass."

I laughed a little louder than normal and suspected the alcohol was starting to take its toll...on both of us. "Seriously, whatever you were going to say, I won't be offended."

He took another long sip from the bowl, licked his lips and said, "Okay...in that case, Nina, not just as your friend, but as a man, I am telling you straight up that you have an amazing body. It's perfect. And your nimrod ex-boyfriend was right about one thing: you do kind of have a big ass."

I spit out my drink. "Excuse me?"

He reached across and tapped my arm. "Let me finish. You kind of have a big ass...but it's the most spectacular ass I've ever seen. You have an hourglass shape and any man with a pulse knows that's the hottest kind there is. You're beautiful, and what makes you even more attractive, is that you have absolutely no fucking idea just how beautiful you really are."

I gripped the seat of the booth, floored by those unexpected words that came out of his mouth.

He thinks I'm beautiful.

He thinks I have a big ass!

He thinks my ass is spectacular?

I wanted to tell him right then and there how I felt about him, that I thought *he* was the most beautiful human being on the planet. But the thoughts wouldn't form into a coherent sentence and just came out as, "Thank you."

"You're welcome."

We sat in silence for a few minutes watching a bald guy and a woman who looked like his mother sing *On the Road Again* before I realized that my bladder was ready to burst.

"Where is the bathroom?"

"I think it's down that hallway behind the stage."

The room spun a little when I stood up. As I walked away, I wondered if he was staring at my butt. I still couldn't believe what he had just said to me. Oddly, it was the nicest compliment I had ever received.

The bathroom was dingy, the floor was sticky and there was only one working toilet. I had to go so badly that I could have easily counted to a hundred while I peed and there would have still been more to come. After I washed my hands, since the mirror only showed the waist up, I couldn't help but jump a few times to check out my rear. I wanted to see what he meant by "spectacular." A woman walked in and looked at me like I was nuts.

When I reentered the dining area and sat back down, Jake was gone from our booth and I assumed he went to the men's room. That is, until I turned to the stage and saw him standing there with a microphone in his hand.

A bunch of girls at a table in the front started whistling at him and shouting things, like "Hey, hottie." I couldn't quite make out everything they were saying, but this whole scenario suddenly made me nauseous.

The announcer asked, "What's your name?"

"Spencer," Jake said, tapping his hand over the mic.

Oh my God. What was he doing?

"What are you singing, Spencer?"

Jake whispered something to him and then spoke into the microphone. "This is a special song for Nina. Please forgive me for being such an ass goblin."

I looked around the room, covered my face in embarrassment and tears of laughter formed in my eyes.

The music started and Jake searched for me. As our eyes met, he bounced his head to the music and flashed me a huge dimpled smile that made me want to rush the stage.

When he started to sing the beginning lyrics, the crowd went wild and several women started to get up and dance near him. Other people were clapping along. He tapped his foot to the beat as he sang, and it wasn't half bad, either.

Everyone except me seemed to recognize the song. I didn't get the relevance until he belted out a certain line. Then, I got it. I completely got it...and began laughing hysterically.

I turned to the guy next to me. "What is this song called?"

"It's *Fat Bottomed Girls*, by Queen."

Jake's eyes locked in on mine, and I shook my head at him. My face must have been red as a tomato. He could see I was cracking up, and he tripped over one of the lines because he started laughing at my reaction. He was rocking back and forth as he sang, looking at me the entire time.

I couldn't blame those women for ogling him. He looked hot beyond words as his hips slowly swayed side to side. I'd probably be right by the stage drooling over him along with them under different circumstances. His green eyes shined under the lights, and the white shirt he wore under his blue plaid button down clung to his chest, leaving little to the imagination. He always wore the sleeves rolled up to show off the tattoos on his forearms.

When he finished the song, the crowd went wild, and I could see his forehead was glistening under the hot lights. He was sweaty and hot as hell. Several women wanted a piece of him. I heard one yell, "You can do whatever you want to this fat bottom."

Ugh.

He started to make his way back to our booth when a couple of the girls sitting at that front table stopped him. They were attractive and jealousy pumped through my veins as he politely made conversation with them. One of them grabbed onto his shirt and slipped a piece of paper into the front pocket, causing my head to throb. My drink started to come up on me as I reminded myself that this guy was going to break my heart.

Jake interrupted the conversation after he noticed I was watching him. He walked away and cut one of the girls off mid-sentence. When he sat back down in the booth, my heartbeat started to regulate again.

"You're a popular guy," I said.

He chuckled. "Well, you can't sing a song like that and not expect to attract all the big-butt girls in the house like a magnet."

"Yeah, I noticed one of them slipped you her number."

"Oh...yeah," he said as he took the paper out of his pocket and threw it in the leftover flame from our Poo Poo platter.

I feigned pity. "That's a shame."

He sighed sarcastically and flashed me a smile. "Isn't it?"

"I guess there is only one fat-bottomed girl you're leaving with?"

He winked. "Yeah, I have a feeling I'm taking you home tonight."

Our waiter came by and collected the empty scorpion bowl and plate, replacing them with the bill and two fortune cookies.

I started to take out my wallet when Jake said, "Put that back."

"I'm paying my share."

"Nina, put it back. I've got it. You don't even work, and it was my idea to go out."

I listened to him and returned my wallet into the purse. "Thank you."

"Thank *you*. We need to get you loosened up and buzzed more often."

"I think I loosened up *a lot* tonight."

"Yeah...I think so, too." He smiled.

I pointed to the cookies. "Aren't you gonna open your fortune? Take the one facing you. That's the one meant for you. I'll go first."

I opened mine and read it out loud. *"When one door closes, another opens."*

I thought about how true that really was. All of the painful moments in my life have led me right here to this amazing night with this amazing person. There was nowhere else in the world I wanted to be.

"Your turn," I said.

Jake reached over, grabbed his cookie and opened it. "Big-butt girl make man smile."

"No sir!"

"I'm kidding. I'm kidding."

"What does it really say?"

He looked down and then up at me. "Now is the time to make a move."

Oh, man.

Even the fortune cookie was wondering what was taking him so long. I had to laugh inside at the irony.

"Interesting," I said.

He let out a deep breath that I could feel from across the table. "It is...very interesting."

He continued looking at me in a way that was giving me a vibe that he wanted more with me. This man was going to drive me insane.

Then, he finally spoke. "Want to get going?"

"Sure," I said.

We started to walk home, but it was pretty cold out, so when Jake noticed a cab approaching us, he hailed it.

Sitting next to him in the backseat was the closest I had physically been to him all night.

At one point, the cab driver took a sharp right turn, and I fell right into Jake. Instead of moving back to my spot, I stayed leaning against him and could feel his chest stiffen under me. He didn't move as he looked out the window.

I had lingered too long to turn away, so I just stayed with my ear on his chest and listened to his heartbeat that was getting faster and faster, a rhythm I was pretty sure I had created. The heartbeat never lies. That told me this was a black and white situation. Either he didn't want me there at all, or he wanted me there badly. I needed to find out which one it was soon before I completely lost my mind.

I closed my eyes and listened to him breathing. On the top of my head, I could feel his warm breath that smelled liked alcohol. The close contact and the scent of his skin mixed with cologne was making me wet. The booze in me and the pheromones in the air had made my usual want for him ten times stronger, almost unbearable. I took my hand and put it on his chest, watching it rise and fall against the thunder of his beating heart.

When the cab suddenly came to a screeching halt at our house, I reluctantly lifted myself off of him, and he paid the driver as we exited the car.

"After you," he said turning to me, his eyes glassy, as he opened the front door to the building.

"You just want to check out my spectacular ass," I joked, trying to lighten the mood after having thrown myself at him in the cab.

"You caught me," he said as he walked up the stairs behind me.

When we entered the apartment, the living area was dark, but there was light coming from Tarah's room, and I was pretty sure she and Ryan were both in there.

Drunk off him, I stopped in front of my bedroom door and desperately wished he would follow me in. "Thanks again for tonight, Jake. It was just what I needed."

"I'm really glad you had a good time." He stood there with his hands in his pockets for a few seconds before saying, "Good night."

And with that, he walked past me back to his room, closing the door.

I wouldn't get the answer to my black and white question until a chance encounter in the bathroom later that night.

TWELVE

Needless to say, I wasn't able to sleep at all. After changing into a pair of cotton boy shorts and a tank top, I just sat up in bed, shaking my foot nervously, trying to figure out what his deal was.

He flat out told me I was beautiful and made me feel like I was the only woman in that entire karaoke bar, but when given the opportunity to make a move, he wouldn't budge. Even the damn fortune cookie was frustrated.

The alcohol was still making its way through me. I pushed off my covers and marched to the bathroom, noticing from under the closed door that the light was still on in his room.

When I entered the bathroom, Jake's bare chest smacked me in the face.

"Whoa! Are you okay?" he asked as he rubbed his calloused thumb over my forehead. There was still a hint of alcohol on his breath. His scent and the quick contact of his chest against my breasts made me feeble.

"Yeah...I'm fine. Sorry, I didn't think to check if you were in here. The light in your room was on, so I assumed you were in there."

He leaned against the sink and crossed his arms. "What are you still doing up?"

"I can't sleep, so I came in here to pee."

He moved away fast from the sink. "Oh...well, I should probably let you do that."

"Yeah, probably."

"Right," he said before walking out and closing the door.

I sat down to pee, but even though I had to go so badly, nothing would come out because I was still focusing on him.

After running the water for about twenty seconds, I was finally able to go since the streaming sound helped me relax.

When I left the bathroom, I saw that Jake had left his bedroom door wide open, and I took that as a silent invitation to enter.

It was one in the morning, and he was sitting on his bed with his laptop. He closed it when he noticed me at the doorway. I walked toward him and sat at the end of his bed. He was still shirtless and wearing a pair of navy blue sweatpants that hung low displaying the top of his gray boxer briefs.

He sat up straighter. "How was your pee?"

"Fantastic."

"Good to hear." His eyes wandered to my chest, causing my nipples to harden.

Bingo.

"What were you looking at?" I asked.

My question broke his staring, and he suddenly looked up in a daze. "Huh?"

"On your laptop."

"Oh...on my laptop...right. Just useless surfing."

"I see."

We were just looking at each other for a few seconds when our silence was interrupted by the sound of the bed next door squeaking repeatedly.

Great.

Not only did I have no desire to hear Ryan, who was basically a brother to me, having sex with my best friend, but it made an already awkward situation so much worse.

You could cut the sexual tension in the air with a knife, but we both laughed it off.

"You think they're having sex?" Jake asked sarcastically.

I looked down in embarrassment. "Should we just pretend it's not happening?"

"Yeah. You wanna do a math lesson?" he joked as the noises from next door continued to get louder.

"Sure."

"Let's see...we can talk about the probability of sixty-nine."

I giggled. "I would say based on that noise, it's very high."

Jake bent his head back in laughter and I could see his tongue ring. It was so incredibly sexy, and I wanted to know what it would feel like against my own tongue.

Finally, the noises stopped, and we were once again left with a loss for words. But I wasn't going anywhere.

Jake was nervously picking at the lint on his comforter, flicking it onto the ground. He was looking down when he made a comment that shocked me. "I bet that prick ex-boyfriend of yours sucked in bed."

Of all the things he could have said, I definitely wasn't expecting that, but I was holding back nothing tonight.

"Actually, he did...big-time."

He stopped what he had been doing and sat up straighter against his headboard, almost backing away from me. "So, you have had sex."

"What's that supposed to mean?"

"See, now I've made you blush. I am sorry. You just strike me as a certain kind of girl."

"What kind of girl is that?"

"It's nothing bad. Just...innocent...maybe a virgin." He looked up at the ceiling and smiled mischievously. "The kind of girl that guys like me are dying to corrupt."

Shit.

I remained silent.

And I'm dying to be corrupted by you.

I cleared my throat. "Well, in answer to your question...yes, I have had sex, but it was just with him."

"He was your only, and he sucked in bed? That's unfortunate."

"Yeah. It *was* unfortunate. I never even actually...you know...with him."

"You never what?" His eyes widened when he realized what I meant. "You never came? You never even had an orgasm?"

I hesitated. "Not from another person."

He was looking down and started picking at the comforter again, but there was no lint left. He looked frustrated and uneasy. For several seconds, the silence in the room was deafening. Then, he said, "So...you come when you touch yourself."

"Yeah."

He closed his eyes briefly and suddenly looked up at me. "Sex doesn't count if he didn't make you come, Nina.

You're basically still a virgin." He bit his lip then said, "He had sex. You didn't."

It was amazing how the same set of eyes could send me so many different messages just in the way he looked at me. The same eyes that could intimidate me, joke with me, comfort me and make me feel like everything was going to be okay...now looked at me like he wanted to eat me alive. And I wished more than anything he would just do it.

I jumped when he moved because I thought he was going to touch me. Instead, he abruptly got up and opened his window. Cold air rushed in as he walked over to the bedside drawer and reached for the cigarettes, taking one out and lighting it. Inhaling deeply, he slowly blew the smoke outside as he sat against the edge of the windowsill.

"Why are you smoking? I thought you quit."

He shook his head. "I did. But I really needed one, and I need to keep my distance right now."

"Why?"

He didn't answer me and continued to alternate between inhaling, exhaling and flicking the ashes out the window.

I repeated, "Why are you smoking?"

His breath hitched, and he finally turned to me. "You really want to know why I'm smoking?"

I nodded. "Yes."

"Because it's keeping my mouth occupied and stopping me from doing something I shouldn't right now." He took another long drag. "You should probably go back to your room."

My pulse raced. "You're smoking and telling me to leave because you want to kiss me?"

He looked up at the ceiling and laughed like he didn't mean it. Then, he inhaled and looked over at me. Smoke streamed out of his mouth when he said, "I wouldn't tell you to leave if I only wanted to kiss you, Nina. I am telling you to leave because I want to taste you and make you come until you scream in every possible way imaginable. It was all I could think about all night long. It's why I couldn't sleep. But now that you just told me no man has ever done that...fuck. That's why I am smoking if you really want to know."

He had managed to render me completely speechless, and I couldn't tell if my panties were just wet or whether I peed slightly.

He repeated in a raspy whisper. "I really think you should go back to your room."

Despite his direct suggestion, my body did not move from that spot at the edge of his bed. He continued to stay by the window, staring outside even after he put out the cigarette. His handsome side profile lit up in the moonlight.

Something wasn't right. If he wanted me, why wouldn't he just take me? And I've shown him that I wanted him. *He's* certainly not a virgin. We knew that from day one.

The air was getting even colder in the room since he still had the window wide open. He finally shut it and turned to me, glancing down at my breasts. I knew he could see them through my thin pajama top. He licked his lips slowly, causing my nipples to harden even further. He continued to keep his distance.

When I looked down and noticed that he was fully hard through his sweatpants, my frustration grew even deeper. He was breathing heavily and swallowed when he saw me notice his arousal. He continued to look at me without saying anything at all.

I stood up from the bed and walked towards the window stopping a few inches in front of him. The heat radiated off of his body, and I could feel him breathing me in. He was consuming me with all of his senses...except touch. Finally, he slowly reached his hand toward my waist, gripping the material of my shirt and caressed my side. I felt his nails digging into me, and his hot breath blew over my chest. Just when I thought he was going to rip my shirt off, he pulled his trembling hand back. "Fuck," he growled under his teeth.

I was panting, and my stomach was in knots thinking about the question I was about to ask him, one I really didn't want to know the answer to. I blurted out, "I want to know what you do when you go to Boston every weekend."

He blinked a few times and broke eye contact, looking down at the floor, then back up at me. He was caught off guard and looked troubled, staying silent for several seconds before he responded. "It's complicated, Nina."

When the words came out of his mouth, it felt like my heart fell through my stomach. He wasn't going to give me any straight answers tonight, but those three words were enough to confirm that there was likely someone else.

There was a massive gray area to this black and white situation after all.

I wanted to come right out and ask what he meant, whether he had a serious girlfriend, or whether it was something entirely different, but I lost the courage and again, truthfully, a part of me really didn't even want to know. At this point, what I did know was that I had been playing with fire and that I needed to take his advice and leave.

"Good night, Jake."

He just stood there without saying a word and let me walk away.

The next morning, my eyes were bloodshot, and I had that foreboding feeling that I remember getting when I was a young teenager and a boy would break my heart. You know, the one where you wake up and forget about it for one split second, and then when you realize it wasn't a dream, complete dread sets in.

I looked at the time: 9:45. I had overslept and had already missed my first class.

Of course, Jake had left for work and would be gone for the weekend again. This time, though, I was relieved to not see him for a few days.

Tarah was in the kitchen making coffee, and the percolating sound was magnified due to my hangover.

"Sup, girly," she said when I walked out into the living area.

"Hey," I said hoarsely. My head was killing me, and I felt nauseous.

"You look like death, sweetie. Is everything okay?"

I wasn't sure if I should confide in her about what happened with Jake. I didn't even know how to sum up last night properly.

We had a scorpion bowl, he told me I had a big ass, the fortune cookie talked, then he got an erection and kicked me out of his room.

"Everything is okay. It was just a late night."

"You were with Jake. I know. He told me."

"He told you what?" I snapped.

"Take it easy...just that you guys went out late last night. Before he left for work, he told me to keep an eye on you today, that you might be hurting because you drank too much or something."

Or something.

He knew I'd be hurting, because he was the one that hurt me.

"Yeah...we went to that Kung Pao Karaoke place."

"So, was it like a date?"

"No. Nothing like a date."

"Nina, are you okay? Because you don't look okay."

Damn it. My eyes were starting to water.

"I am not, T. I am not okay at all."

"Are you gonna tell me what's going on? What did he do?"

"It's not what he did. It's what he didn't do. It's what he wouldn't say. It's what won't be happening between us. Let's just say, I needed to know whether we would be more than friends, and I basically got my answer last night."

"I am sorry, sweetie."

"Don't say anything to Ryan, okay?"

Tarah pulled me in for a hug. "I've seen the way Jake looks at you when you don't even realize it. I don't know what he did or said or didn't say last night, but that dude does have feelings for you."

"I guess it's just...complicated," I said rolling my eyes.

As I was leaving English class that afternoon, I made an impulsive decision to take the building elevator instead of the stairs. I no longer had the same fear of them that existed before meeting Jake and before our elevator picnic, but I found that I still avoided them everyday.

Maybe I just needed to prove to myself that I didn't need him anymore.

Thankfully, the elevator was empty. I was extremely jittery but felt in control when I pushed the button and closed the doors.

I shut my eyes and worked through the anxiety and building panic, counting to myself as the elevator descended down six floors.

When the doors opened, I felt immense relief because I knew now that I could do it on my own. It was only six floors, but this meant everything to me. I became extremely emotional as I made my way out to the sidewalk.

On the way home, my thoughts turned to Jake and that day in the elevator when he played the song that moved me deeply, *Stuck in the Elevator*. I had downloaded it to my iPod and scrolled down to play it while resting on a park bench.

The song brought me right back to that moment with him where I had been so filled with hope and excitement about the way he made me feel. It was painful to accept that I would have to stop those kinds of feelings in their tracks moving forward. They weren't going to go away. I just needed a way to bottle them up because that was the only way I could survive living with him.

A teardrop fell down my cheek as the song continued to play. My phone then vibrated on my leg, and I looked down to see that it was a text from Jake.

Please tell me I didn't lose you as a friend last night.

My emotions went into overload with the song still playing as the text came in. I had no idea how to respond, but regardless of the exact wording, the answer would have been the same.

> *Nina: Of course not.*

> *Jake: I know I was acting all sorts of fucked up. I am sorry.*

> *Nina: It's okay. We were both probably still drunk, right?*

There was a long pause, and I didn't think he was going to write back, but then my phone vibrated again.

> *Jake: I care about you. I am sorry if I hurt you.*

> *Nina: You didn't.*

Liar.

> *Jake: I'll see you Monday.*

> *Nina: See you then.*

> *Jake: We're still friends?*

> *Nina: Yes. Still friends.*

> *Jake: Just checking.*

And with that, still feeling hurt beyond belief, I resigned myself to the fact that friends were all we would ever be.

THIRTEEN

For the remaining days before the end of the semester, both Jake and I did a good job of pretending that night in his room never happened.

He seemed to really be trying hard to act like a "friend" lately, careful not to cross any lines. Despite that, our non-physical connection seemed to be growing. He was hanging out more in the living room with Tarah, Ryan and me at night. He and I would sometimes linger, staying up late, eating ice cream or a dessert I made while we talked in the kitchen.

Our conversation topics became more personal, too. He opened up more about his childhood. I learned that he actually grew up in Chicago, not Boston and that his mother had been a drug addict as a teenager but straightened up when she met his father. Even more surprising: the fact that the sister he is close to, only came into his life eight years ago because she had been given up for adoption when Jake's mother was fifteen. He told me a story that blew me away about how he first met her accidentally during a bizarre chance encounter in a cemetery.

It was adorable how his eyes would light up when he talked about his twin nieces. He used to babysit them when they were infants and shared a lot of funny memories about those days; it thoroughly amused me to picture this tough-looking guy changing diapers and getting spit up on.

We had a lot of laughs and sometimes, I would catch his eyes lingering on mine or traveling down to my mouth. These were subtle hints that a part of him wanted more, even though something was obviously holding him back.

Every night, he would go back to his room, and I would go to mine, replaying everything we had talked about. Despite my vow to bottle up my feelings for him, they were still growing stronger than a batch of sea monkeys trapped in a jar.

The last Wednesday of the semester rolled around, and when I turned my final exam into Professor Hernandez, I knew that this one wasn't going to be an A. In fact, I hadn't even completed the last two problems. Maybe it was because Jake and I had done more talking lately than studying or because secretly, I wanted this last punishment from him.

That night, when Jake arrived home from work, I stood in his doorway with my laptop.

He was taking off his jacket and looked amazing in a black button down shirt that was open slightly at the top. He smelled of cologne mixed with cold air, and it annoyed me that my body would consistently react to him in a way that was not befitting a platonic friend.

He hung up his jacket and looked over at me. "What's up?"

"I got my grade."

A slow and devious smile spread over his face because he could tell from my expression that it wasn't good. He held out his hand. "Let's see it."

I turned the laptop toward him, and he gasped. "Sixty-nine!"

Of all numbers, I know.

"Nina Kennedy...that is perversely horrible," he said trying to stifle his laughter.

"I know it is! But it still brings me to a B average for the semester." I feigned a smile.

He didn't look too pleased with my answer. "In all seriousness, why did you bomb so badly?"

"I don't know. I guess I just got lazy. I knew with the other grades, I'd get at least a C+ average no matter what, and I haven't been sleeping well the past few days."

"That's no excuse. You could have had a B average too if you had done better on this one," he said in a serious tone.

I sighed. "I'm sorry if I disappointed you."

His frown turned into a slight smile, and he seemed to perk up real fast, smacking his hands together. "That being said, I'm fucking stoked it wasn't an A." He was now beaming.

"I know you have been waiting for this."

Jake scratched his head, spun around searching for his laptop, then lay on the bed, kicking his feet up. "You don't have classes tomorrow, right?" he asked as he typed.

"Nope...done until after Christmas."

His smile grew bigger as he clicked away. When I walked over to the laptop, he shut it and waved me away. "Get outta here. You can't see this."

I stood across from him nervously tapping my foot, watching him type and wondering what he was up to. "What are you doing, Jake?"

"I'm planning our day tomorrow."

"Can't you just give me one little hint?"

"All I will say is that you need to be ready very early in the morning, like five-am. Can you do that?"

I nodded. "Yes."

He continued typing. "Good. I have to take tomorrow off from work for this."

"You're taking time off from work to spend the entire day scaring the shit out of me?"

"You're welcome."

"Seriously? This is a day trip?"

"I have the time."

"Can you please just tell me what we are doing? Come on, I am starting to freak out."

"What else is new? No way. You'll find out soon enough."

I made sure to shower that night because I wouldn't have the chance to do it in the morning. Under the water, my heart was palpitating, filled with anxiety over tomorrow. It had been too long since I had faced my fears on Jake's terms and tested my nerves. Not to mention, I had an ominous feeling about this one.

When I got back to my room, low and behold, there was an origami bat greeting me on the nightstand. He would always wait for me to take a shower, so he could sneak one into my room.

When I opened it and saw what it said, my heart nearly skipped a beat:

**For our last stint,
I will give you a hint.
It's a windy city...
Where Jake was itty bitty.**

He was taking me home to Chicago.

Maybe by some miracle there would be a terror threat or a medical emergency, and this spaceship would stay on the ground. Actually, I was probably going to become the medical emergency. That was my last hope because the passengers had boarded, and the doors to the Boeing 737 were now closed, trapping us all inside.

Officially out of control of my life. Why did I let him do this to me?

Because I would do anything he asked me to.

"Hold my hand, Nina. Squeeze it as tight as you need to. Breathe," he said.

The smell of the engines turning on reminded me of burning cheese.

With the way I was breathing in and out and the way Jake was squeezing my hand, row nine, seats E and F, looked more like a labor and delivery area.

Even the flight attendants were seated now in those strange side seats, belted and useless. Their fate was in the same hands, those of a man who might have just had a couple of whiskeys in the airport lounge.

Forget the elevator, this was the single most terrifying moment of my life. Flying was at the very top of the list of things that scared me. As queen of the "what ifs," I created too many possible scenarios of what could go wrong and couldn't even wrap my head around them all.

As the jet taxied toward the runway, my breathing had gotten completely out of control, and my entire body shook involuntarily. How was this thing going to possibly lift off the ground and stay up in the air? I knew nothing about the mechanics of the situation, and even if properly explained, it likely would still not seem logical.

Rosary beads in hand, the old lady across the aisle made the sign of the cross. She certainly wasn't helping my situation in the least bit.

Jake could see he was losing me fast. I was starting to hyperventilate. He reached into his trusty black backpack of doom and took out a brown paper bag. "Breathe into this."

It wasn't helping, because I had myself convinced I couldn't breathe and panicked, which fed the hyperventilation.

As the plane picked up speed, the concern in his eyes grew when my breathing became shallow.

The last thing I remembered before we were completely airborne was Jake bending down to tie his shoes. How bizarre, I thought, for him to do such a thing when I am on the verge of collapse. I soon realized that he wasn't tying his shoes.

He was untying mine.

Near hyperventilation morphed into uncontrollable and hysterical laughter, as he stayed bent down attacking my feet in the worst foot tickle ambush of my life.

I fidgeted in my chair and kicked him repeatedly, crying tears of laughter, and so was he.

"Jake...stop!"

"Stop."

"Stop."

"Stop."

"Stop" was all I could manage to say in between my cackling and hitting him. It was not an exaggeration to say that the entire plane was looking at us like we were nuts.

By the time he finally did stop, we were at cruising altitude, and my nerves calmed down after realizing that we had not crashed upon takeoff. His tickles had distracted me so much that it was impossible to focus on anything else.

My breathing was still heavy, but I was no longer close to hyperventilating. I finally turned to him worn out. "Why on Earth would you do that to me?"

"I had no choice. There are only so many things I can do from this seat to get your mind off your fear. You can only handle one thing at a time. I figured if I made you totally lose it that way, you couldn't possibly become scared enough to panic." He could see I was starting to crack a smile and returned it. "It worked...didn't it?"

"I guess. But don't ever do that again to me."

He flashed a wicked grin. "I'll do whatever I have to do to save you from yourself."

A few minutes later, my breathing had calmed down significantly, and I gave in to the fact that I had no choice but to try to relax.

Jake took his iPod out of the backpack and handed it to me. "Here. I made you a playlist for the ride." He scrolled down to it, and I could see it was titled, *Crash and Burn*.

"Thanks a lot."

"You're welcome."

I put the headphones on and breathed through *Leaving on a Jet Plane* by John Denver.

When the next song played, I didn't quite get it until the chorus: *I'm Goin' Down* by Mary J. Blige.

I looked at him and shook my head. He was listening to my iPod and took off his headphones for a moment. "Mary J. Blige?"

I nodded and rolled my eyes.

He snickered and returned the headphones to his ears, lying back and closing his eyes again.

The next song, in typical Jake fashion, completely threw me for a loop. It was a mellow country tune about how the chances of surviving at love are slim, comparing it to an airplane that people wouldn't get on if they knew the odds of crashing were high. Yet, despite knowing the odds, people get on board in love all of the time. The song was aptly titled, *If Love Was a Plane* by Brad Paisley.

I looked over at him, and he looked back at me and smiled. I wasn't sure if he realized which song I was on or if it even had any meaning to him. But it had meaning to me. I wished that he knew how strong my feelings were and that I would be willing to risk anything to be with him. Hell, in my mind, I was doing it right now on this vessel to Mars. Despite whatever was stopping him from taking the next step with me, nothing had been able to prevent me from needing him, not even knowing that he was hiding something from me.

The drink cart was parked in front of our row, and Jake wouldn't let me order anything but a Bloody Mary to relax. Of course, the older, busty flight attendant licked her lips and made a flirtatious face before handing him his beverage and moving past us. He smiled back at her, and this prompted me to down my drink, which immediately went to my head.

He lifted my empty glass. "Thirsty?"

"Yes."

The two hour flight seemed to take forever, but when the pilot had put on the fasten seatbelt sign, and the old lady across the aisle had taken out her rosary beads, I knew we were close to landing.

The turbulence from losing altitude brought my panic symptoms back in full force. My ears were popping. He didn't say anything, just grabbed my hand because he knew I needed it.

One jolt in particular forced me to squeeze his hand even harder. He surprised me when he reached over me, locking both of my hands in his. "It's almost over, Nina. You did good," he whispered in a soothing tone.

I focused only on the warmth of his grip, melting my body like butter, to get me through the slow descent. When we finally touched down, I looked over at Lady Rosary. We smiled at each other and simultaneously made the signs of the cross.

FOURTEEN

I was so incredibly happy to be back on land. We had no bags to retrieve, so Jake and I made it out of the crowded airport in no time. It was energizing to feel the air of a foreign city on my face as we exited the sliding doors. This was a place I probably would have never otherwise visited over the course of my life, and again, I was grateful that Jake had pushed me this far.

Sinatra's *My Kind of Town*, the song about Chicago, played in my head as giddy excitement to explore this new city built up inside me.

We hopped into a waiting cab, and he told the driver to take us to Willis Tower.

"What's that?" I asked.

"You'll find out soon enough."

I spoke too soon about being grateful for his pushing me and had been hoping to catch a break for the rest of the trip. I took my phone out to google it and soon learned that Willis Tower was the site of a famous Chicago landmark known as the "The Ledge," a glass box that extends out from the building's Skydeck, 1,300 feet in the air. Apparently, even people who are not normally afraid of heights get scared standing on this thing.

He leaned over my shoulder. "So, you figured it out, hey, Sherlock?"

"Haven't I had enough torture for one day?"

"We're just going to do this one thing, and then I promise, the rest of the day, we'll just chill." He crossed his heart with his hand.

"What time is our return flight?"

"Late...not until nine."

I was officially on the old wooden roller coaster of anxiety again, rising up slowly.

When the cab let us off at the building on South Wacker Drive, I looked up and gulped. "You're kidding me, right?"

"Come on." He waved and led me through the front doors to the elevators.

My panic didn't even have time to fully build because in what seemed like less than a minute, we had arrived on the 103rd floor in lightning speed.

I didn't know if it was because I had just survived a flight thousands of feet into the sky, but being up there wasn't as bad as I was expecting. I couldn't wait to be done with it, but compared to flying, it produced so much less anxiety because there was a means to escape.

Jake made me feel like a kid when he stopped to tell the staff it was my first time, and someone actually gave me a sticker.

An unexpected calmness came over me as I looked out at the view.

There were details posted all around that explained what part of the city we were viewing on each side.

Jake led me over to this high-tech set of binoculars. "Look, that's the south side of the city, where I grew up." He pointed to his old stomping grounds. It made me both sad and happy for him because he hadn't been back here in years. I wondered if he was thinking about his father or what he left behind when he moved to Boston.

After about ten minutes, I knew there was one last thing he was going to make me do.

"Come on, let's go take a picture on the ledge," he said.

Shit.

I knew I wasn't getting out of this, so I hung onto him, gripping his jacket as he practically dragged me over to the terrifying glass platform.

I continued to nervously cling onto him, floating through the moment, developing vertigo as my legs shook. As the staff took a professional picture of us, I was careful not to look down.

Luckily, he didn't force me to stay on it for very long. When we stepped off, it was an immense relief, but I was glad I had done it. I could have never dreamt of attempting that without him by my side. They gave us our picture, and it took my breath away. The two of us were basically on top of the world, and that was exactly how I felt.

The next leg of the adventure was a subway ride to Jake's old neighborhood.

It was run down with dilapidated houses very close together. There was a bodega on the corner that he used to frequent as a kid. He told me he would buy penny candy there after scrounging up all of his change. He took me inside and bought me some Lemonheads and Laffy Taffy.

We dodged children playing on the narrow sidewalks as we approached a beige house with a rusty railing along a steep set of stairs.

"This is it. This was where we lived," he said with a look of childlike awe, as I followed him up the front steps.

He knocked on the door, but there was no answer. "That sucks. I was hoping to see the inside."

I felt bad that we had come all this way, and he wouldn't be able to see his old house.

Jake put his hand on the small of my back as we walked back down, and it gave me goosebumps. "Come on, let's go out back," he said.

He didn't seem to care that we were trespassing; it was clear he felt that the memories here gave him some ownership.

There was no fence preventing access to the backyard, which was a small rectangular area of grass with a concrete border surrounding it.

"Check this out," he said, leading me over to a shady corner.

Carved into the concrete were the words, *Jake Loves Buffy.*

"Buffy, huh? Lucky girl," I said as we both sat on the ground next to the carving.

"Buffy. I was nine. She was basically my first love."

I did not just get a twinge of jealousy over a nine-year-old girl!

"What was she like?"

"She loved to nibble on things if you know what I mean."

"Nibble?"

"She'd do anything for me. I had her eating out of the palm of my hand."

"Seriously? I mean, I figured you had skills, but nine-years-old?"

"Buffy was portly. She loved to eat. So, as long as I fed her, she was happy." He noticed my disturbed expression and chuckled. "A hamster, Nina! Buffy was my first pet."

I looked up at the sky and shook my head. I felt so stupid. "Seriously?"

"Yeah. This grassy area right by the carving is where I had to bury her. That was a tough day."

"I am sorry, Jake." I hoped it wasn't bad that I was laughing somewhat when I said that.

"It sounds so stupid, but for a kid, when a damn hamster is the only thing you came home to everyday and then it dies, well, that was a shitty day."

"What do you mean the only thing you came home to?"

"I was a latch-key kid. My mother had to work two jobs after my father died, and she couldn't afford a babysitter. So, when the bus dropped me off at the corner, I would walk home and come in to an empty house. I'd lock the door with like five different dead bolts, make a peanut butter and banana sandwich and hope for the best."

I definitely wasn't laughing now; my heart ached for that little boy. "God, that is so sad."

"It was fine. I didn't know any different. My mother worked hard, and she had no choice. She taught me to take care of myself, and the old lady next door would look in on me from time to time. But the thing is, for two years, I looked forward to seeing that little critter every day."

I was not about to cry over a hamster.

I was...about to cry over a hamster.

My eyes became watery, and I ran my hand over the carving. "Well, for a latch-key kid, you turned out really well." I nudged him playfully with my shoulder. "You're seriously the smartest person I have ever met."

He didn't say anything. He just closed his eyes with a placid look on his face as the wind blew on us. I felt honored to be here with him at the place where he experienced so many things that shaped him.

He opened his eyes and rubbed my shoulder. "Are you cold? You wanna get going?"

The truth was, it was the warmest I'd felt all day. "Let's stay for a little bit longer. We came all this way."

"Okay. Thank you."

We just sat, taking in the cold air and listening to the sounds of sirens and children in the distance. I wanted so badly inside his head as he looked around. It was clear this place still meant a lot to him.

I really wanted to hold his hand, so I reached for it, and he opened his palm for me, taking mine in his and said, "Thank you for tagging along with me."

"Does it make you sad to be back here?"

"Not if I take my own advice and only think about the good memories. It's all about focusing on the good ones, remember?"

I squeezed his hand tighter. "What are some of the good ones?"

He looked up over at the house. "Oh, I have a lot at this place. Christmases with my mother were definitely good ones. She would save up her vacation days and use them all up during the holidays. She'd do up the whole house in cheesy tinsel and plastic mistletoe, and we'd eat greasy Chinese and play games like Monopoly. We'd watch *A Christmas Story* over and over because that's the best fuckin' movie ever." He laughed. "Then, of course, there were the teenage memories. Let's just say being a latch-key kid ain't so bad when you want to sneak girls in at fifteen."

I cringed. "I bet."

"Then, there was the day I found my sister...coming back here and telling my Mom. Or the day I checked the mailbox right out front there and opened a letter that said I had gotten a full ride to Northeastern. Man, I'll never forget that day."

"Wow, I never knew that."

"Yeah. As they say in Boston, I was pretty *smaht*."

"Well, I knew that part."

"Anyways, lots of good memories...focus on the good..."

"I am trying. I don't know how I got to be such a negative person...so flawed."

He turned to me. "Flawed?"

"Yeah, you know, with all my crazy fears."

He didn't respond right away and seemed to be thinking about something. "When did your first panic attack happen again?"

"I was a senior in high school."

"What was going on in your life then?"

Maybe it should have seemed obvious, but for some reason, until this very moment, I had never connected my own issues to my brother's death. The truth was, "My brother had just died...a month before the first attack."

My brother had just died.

"See, Nina, I hadn't even realized that part. Is it really that unusual for someone who experienced a traumatic event to lose control? That doesn't make you flawed. It makes you real."

I looked down at our intertwined hands and back at him. "I have honestly never thought about it that way. I always just assumed my panic attacks were a sign of weakness."

Jake scratched his chin and turned his body toward mine. "I've been thinking about something a lot since I met you. Everyone has fears. Yours are just more tangible. You wear them on your sleeve. You think you're weak, but you're one of the strongest people I know, because as of today you've knocked the top two things you feared down one by one in a relatively short amount of time. Do you realize how rare it is for people to actually do that? Some people never have the courage to face their fears in an entire lifetime, let alone a matter of months."

I pushed my shoulder into him playfully. "Most people don't have crazy roommates who take an interest in helping them do it."

"You think I've helped you...but you inspire me, Nina, without even realizing it. Seeing you and how you've trusted me enough to guide you through your own fears, makes me think about facing some of my own."

"I can't imagine you being afraid of anything. What do you fear?"

"What are my fears?" He looked up at the sky, and his lip twitched as he pondered my question, then looked back at me. "Hurting people...like letting people I care about down. Stuff like that."

That was all I was going to get because he looked away from me, and I knew an imaginary wall had just gone up. Jake was like a puzzle. He'd offer me small pieces of his life, but none of them fit together to tell a complete story. The more silence that ensued, the more sure I became that he wasn't going to elaborate on why he was afraid of hurting people and who he was afraid to hurt. I decided not to press my luck in prying further.

A plane flew overhead, and we both looked up at it in unison. More time passed in silence as we sat holding hands while we continued to trespass on the back lawn of this house.

A sudden blast of wind blew my hair right into his face, and I said, "They're not kidding when they call it a windy city. Sorry about that."

"Don't apologize," he said, still looking up at the sky, before whispering, "I love your hair." He said it so softly I wasn't sure he intended for me to hear it.

But I did.

He let go of my hand abruptly, and his eyes popped out of his head. "Do you like milkshakes?"

Holy random transition.

"Sure."

He stood up, and I followed suit. "Let's get out of here."

FIFTEEN

"This place is awesome," I said as I followed him into Bernie's diner, a retro-style joint about six blocks from his old house.

The smell of French fries and burgers was absolute heaven because I was starving.

"Wait 'til you taste the food." He was grinning from ear to ear as we sat ourselves in a booth by the window. The table had one of those mini jukeboxes, and for a dollar, we could play our choice of about twenty-five different oldies from the 50's and 60's.

"These music boxes have been here since I was a kid. The songs are exactly the same. It's wild."

"What are you gonna play?"

He put some change into the machine. "My father used to always play this one."

I recognized it immediately, and my mouth dropped because I couldn't believe my ears. "*Crimson and Clover,*" I said.

"You know it?"

"This was one of Jimmy's favorite songs. It was from way before our time, but he loved it. Except, it was the Joan Jett version he would play. Who sings this one?"

Jake closed his eyes and moved his head slowly to the rhythm of the haunting song before answering me. "That's wild about your brother. This was my Dad's absolute favorite song. This one's the original by Tommy James and the Shondells. It's one of the few songs that remind me of my childhood, because he'd play it every Sunday when we'd come here."

"I didn't realize the other one was a remake."

"I like the Joan Jett version better, but this is the one my Dad always listened to."

When the song finished, a waitress came by to take our order. We hadn't even looked at the menus, so she said she'd come back.

He handed me one. "I know what I'm getting, but you should decide. The milkshakes are legendary, and the burgers...don't even get me started."

"I'll have whatever you get."

"Anchovy pie, then?" He winked, then flagged the waitress down and said, "We'll take two Bernie burgers and two strawberry milkshakes."

While we were waiting for our food, he played with the straw to his water then looked up at me and asked, "What made you decide to become a nurse?"

"Honestly? My brother. There was this one nurse who was with him the most. Her name was Kerri. She was younger, just out of school. I think he actually had a crush on her." I laughed thinking about how cute my brother was. "I just remember being so grateful for the times that she was with him when we couldn't be because of work or school. He was so sick but would just light up whenever she was around. And I remember thinking back then, God, if my brother makes it, I swear I am going to give back and do the same thing for someone else's brother or son."

"So, after he died, you still decided to do it."

"Yeah, I did." I focused on his dragon tattoo, trying not to lose my composure.

He could tell I was about to cry.

"It's okay, Nina.

My voice was now shaky, but I managed to get it together. "It just made me so thankful that he had her... someone that brought a little light into his life, during such a dark time."

"I can relate to that," he said looking down, playing with his straw again.

"What do you mean?"

"Much needed light during a dark time...being on the receiving end of that."

Then, he looked straight up at me suddenly. I didn't fully understand what he meant, but before I could ask what he was referring to, our food had arrived.

I gasped when the waitress set my plate in front of me. "Okay, this burger is bigger than my head."

He chuckled. "Don't worry. Whatever you don't finish, I'll eat."

Our hands collided when we both reached for the salt at the same time. Even a split second of touching him sent a shock wave through me.

As usual, we ate in comfortable silence, and the sounds he made while devouring the burger reminded me of his reaction to my desserts. He definitely let it be known when he was truly enjoying something.

The shake was so thick I could barely get it through the straw.

"You need to suck on it harder," he said with a smirk, wiggling his eyebrows.

He was the king of sexual innuendos. I usually didn't play along but was in a different kind of a mood today. "I guess my mouth is just out of practice."

He nearly choked on his own shake and that topic of conversation pretty much ended there.

Suddenly embarrassed at my boldness, I changed the subject. "So, you asked me why I decided to become a nurse. Why did you choose engineering?"

"From a young age, I liked to take things apart and put them back together. So, I guess it was the field that fit the bill."

So, when he rips my heart out, he'll be able to fix it.

I looked down at his sexy arms. "I am sure you get asked this all the time, but what are the meanings behind your tattoos, like the dragon, for example? That's my favorite one."

Squinting his eyes sarcastically, he said, "No...no one *ever* asks me that!" He chuckled. "Seriously, though, nothing profound. Everyone thinks there's got to be some fucking deep meaning behind ink, but I just thought the dragon looked cool. The same goes for these." He pointed to his right arm that sported various Celtic and tribal markings, along with crosses, roses and other artwork. "All meaningless, except for this one right here, the moon with my father's initials on it. I got most of these when I was a teenager."

I reached across the table and rubbed my index finger over the half moon tattoo that had the letters A.B.G. surrounding it.

"What does it stand for?"

"Alan Boyd Green."

"What does the moon mean?"

He looked down at my finger, which was still brushing against his arm and said, "My Dad used to say this thing to me before he left the house or tucked me in at night. I would tell him I loved him then he would say he loved me too. But I would always ask him how much. He would say, 'to the moon...I love you to the moon.'"

"That is so incredibly sweet."

He was staring out the window. "Sometimes, I look up at the moon at night and think of him. I know that's fucking cheesy...but I do."

"I think that's beautiful."

I think you are beautiful too, and God help me, I want to kiss you so badly right now.

"He was this big biker dude, you know? But he had a heart of gold, and he would have been a great father to have growing up." He lifted his thumb, pointing to the band he always wore around it. "This was my Dad's wedding ring, actually."

Wow.

"He knew that you loved him, Jake. I regret not telling my brother I loved him more like that."

"We all have things we regret...decisions we make that we have to live with. You can't dwell on them and beat yourself up for it. It doesn't change anything."

We stayed in that diner booth for at least three hours. We played more music from the jukebox, and I told Jake stories about growing up in the boonies; he couldn't believe I actually drove a tractor and said he'd pay money if I let him come home and watch. He joked that he would pay more if I did it in a bikini.

Then, we shared a huge slice of "death by chocolate" cake. He had asked me if I wanted to go explore more of

Chicago, but there was something so peaceful about this nostalgic place. I told him I preferred to just hang out here until we had to head back to the airport.

The sun had set, and the evening dinner crowd started to fill Bernie's. Every time the bell on the door chimed, it reminded me I was one step closer to getting back on another plane. The anxiety started to build up again.

I took the last bite of cake, and with my mouth full, said, "This day really surprised me. I had no clue what you had in store, but it turned out to be one of the best days I've had in a really long time. To think I was dreading it. Now, I just have get through the flight home."

"You can choose right here and now to stay in the present and let go of the fear or you can choose to engage it. Nothing can hurt you on that plane, unless you let it."

I put my fork down. "How did you get to be so wise? Seriously, you're like an 80-year-old man stuck in a hot, tatted body."

What the hell did I just say to him?

His gaze was penetrating, and the amused smile on his face showed me that my admission hadn't escaped him.

"So...you think I'm hot?" His smile was devious now. He was going to torture me.

I didn't know what to say, so decided on an answer that made no sense. "Well, you know what I mean."

"Are there other meanings for hot?"

"Jake—"

"You're turning red...stop. I'm messing with you. You make it so easy sometimes." He laughed and startled me when he reached across the table and swiped his thumb gently across my lip then licked his finger. Chills radiated down my spine as he did it.

"You had chocolate all over your mouth. It was cute for a while, but I didn't want you leaving here like that."

"Oh...thanks," I said looking away, still embarrassed about what I had just admitted. I was also desperately wishing he had licked the chocolate directly off of my mouth, so I could taste him.

It was now completely dark out, and I knew we had to leave in a few minutes. I wished we could just stay here in this booth longer. Somehow we were able to drown out the whole world for the past few hours. He had me crazy in lust and had a way of making me want to tell him everything, like my deepest fears and desires. Sometimes, I made an ass out of myself in the process because if I was being honest...*he* was my deepest desire.

"Ready to go? We should get to the airport," he said as he took out his wallet and paid the bill.

"As ready as I'll ever be."

As we exited Bernie's, he put his hand on the small of my back again, and my breathing quickened immediately. Anytime he so much as brushed up against me, let alone touched me directly, my body responded, and lately, the effects have been cumulative; I was slowly wearing thin.

On the flight home, before takeoff, he grabbed my hand without my asking him to.

I think he could see my nerves starting to work their way up to panic mode.

This plane was bigger and nearly empty, and we had a large middle row all to ourselves. I was scared but didn't feel as out of control as I was at the start of the first flight. It was nighttime, and somehow that was more calming than the sun pouring in.

"You think you can make it through takeoff without a tickle?"

I nodded. "Just don't let go of my hand, okay?"

"I promise. I won't."

And he didn't, for the entire flight. Even when we had reached cruising altitude, even when the flight attendant came by with drinks, even when he would reach into his backpack for something, he kept my hand in his. It was a small gesture, but it was the first time I truly felt that he was holding it because he wanted to, not because I needed him to.

It was dark inside the plane aside from some small interior lights. Sitting close to him in the dim lighting of our otherwise empty row felt intimate.

Jake came up with a game to get my mind off a patch of turbulence. "We are going to take turns shouting out a word, and then we both have to say the first thing that comes to mind.

I breathed out, still shaken from the constant bouncing of the plane. "Okay."

"Ready?"

"Yeah," I said.

"You first," he said.

The first subject that came to my mind was "Chicago."

Me: "Bernies."

Jake: "Home."

"Math," Jake said.

Me: "Torture."

Jake: "Fun."

"Mrs. Ballsworthy," I said laughing.

We looked at each other, amused and said in unison, "Fuck."

He threw out his own name. "Jake."

Me: "Bananas."

Jake: "Hot."

I smacked him.

I threw out, "Nina."

Me: "Spectacular."

Jake: (Silent pause) "Let me think about that and get back to you."

I whacked him playfully again.

We continued to play the back and forth game until the turbulence let up. He had succeeded in distracting me from it.

It had been a long day, and I decided to lay my head back and close my eyes, even though I was too nervous to actually nap. Jake was still holding my hand, and at one point, started rubbing his thumb softly back and forth across it. My eyes were still closed, but I was melting into the seat, quivering between my legs at the small but sensual gesture. I squeezed his hand in an attempt to communicate that I liked it when he did that. As he continued to brush across my hand with his thumb, I mimicked him and started rubbing my own thumb across his. Eventually, our two thumbs were moving in soft circular motions.

When I opened my eyes suddenly, I was surprised to find him turned in his seat completely toward me. I had assumed he was looking straight ahead with his eyes closed, like I was. Instead, he was just staring at me, and I seemed to have caught him in the act. Was he doing that the entire time our thumbs were making out?

His breathing was rapid, and he was looking at me like he was struggling to say something, like he definitely wanted to kiss me, like he wanted inside my soul, but something was holding him back.

He took his hand from mine and used it to push my hair behind my ears, sat up and then said, "You better put on your seatbelt. The light just came on."

We said nothing else for the rest of the flight. My heart was pounding, but this time, it wasn't because of my fear of flying. It was for fear of Jake. Because I had really thought that something was about to happen between us in that moment, yet in typical Jake fashion, he stopped at the tipping point. And those butterflies in my stomach? They were dead from exhaustion.

When I returned from the shower to my bedroom that night, in place of a paper bat on my nightstand, was a pair of plastic gold pilot's wings that I had apparently earned as a brave flier. So, once again, Jake managed to make me feel like a child.

I was damn proud of myself, though. The feeling was bittersweet because even though our trip rocked, it created more confusion. After today, I was absolutely sure he felt something for me.

The next day, I'd leave for almost two weeks to go home for Christmas break. What I didn't know was, once I returned to Brooklyn after the holidays, nothing would ever be the same there again.

SIXTEEN

I was back at my parents' house all of one day, and I was already itching to see Jake again. It was the weekend, so he would have been in Boston anyway, but it was psychological because I knew I'd be here for several days. It would be the first whole week since I had known him that we would be apart.

I felt empty and hopeless, and it was my first realization that I was truly becoming addicted to him. It was snowing heavily, and while I should have appreciated the beautiful white landscape outside the window, it just made me feel more trapped here.

I sat on the red suede couch, mindlessly flicking through cable channels, while really focused on thoughts of Jake's thumb brushing against mine.

Then, my mind wandered to that night in his room when he basically kicked me out. I tried really hard in general not to think about that night, those words that came out of his mouth that were so brutally raw. I nearly had an orgasm from just replaying them alone and believed that he meant what he said about the things he wanted to do to me. He *was* trying hard to stay away. The thought both turned me on immensely and angered me.

At dinner, my parents grilled me about life in New York. They were pretty conservative, and if they thought I was shacking up with someone I wanted to have sex with, they would flip. So, I chose to continue to keep my feelings for my roommate a secret.

"So, honey, have you met any nice young men yet in the city?" my mother asked.

"No one special."

Someone amazing.

"Do you think you need to get out more? Maybe join a college club or something? I bet you would meet a nice guy if you joined some kind of group."

Unless he has piercings, a dragon tattoo, wants to make me come until I scream in every way possible and his name is Jake Green...not interested.

"Yeah, maybe," I said with absolutely no feeling whatsoever.

My mother, Sheryl, always tried to offer up advice on ways I could meet men. Unfortunately, her judgment could not be trusted. Aside from the fact that she thought Spencer was the best thing that ever happened to me, she once tried to set me up with a co-worker's son who, at first, sounded interesting on paper. He supposedly worked in "makeup" and resembled a famous actor. Very "Hollywood," right?" It turned out to be a different story once I met the guy. He was a funeral embalmer, which although it weirded me out, I could have lived with, had the celebrity he *actually* resembled not been Pee Wee Herman. So, I kept my mother out of my love life.

After dinner, I went to my bedroom to daydream in private, while looking out the window at our neighbor's holiday lights. We had stopped putting lights up after Jimmy died, but our neighbors, the Hardimans, had always put up the same exact decorations every year since I was a kid. Looking out at their front yard was nostalgic because despite everything that we lost when Jimmy died, seeing the same old pair of lit up reindeers and the same inflatable Santa was a glimpse back to the way things were in happier times.

The next night was Christmas Eve. It used to be a huge deal in my house growing up, with lots of presents under the tree and a huge nativity display outside. After Jimmy died, my mother scaled back significantly. All we had this year was a modest tree and two stockings—Jimmy's and mine—over the fireplace.

Our plans were to go to a late afternoon mass at St. Margaret's Church, followed by a small gathering of my parents' close friends back at the house.

It was in the middle of mass that evening, when my solemn Christmas Eve took an interesting turn. My phone had been on vibrate when I felt it buzz against the pew. It was a text from Jake.

I didn't want to be rude and read it during the sermon, but I couldn't help myself.

> *So, I'm in the middle of a Christmas get together at my sister's house, and she has Pandora radio on. That Divinyls song comes on, and now all I can think about is you. Thanks a lot.*

What Divinyls song?

It was killing me not knowing what he was talking

about. I managed to hold off on googling it until we left the church. Once in my father's car, I searched *"Divinyls songs"* and found it: *I Touch Myself*. I knew the song but not who sang it.

Of course. Very funny, Jake.

I happened to notice another song by The Divinyls on the list. It was the perfect title of a song that would describe how he made me feel. So, I texted him back:

> **That's funny, because there is a Divinyls song that reminds me of you too. It's called Pleasure and Pain.**

I was expecting him to respond in typical Jake fashion with a wise comeback.

> **Jake: ;-) So, what are you doing tonight?**

> **Nina: Christmas is kind of sad at my house. We just went to church. Now, going home for some dinner. What about you?**

> **Jake: Playing dolls with my nieces. Don't tell anyone.**

> **Nina: LOL. You never cease to amaze me.**

About three minutes later...

> **Jake: When are you coming back to the city?**

Nina: Not for almost two weeks.

Jake: Damn.

Nina: Are you gonna miss me that much?

Jake: Actually, yeah. I miss you already, to be honest. A lot.

Oh.

Nina: I miss you too.

Jake: Merry Christmas.

Nina: Merry Christmas.

After dinner, my parents stayed in the dining room eating roasted chestnuts with a few friends while I excused myself back to my room yet again. I lay back on my canopy bed (don't laugh) and closed my eyes, looking up at the glow-in-the-dark stars (don't laugh) that I had stuck on the ceiling years ago.

All I could focus on was Jake saying that he missed me. And you know what? It was a hell of a lot better than focusing on how much I missed my brother. In fact, these past few months living in Brooklyn have been the first time since Jimmy died that I have felt alive again.

He brought me back to life.

He brought me back to life, and he could very well be the death of me all over again.

It would be worth the risk.

But he's holding all the cards.

An hour later, it was about ten o'clock when my phone vibrated.

Did you see the moon tonight?

I smiled and immediately walked over to my window. The moon was not quite full but almost, and it was amazingly bright. Along with the snow on the ground and the holiday lights shining from across the street, the combination was astonishingly beautiful. It absolutely warmed my heart to think about Jake looking up at that same moon, thinking of his Dad tonight.

> **Nina: I would have never thought to look out at the moon on Christmas Eve, but I am glad I did. You always have a way of opening up my eyes to things.**
>
> **Jake: There is nothing more I'd rather look at right now, actually.**
>
> **Nina: The moon is beautiful.**
>
> **Jake: I was talking about your eyes.**

On reflex, I touched my hand to my heart, as if to stop it from leaping out of my chest. He had the ability to completely shake me to the core and transform my body to mush with a simple sentence. I needed to respond but couldn't form a coherent word. He texted again before I could try.

Jake: They're the most beautiful eyes I've ever seen. I get lost in them sometimes. They comfort me in a way that nothing else can.

My hand was shaking as I wrote.

Nina: I love your eyes, too.

Jake: I know I've been confusing you. I am sorry. We need to talk when you come home.

My heart was palpitating because it didn't know how to react to "we need to talk."

Nina: I think we need to talk, too.

I waited for a response, but apparently that was the end of the exchange. I fell asleep confused, not sure whether to be heartbroken or happy that he wanted to talk about us.

My phone was still in my hand when I woke up the next morning, Christmas day. I looked down and realized he had, in fact, texted me one more time, hours later in the middle of the night.

Jake: I've got it...Angel. That's my answer to your question from the plane. What Nina reminds me of.

I didn't know what exactly had gotten into him, but I was sort of liking it. As I got out of bed, though, giddiness transformed into a lingering fear that had begun to gnaw at me.

Throughout the course of that day, his admission that we needed to talk when I got back, had started to consume me.

I had no appetite during our Christmas ham dinner because my body had basically shut down from worrying.

When my parents and I sat down later to watch, *Elf*, my mind was not focused on the movie, and I wasn't finding parts funny that used to make me laugh out loud. The different theories about what he wanted to say to me were flooding my brain.

Then, I came to an unhealthy realization. I seriously didn't think I could live without Jake and felt like my entire world would crumble without him in it. Even though I wanted to take the next step with him so badly, at the same time, I knew if things stayed the same, I would never have to worry about losing him. There was something to be said for keeping things just as they were.

The fact that he hadn't texted me again that Christmas Sunday put me further on edge.

The following Tuesday Jake was back in New York when he texted me for the first time since Christmas Eve.

> *Jake: The house is fucking boring without you. Even sniffing your underwear hasn't put me out of my funk. If I sniff this one five times, will you magically reappear?*

Nina: LOL. Get out of my lingerie drawer!

Jake: 36C? I knew it.

Nina: Now, I know you're lying because you're off by a cup size.

Jake: 36D? Really? Damn.

Nina: 34D but yes.

Jake: That was a clever way to get your bra size, though, wasn't it?

Nina: What are you really doing?

Jake: Just sitting around, actually. Tarah and Ryan are going downstairs to Eleni's for dinner. I might go with them because I have nothing better to do without you here to bug.

The fact that he'd be going downstairs tonight irked me and made me want to jump on the next bus back. If Desiree were working, she would use the opportunity of Jake being a third wheel without my being there, to sink her nasty paws into him.

Nina: That's nice. Have fun.

Jake: What day do you get back again?

Nina: Sometime during the week-end of January 8ᵗʰ.

Jake: Shit. I won't be home. I'll see you that Monday, the 9ᵗʰ, then?

Nina: Yeah.

Jake: Let's plan to go out that night.

Nina: Okay. Have fun at dinner.

Jake: Where is this lingerie drawer, btw?

Nina: (Rolls Eyes)

Jake: ;-)

At the end of the two weeks, I ended up arriving back in Brooklyn on a Saturday afternoon. A part of me was hoping that by some miracle, Jake would have skipped Boston just this once, but he was gone.

Tarah and Ryan were nowhere to be found either, so I decided to go out for a jog, since the weather was actually mild for January. Running would be a good way to expend some of the nervous energy that had built up over the past couple of weeks.

After changing into spandex and a hooded sweatshirt, I grabbed my iPod and a bottle of water from the fridge and flew out the door. On my way down the stairs, I could hear groaning coming from Mrs. Ballsworthy's apartment which prompted me to stop in the stairwell outside of her door and listen in.

Strange.

Usually, the only sounds coming from that place were an expletive or a game show blaring on the television.

The noises continued, and I stood paralyzed, unsure of what to make of it. Suddenly, came the words, "Help! Help me!"

Oh God!

What was I supposed to do? I was terrified of that woman. She scared the bejesus out of me.

Putting aside my terror, I turned the knob, surprised to find that the door was open. I nervously trotted on my tippy toes to the back of the apartment and followed the sound that was coming from one of the bedrooms.

She was on the floor, clutching her chest and turned to me. "Help me, Nina. Help...me."

"Mrs. Ballsworthy?!" I rushed over to her, and she grabbed by hand squeezing it. I dialed 911. "Yes, I need an ambulance right away to 1185 Lincoln. I think my neighbor might be having a heart attack. Mrs. Ballsworthy, what are you feeling? Can you talk?"

She could barely get out the words. "Chest...tight... pain...arm."

I responded to the directions of the dispatcher. "Okay...okay. Yes, of course, I'll stay with her. Yes...she's lying down. Do you have any aspirin?"

She pointed to bathroom across the hall.

I ran and grabbed a bottle of Bayer that was in the cabinet, rushing back to her and placing one in her mouth in a panic. I opened my water bottle and helped her drink some down.

"Don't leave me, Nina."

"I won't. I'm right here. I'm not going anywhere," I said holding her hand for about five minutes until the sound of sirens in the distance got closer.

As my father always used to say, "We make plans, and God laughs." I was heading out for a jog and somehow ended up in the back of an ambulance with a woman whose only words to me prior to today had been, "Go fuck yourself."

The woman next to me was no longer that miserable person I thought I knew; she was just...scared. Somehow, the man upstairs chose me to hold her hand through it, and I was damn well going to do my job.

"Mrs. Ballsworthy, do you have any family I can call?"

She was still having trouble speaking but managed to say, "My...daughter."

"Can you tell me her number?"

She slowly threw out the digits in between breaths, and I dialed as she spoke.

A woman picked up. "Hi, my name is Nina Kennedy. Is this Mrs. Ballsworthy's daughter?

"Yes," the woman answered.

"I'm her neighbor. Your mother may be having a heart attack. She is okay right now, but we are in the ambulance headed to the Brooklyn Hospital Center."

The woman said she'd be following us there right away and hung up.

When we got the hospital, they rushed her into the back and asked me to stay in the waiting area. I discovered her name was Laurice.

A beautiful woman with caramel colored skin and long thinly woven braids rushed into the waiting area, and I stood up. "Are you Laurice's daughter?"

"Yes. Where is my mother?"

"They just took her in and wouldn't let me go back. They told me to have you wait here and that a doctor would be out with an update."

She covered her mouth in shock, pacing the floor. "Is she going to be okay?"

"I think so. She was coherent and breathing."

"How did you find her?"

"I live upstairs. I was going out for a jog and heard her yelling for help."

"Oh my God," she said then surprised me when she pulled me in for a hug. "You may have saved her life."

"Anyone would have done the same thing."

"Thank you for being so diligent." She held out her hand. "I'm Daria."

"Nina. Nice to meet you."

Several minutes later, a nurse had come out to tell us that Mrs. Ballsworthy was stable but going into the operating room. I insisted on staying with Daria until her mother was out of surgery. I knew I wouldn't have wanted to be alone in this situation.

A doctor came out about an hour and a half later, and we both stood up. "Hi, I'm Dr. Tuscano. Who's the daughter?"

Daria raised her hand. "I am."

"Your mother is going to be fine. She had a clogged artery that caused a mild to moderate heart attack. We performed an angioplasty immediately and put in a stent to keep the artery open. You are very lucky that she was found when she was, because the risk of damage to the heart rises significantly if left untreated for more than ninety minutes. In your mother's case, I think we got her in time for everything to be okay."

"When can I see her?" she asked.

"Someone will be out in about twenty minutes to let you know when you can go in. She is stable right now in the recovery area."

"Thank you, doctor. Thank you so much."

A look of immense relief appeared on Daria's face, and we hugged each other.

"Nina, you *did* save my mother's life."

"I am just glad I was there."

We sat back down and she glanced to the side at me. "Had you known my mother before this?"

"You could say I had met her, but didn't really know her."

"Did she ever say anything *inappropriate* to you by any chance?"

I didn't know if I should tell her the truth under the circumstances, but there was only one answer. "She told me...to go fuck myself...multiple times."

Daria looked down at the ground and shook her head. "I am so, so sorry. I need to explain her behavior."

"It's okay. I knew it was nothing personal. She does it to all of my roommates and some of the neighbors. Why, though?"

"My mother has had these episodes for the past ten years. One minute, she's fine and the next, she's swearing at everyone. It's some sort of post-traumatic reaction. It started after my father was killed. He was walking home from work late at night, and he was robbed and shot to death. They caught the guys. That's a long story in itself... but that day, my parents had gotten into a terrible fight. The last thing she said to him from the window as he left was 'Go fuck yourself.' Nine hours later, the cops had woken us up to say my father had been murdered."

Holy crap.

"I'm so sorry, Daria."

"These episodes didn't appear right away, but over the years, she started developing flashbacks, and it's made her act out sometimes. She never forgave herself for the way things were left between them. These swearing episodes seem to be some sort of strange coping mechanism. She is truly a good woman and doesn't mean anything by it. It's just a very strange reaction to a devastating event. So, on behalf of my mother, I apologize."

I placed my hand on her back. "You didn't have to, but thank you for explaining it to me."

Lesson learned. People are not always what they seem on the surface.

I stayed with Daria until she was able to see her mother. We made plans to go to lunch soon, since she insisted on it as a thank you.

As I was walking down the hospital corridor to leave, I got stuck in a maze of hallways. Each time I would turn a corner, I'd find myself lost again.

After about five minutes of hitting dead ends, I happened to stop to catch my bearings in front of one of the patient rooms. A young teenage girl who had lost all of her hair was sitting alone staring blankly up at a television.

Just as I was about to move on, the girl noticed me staring and said, "Are you a candy striper?"

"I'm sorry?"

"You know...a candy striper. They're those lame hospital volunteers. They've been coming around a lot lately."

"No, no, I'm not."

"Good...because they suck. They come in here with their fake smiles, like I'm supposed to believe this is Disney World or some shit." She paused. "I have cancer, by the way."

"I know...I...I figured—"

"Because I look like Caillou?"

"Caillou?"

"Awkward cartoon character on PBS, bald for no good reason."

"Ah."

"Seriously, what are you here for? Are you here for me?"

I looked into her hopeful eyes. "Maybe I am."

"Good. Because today, I want to talk about sex."

"Excuse me?"

"What's your name?"

"Nina."

"Don't be a pussy, Nina."

"What?"

"Pardon my language, but I don't really hold back anymore. Life is too short not to get the point. Anyway...I said I wanted to talk about sex, and from the way you're dressed, you seem like you'd be open to that. I have been waiting for someone just like you to show up, actually." She waved her hand. "Get in here, and close the door."

I looked behind my shoulders, then down at myself self-consciously and entered the room. Was I on *Candid Camera*? I swear, between Mrs. Ballsworthy and now this, today definitely felt like the Twilight Zone.

Landing on a chair next to her bed, I asked, "How old are you anyway?"

"I'm fifteen."

"What's your name?"

"Skylar," she said, shutting off the television.

"What do you want to know, Skylar?

"I can't talk about these things with my mother. She'd die."

I sighed, gearing up for her questions. "Okay..."

"My first question is...how early is too early to have sex?"

Oh goodness. Why me?

I laughed to myself at the absurdity of the situation I had just gotten myself into then thought about how to respond. "There is not really one answer to that question... but fifteen is definitely too early."

"What if someone might not live to be old enough?

You could have heard a pin drop. I was at a complete loss for words.

Thankfully, she continued before I had to come up with an answer. "See...there's this boy. His name is Mitch. He's my best friend and has been since we were young, but he doesn't know I am actually in love with him. We live in New Jersey, but I've been here in Brooklyn for my treatments for the past few months because my father lives here, and my doctors are based here. So, I moved temporarily and haven't seen him in a while. I'm really afraid he is going to forget about me."

"Why would you ever lose him if he's truly your best friend?"

"I don't think he'd intentionally stop being my friend, but a lot of girls are into him because he's hot. They don't even know him like I do. They just want to get a piece and well, he's a guy, so..."

"Have you told him how you feel?"

"Things started to get a little weird between us right before my diagnosis. He was looking at me differently, and I was starting to think something might happen. I have always held onto this fantasy that I would be his—you know—first. And he would be mine. If I'm not around, though, whether it's because of my treatments or...otherwise and he meets someone, I may never get the chance. Every second that I'm away, I feel like I'm losing him."

A stiff drink would have really come in handy right about now.

"Does he come visit?" I asked.

"That's the thing. He's been begging me to let him. He doesn't know which hospital I am at because I won't tell him. I don't want him to see me like this, but I miss him so much...it's killing me." She reached over to her phone and pulled up a photo. "That's him. That's Mitch."

"He's really cute," I said as she handed it to me. He was. With dark, longish hair under a Yankees cap and big blue eyes, I could see why she was feeling like that about him."

She looked hopeless. "What am I gonna do?"

"Well, Skylar, I would say a wise old man, but in reality...a wise, pierced, tattooed man once told me, you can choose to stay in the present and let go of the fear or you can choose to engage it."

"He sounds hot."

"He is. The point is...you are worrying about what might happen instead of using this time to be with the person you care about. He wants to see you. What are you afraid he'll think? You're beautiful." *She was.* Not many people can pull off bald, but she looked angelic.

"You want to see beautiful?" She scrolled through her phone and handed me another photo of Mitch and her. She had long flowing auburn hair, a little more meat on her bones and color in her cheeks, and the two of them looked like an Abercrombie and Fitch ad.

"You were gorgeous then with your hair, and you are gorgeous now without it. What can I do to make you see that? You need to let him see you."

She seemed to be struggling with my suggestion but eventually shook her head in agreement. "Okay, then. I'll need your help. I'll need props."

"What?"

"Props! For the *Skylar Seymour Pretend I Don't Have Cancer Extreme Makeover Edition*. I have a wig, but it's lame. I'll need a really good one, like with real human hair and highlights like yours. It needs to be *unbeweave-able*. And I'll need some makeup and chicken cutlets."

"Chicken cutlets?"

"Those boob enhancers. I wouldn't expect you to know what those are, Dolly Parton."

I looked down at my breasts. She had a point.

"I need to look even better than before."

"Even though I think you look perfect right now, I will do whatever it takes to make sure you feel confident enough to see him."

Because I know what it feels like to be crazy for a guy who's also your best friend.

I put my hand on her knee. "Give me a few days, okay? My roommate works in a salon downtown. I think she can hook me up with some human hair."

"Good."

What have I gotten myself into? Whatever it was, it invigorated me and gave me a sense of purpose. If it was possible to fall in love at first sight with this person, I think I might have.

"Skylar, how often to do those candy strippers...*strip-ers*...come to visit you?"

"They'd be more exciting if they were strippers. They come by a couple of times a week."

"Well, I'm gonna talk to someone and figure out how to be your candy striper from now on."

"Do you have a boyfriend, Nina?"

"No, but there is someone special who I really care about. He's kind of like my Mitch. His name is Jake."

"Have you screwed his brains out yet?"

"Skylar—"

"Well, have you?"

"No."

"What are *you* waiting for? You're old enough."

"I know that. But things are complicated. We're supposed to talk soon, so..."

Why was I getting into this?

She sat up eagerly. "Will you text me if something happens?"

"I...I guess."

"Good." She grabbed my phone and programmed her number into it.

I stared at her smooth head and her beaming eyes that I had just put a glimmer of hope back into and realized I hadn't been lost at all earlier. Something had led me to exactly where I was supposed to end up. I just couldn't figure out who was meant for whom.

SEVENTEEN

The next day, Sunday January 8th was my twenty-third birthday, but I hadn't told anyone, not even Jake. Ryan knew when my birthday was somewhere in the back of his head. He certainly hadn't given me any indication that he remembered this year. So, there would be no fanfare. I was planning on a quiet day (after yesterday's events), trying to get all of my ducks in a row prior to Jake's return from Boston. He said he would be coming in really late tonight and that we would be going out tomorrow and having that "talk." My stomach was in knots. It had been two weeks since we had seen each other. I missed him something fierce.

I had arrived home after an early afternoon run to find a large gift-wrapped box sitting on my bed. I opened the small note card. *If you thought we were going to forget your birthday, think again. Dinner. Tonight. 7pm. Eleni's. Drinks are on Telly. Drunk Greek Circle Dancing. Wear Your Party Dress. Love, Tarah and Ryan*

I clutched the card to my chest and giggled, secretly happy they figured it out. I immediately unwrapped the purple paisley wrapping paper. Inside the box, was a beautiful strapless, red mini dress. Tarah and I had gone shopping a few weeks ago, and I had tried this exact dress on but decided I couldn't afford it.

"You're gonna look so sexy in that, birthday girl."

I turned around, and she was standing in the doorway.

"Thank you so much, but I can't believe you spent that kind of money on me."

Tarah walked into the room and hugged me. "It was nothing. I made some good tips yesterday. You can make it up to me by letting me make you over again tonight."

"Why would you go through the trouble? It's just Eleni's."

"It's not just Eleni's. It's your birthday and open bar for us. You never know, you might meet some hot Greek down there, named Taso or Christos."

"And we'll fly away and live happily ever after in Mykonos."

"See, now you're talking!"

"Wearing my bikini, sippin' a martini in Santorini." I wiggled my hips as I said it and cracked myself up.

"That's my girl! But seriously, trust me, you're going to want to look good tonight. I've got this idea for your hair."

"Speaking of hair, how's that human hair wig search going?"

"Oh! I meant to tell you, I found the perfect one. It matches that picture you sent me of her with the hottie guy."

Skylar had texted me the picture of her and her friend Mitch, so that I could use it to find a wig that matched her original hair.

"You do realize he's fifteen..." I said.

She shrugged her shoulders. "Yeah, whatever. Anyway, it's beautiful, long, auburn, just like in the photo. It should be delivered to the salon sometime in the next week."

I couldn't wait to tell Skylar when I went to visit her this Wednesday.

Tarah had really outdone herself. I wore my hair down and she created two thin braids, which she tied back over the top. It was very Roman. For makeup, she insisted I wear red lipstick to match my dress.

As I slipped into the strapless frock, I received a text from Skylar.

Have you tapped that yet?

I shook my head. That girl was sex crazy. I'd text her back later.

Ryan peeked his head into my room. "Almost ready?"

"Yeah...just give me a second."

He stood in the doorway. "Tarah had to run to the drug store. She is gonna meet us downstairs. By the way, a friend of mine from work is going to join us for dinner. His name is Michael Hunt. I think you'll like him."

"What do you mean...you think I'll like him?"

"I mean, he's good looking, single and I told him about you."

Shit. Shit. Shit.

This is why Tarah wanted to dress me up. This was a set up!

"Please tell me you didn't plan this birthday dinner as a setup."

"No, it's not like that. It's more like I planned this set-up as a birthday dinner."

"Ryan!"

"Come on, Troll. You haven't been on one decent date since that preppy guy, and I really think you'll get along with Michael."

It was evident that Ryan had no clue about my feelings for Jake and Tarah had kept her word about not spilling to him. I couldn't blame him for trying. Anyway, it was too late now. I'd have to make the best of it.

I shrugged. "Okay, but please don't expect anything to come out of this. It's just a friendly dinner."

"Of course. Relax."

When we made our way into Eleni's, Telly greeted us at the door. "There's the birthday girl!" he shouted.

"Hi, Telly. Thanks for the open bar tonight," I said.

"Anything for my best customers."

Ryan and I had just sat down when he waved over to a tall lean guy with short reddish hair who walked in the front door and made his way over to our table.

Ryan stood up, and they clasped hands. "Hey, Michael. Glad you could make it." He turned to me. "Nina, this is Michael Hunt. Michael, this is Nina Kennedy."

"Pleasure to meet you, Nina." He smiled and reached his hand out.

"Same here."

There was nothing wrong with him. He was cute enough, nice enough, but I knew immediately this wouldn't go anywhere.

"So, Ryan's told me a lot about you. He said you guys are like brother and sister."

"We are."

Maybe if I bored him to death, he would just leave.

Ryan waved at the door again, and I turned around to see Tarah clicking her heels toward our table.

"Sorry I'm late. I had to get money." She bent down to kiss me on the cheek then looked at Michael and Ryan. "And who's this?"

Was she really playing dumb?

"This is my co-worker Michael. Michael, this is my girlfriend, Tarah."

"Nice to meet you, Michael."

"Likewise," Michael said getting up and extending his hand.

Tarah squinted her eyes at Ryan. I wondered why. Had she not known about this?

The four of us sat there like the perfect double date when Desiree approached our table looking smug. "Hi guys. What'll it be?"

We placed our drink orders, and as she took the drink menus away, she looked at Ryan. "No Jake tonight?"

I wanted to throw up.

Ryan shook his head. "He's in Boston."

"Too bad," Desiree said.

Go away. Shoo!

She walked away, and I could breathe again. Michael started making small talk with me, and I went along with it. Like I said, there was nothing wrong with him. I was going to have to get through this casual date whether I liked it or not.

When Ryan started a conversation with Michael about work, I whispered to Tarah. "So, now I know why you tried to get me all dolled up. Nice try but no cigar."

She sighed. "Nina...I knew nothing about this."

"Liar," I whispered.

She looked over at the guys as if to make sure they weren't listening. "I did want you to get dressed up for a guy tonight...but it wasn't for this one. It was for—"

"Jake!" Ryan shouted.

I turned around to see Jake walking toward our table. It felt like my heart started beating again after a two week hiatus. He was dressed up, wearing a sexy navy button down shirt rolled up at the sleeves and dark jeans. His hair was slightly wet. He looked so incredibly hot. I felt like I was going to crawl out of my skin.

He was looking straight at me when he approached and said, "Sorry I'm late. Happy birthday, Nina." I flinched when he moved in and kissed me on the cheek, the scent of his cologne now permanently invading my senses. Then, his eyes darted over to Michael and Ryan across the table. He took notice of the seating arrangement: Ryan across from Tarah and Michael across from me. There was an awkward silence.

I looked over at Jake who was now giving them a dirty look. He had figured out what he had walked in on.

Ryan spoke first. "This is our roommate, Jake. Jake, this is Michael Hunt, my co-worker."

Jake reached out his hand. "Mike, is it? Mike Hunt?" Jake had a devious look on his face, and I knew immediately what he was doing.

Mike Hunt. My cunt.

No one said anything. Then, the shit show continued when Desiree walked over with our drinks. "Jakey...there you are. I thought they said you were in Boston."

"Funny you should point that out, Des. Tarah had told me it was Nina's birthday dinner, so I came home early to surprise her." He looked at me. "Turns out, I was the one surprised."

Oh...God. Did he think I planned this date?

He handed her his drink menu. "I'll take a vodka straight, Des."

I hated that he called her "Des" and wanted to rip my hair out.

"You got it," she said, batting her lashes flirtatiously before trotting away.

Tarah stood up. "Jake, there is something upstairs I forgot to show you. It's broken, and I don't want to forget to tell you about it. Do you mind...before we order our food?"

He raised an eyebrow at her and glanced over at me. He looked upset, and I wanted to scream out in frustration. Then, he got up and followed her out the door.

Trying to regain some semblance of composure, I made small talk with Michael and sipped my white wine, which I really hoped started to kick in soon. He started asking me about my nursing aspirations. While I was answering his questions, all I could focus on was what Jake and Tarah were discussing upstairs.

When they returned to the restaurant, Jake sat back down next to me and downed the vodka that Desiree had brought for him, smacking the empty glass down on the table. He looked over at me and cracked a smile. There was no longer any anger lingering in his beautiful green eyes.

After we ordered our food, Michael continued asking me questions in an effort to get to know me. I stumbled on my words when Jake's warm hand suddenly slipped under the table and onto my bare thigh. My breath hitched, and I froze as his hand moved under my dress. His thumb grazed the edge of my bikini line. Then, he squeezed my thigh and slid his hand forcefully down the length of it. My skin burned from the friction of his touch. He was staking his claim and my body was getting the message loud and clear. I was wet and so turned on that it felt like I was about to go insane.

Thankfully, Ryan had started a different topic of conversation with Michael, so I no longer had to use what little brain juice I had left to formulate sentences. I bit my bottom lip and looked over at Jake who was sliding his tongue ring between his teeth, looking frustrated again, almost angry.

He pulled his hand away from my leg and got up from the table. I assumed he was going to the bathroom until my phone buzzed.

Meet me in the hallway.

There was a side door that led to the staircase leading up to our apartment. I assumed that was what he meant. My heart palpitated as I excused myself from the table "to go to the bathroom." When I opened the door, he was standing in the stairwell with his hands in his pockets, looking uncharacteristically shy.

"Hi," I said.

"Hi." A slow smile spread across his face. *Those dimples.*

It was as if we were actually greeting each other for the first time tonight and everything that happened up until now didn't count.

"What's going on?" I asked.

He exhaled. "That guy was looking at you like he wanted to rip your dress off with his teeth. I had to get out of there before I killed him with my bare hands."

"Why would that bother you?" I teased.

"You know why."

My heart beat faster as he walked toward me until he was just inches from my face. "Why didn't you tell me it was your birthday?"

"I figured you'd be away anyway, so I just never mentioned it."

"I would *never* miss your birthday. Never. You underestimated how important you are to me, Nina."

"I am sorry."

"You should have told me. Tarah called me Friday when I was already in Boston, so I decided to surprise you tonight."

"You're sneaky," I said.

"You're fucking gorgeous."

His eyes closed suddenly after he said it, like maybe he regretted coming on strong or was still struggling with his feelings. Then again, his hand was up my dress out there.

My body was humming between the words coming out of his mouth and the smell of his cologne mixed with vodka scenting me. I had never wanted to kiss him more than this moment. "Thank you. You're not so bad yourself," I said, tugging playfully on the material of his shirt but really wanting to tear it off of him. It felt like I was losing control fast.

"Tarah explained about what's his name in there. She didn't know he was going to be here when she invited me. She told me Ryan ambushed you."

I couldn't help but ask, "What if I *were* on a date?"

"I guess if he made you happy, I'd be okay with it."

"I see."

"That was a lie."

"Oh."

"I wouldn't be okay with it. Fuck...I missed you." The depth of the emotion in his voice resonated throughout my entire body. Then, he put his hand on my waist and squeezed my side.

I closed my eyes for a brief second when he grabbed my hand and kissed it. It wasn't the kind of kiss I yearned for, but the touch of his wet lips on my skin nearly put me over the edge. I almost wrapped my arms around him but refrained. "I missed you, too."

"Go on a date with me."

"What?"

"Spend the rest of your birthday with me tonight. Let's get out of here right now, go somewhere, anywhere. I just want to be alone with you. I can't say what I want...do what I want...in this hallway."

Shivers ran down my spine. "How are we going to manage that?" I breathed.

He gave me a mischievous smile. "We'll go back to the table. I'll make up a story and leave first. Then, I'll call your phone from outside, and you can pretend it's some kind of emergency."

"I can't worry Tarah like that."

"It was her idea, Nina."

Oh.

"Okay...okay." I smiled.

He winked. "Let's go."

I started walking back into the restaurant then turned back around toward him. "I'm just going to go the bathroom first, while you go to the table and tell them you're leaving. Then, I'll text you when I'm out so you'll know to call my phone in like five minutes."

He put his hand on my face and leaned in. I could feel his breath when he said, "I love sneaking around with you."

I got goosebumps, and my body was on fire as I made my way back into the crowded restaurant and walked to the bathroom on cloud nine.

There was no doubt he was going to kiss me tonight.

After I peed and exited the stall, Desiree walked in. Talk about a buzz kill. She didn't actually have to use the bathroom apparently, because she just stood near the sink with her arms crossed. I soon realized that she had come in to confront me.

"Nina...right?"

"Yeah."

"I saw you sneak out to the hallway with Jake. I kind of figured something was going on between you two. Anyway, I came in here to make sure you knew, that despite what he might be saying to you, he's not the boyfriend type. He just isn't. I mean, don't get me wrong—he was the best fuck I ever had—but he made his intentions very clear. It would never be more than just sex. I see the stars in your eyes when you look at him, so I thought I would save you some time and heartache."

I stood there frozen against the hand dryer and didn't even flinch when it turned on after I accidentally pushed into it. I wasn't sure exactly when the room started spinning. Was it when she finished her monologue or was it when I looked down and saw the large purple rose tattoo on her ankle? It was the same tattoo I saw on the girl leaving Jake's room the day I moved in.

I had been listening to Jake having sex with Desiree that day.

She just stood there eating up my shock with a satisfied expression.

Don't cry.

Don't cry.

Don't cry.

I started to cry.

Should I go back into the stall and throw up there or see if I can make it upstairs? I burst through the bathroom door and texted Jake.

You fucked Desiree???

When I reentered the dining room, he was just getting up from the table when I saw him look down at his phone. The moment he noticed the text, he looked up into my tearful eyes.

His voice shook. "Nina..."

He looked terrified as I ran past him and weaved through tables to the restaurant exit.

As I was almost out the door, I could hear him in the distance shouting at Desiree, "What the fuck did you say to her?"

EIGHTEEN

I wanted to run as far away from the restaurant and from him as I could. If it weren't starting to snow heavily outside, I might have.

Everything was foggy as I made my way up the stairwell in a haze. My heart was beating faster than I ever remembered, as the worst kind of jealousy-induced rage consumed me.

I couldn't believe it.

He had done everything in his power to stop things from becoming sexual between us. He wouldn't give himself to me, yet he very willingly gave himself to that whore.

I hated him.

I loved him.

I had planned to pour my soul out to him tonight and almost told him how I felt moments ago in that hallway. How stupid of me to think that his feelings for me were equally as strong. On top of that, he treated Desiree like he barely knew her in front of me. Apparently, women were a dime a dozen to him.

Without thinking, I began to pack some of my belongings into a duffel bag: underwear, bra, pajamas and an extra shirt. I had no idea where I was going or what I was going to do, but I knew I needed to be far away from this apartment tonight. I couldn't even look at him right now, let alone sleep here.

As I began to run out of my room with the bag in hand, the front door flew open. Jake was panting, and his eyes were frantic as he stormed toward me. "Nina, please... talk to me. Please," he said hoarsely.

I clutched the bag to my chest, using it as a barrier between us. "Stay away from me. I have nothing...*nothing*... to say to you."

He kept his distance, backing away but stood in front of the door, blocking it. His voice was low and his breathing rapid as he held out his hands in protest. "You have to let me explain."

"Explain! You want me to stand here and listen to you explain how you fucked that whore so easily while you put my feelings through the wringer for months, confusing me and sending me mixed messages? You had no problem 'making her come until she screamed'...did you? And believe me, it was a doozy. I heard it for myself."

He stepped back in shock and gave me a belligerent look. The wind howled outside, but that was all you could hear in the room until he shook his head and asked, "Fuck...what? What are you talking about?"

I was about to cry but managed to hold it in. "That's right. The day I moved in. You were fucking her in your room. Remember that day? Well, I was here unpacking. I thought I was alone and didn't realize what was going on until it was too late. I heard *everything*, Jake...everything." A teardrop escaped and fell down my cheek as I recalled hiding in my room, blissfully unaware that I was listening to the man I'd eventually fall in love with, screwing another woman.

His breathing intensified as he ran his hand through his hair, closed his eyes and looked down at the floor, computing what I had just revealed. He said nothing for several seconds. Then, he finally whispered under his breath. "Oh my God." He slowly approached me. "I am so sorry," he said, his voice quivering.

"If you'll excuse me, please get out of my way. I need to find somewhere else to stay tonight," I said trying to pass him again.

"You're not going anywhere. Not until you hear me out."

"I told you. I have nothing to say to you."

He blocked me as I attempted to get to the door and wouldn't let me by. My body reacted instantly when he held out his hands and placed them firmly on my arms. "I'll leave tonight, but I'm not going anywhere until you let me explain. Do you hear me?"

I looked down, still clutching my bag and felt one of his hands leave my shoulders and touch my chin, pulling my face in line with his. "Look at me," he whispered.

Even though my face was turned toward his, my eyes were facing the floor.

His voice was deeper and more insistent when he repeated. "*Look*...at me."

When I did, he finally spoke. His eyes were glistening with a fiery intensity, and he didn't take them off of me for a second. "I slept with Desiree...twice. The first time was about a week before I met you; the second and last time was the day you moved in. I am not proud of it, but it was just sex. I know that sounds really bad. It's the truth, though. She doesn't mean anything to me, and we had a clear understanding beforehand that it wouldn't go any further than that, which was why I agreed to it."

"I see. So, you're also a whore who wants nothing more than sex from a woman, so much so you agree to that stipulation beforehand? Well, you would have gotten exactly what you wanted that night in your room from me, but you didn't even try. Clearly, it wasn't *me* that you wanted it from."

He said nothing in response, just grabbed my bag and threw it down on the ground. Then, he took my hand and led me forcefully down the hall. I hated the fact that my body so easily submitted to him while my mind resisted.

"What are you doing?" I asked.

"We can't have the conversation we're about to have in the middle of the living room in case they come back upstairs."

My heart rate accelerated because I didn't realize there was going to be a "conversation."

Jake led me inside my bedroom and closed the door, turning on the small lamp for some light.

We both stood facing each other, and I crossed my arms as a protective mechanism when he walked toward me and backed me gently against the wall.

I could feel his breath on my face. "You think I don't want you?"

I shook my head no, but didn't respond.

"That thing with Desiree...was a huge mistake. If I had even known you existed and that it would come back to haunt me and more importantly, hurt you...it never would have happened. *Never.* Do you understand me?"

I had been looking at him but suddenly looked down because the thought of him and Desiree made me sick. I continued to remain silent.

"You need to believe me. I haven't so much as thought about another woman that way since the day you walked in the door." He stopped talking until I looked up at him again. "Before I met you, I had only been going through the motions of life. I hadn't really felt...anything...for a really long time."

I looked up. His eyes were passionate and sincere when he said, "My heart hasn't beat the same since I laid eyes on you, Nina. Ever since that day, my entire life has been about doing everything in my power *not* to want you like this...because I don't want to drag you into my fucked up life." His voice cracked. "But despite doing what I thought was right, I want you more everyday, more than I fucking want to breathe."

My chest tightened upon hearing those words, which unraveled me. Despite the shock of finding out about Desiree, I believed him. He had always given me his full attention, and I never once saw him with anyone else since the day I moved in.

He placed one arm on each side of me, locking me in against the wall. I was losing my breath but stayed silent as he whispered, "I have been trying so hard to stay away from you...because with you...it would be so much more than sex. I would need to be all in because you deserve all of me, and there is something I haven't had the nerve to tell you. I don't know if you'll understand it." His voice trembled. "I'm so fucking scared because I don't want to lose you. I have never felt this way about anyone before... not in my entire life."

My throat closed up, and I still couldn't speak.

Neither have I. I love you so much. I don't care what it is because I don't think I could live without you.

Words could not do justice to what I was feeling inside for him right now.

He moved his face closer to mine. "You're the first thing I think about in the morning and the last thing I think about at night. And then, you invade my thoughts and dreams in between. I have tried so hard to stop these feelings. I have put up as many barriers as I could stand to, but they are crumbling down. I can't do it anymore." He placed his mouth on me whispering into my neck huskily, "I can't do it anymore...I can't do it anymore...I can't do it anymore." His hands moved slowly down my sides gripping my hips, and his lips moved over mine when he said, "I've come undone."

He grabbed my face and startled me when a rush of wet heat met my starving mouth. My entire body went limp the exact moment his lips finally swallowed mine whole. He opened and closed his mouth slowly over mine, before nudging my lips open impatiently. I tasted the metal of his tongue ring, a little vodka and the sweetness of his breath. The feel of the cold metal, mixed with the heat of his tongue circling mine made me instantly wet and weak in the knees. I felt like a rag doll in his arms.

He kissed me vigorously and gripped my sides harder as he pulled at my dress. It might have even ripped, but I was too wrapped up in him to notice. I grabbed the back of his head, running the tips of my fingers up and down his hair, noticing it was slightly coarse. I pulled his face into me harder because I couldn't get enough of his mouth on mine. He groaned, and the sound resonated through my body. I pulled him further into me and that's when I felt him rock hard against my stomach. I could feel the heat of his erection through his jeans and began to rub against it, causing his breathing to become even more shallow.

A need so strong developed in me that I thought I might die if I couldn't have him inside of me. My body ached in desperation when he pushed back, moving his hands away from my waist then cupped my cheeks. "I need to tell you something, Nina. We need to have that talk now."

Elation quickly turned to fear, because I was more terrified of what he had to tell me next than I had ever been of anything. I knew whatever it was could never change my feelings for him, but it might steal this moment that I will never get back again. I wasn't ready to hear it. I panicked. I just needed him tonight. Just *him*...not his skeletons or whatever it was he thought I wouldn't accept. He was wrong anyway. I loved him and knew I would take whatever came with him, no matter what it was. I wanted to know everything, just not tonight. My body couldn't take it, and my desire for him drowned out all logical thinking.

I spoke for the first time since before we kissed. "I don't care about your past or what's going on in Boston. Please...I'm begging you. Let's not do this now. Don't say anything tonight. We'll have the talk tomorrow, like we were supposed to. What I need right now more than I have ever needed anything is for you to make love to me, Jake."

He closed his eyes, let out a long deep breath, and his hands were shaking as he held my face. "You have no idea how badly I need to be inside of you right now."

"Please...I don't want to have the talk tonight, okay?"

He caressed my mouth with his thumb. "Nina, either we have this talk now, or you are going to have to make me a blind promise."

"Okay..."

My lips quivered, and he placed his forehead on mine. When he saw a tear fall down my cheek, he licked it away slowly and whispered against my face. "I need you to promise me...that you won't leave me." I nodded, and he grabbed my chin. "Make sure you mean that. Because I can't make love to you the way I want to tonight, only to lose you the next day. It will fucking *destroy* me. I need to know you will be mine, no matter what I throw at you. Promise me."

"I'm yours. I have never belonged to anyone before... but I know that I belong to you," I said into his chest.

"Look at me and say it."

I looked up into his eyes on command. "I'm yours. There is nothing that could make me leave you, because I don't think I could live without you."

His eyeballs moved back and forth in a fast motion as he looked into my eyes. He seemed to be searching them for sincerity. Finally, he pulled me into him and held me, pressing his body hard against mine. "Well, that's good, because I *wasn't living* before you."

He just held me for what seemed like several minutes. It still felt like he was hesitant. He probably didn't realize how badly I needed him. So, I decided to speak in a language he could understand. "I need you to fuck me, Jake."

I just wasn't expecting him to burst into laughter against my shoulder when I said it, though.

I smacked his arm. "Why are you laughing?"

He kissed my neck. "Say that again."

"I want you to *fuck* me."

He looked at me, smiling and kissed my forehead. "See, only you would say something so dirty and turn red as a beet."

"Dirty talk is new for me," I said, looking down at the ground and biting my lip to stifle my own laughter.

He grabbed my chin to look at me. "I know it is. You're so fucking adorable...so sweet and innocent. I love that about you. It turns me on like you can't imagine. I fully intend to fuck you tonight, baby. Then, I'm going to make love to you. But not before I feast on you."

He wasn't laughing anymore when he let go of me and walked out of the room. I gulped in nervous anticipation, breathing a sigh of relief when he returned with a strip of condoms and locked the door behind him. The clicking sound of the lock gave me chills. It was the assurance I needed that I was about to get what I yearned for.

He threw the condoms on the nightstand and sat on the bed. I was still standing up against the wall where he left me. I suppose I was waiting for his direction.

"Come here," he whispered, gesturing with his index finger.

I walked over to him. He stayed seated as I stood before him while he traced the contours of my body with his fingertips, following them with his eyes.

"Incredible," he said as his fingers moved over my breasts. "Do you know how many nights I would sit in my room dreaming about touching you like this while you were just across the hall? Every single night since I met you, I ached for you. This seems surreal." He swallowed and licked his lips, which caused my body to stir.

I needed those lips on me. "Kiss me," I whispered, my voice desperate.

"Where?" he asked.

"Everywhere."

He reached behind me and slowly lowered the zipper to my dress, letting it fall to the floor. I kicked it away, and he stood up from the bed towering over me after I had slipped off my heels.

I couldn't wait any longer. I stood on my toes and kissed him, sucking his bottom lip into my mouth and flicking my tongue repeatedly over his lip ring, something I had often fantasized about doing when we studied together in his room.

He moaned into my mouth as I tugged at his lip with my teeth. The pace of the kissing became more urgent then he pulled back.

"Nina, you're driving me crazy with that tongue, pulling on my lip like that. I could come from just kissing you."

"I've always wanted to kiss you there."

"I've wanted to kiss you in a lot of places." He caressed my chest with both hands gently before unhooking the back of my strapless bra, letting it fall to the ground. "Good God," he said gruffly as he looked down at my bare breasts. "Like here, for starters."

He continued to massage them before taking each one into his mouth. My nails dug into the back of his head as he alternated between licking and sucking, taking turns with each one.

I looked down and took notice of how hard he had become, so I started rubbing my hand against his jeans as he sucked on my breasts. I could feel the change in the rhythm of his breathing as I touched him.

He stopped sucking and whispered in my ear, "Now you know what you do to me. I want to feel what I do to you." I knew how wet I was, but as he tugged at my underwear and slipped a finger inside, he realized it and said, "Holy shit, Nina."

He continued moving his fingers in and out, and I could feel myself losing control. My eyes began to roll back and my muscles contracted. I had almost come in less than a minute from his hand alone. I think he knew I was going to lose it, because he stopped. Then, I almost lost it again when he licked his fingers slowly and made a guttural sound.

"You taste better than I could have imagined."

"I almost came."

He squeezed my ass. "I know. I almost lost it myself because I love how turned on you are. That's why I stopped. But that's not how I want your first time with me to happen. And believe me, Nina, this is gonna be your *real* first time."

I had to clench myself, because just those words alone were enough to do me in again.

He pulled my underwear all the way down so that I was completely naked and brushed his hand over my vagina gently. Normally, I would feel vulnerable standing like that in front of a man and had never allowed it before. I always hid myself, but the look in his eyes was one of complete adoration. He had always made me feel safe and laying myself out bare like this was no exception.

He held my face with both hands and kissed me. "You're the most beautiful woman in the entire world."

"I want to see you naked too," I said.

He gave me a naughty grin and said over my lips, "Undress me. I'm yours."

Even his voice alone caused my muscles to contract.

My mouth was watering, knowing full well the masterpiece that lay underneath his clothes. I felt like a little girl on Christmas opening that one special gift that she knew was in the last box, as I unbuttoned his shirt and threw it on the ground. I stopped to relish in the beauty of his defined chest, which I had only ever been able to admire in detail from afar. His heart was beating fast as I kissed over it and moved my mouth and tongue over each and every tattoo on his arms, saving the best for last. The tribal marking on his left lower side torso had always teased me the most. I loved being up close and personal with it as I bent down to lick over his salty skin.

218

I stood up and undid his jeans, and he kicked his shoes off. He put his hands over mine helping me pull his pants off. His black boxer briefs were like the last piece of wrapping paper. I could feel the heat of his erection bursting through them. He removed my hands just as I was about to pull his underwear down.

"I think I need to keep these on for a little while."

"How come?"

"Because I don't want to lose control and bury myself inside you before I have a chance to make you come with my mouth."

Holy. Crap.

"Oh."

"Lay down, beautiful," he said.

I immediately complied and lay down on the bed as he hovered over me. His green eyes were brimming with desire, and I could see my reflection in them as he looked at me for several seconds. He shook his head as if in disbelief, then lowered his mouth and slowly licked my lips before kissing me hard and passionately. I loved the way the weight of his body felt on me as I wrapped my arms through his and caressed his back.

My hands dropped to his waist, and I squeezed his ass pushing him into me. He moaned into my mouth and quickly moved my hands off of him. "Don't do that, baby. It's my weakness. I want to last for you," he said.

I loved it when he called me "baby." I took a mental note to squeeze his ass again very soon, so I could make him lose control because I wanted to see what that looked like.

He slowly lowered his mouth down to my neck and then to my breasts, alternating between sucking on each nipple and rubbing his thumbs across them in slow circular motions as my legs rustled beneath him.

He then trailed his tongue down the length of my stomach in one quick line, like a plane taxing down a runway, and his mouth landed...well...on *my* landing strip.

I closed my eyes in ecstasy as I relished the foreign sensation of his hot lips opening and closing on me.

Spencer had never gone down on me, not even once. He expected me to do it to him, and I did, even though I never enjoyed it. But he didn't return the favor and I never asked.

Jake began flicking his wet tongue in slow controlled motions with the ball of his tongue ring over my tender clit. There was no other feeling like it. Add to that, the sight of him between my thighs, his hair, dark and sweaty. I knew I was going to climax within seconds.

My legs were restless, and my hands were gripping the sheets. "It's okay...let go," he said in between devouring me.

I was still fighting it because I wanted this feeling to last forever.

He lifted his mouth off of me, stuck his fingers inside me and rubbed me with his thumb, kissing my stomach. It felt good, but I wanted his mouth back down where it had been.

I could barely speak. "Jake..."

"What do you want, Nina? Say it."

"I want you to lick me there again."

"Good, because I want to taste you while you come."

Those words were more powerful than anything he had done to me. Literally, the second his tongue bore down on me again, I screamed out in ecstasy and could feel the vibration of his mouth moaning against me while I came. It was the most mind-blowing feeling I had ever experienced.

He slowly kissed his way up my stomach, over my breasts and up to my mouth. I tasted myself on him, and it turned me on all over again. I had just had an orgasm seconds ago, and my vagina was tingling, buzzing, ready for another.

Jake was a drug, and I was a junkie looking for my next high before I even came down from the last. Up until this moment, he had been my emotional addiction, but now it was officially physical too. I might spend the rest of my life walking around completely strung out, and I didn't care. I wanted more.

"I want more," I said, breaking from his kiss.

Did I just say that out loud?

He smiled against my lips and said, "Now, I want... *you.*"

I didn't ask for permission when I pulled his briefs down and wrapped my hand around his cock and began to stroke him. He was hot and slick in my hand. His breathing quickened, and he stood up onto his knees, as I got my first glimpse of him fully naked. He looked down at me with a hunger in his eyes and spread my legs apart gently. It was all too much to take in: his handsome face, his perfect tattooed body and his beautiful cock, which was bigger than I had ever anticipated and surprisingly...not pierced. The tip was beautifully untouched and glistening and I reached my hand out and rubbed him some more, circling the top with my thumb, as he closed his eyes and leaned his head back, almost losing control. "Stop," he urged as he smiled down at me. He then reached over to the nightstand for a condom, ripping it open with his teeth and sheathing himself.

He looked down at me and ran his fingers through my hair. "Nina...my angel," he said softly, as his fingertips moved over my mouth. No one had ever looked at me like that. He hadn't said *those three words* yet, but his eyes were telling me a story again. This time, they were telling me that he loved me and that he was scared that things were about to change between us. If things didn't work out, there was no going back to the way things were. We both knew it.

He kept his gaze on me when he lowered himself down, and I immediately felt him between my legs. The heat there was immense, and he wasn't even inside of me yet. I was looking down at us and not at his face. "Look into my eyes," he said.

He stared at me with his beautiful green irises with gold speckles spread out like stars in a night sky and said, "I want you to forget the other sexual experiences you think you had, because *this* is your first time. You will always belong to me and unlike your prick ex-boyfriend, *I'm* gonna finish the job." We smiled at each other, and my heart nearly combusted. I was dying for him and just like that, I felt the friction and then the unprecedented pleasure of him fully inside of me.

He kissed me as he moved in and out of me with a graceful intensity. Every movement was intentional, as he started off easy, pulling almost completely out each time before slipping slowly and deeply back inside. When I tightened my muscles around him and grabbed his ass, he laughed over my mouth because he knew I was egging him on and said, "You want to play like that, baby?"

I giggled into his mouth and nodded. He then began to thrust harder and faster and I moved my hands off of his ass, so he wouldn't lose control.

"Nina...God, you're so wet. It's so beautiful. You feel amazing. Better than amazing. Better than anything I have ever felt."

His kiss became more urgent, and we developed a rhythm for several minutes that was all-consuming. I never understood the meaning of becoming one during sex until this moment. I was lost in him and had no concept of time.

When I returned my hands to his ass, he let out a growl and broke from my mouth. "Tell me you're close... because I don't know how much longer I can go. You feel too good. I'm losing control. I need to come."

"I've been holding out for you."

"Don't hold out, baby."

I closed my eyes when he said, "Open them...look at me. I want look in your eyes when we come together."

He thrust into me harder, never taking his eyes off of mine. I wanted to let go at the exact moment he did. I squeezed my muscles and watched as he groaned loud and deep as his eyes rolled back once before returning to my gaze. He began to pulsate fast inside me and I finally let go and screamed as I surrendered to the best orgasm of my life.

Holy shit. I just had sex with Jake.

Our hearts beat against each other as he collapsed onto me and buried his face in my neck. All I could think about was how right he was. Tonight had been my first *real* sexual experience.

NINETEEN

I hadn't counted the number of times or ways we made love that night, but we didn't stop for hours. I kept wanting more, and he kept accommodating me, making good on his promise to "make me come until I screamed in every possible way imaginable." We might have even been in the midst of another round when I fell asleep because when I woke up at three in the morning, I hadn't even remembered nodding off.

The lamp was still on, and to my relief, he was right next to me fast asleep. He locked me into his warm grasp with his arm across my belly. As I looked down at his handsome face, I wanted to cry because I had never been so happy and so scared at the same time in my entire life. This moment in time was like a dream I didn't want to wake up from. I was terrified of what he needed to tell me later today.

My thoughts kept me up, and I really needed to use the bathroom, since I hadn't peed at all after leaving Eleni's last night. Quietly slipping from underneath Jake's arm, I tip toed down the hall. There was a note on the mirror.

Glad to see you two made up. From what I could hear, you actually made up multiple times last night. --T

I would deal with her later.

When I returned to the bedroom, he was in the same position sound asleep on his stomach with his arm reaching across my side of the bed. Lifting it, I slid back underneath him. When I glanced over at my nightstand, I noticed a folded piece of paper that hadn't been there last night and opened it.

I met a girl, a few months back
With huge blue eyes and an amazing rack.
Turned out she was moving in
And kind of looked like an Olsen twin.

She put up with my shit and sarcastic wit.
And faced my wrath when she sucked at math.
Until her, it had been a while
Since anyone truly made me smile.

It might have been fate, in a way...
Her moving in that day.
I found the more time with her I'd spend
She actually became my best friend.

When we made love, things did change.
In fact, it's really strange.
That friend delivered by fate?
Turns out...she was my soulmate.

And as I lay here watching her sleep,
I realize my feelings run deep.
Because they burn and cut like a knife.
I think I love her more than life.

P.S. On my second birthday, you came
into the world and were the best present
I never knew I got. And this year? Best.
Birthday. Ever.

The paper shook in my hand as I reread his beautiful words and took it all in.

Soulmate.

He loved me more than life.

It was his birthday too?

After a few minutes, his body stirred, and I jumped as his hand squeezed my side. His eyes opened, and he smiled groggily. "I see you got my note."

I turned to him so our faces were just inches apart and pulled him into a gentle kiss. "I love you, Jake. The days since we met have been the happiest of my life."

He kissed me harder, then said, "I meant every word... except the Olsen twin part." He chuckled. "You don't really look like them to me, actually. Ryan mentioned it before you moved in, and I messed with you about it that first day. You look more like a young Brigitte Bardot."

Note to self: Google Brigitte Bardot.

He caressed my face. "You fell asleep in my arms, and I couldn't sleep because I was so overcome with emotion. I had to get it all out. So I did it on paper. But now, I need to *tell* you that I am so crazy in love with you, Nina Kennedy."

He pulled me in for another kiss, sucking on my bottom lip gently before slowly releasing it. My panties were already moist again. My appetite for him was insatiable.

"Your birthday was really yesterday too? Seriously... January 8th?"

He ran his fingers through my hair and nodded. "I couldn't fucking believe it when Tarah texted me Friday about your birthday being Sunday. My nieces had planned this party for me that day. They are so cute. But I wasn't about to miss being here with you, so I promised them a rain check next weekend. I couldn't wait to tell you we shared a birthday. I was gonna say something last night when we broke away from the crowd. I had this whole funny thing planned out about how I was going to tell you, but as you know, the date never happened. Believe me, the alternative was so much better."

A thought occurred to me and I laughed. "I guess I'm going to have to break the news to my parents, that I've fallen in love with my nerdy roommate."

"Say what, now?"

"I've...sort of...painted a picture of you that's not entirely accurate, so they wouldn't think I was living with a guy I was attracted to."

His eyes widened as he grinned. "And so, they think I'm a nerd?"

"Yes. A nerdy engineer." I laughed.

"You know what I think would be really funny?"

"What?"

"If I actually played the part. Like, put on some glasses, wore a pocket protector, took out my piercings and covered my tats when you take me home. We could have some fun with it. They'd be happy and trust me enough to let me in your room. We could say we were studying. Then, I'd close the door, take off my disguise and fuck you on your canopy bed."

We both started laughing hysterically at the thought.

He made me so happy.

I kissed him. "No way. I want you just the way you are all of the time. And I want them to meet you."

He jumped up. "Shit. You had me so distracted last night, I totally forgot about your birthday gift."

"Where are you going?" I asked.

"It's in my room."

Jake ran down the hall and returned with a small black velvet bag with a rope string and sat down on the bed. "My brother-in-law had given one of these to my sister on Christmas. It made me want to get one for you, so I went online that night and ordered one. I didn't even know when I was going to give it to you. It happened to come in the mail yesterday. I would say after last night, the timing was perfect. I hope you like it."

Prying the drawstring open, I pulled out a beautiful sterling silver charm bracelet.

I held it in my hand and turned to him. "Jake..."

He took it from me, opened the lobster clasp and placed it on my wrist. "You can actually go online and custom make these with whatever charms you want. They have literally every single thing you can think of. These are all the things that remind me of you." He lifted my hand to his mouth and kissed it.

I touched each charm with my fingertips and was floored by the thought he had put into selecting them. There was an airplane, a pair of dice, a four-leaf clover, an angel...even a little bat.

"*This*...this is the most thoughtful present I have ever received. I can't believe you were thinking of me like that over Christmas."

"I couldn't get you off my mind over Christmas. You knew that. Didn't I make it painfully obvious?"

"Sort of. But I loved it. I love this. I love you."

"I love you too, baby. I am glad you like it."

I got up and straddled him. "I haven't even had a chance to get you a gift."

"You *are* my gift."

That moment was the single most precious of my life. I might as well have handed him my heart on a silver platter; it was his.

It wouldn't be long, though, before he would shatter it into a million pieces.

TWENTY

The alarm went off at noon, and I was still exhausted. Jake must have set it before he left for work so that I wouldn't sleep the entire day away. I had fallen back asleep in his arms shortly after he had given me the bracelet in the middle of the night and slept like a log after that.

I stretched my arms in the air and yawned, smiling when I noticed a new origami bat on the nightstand. I opened it.

I am batshit crazy for you. See you tonight.

I kissed it and put it in the drawer with all of the rest, but that one was, by far, my favorite. Last night changed everything between us, and there was no going back. I sniffed my hair and could smell Jake all over it, all over me. His cologne and the scent of his body coated me after our long night of lovemaking. My lips were swollen, and I was sore in all the right places, still intoxicated by him.

Six o'clock could not come soon enough because I was craving him again already. I was distracted and giddy, barely able to focus on what to wear. I looked down at the charm bracelet and closed my eyes. How had I lived my entire life without him?

Dread soon set in as I reminded myself that we were having that talk tonight. I just wanted to get it over with, so we could move on. Whatever he needed to tell me, I would deal with it. It would be okay. We would be okay. We were in love, and that was all that mattered.

Tarah was in the kitchen making a smoothie when I emerged from my room. I was startled to see her because I had forgotten that the salon was closed on Mondays and that she would be home at this time. I prepared myself for the third degree.

She stopped the blender. "Well, good morning at half past one."

"I know. We didn't get much sleep last night."

"Oh, believe me, none of us did."

I covered my face in embarrassment. "Shit. Were we that loud?"

"I'm pretty sure my parents in Staten Island and my cousins in Jersey heard you. Yes, you were definitely loud. Was it as good as it sounded?"

"What do you think?"

"You're flushed. I think he was just as good in bed as he looks like he'd be, if not better."

"You would be correct."

"Uh, yeah...I figured. Actually, I almost wish you had let me tell Ry about your feelings for Jake all this time, because he was seriously shocked. He had no idea that you two were more than friends."

"I know."

"I never realized how protective of you Ryan was until last night. He was tossing and turning and kept saying that Jake better not hurt you or he would fuck him up. And you know, he doesn't normally talk like that."

"Shit. No he certainly doesn't. Well, he is the closest thing I have to a brother, but he really shouldn't be worried. Jake has been the best thing that's ever happened to me. He's helped me through so much. I've never felt safer with anyone in my entire life."

"I am glad that you two finally figured it all out last night. I knew it would happen eventually." She paused and looked down. "Nina, I have to tell you something. I...knew about Jake and Desiree."

Silence.

"I am sorry I never said anything. It was before you, so I didn't think it really mattered. I didn't quite know how to bring it up. She spent the night one time, like a week before you moved here. The bitch had always thrown herself at him. I knew it was just a cheap fling, and I didn't want you to think badly of him because I could always tell he really liked you. Plus, I didn't want you to be uncomfortable downstairs at the restaurant since we're always there. I was trying to protect you, but I still should have told you."

I let out a deep breath. "It's okay. I understand why you didn't. I mean, how can I fault him for something that happened before he even met me?"

"I'm glad you're not upset with me," she said.

I was...a little.

I quickly changed the subject to rid my mind of Desiree. "Did you know Jake's birthday was yesterday too?"

"What? You're kidding!"

"Dead serious. And look what he got me for mine." I stuck out my arm to show off the bracelet.

Tarah held my wrist, and her jaw dropped. "A charm bracelet. Sweet."

"Yes, with all the things that remind him of me."

"I knew he had it bad, but damn, girl." She shook her head at me. "Look at you...you're beaming."

"I can't help it. I've never felt this way. I'm in love with him, Tarah."

She hugged me tightly then pulled back. "Make that two people who'll fuck him up if he ever hurts you, then."

Jake called me from work at 2:45 that afternoon, and I answered the phone in my best throaty voice. "Hi, handsome."

"Nina?"

"Yes, of course it's me, silly. I've been thinking abou—"

"Listen to me, okay? I have some bad news. Everything is okay, but I have to go to Boston tonight."

"What?"

"There's been an emergency, so I am actually flying instead of taking the train. I'm on my way to LaGuardia now."

My heart fell to my stomach. "You're scaring me. What kind of emergency?"

"It's nothing to be scared about. There's a situation that's related to what I needed to discuss with you. We can't have this conversation over the phone. We were supposed to talk tonight, but it's going to have to be as soon as I get back. Please trust me. Everything is okay with us. Everything is going to be fine, and I promise to explain it to you in a couple of days. Nina...are you there?"

I was silent for a few seconds then said, "Yes."

"I'll call you as soon as I can later tonight." He repeated, "I need you trust in me."

"I do trust you...but you can't blame me for wondering and worrying."

"I know, baby. I know. It's easier said than done, but please don't worry, okay?"

"As soon as you get back, we need to have that talk. The not knowing is starting to kill me."

"I promise," he said amidst car horns and people shouting. "I just pulled up to the airport. I'll call you later. I love you, Nina."

"I love you, too."

I spent the rest of the day Monday on pins and needles unable to eat or concentrate.

Ryan had asked me where Jake was that night, and I explained that there was an emergency in Boston. He spent most of the evening interrogating me about what I really knew about Jake, trying to convince me that something didn't seem right and warning me to be careful. I tried not to let him see that he was scaring me.

Jake ended up calling me about midnight.

He sounded extremely tired. "Did I wake you?"

"No. I haven't been able to sleep. I have been so worried."

"I am so sorry that I couldn't call you until now. Everything is okay. There is nothing for you to worry about. Believe me. My being here does not change *anything* between us. Do you hear me? Just give me a chance to explain this to you in person. It's not something I can do over the phone. I'll be here one more day then flying home late tomorrow night and coming straight to you."

It was quiet wherever he was.

"Okay. Where are you?"

"I just got to my sister's house. I'm spending the night here."

"Call me tomorrow?"

"I promise. I love you, Nina."

"I love you too, Jake."

I hung up the phone and prayed for tomorrow to come quickly.

It was about 5:30 Tuesday night when Ryan came home from work. He walked in the door and hung up his coat.

He hung up his coat.

Normally, the act of hanging up a coat is a very insignificant thing. But for me, the moment when Ryan hung up his coat meant everything.

It was the last moment that I could remember when things were normal. It was the moment before everything changed. Because the second he turned to me and looked into my eyes, I began to suffocate.

"Nina, you need to sit down."

"What's going on?"

He gently patted my arm. "Sit down."

I walked over to the couch and sat. My palms were sweaty, and my heart was beating a mile a minute.

"Nina, I don't know how to tell you this…"

I gripped the seat cushions. "Just say it. What is it? Did someone die?"

"No…it's not like that."

"What?"

"After our talk last night, I did some digging. You know, at work at the D.A.'s office, I think I told you, we have quick access to public records and such."

Thump.

Thump.

Thump.

He continued, "I looked up Jake's information, did a background check and found this document. Do you know what this is?"

He handed me a piece of paper and I glanced down at it. He immediately moved to the couch next to me and put his arms around my back. It felt like a drum was beating in my ears and my body started to shake uncontrollably.

I had suspected that maybe Jake was in some kind of trouble with the law or that he had a girlfriend in Boston. But I never expected this.

I looked down at the printout again and felt like my head was on fire.

Jake Alan Green

Ivy Marie Macomber

No. Jake didn't have a girlfriend. He had a wife.

He was married.

PART TWO

JAKE

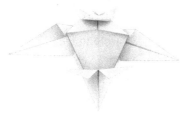

TWENTY-ONE

*"Mr. Green, your wife has been trans-
ported to McLean Hospital. We think she
tried to take her life last night."*

It wasn't the first time I had received a call like that, and it probably wouldn't be the last. Talk about going from heaven to hell in a matter of hours.

Before Nina, that was all my life amounted to...a living hell. Maybe escaping to New York for work during the week was my purgatory. But there was certainly no heaven, no respite, never any peace or true happiness...until she came along. Nina had become my only solace from the nightmare I had been living over the past five years.

The beverage cart stopped in front of my seat, and I asked for the strongest thing they had. It didn't even matter what it was. I needed to take the edge off because I never knew what I was going be to walking into, especially this time. Thank God, at least from what they told me, Ivy was stable in the safety of a hospital.

The flight attendant nudged me. "Excuse me? Your drink, sir."

I had been deep in thought staring out the window and hadn't noticed her handing it to me. "Thanks," I said, taking the hard liquor, whatever it was, and downing it.

I let out a long breath and closed my eyes. My focus should have been on Ivy, but I couldn't bear to let my mind drift to the reality that was about to slap me in the face when this plane touched down. There would be no way to escape it then.

These minutes, miles up in the sky, were going to be my last moments of peace for a while. So, I chose to close my eyes and focus on the only thing that took the pain away.

I never should have let things get as far as they did with Nina. But what should have happened and what I wanted to happen with every fiber of my being were two very different things.

I became addicted to her from the moment I first shook her hand, and it trembled in mine. Women have always had strong reactions to me but never like that. I had never met someone so beautiful and sexy, yet humble and innocent at the same time. I wanted to lift her over my shoulder, carry her right then and there back to my room and make her mine, which was a crazy thought to have seconds into meeting someone. That was just the physical pull. Within a few minutes though, when I really looked into her eyes and she was talking about her phobias, there was this darkness there. She looked the same way I imagined I appeared to anyone that could see through my façade. Here was a girl I had just met, and I was sure our life stories couldn't have been more different. Yet, somehow, I knew we had both been living the same *kind* of life, just going through the motions, trying to find something to make it worth living. For some unexplained reason, there was a connection with her that I hadn't even known I was searching desperately for. But it was too late. My life was already laid out for me. So, I had to figure out a way to ignore what I was feeling.

What a mind fuck.

Any sane man in my situation would have just gotten the hell out of there that first day, taken a long walk and sorted out my head...maybe moved out of the apartment even.

Instead, you know how I handled it? I went straight to my room and made her a fucking paper bird. Because, after meeting her, the only thing I could think about was that I just wanted to make her smile, take some of the darkness out of those beautiful blue eyes.

What a pansy.

It only got worse from there. I'd keep looking for excuses to be around her. I knew she had these fears, and I really did want to help her through them. But I also really wanted to get my fix, be near her, smell her vanilla scent and touch her in subtle ways every chance I got, even if it was just her hand or her back.

She made me feel alive after years of being emotionally dead. I lived for every moment spent with her and dreaded the weekends when I had to leave. I thought I could handle being close friends with her, as long as I paced myself without letting it go too far.

Which is why I came up with the brilliant idea of tutoring her and of course, our bet. Everybody won. She'd get good grades, overcome her fears, and I got my angel fix. She got what she needed, and I needed...*her*.

Things started to get complicated because each day I fell harder, and I craved more. The fact that I sensed that she was attracted to me too didn't help; it only turned me on, and there was no goddamn shut off switch. I tried my best to curtail the physical need. I really did. Let's just say, I jerked off so much that I was able to prove once and for all that the myth my grandmother told me about was false, because I never did go blind.

Aside from wanting her physically, there was this constant need to make her happy. I got off on it. I noticed Nina changing the more time we spent together. Her eyes started to transform. Light replaced the darkness, and I wondered if I had put it there. She always looked at me like no one ever had and was so attentive; she ate up every word I said. I made her laugh, and she comforted me. I wanted to be around her all of the time like a fucking bee on honey.

The way I saw it, we were two fractured souls that fit together like the last two missing pieces in a "fucked up life" puzzle. When we were together, life finally made sense; it wasn't all work, obligation, guilt and fear. It was just amazing to be alive. She needed me to help her, but she didn't realize I needed her so much more.

The first time I knew I was really in trouble was when she cut her finger that night trying to make me dessert. I physically felt the pain—a shooting pain—when I saw her blood. I had never experienced anyone else's pain before. It felt like she was an extension of me. That was when I began to suspect that I might have been falling in love with her.

The moment I absolutely *knew* I loved her, though, was in Chicago. I was telling her things I hadn't ever told anyone, like the story about my father and the moon. On the plane ride home, when we were holding hands and I watched her with her eyes closed, I had wished that the plane were taking us somewhere far away, where I could spend the rest of my life just being with her, making love to her and not worrying about anything else. I knew it was selfish, but I would have given anything for that.

I hadn't even planned to take her to Chicago initially. My original idea had been a helicopter ride over Manhattan, but she kept getting A's and putting it off. During that time, we became closer, and I wanted to share more of myself with her. Maybe it was to make up for not letting her in on the most important piece of information. Something she had every right to know, even as my friend.

Over Christmas, I had missed her so much that it was like going through withdrawal. I realized that staying in the friend zone just wasn't working for me. I needed her. The only way I could be with her was to tell her the truth and hope that she would understand. She promised that nothing could make her leave me, but would that really still be the case once she found out about Ivy? Maybe I was kidding myself.

If she didn't want to be with me after I told her the truth, I'd move out and walk away, because living under the same roof with her would be like strapping a bottle of vodka to an alcoholic.

I wished she had just let me get it off my chest last night, because the truth was, there was never really going to be a right time to explain my fucked up situation to her. But she convinced me to wait a day to have the talk.

When I realized she wanted me as much as I wanted her, I became like a caged animal unleashed for the first time; I wanted to ravage her so badly that I gave in and waited to say anything. If all else failed, last night will stay with me for as long as I live, and nothing could ever take it away.

Now, I needed to figure out how to explain my sudden disappearing act and everything else, the second I get back to New York.

How exactly *was* I supposed to tell the person I love that I'm married to another woman I may never be able to leave?

The halls were eerily quiet as a nurse led me to her room. Ivy was sitting up in bed staring at the clock on the wall. That was a habit she developed about a year ago. She just watches the hands go by. It seemed to calm her.

"Ivy?" I said as I slowly approached the bed. She wasn't in the middle of a delusion, but she also didn't seem to be affected by my being there one way or the other. She looked at me and then looked right back at the clock.

She winced when I grabbed her hand. She didn't like to be touched, but she gave in and let me hold it. I was just relieved she wasn't telling me to go away this time or accusing me of trying to kill her. That one was the worst.

I squeezed her hand lightly. "Are you okay?"

She nodded repeatedly in quick motions without making eye contact with me then said, "Did they call you?"

"Yes. They said you—"

"Well, I didn't. They're lying. They shouldn't have called you."

I didn't want to argue with her. The truth was, only she really knew whether she meant to take her own life or whether it was a misunderstanding. She never admitted to intentionally trying to commit suicide the past few times something like this happened.

"What did you do, Ivy?"

"I was just trying to get some air."

"They thought you tried to jump out a window?"

"I was on the roof."

"Ivy—"

She cut me off and shouted. "I was just getting air!"

I decided not to grill her any further. It was pointless. Even this little amount of clarity from her was rare, and I didn't want to push her into an episode. She just needed to know I was there for her. Thank God, this time, my being here didn't set her off.

She kept her hand in mine, and I watched her eyes return to the clock on the wall. Aside from the faint traffic sounds through the glass from the street below and the clock ticking, it was quiet. Then, came a light knock on the door.

"Mr. Green?"

I turned around to see a tall middle-aged woman with a white coat standing at the doorway.

"I'm Doctor Greally."

"Hi," I said, standing up as we shook hands.

"May I have a word with you?" She gestured for me to walk out into the hallway with her.

I looked back at Ivy who was still staring at the clock. "I'll be right back."

"What happened, doctor?" I whispered.

"She was apparently naked on the roof threatening to jump if someone didn't leave her alone. There was no one actually bothering her and no one in the vicinity. The staff at the home had a tough time getting her down safely. They brought her in because they didn't know what else to do."

I rubbed my forehead vigorously with my fingers. "How long is she going to be hospitalized this time?"

"At least a few days. I wanted to talk to you about treatment options."

"You obviously looked at her records? Nothing has ever worked for her," I said.

"Yes, but I noticed they've never tried Clozapine."

"What is that?"

"Well, it's usually prescribed as a last resort in patients who have never responded to any of the other anti-psychotics."

"Why is it a last resort?"

"There are some potential troubling side-effects, like dangerously lowering white blood cell count. People who take it have to have frequent blood tests to monitor the situation. However, aside from that risk, it can be a very effective treatment in some people."

My stomach felt sick. "When do we have to make a decision?"

"You can take all the time you need. Just know that it's an option."

"Thank you," I said as I rubbed my chin, unsure about whether it would be worth the risk. I'd have to do more research.

As I reentered her room, she was fast asleep. I sat down beside her and once again, felt helpless as I watched her peaceful face.

When she was sleeping, it was easy to imagine the old Ivy. I only got to experience that girl for under a year before things started to dramatically change. The past five years have been a steady decline.

Ivy and I dated for six months before we eloped to Vegas on a whim and were only married for about six months more when her behavior started to deteriorate. At first, I didn't understand what was happening or what to even call the episodes; I just referred to it all as *hell*.

The first time I ever took her to the hospital, by the time she was discharged, it finally had a name.

"That went well, don't you think?" my co-worker Henry said as we exited the meeting.

"Yeah. Lunch?"

"Sure. The Ninety-Nine?" he asked.

I turned the corner toward my cubicle. "I'll meet you in five."

I had been doing my co-op for a technology company north of Boston. It was a hip start-up, and I loved the fact that they didn't give a shit about my piercings. As long you worked hard, they left you alone. Management had called some of us in to talk about possible job opportunities after graduation. They were scoping out the co-op students for computer hardware engineering positions. We would be developing computer chips, circuit boards and routers.

I didn't like working so far outside the city, where we lived. Ivy's behavior had deteriorated lately, and she was really starting to worry me. She had dropped out of school and lost her job several weeks ago, which meant she was now home all day. She wasn't in any condition to work, but not having anything to occupy her was making an already bad situation worse. I didn't know how to help her anymore, but losing my job too wasn't going to help either one of us. So, I drove the forty-five minutes every day and left her alone, hoping for the best.

Rachel, the receptionist, spoke through my phone intercom as I was counting my cash for lunch.

"Jake?"

"Yo."

"Please come out front."

Her tone was strange. I immediately grabbed my wallet and walked to the front desk.

My heart dropped.

No.

No.

Not here.

She was standing there in the lobby with mascara running down her eyes, wearing her pajamas, her hair disheveled.

"What are you doing here, Ivy?"

She kept her distance and pointed at me, her index finger shaking. "You know what I am doing here. You know what you tried to do to me this morning. I know you tried to poison me!"

No.

I briefly closed my eyes unable to believe this was actually happening at work. Her words shouldn't have shocked me, yet every time she accused me of something like that, it fucking ripped my heart out. This was the first time other people would witness it.

I looked behind me to see Rachel looking at us like a deer caught in headlights. I could only imagine what this must look like to someone who didn't know my wife.

"How did you get here?"

She didn't answer, but through the sliding glass doors of the lobby, I saw there was a cab waiting outside.

I grabbed her arm. "Let's go. Now!"

"Don't touch me!" she yelled.

I started to push her out the door when she resisted.

Her scream echoed in the lobby. "He tried to kill me this morning. He put something in my coffee before he left for work. He's wanted me dead for a while."

I looked over toward the desk and saw my three co-workers who were supposed to be meeting me to go to lunch, staring at us speechless. I shook my head at them to let them know this wasn't what it seemed.

Bob, the office manager came out. "What's going on out here?"

I started to sweat. "Bob, we were just leaving. This is my wife, but she's ill and doesn't realize what she is saying. She shouldn't have come here. I apologize for the scene."

She was crying, and I pulled her out the door, as she struggled with me. I held onto her arm so she couldn't run away as I stuck my head in the open cab window. "Did she pay you?"

The cabbie shook his head, so I took out my wallet with the one available hand I had. "How much?"

"Ninety-seven dollars," he said.

I didn't have enough cash. Fuck.

Humiliated, I held onto Ivy, as we walked back into the lobby. More people were now standing there to witness the drama. Henry came up to me. I told him I would explain everything later and he gave me the extra cash to pay the cab driver. As Ivy stood there whispering to herself, I think he was starting to get the drift of what was really going on.

I paid the driver before dragging Ivy to the far end of the parking lot where my Jetta was parked. She was still trying to get away from me and was threatening to call the cops. Cars were speeding by on the nearby highway and I feared if she got away, she'd run into traffic and get herself killed.

Her spit sprayed my face when she said, "I fucking hate you, Jake." I pushed her into the passenger seat and shut the door. Those words went right through me. As I started the car, she turned away from me looking out the window. I looked over at her, feeling helpless, not sure if I should take her home this time.

I just sat there with the car running. I couldn't fucking do this alone anymore. Ivy's mother died shortly before we got married. She had no father in the picture and no siblings. I was all she had. It was the reason I was still here.

Taking her to a hospital had been something I'd been avoiding. I was scared for her, what they might do to her there. Visions of padded white walls and isolation haunted me. I thought I could keep her safe myself, but I was losing control faster than she was losing her mind. My poor Ivy. This wasn't her fault.

She turned and looked at me, and I knew she was coming out of it. Each episode was like a cycle. It always passed, but once she came through it, a new one was never far behind. Feeling defeated and hopeless, my chest tightened as I reached for her hand. I almost wished, this once, she stayed out of her mind, so that she didn't realize what was about to happen. Because as we pulled out of the lot, I knew that this time, I wasn't taking her home.

"Where are we?" she asked when we pulled up to a large brick building just outside Boston.

We hadn't spoken the entire ride to the hospital.

I touched her hair gently. "We're going to get you help, baby girl."

I helped her out of the car, and this time, she didn't resist.

A couple of days later, she was still admitted when the doctor pulled me into his office. I knew something was coming, but I was never going to be ready to hear it.

I was looking at the pictures of the doctor's smiling children as he said, "Mr. Green, your wife has schizophrenia."

I continued to stare blankly at the photos. A snapshot of a little boy lifting a fish on a boat would forever be etched in my mind as the image I was looking at when I heard those words come out of the doctor's mouth. The rest of that one-sided conversation was a blur that I could only recall bits and pieces of.

Auditory Hallucinations

Delusions

Anti-psychotics

Manageable with meds

No cure

No cure

No cure

He was sending us home with a few prescriptions for medications to start.

Ivy took my hand as we walked through the hospital's revolving doors that symbolized our new normal, in and out of hospitals until I would eventually reach my breaking point.

TWENTY-TWO

JAKE

I took a cab from the hospital to my sister Allison's house in Brookline. Ivy had stayed sleeping, so I decided to get some sleep myself. I'd go back to the hospital in the morning.

I had placed a quick call to Nina around midnight, letting her know everything was okay here and to reassure her about us, but I could tell by the tone of her voice, she was scared. Who could blame her? She needed to know what the fuck was going on with me, but I wasn't about to tell her everything about Ivy over the phone.

Allison and Cedric had a big Victorian-style house with plenty of space, so I always crashed in their guest room on weekends. They weren't expecting me on a weeknight, though. I knew my nieces would be asleep and hoped someone would be up to let me in.

Crickets chirped as I waited out front wondering if I should text one of their cell phones because I didn't want to ring the doorbell and wake the girls.

Then, I remembered that my sister left a spare key under a rock in the side yard, so I grabbed it and let myself in.

My eyes nearly bled as I entered the living room to the sight of Cedric's bare ass...while he was mounting my sister on the couch.

I covered my face. "Aw, man, what the—"

"Jake?" I heard my sister's voice but refused to open my eyes.

"What the fuck are you doing here on a weekday in the middle of the night?" Cedric growled.

"Haven't you guys heard of a bedroom?" I said with my eyes still shut.

Cedric chimed in. "Haven't you heard of a fucking knock?"

When I opened my eyes and got a look at my sister, I couldn't help but laugh. She was wearing red thigh high boots and was dressed as...*oh, Christ.* "Seriously? What the hell are you wearing? Are you supposed to be fucking Wonder Woman?"

Allison blushed and covered her face. "Shut up. He likes it. Sometimes I wear it."

"Gross. That's my sister, dude. You are one sick fuck." I glared at Cedric.

He sneered as he finished putting on his sweatpants. "That'll teach you to barge into our house in the middle of the night."

"Yeah, I'm gonna fucking need therapy," I said, causing Allison to laugh.

Then, her tone turned serious. "Jake...what happened? Why are you here? Is everything okay?"

I let out a deep breath. "I flew home this afternoon. It's Ivy. She's okay, but she's in the hospital again. They found her naked on the roof of the group home. She claims she was trying to get air. They thought she was trying to jump. Who knows what really happened. It's a fucking mess. The doctor wants me to try this medication that might have some serious side effects. She's fine, for now, though...stable. She'll be in the hospital for a few days, same as always when this happens. I'm wiped."

It was sad that neither of them seemed shocked. But the truth was, you became immune to it after years of the same pattern with Ivy.

I was about to go up the stairs to the guest room when my sister came up from behind me and pulled me into a hug. "I'm so sorry you have to deal with this. You're a friggin' saint, you know that? I love you."

"I love you, too. Good night."

"Good night, Jake," Cedric said as I was halfway up the stairs.

When I entered the dark room, I pulled off my shoes, undressed and collapsed onto the bed. As tired as I was, I couldn't sleep, tossing and turning, worried about the medication decision I had to make. So, I decided to take a shower in the guest bathroom.

It was the first time since the plane ride that I allowed my mind to escape back into thoughts of Nina. I would have given anything to have her there with me under the water. With my eyes closed, I ached to be inside of her again. It had been only twenty-four hours, but it felt like an eternity ago.

Sex with her had been incredible, better than I had imagined it...the best I ever had. She was so eager, so wet, and it turned me on to no end, knowing I was the first guy to ever make her come like that. We did it as many times and in different ways as we could until the strip of condoms was gone. Then, we got creative and used our mouths and didn't stop for hours. It was the most sex I had ever had in one sitting in my entire life, and it still wasn't enough. I guess that's what months of mind numbing sexual frustration will do to you.

I licked my lips remembering how sweet she tasted and squeezed some shampoo out of the bottle to jerk myself off. I pretended I was pumping into her and came within seconds as I thought about how she looked at me with those beautiful innocent blue eyes when she climaxed. Her blonde hair was spread out all over the pillow like spun gold.

Back in bed, I prayed that I would get to experience all of that again with her and that she would just let me love her, despite all of my baggage. Something told me I would need those prayers because I had a feeling it wasn't going to be that simple.

The next morning, I woke up to find one niece on each side of me pulling me out of bed. They begged me to take them to school, which turned out to be a welcome distraction. I decided to go back to the house afterward for some breakfast before returning to the hospital for the rest of the day.

Allison didn't have to work until noon, and Cedric decided to go into work late, so they were both having breakfast together in their massive kitchen when I walked in. I had a feeling they were waiting to grill me about stuff. I had confided in them about my obsession with Nina over Christmas. Even though I had been struggling with guilt, they both had encouraged me to pursue her.

"Hey," I said as I walked in.

"Hey, little brother," Allison said smiling.

I grabbed some cereal and sat down at the table, noticing they were both staring at me.

"What's going on?" I asked.

Allison laughed. "I should be asking *you* that. By the look on your face, something is going on."

"What are you getting at?"

I knew what she was getting at.

"She wants to know what happened with blondie, but she's waiting for you to tell her because she doesn't want to seem like the nosy sister that she is," Cedric said, giving Allison a peck on the cheek after she nudged him.

My mouth was full of cereal. "Ah, I see. You really want to know what happened?"

She leaned in. "Yes."

Suddenly, the tone of the conversation changed from jovial to serious. I sighed, pushed my bowl away and answered her. "Everything fucking happened, almost at once, and I might be about to lose it all just as fast."

"You mean...you..."

I nodded. "Yes, multiple times. And I told her I loved her. I am...in love with her."

Cedric eyes widened. "Whoa. That serious, huh?"

"I've never been more serious about anything in my life. The problem is, I haven't had a chance to tell her about Ivy. I had planned to tell her everything last night but had to fly here instead. She knows nothing, and I think I might be fooling myself into thinking that she's going to accept it all."

He shook his head. "You'd be surprised what people can accept when they love each other. If she truly cares about you, she'll find a way. Look at your sister and me...all that I had kept from her when we first started dating. But we got through it because we were meant to be."

Allison reached out for my arm. "I want you to be happy, and this girl clearly makes you happy. I had never seen you with the look in your eyes that you had over Christmas when you first told me about her. You have suffered alone for five years with Ivy. You have your whole life ahead of you. You are the most loyal person I know. That is what I love about you...how you are with Hannah and Holly and how you're always there for me. You love hard, but in this case, that's also been a curse. No one your age should be expected to live like you have been, Jake...no one. You deserve to have the kind of love that fulfills you, like I have with Cedric and not feel guilty or like you don't deserve that because of the hand you've been dealt."

"I know I deserve it, but it's not that simple. I can't just fucking leave Ivy. I made a vow. What would happen to her? I'm all she has. My name is on everything. She's on my insurance. I have power of attorney. Whoever I'm with is going to need to understand that. What if Nina can't? This is why I didn't want to get involved with anyone. Nina doesn't deserve to be dragged into this."

"Do you love Ivy?" Allison asked.

"I don't think I even knew what being *in love* was until I met Nina...eating, sleeping and breathing someone, feeling like I can't live without her. I thought what I felt for Ivy when we were eighteen was love. Looking back, it was more infatuation. But to answer your question, I do love Ivy in the same way that I love you."

"So, you're staying married to someone you love like a sister because you're afraid of what will happen to her? Don't you ever want to have a family someday?"

"I want that, sis. I do. You know how much I love the twins. I would love to have kids of my own. But I pretty much wrote that off when Ivy got sick. I never thought about those kinds of things again until Nina. But divorcing Ivy…I just don't know how I would live with myself if I did that and something happened to her."

Cedric put his coffee down and looked at me. That dude has some intense blue eyes. "Let me tell you something I learned a long time ago, Jake. Love has no conscience. It doesn't know right or wrong. It's a feeling you can't shake that penetrates your soul, and it cannot be broken. If you're truly in love with this girl, that's not going to change no matter what your life circumstances are. Time will tell whether it's true love or not. If it is, you won't be able to live without her. End of story." He looked at my sister.

I knew he was right.

Allison got up from the table and hugged me. "We just want to see you happy. We'll help in any way we can. Divorcing Ivy doesn't have to mean deserting her. I'll look into alternative insurance plans and state aid. We'll help, even if Cedric and I have to pay for some of the expenses. We've already discussed it."

I would never let them do that, but damn, I truly had the best family in the world.

"I am not ready to think about divorce, Al. Just let me tell Nina what's going on first, and then we'll see how she reacts."

"Hi, baby girl."

Ivy was looking out the hospital window when I arrived. She turned around, smiled and ran to me, giving me the biggest hug I had gotten from her in a while.

"There's my handsome man," she said.

My stomach was in knots with guilt. She and I hadn't had an intimate relationship in years, but sometimes, it was like her mind would revert back to the past for a fleeting moment. It came in waves and never lasted. It freaked me out when it happened.

"How are you feeling?"

"So good...so good," she said leaning her head on my chest.

"I want to spend the whole day with you before I have to go back to New York, but I'll be back again this weekend."

She pulled back abruptly. "Where were you last night?"

"I was here the whole time until you nodded off. Then, I went to Allison and Cedric's to sleep."

"Why did you leave?"

"I just told you."

"What were you really doing?"

"Sleeping, Ivy."

"I don't believe you."

Here we go. It was always like a light switch.

"Where do you think I was?"

"I think you were with them."

"With who?"

"With the police."

"No, baby girl. No police."

"You're trying to get me out of the country again, aren't you?"

It was pointless to defend myself in any great detail when Ivy's paranoia started up like this. I learned over time, it was better to just simply deny what she was accusing me of with one or two word answers. If she became overly upset at me, I would just leave until she calmed down.

"No, Ivy."

"I can't believe you're doing this again. Why are you trying to get rid of me?"

"I'm not."

"Don't you love me?"

"I love you very much."

"Then, why are you trying to hurt me?"

"Ivy—"

"Get out! Get out of here before I scream!"

I looked up at the ceiling, focusing on a crack in the paint as she continued to yell. I really didn't want to leave her since I had to go back to New York tonight. When she started to push me, I left the room to see if I could talk to the doctor. After a fifteen- minute wait, Dr. Greally came out to the sitting area and asked me to go back to her office.

"Have you made any decisions about trying the Clozapine?"

"I am still on the fence. I am not around during the week because I work out of state, and I am worried about the side-effects. I don't know if I can trust the workers at the group home to keep tabs on her."

"We'll have the social worker make sure she gets to the lab safely each week for the blood work. I can also do daily check-ins with the supervisor over there. If there is any indication that she's experiencing anything abnormal, we can always stop it."

"Okay...I'll let you know in a couple of more days, if that's okay?"

"Take your time."

When I returned to Ivy's room, she had the television on and was watching an episode of *House Hunters*, that real estate show where the people have to pick between three houses to buy. I sat down next to her and searched her face to see if I was welcome again.

She looked at me. "I don't know which one they are going to pick. It's a tough decision."

I half-smiled.

Yes, it is.

I leaned my head on her shoulder, and we spent the next hour watching television, before she sent me away again.

TWENTY-THREE

Nina never responded when I texted her from the airport about six o'clock that night, letting her know I
was getting on the next commuter flight home. That was
unlike her and made me uneasy, especially knowing I was
going to be coming clean to her about everything tonight.

By the time I landed at JFK, there was still no response. It was raining, and I couldn't seem to catch a cab.

Fuck.

When I finally hailed one, I texted her again.

> *I am in a cab on my way to Brook-
> lyn. Please let me know you got this.*

No response.

After five minutes, still nothing.

I dialed her number three times in a row and her
phone went straight to voicemail each time. I left a message after the fourth call.

"Nina, it's me. I'm starting to worry. You haven't responded to me all day. I'm almost at the house. I guess I'll see you in a few. Call me if you get this. I love you."

She never called me back, and by the time the cab pulled up to the house, a feeling of dread came over me.

When I opened the door to the apartment, I yelled, "Nina?" before realizing that no one was home. I double-checked her bedroom. It was empty.

Sitting on her bed with one hand on my head and the other on the phone, I texted her again.

I am home. Where are you? You've got me worried sick.

I lay down on my back, tossing the phone across the bed.

Five minutes later, I looked over at her closet and noticed that the small pink suitcase she normally kept underneath her hanging clothes was gone.

Her suitcase was gone.

What the fuck?

I began to pace the room, rubbing my temples.

Think.

Think.

Think.

Then, the front door slammed shut, and I ran out to the living area to see Ryan standing there.

"Ryan, where is Nina?"

He shook his head with a smug look. "You have got some nerve, you know that?"

"Excuse me?"

"You will not find out where Nina is. You will stay the fuck away from her. Do you understand me?"

My blood was boiling, and I was ready to pounce, but I decided to play it cool until I could find out where she was. That was all that mattered.

"What the fuck are you talking about, Ryan?"

"I am talking about the fact that you fucked my best friend, then took off to Boston to fuck your wife, you dirty mother fucker."

My heart felt like it was going to leap out of my chest.

No.

This could not be happening.

My hands began to shake, and I had to clench my fists to keep from throwing a punch.

My voice was low as I spoke through gritted teeth, resisting the urge to charge at him. "What...did you...tell her?"

"You know, I always knew something wasn't right with you. After having to listen to you fuck her ten times in the middle of the night, I was sure as hell going to make sure she wasn't getting involved with someone shady. When you didn't come home Monday night, that was it. I looked your information up in the database at work the next day and guess what came up? Your fucking marriage license! Everything made sense all of a sudden...your Boston trips, your secrecy—"

Ryan's head slammed against the wall after I grabbed him in a choke hold. My breathing was erratic. "You don't know *anything* about me. You think you figured it all out, but you don't know shit about my life! Now, tell me where Nina is or my hands stay where they are."

He didn't have the strength to break free or speak, so he spit in my face.

"Tell...me...where...Nina...is," I repeated through my teeth, tightening the hold with each word.

His head bounced back and hit the wall as I released him.

He coughed. "She's staying with a friend, but she doesn't want to see you."

That stung.

I stood there glaring at Ryan. When I calmed down, I decided that considering he knew nothing about my situation, I couldn't blame him for thinking he was protecting her. I needed to calm down and play nice to find out where she was.

"Listen, I am not going to explain everything to you until I've had a chance to talk to her. It's not what you think. I am *legally* married, yes, but it hasn't been a marriage in the real sense for years. It's complicated, okay? Ivy...she's mentally ill. She lives in a home. I rushed back to Boston because they thought she tried to kill herself." I rubbed my temples in frustration.

Ryan just stood there speechless.

What do you have to say now, asshole?

"If this is true, I really don't even know what to say. You should have told Nina you were married and you certainly shouldn't have slept with her."

I wasn't going to waste time explaining my actions to him when the only person that deserved an explanation was Nina.

"Where is she, Ryan?"

"She's crashing with Mrs. Ballsworthy's daughter. She came by right after Nina found out about you. Daria had stopped in to give her a thank you basket and saw her crying. I pulled her aside and told her what happened. She insisted Nina come stay with her for at least a few days. She lives in Park Slope."

"What's the address?"

"I promised her I wouldn't tell you."

"Ryan, I like you. I do. So, I'm gonna be up front and tell you that I'm going to beat the snot out of you if you don't tell me, and I really don't want to have do that."

He huffed and pulled out his phone, texting me the address.

"Thank you," I said as I ran out the door.

I took a deep breath and tried to gather my thoughts before entering the brownstone. The front door was open, but you had to get buzzed in to enter the second door. I pressed the button for Unit Six.

A woman's voice blasted through static. "Hello?"

"Hi, this is Jake. I know Nina is staying with you and doesn't want to see me, but please, I need to talk to her. Can I come up?"

Silence.

It felt like it went on for an eternity. Then, came more static. "I'm sorry, Jake. She doesn't want to see you. Please leave."

I pressed the buzzer again but no response. This went on for about fifteen minutes with no luck. They were just ignoring me.

I went back outside and walked around to the back of the building to see if there were any windows. A fire escape led up to the sixth floor. If I could get up there and knock on a window, maybe they would see how serious I was and let me in. Shit, I would camp out here all night if I had to.

I began to crawl up the fire escape, unsure of whether the apartment at the top was even the right one. When I got to the sixth level, I looked in the window at a dark, empty room. Just as I was about to knock on the window and beg whoever lived there to let me in, a light came on.

The sight of her nearly knocked the wind out of me. Nina closed the door and sat down on the bed. She didn't see me. Her beautiful long hair covered her face as she cried into her hands, her shoulders shaking up and down. Then, she looked up at the ceiling and muttered something to herself. I felt like I was about to suffocate as I watched her suffering because of me. I hated myself for causing the person I loved more than anything so much pain. It was tearing me apart. I didn't want to scare her, but I needed to do something.

Her body jolted when I knocked on the glass. Her hand over her heart, she turned and noticed me staring through the window.

"Nina...let me in."

She sat there just looking at me, her chest rising up and down.

"Let me in," I repeated. "I'm not going away. You have to let me explain."

She stayed frozen, her beautiful eyes, dark again for the first time since I met her.

"Please...I love you," I said.

It pained me to think that she probably thought I was a horrible person who was using her.

I decided to attempt to carefully break through the window, but low and behold, it opened right up. I crawled through and closed it behind me.

It sickened me when she backed away and leaned against the wall on the opposite side of the room. I didn't want to upset her, so I kept my distance.

"Nina...it's not what you think."

A tear fell from her cheek.

I decided to get right to it. This story needed to be told from the beginning, and I only had one chance to do it right. I sat down on the bed and took a deep breath, looking away from her sad face.

"I was eighteen when I met Ivy. She was like no one I had ever encountered before...so full of life and vibrant. The first time I saw her, she was dancing in the middle of a torrential rainstorm. I walked up to her and made small talk. We made plans for later that night. She was a guitarist, played some small gigs and I went to see her perform in a coffee house. I just thought she was really cool. I guess it was infatuation. We became inseparable and started dating. About six months later, we got a little drunk one night, and she decided that it would be a brilliant idea to hop the next flight to Vegas and get married. What did I know? I was an impulsive teenager with a hot girlfriend and figured it would make a really cool story someday to say I got married by Elvis. I thought I knew what love was then. I thought I loved her enough to spend the rest of my life with her."

I looked over at Nina to gauge her reaction, and she was looking down at the ground.

"That Vegas trip was just about my last good memory...until I met you. Anyway, we moved in together after that. My family was pissed at me for eloping. My sister didn't talk to me for weeks. They didn't like her and thought she was a bad influence. But I was still in the honeymoon phase and didn't care what anyone thought. About six months later, our relationship began to change. She started calling in sick a lot to work and stopped going to her classes. We were fighting all the time about her behavior. I started to realize that getting married was a really big mistake. I'd get home from work, and she'd accuse me of having affairs all day. Then, the next day, she would tell me she was hearing voices and that they were telling her I was trying to kill her and that she'd better kill herself before I got to her. At first, I thought it was just stress, because she had recently lost her mother to a heart attack. She had no other family, except me. Every day, though, it was something different. The erratic behavior went on for months. One day, she showed up at my job and in front of my co-workers, screamed about how I was trying to poison her. That was when I took her to the hospital for the first time. By the time we left, she had been diagnosed with schizophrenia."

I turned to look at Nina, who was now looking back at me.

"A lot of people can live very normal lives with it, because it can be managed with medication. We tried every medication out there, Nina. Nothing worked. They call her condition 'treatment-resistant' now. She was in and out of hospitals, and I just couldn't take care of her anymore. I was worried she'd kill herself while I was at work. So, about a year after she got the diagnosis, I reached my breaking point and put her in a group home. Shortly after that, I got a job offer I couldn't refuse in New York with the kind of benefits I needed to help take care of her. She made me promise I would visit her every weekend. That was four years ago, and I've kept that promise."

Nina let out a deep breath. I stopped talking for a few seconds to let her process what I had told her so far. She finally whispered, "Jake...I—"

"Please...don't say anything yet. I need to finish this."

She nodded.

"I was scared shitless those first couple of years, but over time, it just became my normal. The way I saw it, I had made my bed, and I had to lie in it. I convinced myself that I could handle it. I was just a 20-year-old. Twenty fucking years old and I was taking care of my mentally ill wife. After those first two years, our relationship changed. It became less like husband and wife and more like brother and sister. We haven't been intimate since she moved to the group home over four years ago. Even in the months before that, it was almost non-existent, and when it happened, it didn't even feel right anymore. I was celibate for a long time. Then, a couple of years ago, I started seeking out women I knew I could use as an escape with no strings. I had needs, and I was so fucking lonely."

"Women like Desiree," she whispered.

I nodded.

"I had accepted that fate. My life was all planned out, and that was it. I'd stay legally married to Ivy so she could have my benefits and so I could look out for her, and the rest of my life would be separate. I was basically dead inside...until you."

She turned to me. "What happened the other night... when you had to go to Boston?"

"They thought she tried to kill herself. They found her on the roof. No one knows what really happened."

Nina closed her eyes as if my words hurt. "So, you were going to tell me all of this the night we—"

"Yes. Yes, Nina. I was going to tell you everything and hope that by some miracle, you'd still want to be with me."

She walked over and sat next to me on the bed. I inhaled her vanilla scent. I wanted to hold her so badly and bury my nose in her hair but held back, unsure of where things stood. She reached for my hand and squeezed it and my body relaxed. We just sat like that for minutes. My heart was breaking with each second that passed. The silence was killing me. "Nina, talk to me," I finally said, my voice hoarse.

"I don't know what to say, Jake. I am so confused right now. I spent the past few hours filled with hate toward you. I thought you were sneaking around on your wife with me. I never wanted to see you again. And now...I don't know what to feel. This was a lot to take in."

I shook my head in understanding, but inside, I was shitting a brick. I don't know what other kind of reaction I expected.

What I wanted to say was, *"you said you'd never leave me."* What I actually said was, "I know this is a shock and can only imagine how you feel. You need to know how much I love you and how you've changed my life."

Her eyes were watering again. "Are you going to stay married to her?"

"I never planned to divorce her because I never planned to fall in love with someone. I don't know what would happen to her if we weren't legally married, what rights I'd have when it came to her care. I still have to do a lot of research before I cut those ties legally. I would never be able to abandon her, Nina. She's always going to be a part of my life. But if divorcing her is a condition of being with you, then I am telling you right here and now that I will do it."

"I would never expect you to abandon her, Jake. That's horrible. I hope you didn't think that's what I meant when I asked if you were going to stay married."

Thank God.

"I didn't think that. I am glad you understand."

She continued, "But I just can't *be with you* if you are married. I can't sleep with a married man."

Fuck. Where was this going?

271

"I don't consider myself committed to her in that way anymore. There would be no marriage if it weren't for my wanting to be able to make sure she is cared for. I can understand your point, though. I am still legally married to someone else."

Just be with me, Nina.

She let out a deep sigh. "Daria asked me to move in with her. This is an extra room, and she had been looking for a roommate anyway. I think it's best if we live apart while we try to figure things out."

No. I can't fucking live without you.

"Okay. If that's what you need."

It felt like I was losing her.

"I am still in shock, okay? I need some time to let this set in."

You said you'd never leave me.

I put my hand on her knee as my chest tightened in agony. "Anything you need."

TWENTY-FOUR

I fell into a deep depression over the next couple of weeks. Nina moved the rest of her stuff out, and the new semester had just started, so I hadn't seen her much.

We met in a park to talk one afternoon. She seemed disconnected and wasn't making much eye contact when I answered some questions she had. She asked me again exactly how long it had been since I had been intimate with Ivy and how many women I had slept with since. She was fidgety and seemed distressed. I was honest with her about everything, but it felt like we had taken a step backwards.

I went home that night pissed at life and ended up punching a hole through the wall in my room. The clincher was, after seeing her, I felt more in love with her than ever. That desperate need to take away the darkness that had returned to her eyes was overwhelming me. I had been dying to touch her as she sat across from me on that bench. She was wearing a white wool coat and looked like a snow angel, her nose and cheeks rosy from the cold air.

That was over a week ago. Now, I couldn't even walk by her empty room without getting angry. One night, I lay down on her stripped mattress, staring at the ceiling and wallowing in the memories of our first and last night together in this room. I opened her bedside drawer and slammed it shut out of frustration after finding every single paper bat I ever made her.

Mostly, I was mad at myself because I hadn't grown the balls to confront Ivy about a divorce. The timing was bad because she had just started that new risky medication. I was hoping that if it gave her some clarity, it would make it easier to explain everything to her. So, I was waiting, but it hadn't kicked in yet. We had no guarantees that it ever would, especially when nothing had ever worked for her.

The more days that passed, the more afraid I was that Nina was going to move on and realize that she was too good for me and all of my baggage. I had asked her to wait for me, but how realistic was that when I had no idea how long a divorce would take? That asshole Ryan was probably planning another blind date for her as we speak. I knew in my gut he was working against me. I needed to keep an eye on him.

One Thursday afternoon, I told my boss I was going home sick, but really, I was sick over Nina. I walked around the city aimlessly until I decided I just needed to go to her. I hopped the next train back to Brooklyn, unsure of what I was going to say or do. I needed to know where things stood. And I just wanted to see her, bury my nose in her hair and tell her that I loved her. It was her day off from school, so I was counting on her being there.

After buzzing the doorbell several times, there was no answer at her apartment. Desperate, I even climbed up the fire escape on the off chance she was in her room and didn't hear me ringing. Her window shade was down. I knocked on the window, but she wasn't there. I sent her a text.

I really need to see you.

I got no response after five minutes of waiting outside her doorstep.

My mind went crazy wondering where she could be, at one point, imagining that she was out with another guy. A jealous insecurity like I had never felt in my life started brewing inside me. I sent her another text:

Where are you right now?

When there was still no reply, I threw my phone, and the screen cracked.

Fuck.

When I got back to my apartment, thankfully, my room-mates weren't home since it was still late afternoon. Ryan made no secret of the fact that he didn't want me with Nina, so he and I avoided each other. I pretty much kept out of the living area entirely when he was home. I was never quite sure which team Tarah was on.

When I opened the door to my bedroom, my entire body shuddered in shock.

The sight of beautiful blonde hair cascading down the side of my bed stopped me in my tracks.

She was sleeping in my bed.

Nina was out like a light, her body rising and falling slowly with each breath. I stood frozen a few feet away, not wanting to wake her.

I noticed her phone on my desk, with the lit up notification of my texts. She wasn't ignoring me; she was asleep...in my bed...the entire time.

My heart filled with love and my body with desire as I sat down next to the bed, taking in her beautiful silhouette curled up on top of my comforter. With each passing minute, I became more and more tempted to curl up beside her and hold her, but I stayed back, afraid if I woke her, she'd leave.

I thought back to the other night when I could have sworn I smelled her on my pillow. I had assumed it was my imagination playing tricks on me. I laughed to myself now, realizing the probability was good that she had actually been in my bed that day. She was always a little sneak.

I loved her so much it hurt.

After about ten minutes, her body stirred and her eyes opened. When she noticed me sitting there, she jumped.

Her eyes were groggy. "Jake...I'm sorry, I—"

"Shh. Baby, it's okay. I can't tell you how happy it makes me that you sleep in my bed when I am in work. It means you're thinking about me, and I can't stop fucking thinking about you. I had to leave early today, because I couldn't focus. I went to your apartment. If I had known you were here..."

She scooted up against the headboard. "I still have my key, so sometimes I come here."

I reached my hand over to cup her cheek. She closed her eyes when I rubbed my thumb across her face. She started to tear up. I was going to lose it. Anytime she cried because of me, it felt like getting stabbed in the chest.

I climbed onto the bed and placed my face on her stomach, afraid she'd resist, but she didn't. Instead, she caressed my hair with her soft fingertips. This was exactly the comfort and reassurance I needed, what I had been desperately searching for today. A firestorm of emotions that had been dormant for years erupted inside of me, and I cried for the first time in my adult life. It felt like the weight of the past six years was finally crushing me, and the core of her body was the only place I felt safe enough to let go.

My shoulders shook over and over as I buried my face into her, my tears soaking through the thin fabric of her shirt. She held me closer, and I could hear her crying too. In that moment, I realized the depth of her love for me; I just worried whether love would be enough to conquer the lack of trust that now existed.

When my tears stopped, I sniffled and kept my head on her stomach. I couldn't resist moving my mouth over her skin. She let out a soft moan that my dick felt instantly. The need to be inside her grew by the second. I began to kiss her stomach more urgently, grazing her with my teeth, nearly ripping her shirt as I pulled at the material.

I knew she was conflicted and could tell she was tensing up. I understood why. Nina was very literal and saw the situation as cut and dry. In her eyes, I was a married man, off limits. In my mind, a piece of paper couldn't dictate who owned my heart. And she owned me in every way that mattered.

Despite her reservations, I also knew that I had a strong physical effect on her. It's why she'd been staying away from me these past few weeks. Her body reacted to me from the very first moment I met her. She would always buckle under me with the slightest touch. That's always made me crazy. If I kept touching her like this, it wasn't a question of whether she would give into me today but when. I just needed to decide whether I would push, knowing that she had asked me for space.

I started to kiss lower and could almost taste her.

Fuck space.

I needed her like my life depended on it, to carry me through the next few weeks, which were going to be the most difficult of my life. Because that cry I just had confirmed what I already knew. I would be going through with telling Ivy about the divorce, because Nina was the love of my life, and I couldn't live a second longer without her.

In an instant, my mouth went lower, and I began to devour her over the material of her yoga pants. She panted, thrusting her hips to meet my mouth.

We were on the same page now.

I pulled her pants and underwear down together slowly, and her breathing became even heavier when my tongue found her bare clit. I knew she loved when I flicked my tongue ring over it fast and repeatedly. I moaned into her. Her legs were restless, and I swore I could taste that she was going to come and within seconds, she did. When she screamed out, I thought my cock was going to burst out of my pants.

I moved up to kiss her, slipping my tongue inside her mouth hungrily, as we grinded against each other. I could feel how wet she was through my clothes. I lifted her shirt off and pulled her bra down, taking turns sucking on each of her beautiful light pink nipples. God, her tits were gorgeous. I squeezed them together and licked up and down the middle of them.

I was in heaven again for the first time since the night we made love.

Today felt different though. I had been calm that first time and wanted to take my time pleasing her so that she would never forget it. But right now, I was starving, feeling selfish, needy and out of control. I was dying to be inside of her and needed to know that she still trusted me enough to let me.

When she put her hands on my ass, I unzipped my jeans and pulled my boxers down, rubbing my rock hard cock against her slick opening. I had meant to just tease her at first, but within seconds, I was fully inside of her raw. The feeling was indescribable.

With every movement, I felt like I was claiming her. That was what I wanted to believe. Because I couldn't survive the thought of any other man so much as touching her. That thought made me crazy, and I fucked her harder, bending her legs back as far as they would go so that I could get deeper inside. I sucked on her neck and squeezed her ass hard, wanting to brand her with my hands and mouth, too.

With each movement, I growled in her ear.

"My body belongs to you."

"My heart belongs to you."

"My soul belongs to you."

"Only to you."

My thrusts got harder with each word. "Do...you...understand...me?"

I abruptly stopped moving when she didn't answer me, pulling her face toward mine and searching her eyes. "Do you?"

She nodded, breathing heavily and looked like she was about to cry again.

"Say it."

She panted and pulled me into her. "Yes. I understand."

I fucked her even harder. I felt the moment her muscles contracted, and when she screamed out in pleasure, I let myself go. "All of you belongs to me, Nina...to no one else...ever," I said as I exploded inside of her.

My dick throbbed in place for what seemed like several minutes. In my head, I had been marking what was mine but started to feel terrified of losing her again, the second I pulled out of her.

"I love you so much," I whispered in her ear.

She didn't say anything. I immediately became worried that I had been too rough with her. We lay for a while together in silence before I stood up and reached out my hand. She grabbed it and silently followed me into the bathroom.

Turning on the shower, I held her up against me and kissed her back slowly as we waited for the water to warm.

"Are you okay?" I whispered.

"Yes," she said leaning the back of her neck against my mouth.

"Was that too much for you?"

She shook her head no and pushed her ass up against me. Jesus. I was hard again as I pulled her into the steamy shower.

Under the water, another primal urge to take her started to build inside me. I knew I needed to control myself this time and slow things down.

I added some soap to a sponge and slowly washed her from head to toe, taking my time over the contours of her body and especially between her legs.

She grabbed the sponge from me, adding more soap and moved it slowly over my body, kissing my chest as she stroked my cock before dropping the sponge to the ground. She bent down and licked slowly over the tip teasingly as she looked up at me. When she swallowed me whole, I closed my eyes, pulling on her hair in ecstasy as she sucked me off. I could feel the back of her throat and almost came before stopping myself because I needed to be inside of her again.

I pulled her up and held her against me under the water for a few seconds to grab my bearings because I didn't want to be rough with her this time, but I was finding it hard to be gentle.

She sucked on my bottom lip slowly, tugging on my lip ring with her teeth. That did me in. I lifted her up over my cock and buried myself deeply inside of her.

My movements were intentionally slow and controlled as I held her over me, gripping her ass as it pushed against the tile wall. My tongue was deep in her mouth, as we kissed feverishly, matching the rhythm of my thrusts.

I was still trying hard to go slow when she began to ride my cock harder, giving me permission to release my inhibitions. I had been dying to take her from behind and couldn't hold off any longer. I pulled out of her and turned her around so that her perfect round ass was facing me. I placed both of my hands on her cheeks and slipped immediately back inside of her. The contact of our wet skin made a slapping sound as I moved in and out, completely incapable of controlling myself.

"Fuck...your ass is so beautiful, Nina. I love it."

She moaned in response as she balanced herself with her hands on the tile wall.

"It's all mine," I said as I pounded into her harder. "All...mine."

Her muscles clenched, and the wet heat of her sudden orgasm set me off. When I came inside of her this time, it felt so good that it was almost painful. I shouted out like a fucking maniac and it echoed through the bathroom.

We collapsed to the shower floor and kissed under the water. I picked up the sponge and washed her gently again, before turning the faucet off.

Grabbing a towel, I squeezed the water out of her hair as I kissed down the length of her body before drying myself.

Back in my bed, as she stared up at the ceiling, the look on her face told me that reality was starting to set in again. She finally spoke. "I didn't mean for this to happen." She turned to me. "It wasn't why I came here. I've just felt like my whole world was falling apart. I wanted to keep my distance until you worked everything out with the divorce, but I still needed to feel close to you, so I've come here a few times. I never expected you to walk in at this time of day. We shouldn't have done what we did...but I've missed you so much."

"You have no idea how badly I needed to hear that," I said, taking her hand in mine and kissing it.

She looked down at our joined hands. "I've felt like I lost my best friend. My life has been empty without you in it. But I still feel like what we just did was wrong. I am just so weak when it comes to you and—"

"Baby, please don't tell me to stay away from you. Remember that night in my room before we got together, when I told you to leave? That was one of the hardest things I ever had to do, but I was able to push you away because I hadn't had you yet. Now that I actually *know* what it feels like to be with you, to be inside of you, to love you, not just from afar, but in every way...I can't ever go back."

"What happened tonight shouldn't have. It doesn't have to be forever. Just until your divorce."

I couldn't promise to stay away from her; it was something I knew damn well I wouldn't live up to. I held her until she fell asleep again. She must have been worn out from the workout I gave her. The sun was starting to set. I hoped that she would just stay with me tonight.

As I watched her sleep, my emotions were running wild. I got the urge to write her something, so I grabbed a piece of white printer paper from the desk and a pen.

Sure, Green. Fuck her hard like an animal then follow it up with a sappy love poem. It's all about balance.

I had never written a thing in my life before I met her. Now, I couldn't stop. It was like Hallmark was going to be knocking on my door any day now. It started out as a joke, but now, it was something I loved to do for her.

Go ahead...say it. My balls were on layaway, and I couldn't afford to buy them back.

Like drawing, it was a way for me to express the feelings I bottled up inside. Lately, all of my sketches have been of her too, some of her naked body. It would probably creep her out if she found that book, which I strategically kept hidden from the rest.

When it came to telling her how I felt, the right words never seemed to come when I spoke them in the moment. But being able to take my time and especially watching her lying here next to me while I wrote, inspired me.

When I was finished, I was satisfied that I had written down everything I wanted to say to her.

She decided against spending the night with me. As she was getting ready to leave, I gave her the folded up poem and told her to read it when she got home and to reread it whenever she felt lonely or had doubts about my intentions.

I thought my life was planned
Until the moment I touched your hand.

Your sad eyes met mine,
And all I wanted was to make them shine.

And every time they did,
I became giddy like a kid.

With each moment together we spent,
I figured out what my father meant.

When he told his little boy long ago,
"When it's love, son, you just know."

I tried to resist and be strong
Since the timing was all wrong.

But I still came undone.
Because You. Are. The. One.

And I'd rather die than have to say
That mine was the one that got away.

Tell me what I have to do
To prove my heart is married to you.

It won't be overnight.
Just give me time to make it right.

Please wait for me, Nina.

Later that night, she sent me a text.

I will.

TWENTY-FIVE

Holding onto the promise she made me as insurance, I gave Nina the physical space she felt she needed. We spent a lot of time talking on the phone, sometimes late into the night. During one of our conversations, she paused out of the blue, changed the subject and said, "Tell me about her."

She hadn't really asked much about Ivy up until that point, aside from wanting to know where things stood. Maybe she wasn't ready or hadn't felt secure enough in our relationship. I spent the next hour of that phone call going over the last six years and shared memories of Ivy, both good and painful ones. It was liberating to get it all off my chest and to finally share everything with her.

A month passed before I was able to take a week off from work to head to Boston. I didn't want to have the divorce talk with Ivy over a weekend in case I needed to stay for the fallout. I also never quite knew what kind of a mood I'd find her in. A week would give me enough of a window to ensure I'd get her on a decent day.

My plan was to use the rest of the time off to research all of the legal issues. If possible, I wanted to be able to keep my power of attorney. She didn't have anyone else who was trustworthy to make important decisions.

We had stopped the new medication because she wasn't benefiting enough to make it worth the risk. So, waiting for that to kick in was no longer an excuse for me to put everything off.

When I arrived at the group home Tuesday night of that week, I had geared myself up to have the dreaded conversation.

Her door was open, so I knocked lightly, but she didn't notice. She was listening to an old c.d. that she had recorded of herself playing the guitar years ago.

My chest tightened as I watched her sitting on the bed with her back facing me. She was swaying side to side to the sounds of her own music. I would have given anything to know what she was thinking about.

I tapped her shoulder, startling her, and she turned to look at me.

"Hi," she said. "What day is it?"

"It's Tuesday."

"What are you doing here?"

"I came to see you. I took the week off."

She turned back around facing the window, and I sat next to her on the bed. We sat in silence, listening to the mellow guitar. *Ivy's music*. She hadn't played in years. Although, she still kept her Gibson propped up in the corner of her room, an eerie reminder of what used to be.

She stood up in front of me. Her long red hair was tousled, and her eyes looked tired. Even so, she was still a beautiful girl. It was the one thing that never changed, that wasn't taken away from her.

She tugged at my arms pulling me up. "Dance with me," she said.

I couldn't help but smile. That was the last thing I expected. Her behavior was always unpredictable, but this was a new one.

She wrapped her arms around my shoulders and placed her cheek on my chest. I closed my eyes and moved my body slowly to the music, matching her rhythm.

Dancing obviously wasn't what I came here for, but moments like this with Ivy were few and far between. If dancing with me gave her some peace, I'd do it all night. I just wanted to take her pain away. There was never anything I could do to make that happen.

Her breathing became shaky, and I realized she was starting to cry. I held her tighter as her tears covered my shirt. I didn't know what to say or do.

She whispered, "Jake, I'm scared."

"Don't be scared, baby girl. I'm here." My eyes started to water when the next song played: Ivy's rendition of *Yesterday* by the Beatles. I caressed her hair as we continued to dance, the last six years flashing before my eyes.

It dawned on me that maybe she was more aware than I had given her credit for. Maybe in a moment of clarity, she put two and two together when I showed up out of the blue on a Tuesday. Maybe she knew she was about to lose a part of me. I wouldn't know for sure, but what I did know was that no talk was happening tonight. No. Tonight, we would just dance. She deserved that.

After leaving Ivy's, my head hurt from mentally preparing for the talk, only to have to put it off again because of her emotional state.

There was only one person I wanted to see right now. *I fucking needed my mother.*

Instead of going back to Allison and Cedric's, I took the Blue Line train straight to my mother Vanessa's house in Malden.

She and my stepfather Max got married a couple of years ago. They had met shortly after we moved to Boston when my mother took a job as a waitress at the diner he owns.

When she opened the door, she could tell from the look on my face that I was having a hard time.

"Honey, are you okay?"

I walked past her into the living room. "No, Mom. I'm not." I sat down on the couch with my face in my hands. I was distraught but felt better already just being in my mother's house.

She sat down next to me holding a cup of Chai tea. The licorice aroma wafted in the air. "Did you just come from Ivy's?"

I nodded and exhaled into the palms of my hands, too exhausted to talk. Even in my silence, my mother knew everything; she always did.

She put down her teacup. "You still haven't told her."

I looked up, pursed my lips together and shook my head.

With her long dark hair and green eyes, my mother looked like an older version of my sister. Their resemblance was uncanny. I was lucky to have two strong women in my family that I could turn to. She put her hands on my shoulders and sighed.

"Jake, I've made a lot of mistakes in my life, more so early on, between the drugs and getting pregnant as a teenager. When I met your father, I was just starting to straighten out, but there were things about my past I needed to tell him and I dreaded it. Each day, I would put it off. The constant worrying about what his reaction would be nearly killed me. But you know what? All of that worrying never changed anything. When I finally got it off my chest, I was free. It's not going to hurt her any less or more if you wait. You're the one breaking down, son. You need to get this over with for your own sanity. I could not be more proud of you. After your father died, you became the man of the house. You took care of yourself, so I could take care of us. You never stopped wanting to take care of people. I know you feel like you failed Ivy. But she was so lucky to have been blessed with you in her life because not many men your age would have stuck around. I know you'll always look out for her. But it's time for you to start living again."

It was exactly what I needed to hear from the one person I needed to hear it from.

The next day, Ivy was making a sandwich in the kitchen when I walked into the group home. A few of the other women who lived there were sitting on the opposite end of the room along with the house monitor.

"You're back?" she asked.

"Yes, I'm here all week."

"Do you want one?" she asked pointing to the bread.

"Sure."

My heart pounded, and my stomach was upset because I knew this was no ordinary lunch date.

We sat along the counter together eating the turkey sandwiches she made.

When we were done cleaning up, I asked her to come sit with me in the yard. There was a patio out back and that was the best place to have the talk.

Ivy was more coherent than I had seen in a long time and I was grateful that I had chosen today.

"What's going on?"

"I need to talk to you about something important."

"Okay."

"Come sit," I said gesturing for her to join me on a bench swing. I grabbed her hand. She was looking in my eyes and waiting patiently for me to start talking. I was amazed to have this kind of attention from her and knew it was now or ever.

Here goes nothing.

I breathed out slowly. "I'll never forget the day we met when you were dancing in the rain outside Northeastern. Do you remember that?"

She nodded. "Of course, I do."

"Something deep inside told me to go up to you. Whatever it was, if I could go back in time, I would have still walked toward you that day. You were captivating, and I was an 18-year-old boy, smitten for the first time. We were infatuated with each other back then. We rushed things."

"I was crazy about you," she said.

"We should have never run away and gotten married that young. But the man upstairs had a different plan because he knew you were going to need me someday. I am glad he chose me to look out for you. I just wish I could make you feel better, make you healthy again. Most of all, I wish I could fight all of your demons for you. I would fucking slaughter them all if I could.

She started to cry and whispered, "I know you would."

"It's been hard watching you slip further into your own mind over the years. Some days, I really miss the girl I used to know...the one who played the guitar for me at night as I sat next to her drawing in my sketchbook and the one who always lit up the room with her smile. It hurts when you don't acknowledge me now most of the time or worse, when you believe I am trying harm you. When you are having an "on" day, like today, I see glimpses of your old expressions, your sense of humor and the connection we once had. I know that the sweet funny girl who loved life is still in there, and I miss her sometimes."

"I can't do this, Jake. I don't want to talk anymore." She started to get up, but I stopped her.

"Ivy, I have to finish saying what I need to say. This is important. I need you to listen to me."

She reluctantly sat back down. "I know where this is going."

"None of this is your fault, baby girl...none of it. Sometimes, bad things happen to good people. You're a courageous soul and have a cross to bear, but you do not have to carry it alone. I'll continue to make sure of that."

She was looking down when she said, "You're leaving me. You said you'd never leave me!"

"I never wanted to let you see me breaking. You have enough on your plate. But the truth is, I have been lonely and broken for a long time. I didn't even know how depressed I really was, until I met someone who brought me out of it."

She turned and looked at me like those words had assaulted her. The sadness in her eyes was palpable, but I had to continue. There was no going back now.

"I fell in love with someone. I never meant to, and I tried hard to avoid relationships with other people because I wanted to be able give you everything I had. You deserve that. But we haven't had a real marriage for years. I am not sure we ever really had a chance at that. I've wanted to make sure I could still support you, so I never considered ending our marriage legally."

"You're...you're *divorcing* me?"

"I have taken the steps to file for divorce, yes. Believe me when I say this is the toughest thing I have ever had to do. I met someone I love deeply. I don't want to keep that from you anymore. It's certainly not fair to stay married to you under the circumstances. I'm ending our marriage legally, but I am *not* leaving you. I'll never abandon you, Ivy."

She shook her head repeatedly and licked the tears that fell into her mouth when she said, "You say that now." She pushed me and repeated, "You say that now! Leave. Just go."

My eyes were welling up, but I tried to remain strong and continued with what I had planned to say. "I will always make sure you are safe. I will make sure you have health insurance, even if I have to pay for it myself. I—"

"Leave!" she screamed at the top of her lungs.

It felt like she was punching me in the gut. The house monitor would probably come outside any minute if she screamed again.

I spoke louder to get through to her. "I am swearing to you that I will not abandon you for as long as I live. I will always be there for you when you need me. Please try not to hate me. I will always love you."

She was rocking back and forth on the swing with her head down and her hands shaking. It was killing me, but what did I expect? I was all she fucking had. I wanted to hold her, comfort her, but I knew she wouldn't want that.

"Get out of here before I call someone," she said.

I stood up and walked toward the inside door, then turned back around wanting to convince her that nothing would change. "I'll see you this weekend, as always, Ivy."

She stayed rocking on the swing as I walked away, feeling like I had just gotten run over by a train.

TWENTY-SIX

I spent the next couple of days of that week meeting with lawyers and social workers, determined to make sure that Ivy was going to be okay. I was told that even after a divorce, I could still be her conservator and maintain power of attorney unless in her right mind, she objected. I still had to figure out a new long-term insurance plan for her and had filled out some applications for state aid. It was a long and grueling week.

When I returned to the group home the following Saturday morning, Ivy was standing up staring at the clock on the wall. The one picture of us that she had on her chest of drawers was cracked; she must have thrown it the other night in her anger at me.

"Ivy?"

She didn't respond and never took her eyes off the wall as she bounced back and forth between her toes and heels.

I sat at the edge of her bed and rubbed my eyes in frustration, wondering if she recalled everything clearly from the other night. I hoped she at least remembered that I told her I would never abandon her.

When my eyes wandered to the corner of the room, my heart dropped when I noticed the strings of her Gibson guitar had been plucked off and mangled. I walked over to it and when I picked it up, my heart felt like it had been ripped apart, too.

"I'll get this fixed, baby girl," I whispered, "I'll fix it. I'm sorry."

She was counting to herself when I looked over at her. I felt helpless.

Her social worker walked in at that moment. "Jake?"

I turned toward the door. "Hi, Gina."

She looked over at Ivy. "Hi, beautiful." Still in a catatonic state, Ivy ignored her.

Gina and I walked out to the hall, and she whispered, "They told me that she threw a fit the other night, throwing things around her room and threatening some of the staff if they went near her. It wasn't quite bad enough for a hospitalization, but they asked me to check in on her every day this week."

"Thank you, Gina. Thank you so much."

"It's my job." She smiled, searching my eyes. "How are you holding up? Are you okay?"

She knew about the talk I had with Ivy and my filing for divorce. I was sure I looked like shit. I hadn't shaved all week and slept like ass.

"Honestly? Not really. I've been dreading this for five years. I don't want to push her into an even worse state. I could never live with myself if anything happened to her."

"Do you know how many of these situations I walk into everyday where the person has absolutely no one looking after them? I haven't seen one spouse in your situation who has stayed as long as you have, certainly not one your age."

"I'll always look out for her."

"You're a good man, Jake."

I wanted to believe that, but the guilt had only just begun to eat away at me.

That Saturday night, back at my sister's house, I closed the door to my room and called Nina. She had just arrived at her parents' house in upstate New York for spring break. She'd be there all week until the following Sunday.

We last spoke on the phone a few nights ago right after I told Ivy about the divorce. I was extremely sad after I left the group home. Nina stayed on the phone with me for hours, just listening to me vent about everything that had happened. It was a relief that I didn't have to keep any part of my life from her anymore. Toward the end of the call, she told me she loved me. It was the first time she had said it since finding out about Ivy. It was only then that I was able to let her off the phone and fall asleep. It was the first good night's sleep I had in a while.

When I called her tonight, though, I needed so much more than her reassurance. I missed her so fucking much and felt like I was going to lose it if I couldn't be with her soon. Even though we had been talking on the phone, it had been several weeks since we had seen each other. The need to be with her physically was becoming unbearable. I wanted to show her just how badly I needed her.

"What are you doing right now?" I asked.

"I just finished the dishes, a typical exciting night here at home here in the boonies. How are you?"

"I miss you."

"That's funny because I was just thinking about how much I miss you."

I closed my eyes wishing more than anything that she was with me. "Well, I was just thinking about how much I *love* you."

"I love you too." She paused then said, "You know that, right? I feel like things have been so stressful lately and I haven't said it much, but that's never gone away, Jake, not even for a second."

I was going to explode.

"Can you go into your room?"

"Yes. Is everything okay?"

"Yeah. I just want to make sure you're alone."

"Hold on. I'm walking to my room." The phone made a staticky sound as she walked. "Okay, I'm here."

"Close the door and lock it."

"Are you sure everything is okay?"

"Yeah, baby, I am. There is just something I really need to show you right now."

"The door is closed. What's going on?"

I let out a deep breath into the phone and made myself comfortable on the bed. I hoped she would play along with me. "You locked it?"

"Yes."

"How much do you miss me?"

"I feel like I can't keep staying away from you. I've really tried to do the right thing, but—"

"I would give anything to bury myself inside you right now, Nina."

"I am pretty sure I'd let you tonight."

"Fuck. I wish you were here. I'm lying down. Are you lying down?"

"Mmm-hmm."

From the sound of her voice, I knew she was on board and had figured out where I was going with this.

"Close your eyes."

"Okay...closed."

"Pretend I am there with you right now, baby. Can you feel me?"

She whispered. "Yes."

"Take off your underwear."

"I'm not wearing any."

"Say what?"

"I'm wearing a dress."

"With no underwear?"

She giggled. "Yeah."

Well, shit.

"Fuck...lift up your dress, then," I said gruffly.

"Okay..."

"Promise me something."

"Yes."

"You won't touch yourself."

"What?"

"You will *not* touch yourself...until I tell you. Okay? Can you do that?"

She breathed heavily into the phone. "Yeah. Yeah, I can do that."

"Promise?"

"I promise."

I knew she was telling the truth. Nina was honest to a fault.

"Spread your legs open for me."

"Okay..."

"Wider."

"Alright."

"I'm going to lick all the way down your body now. Can you feel my tongue? It's at the base of your neck, and I'm slowly...going down."

It felt like her breathing was penetrating the phone. "Uh-huh."

"Lift one of your breasts to your mouth and lick it. Pretend I'm doing it to you."

She didn't say anything, but I could hear the sound of her tongue lapping against her own skin, and I nearly came from it. I closed my eyes and tried to bring myself back from the brink.

"I'm licking in between your tits, going lower. I have my thumb on your clit while I am kissing your stomach, and I can't wait to taste you."

Nina sighed again but wasn't saying anything.

"Are you turned on right now?"

"Yes," she breathed out.

"I know. I can practically taste it from where I am. My mouth is watering. Can I devour you?"

Her breathing became heavier. "Mmm-hmm."

"I am moving my tongue up and down your clit now. Shit...you taste so sweet. Does that feel good?"

"Yeah."

"Where are your hands?"

She let out a slight laugh. "Clutching my sheets for dear life."

"Good. Keep them there while I tease you with my tongue ring. You like it when I flick it hard over your clit, don't you?" I smiled to myself. I *knew* she loved that.

"Oh...God."

I was so turned on but vowed to not touch myself either. It was extremely hard...and I was harder.

"Do you want me inside of you?"

"Yes…very much."

"I am going to rub my cock against your opening now. Are you ready, Nina?"

"Yes…I am so wet."

"Yeah, I know you are. I can feel it now as I am rubbing my tip against you."

"Jake…"

"I don't know who's wetter right now, you or me. Open your legs wider," I commanded.

"I need to touch myself, Jake."

"Not yet. Just a little longer, baby."

"Ugh." She sighed in frustration.

"How much do you want me inside of you?"

"More than anything…so badly."

"My dick is so hard right now. I need to fuck you."

"Please…fuck me."

"Do you want to touch yourself while I do it?"

"Yes…yes…please…now."

"I'm gonna fuck you a little first, and then I'll tell you when it's okay."

"Now."

"Not yet."

"Please."

"I'm entering you now. Can you feel me filling you?"

"Yes…yes."

"I'm balls deep now. Shit…you feel incredible."

I couldn't take it anymore. I unzipped my pants and started stroking my cock.

"Jake…I need to touch myself."

"Do you feel that, Nina? How much you want it… like you'd die for it? That…*that*…is what I wanted to show you…how I feel when I can't touch you and when you tell me I can't have you. I never want to feel that again."

I jerked myself off faster knowing she was going to lose it. I wanted to come the moment she did. "Touch yourself now...now."

Her breathing became rapid, and I knew she was finally satisfying the need with her fingers. My own need to come was overpowering. When I heard her scream out, I finally let go and came instantly. "Fuck," I groaned. "I love you, Nina. I love you so fucking much."

That had been torture for me too.

I heard a knock in the background and could hear a woman's voice. *"Nina, are you okay in there? Dessert's ready."*

Shit.

"Yes...I'm coming!" she yelled.

We both broke out in laughter at the irony of that. It was nice to laugh again. I felt better than I had in a long time, like maybe things were going to be okay after the toughest week of my life.

God never gives you more than you can handle, right? Well, I was about to find out that when it came to Nina, God would be testing me soon in a big way.

TWENTY-SEVEN

Ivy had been stable, so I was able to return to Brooklyn with a clear conscience after my week in Boston.

Before heading back to New York, I spent all of Sunday at the group home with her and never mentioned the impending divorce, although I brought her a letter I had written that summed up most of what I had already told her, so she would have my feelings in writing.

I didn't know whether she read it or not after I left, but it made me feel better to give it to her. I stayed with her until she kicked me out that afternoon, accusing me of planting a chip in her arm while she was napping.

It was a relief to be back in New York for the week, but I had wished Nina were with me. I overnighted her an origami bat for every day she was at her parents' house. Stopping at Fedex on my way to work each morning was the highlight of my day.

A week later, it was the Sunday night that Nina arrived back in Brooklyn, and I had come home from Boston early. I had planned to rush over to her apartment the second she got home. A text came in from her just as I was heading out the door.

I don't think I can see you tonight.
I'm not feeling so good.

Fuck that.

I immediately picked up the phone and called her.

"Are you okay?"

She sounded tired. "Hey...no. I'm just feeling really crappy. My stomach hurts. It's that time of the month, and it was a long bus ride. Rain check?"

"I guess so, baby, but I was really looking forward to seeing you. How about I come over and take care of you?"

"That's really sweet. I think I just need to sleep, though. I'm sorry. I know we were supposed to spend the night together."

"It's alright. Tomorrow night, though, wild horses won't keep me away, okay?"

"Okay. Good night, Jake."

"Sweet dreams, baby. Feel better."

The next night, desperate to see her, I didn't even call before heading to her apartment straight from work.

When she opened the door, her long blonde hair was tied into two pigtails, and she looked really tired. She also appeared to have lost some weight.

I pulled her into a tight embrace. "Baby, I missed you so fucking much."

"I missed you, too."

I lifted the brown paper bag in my left hand. "I brought Chinese from your favorite place."

"Oh," she said.

"What's wrong, Nina? Talk to me."

"Nothing. I just...don't really have an appetite. I'm still not feeling well."

"I'm sorry," I said as I put the paper bag down and felt her head then kissed it gently. Her skin was cold.

My mouth lingered on her forehead when she looked up at me. "I'm the one who should be apologizing for being such a party pooper."

"That's okay. You can't help it if you feel like crap." I took her hand and pulled her over to the couch. "C'mere. Let's sit down."

She laid her head across my lap, and I caressed her hair. Her skin was pale and her breathing shallow.

I would take being close to her to anyway I could get and became angry with myself for getting turned on. Seriously, had I no shame? It just happened. The feel of her breath so close to my dick made me hard. It had been too long since I had been with her, and it was my body's natural reaction. I closed my eyes and imagined the wart on my seventh grade teacher Mrs. Mortimer's chin. Hairy. Wart. Wasn't working. Shit.

She didn't seem bothered by my erection, or at least, she didn't say anything to that effect. She didn't say much of anything at all, in fact. When I peeked down at her face on my lap, it surprised me that her eyes were wide open, like she was deep in thought. I had assumed the reason she was being so quiet was because she was falling asleep.

Yeah, she wasn't feeling well, but something else was wrong. Something was bothering her. I didn't know how to explain it, but I could feel when Nina was sad in the same way I felt her pain when she cut her finger. It was a connection I had with her and no one else. Unfortunately, it did not extend to being able to read her mind.

"Baby, is everything okay?"

"I just have a lot on my mind. I have two exams this week, plus I told you about my friend, Skylar."

"The girl with cancer?"

"Yes. I go see her every Wednesday. I talked to her today. She hasn't been doing well. The chemo has been making her really sick."

"Shit."

"I am hoping I don't have to skip going to see her this week."

"Because you're sick?

"I can't be around her if she could catch something."

"I think that's awesome that you're there for her every week like that."

"Believe me...I'm the lucky one. If you met this girl, you'd know what I mean."

"Maybe I could go with you and meet her some Wednesday."

She laughed. "She'd love that more than you know."

"Why do you say that?"

"She's a sex-crazed teenager, and she saw a picture of you. She's been asking me to bring you around. She calls you 'Jake the beefcake.'"

I laughed. "She's a hot ticket, huh?"

"You have no idea."

Nina ended up falling asleep on me. I carried her into her room and tucked her in then went into the kitchen to heat up some Chinese food. Her roommate was away visiting her boyfriend in D.C., so we were alone in the apartment. As I ate in the quiet of her kitchen, I thought about how this night was nothing like I had hoped it would be after such as long absence. I wasn't sure whether to wake her to say goodbye, leave a note, or just slip into her bed.

I opted to stay the night. It was just too tempting to lie next to her. She was still fast asleep when I took off my shirt and pants, leaving my boxer briefs on. I lifted the covers and lay down behind her, placing my hand on her waist. She didn't even flinch. I listened to her steady breathing until I fell asleep.

At some point in the middle of the night, she sat up in bed and it woke me up. She seemed to be anxious and her breathing reminded me of how she acted during our plane ride to Chicago.

"Nina?"

She was shaking a little. "I just had a bad dream, that's all. I'm fine."

I began to cradle her. "You don't sound fine."

"Just hold me, okay?"

"Of course. I'll hold you until the morning if you need me to."

After a long silence, I thought she was about to fall back asleep when she asked me, "Are you going back to Boston again this weekend?"

She knew I went to Boston every weekend, so it was a strange question. "I was planning on it, yeah."

"So, even after the divorce, you still plan to go every single weekend?"

She caught me off guard. "Yes. I mean…she's alone all week with no family looking in. Does it bother you that I plan to go back every weekend?"

The fact that she didn't say anything right away told me that it did.

It was dark, so I couldn't tell whether she was crying when her voice shook. "It's just going to be hard."

I held her close to me, feeling suddenly petrified. "I know, Nina. Believe me, I know. This is why I didn't want to get involved with anyone. But shit, I am in deep with you, and there is no going back. We'll figure it out. We have to. Maybe you can come with me some weekends. I know my sister is dying to meet you."

"Come with you to visit Ivy?"

"No, not to visit Ivy, but you and I will spend the mornings and nights together in Boston."

"So, you'll be with Ivy all day while I roam the city alone?"

Fuck. Fuck. Fuck.

"Nina..."

"It's okay, like you said, we'll work it out," she said abruptly.

A sinking feeling came over me as we sat in silence. Suddenly, the seeds of doubt had been planted. Had I really thought this through? Was it realistic for me to expect her to accept my putting Ivy before her for the rest of our lives? It wasn't fair. My sense of obligation to Ivy was strong, but it wasn't stronger than my love for Nina. I had some serious thinking to do about how I was going to handle things. One thing was for certain: I wasn't going to figure it all out tonight.

For the rest of that week, Nina made up an excuse every night not to see me. Tuesday, she claimed she was still sick.

Wednesday, it was that she had returned late from visiting Skylar and needed to study. Then, it was more studying on Thursday. I knew better. If you want to see someone, you always make time, even if its just five minutes.

So, we never got together before I had to go back to Boston the following weekend. Ivy was having a tough stretch and had to be hospitalized again briefly while I was there. I had gotten very little sleep.

The entire weekend was a blur. Before I knew it, I was home in Brooklyn again. It was a never-ending cycle, and I was tired of it.

So fucking tired.

To make matters worse, Nina had not responded to me at all the Monday after I got back. It was the first day she had completely ignored my texts. The more time that passed without a response, the more hopeless I became. Add to that, the fact that Ivy was a mess when I left Boston, and I was in a bad place.

I had let down the person who needed me most, for the person I needed more than anything and managed to fuck up all of our lives in the process. The future was just one black hole now.

If Nina chose to leave me, a day wouldn't go by when I wasn't pining for her. The thought of her moving on, having sex with other men, marrying someone else, having children with him, seriously made me want to hurt someone. I honestly didn't know how I would handle it. She could leave me physically, but she would still be in my heart and in my soul forever. There would never be anyone else.

I had to get out of the apartment before I lost it. I grabbed my keys and jacket and left, walking down the street with nowhere to go. As it started to rain, I stopped inside a bar several blocks from home.

It was dark and loud and just what I needed to drown everything out. I sat at the counter fully intending to get fucked up tonight.

"Grey Goose straight," I told the bartender.

As I sucked the first drink down in one shot, the two voices in my head were battling one another. There was the louder one telling me to never give up on Nina because she was mine and because I felt with all of my heart that she truly loved me. Then, there was that other voice telling me to let her go because she deserved better than to be with a man who could never give her a hundred percent. I wanted to destroy that voice completely, so I ordered another drink.

"I've never seen you in here before." For the first time, I looked up at the bartender and noticed that she was an attractive blonde. She placed the small glass down in front me, her tits bursting out of a black leather bustier. Suddenly, the dark dingy bar had somehow transformed into *Coyote Ugly*.

"That's because I have never been in here before," I said, before drinking down the vodka.

"I would have remembered you," she said flirtatiously before walking away to serve another customer.

Within a few minutes, she was back with another drink. "This one's on me. What can I say? I have a weakness for guys with tattoos, especially gorgeous ones." She winked.

"Thanks," I said, guzzling that one down too.

She leaned in. "You seem down about something."

"You could say that."

"You want to tell me about it?"

"It's too long of a story...um...what's your name?"

"Lexie."

"Lexie, it's too long of a fucking story," I repeated.

She moved closer up against the counter. It was hard not to look at her chest because it was staring me in the face. "Well, it's a good thing I have time."

I laughed under my breath. "You don't. Not for this one."

"What's your name?"

"Jake."

"Try me, Jake."

The "fuck me" look in her eyes suggested she was referring to trying more than her attention.

"I'd really rather not get into it with someone I just met."

She reached across the table and caused me to flinch when she planted a kiss on my cheek.

What the fuck?

"See...now, we're old friends, Jake."

"Well, *old friend,* I really don't feel like going into it."

"Does it involve a woman?"

"Yeah...a couple of them."

"Well, any woman who would be dumb enough to let you go would have to be out of her mind."

I shook my head in disbelief at how messed up and ironic that statement was. How did I end up here...both in this bar and in this miserable state? I checked my phone.

Where are you, Nina? Goddammit, I need you.

I didn't know what came over me, but I started telling Lexie my entire life story. I must have been rambling for almost an hour. I guess I needed to let out everything that was eating away at me. By the time I had finished, she had served me more vodkas on the house, and I was off my ass.

When she walked away to tend to some new customers, I no longer had a distraction and the pain returned in full force. I checked my phone again to see if Nina had returned my calls, and of course, she hadn't. I did have a voicemail...from Ivy.

I went outside to escape the noise of the bar and played the message. She was somewhat incoherent. Given that my mind was fuzzy on top of that, the only thing I seemed to be able to make out was 'good bye.'

Shit. What was Ivy trying to tell me? She rarely called my phone. I speed dialed the main number for the group home as my heart raced. The night staff confirmed that she was in her room and okay after they checked in on her. Hearing her say "goodbye" had scared the shit out of me, though.

Still feeling uneasy, I walked back inside and stayed sitting at the bar until they closed. I think I almost passed out in my seat. That was the most I had to drink in a long time. It was time to get the hell out of there.

Things were hazy as I exited the bar. Even the cold air hitting my face did me no good. As I started the long walk home, an older white Volvo pulled up beside me.

"Jake...come on. Get in. I'll drive you home."

It was Lexie.

Without really thinking it through, I got in the car. It beat walking several blocks, feeling like crap.

Her car smelled like peaches, or was it her hair? I didn't know. What I did know was that Lexie was bad news, and so was this decision I just made.

"Where do you live?"

"1185 Lincoln. It's right over this Greek restaurant, Eleni's."

"Yup. I know that place."

The streetlights and buildings we passed merged into one big blurred line. In less than ten minutes, we had arrived at my doorstep.

I turned to Lexie. "Thanks for the ride. I definitely had too much to drink...thanks to you."

"Well, you were pretty upset when you walked in, and you needed to loosen up. After you told me why, I wanted to help even more."

I slurred my words slightly when I said, "You did succeed in helping me get fucked up." I laughed. "So, thanks...I think."

"Anytime," she said putting her hand on my knee. "And I mean that."

"Okay...well, goodnight. Thanks again," I said as I exited the car unusually fast, stumbling a little. I could tell she was disappointed that I wasn't asking her in. Lexie was the type of girl I probably would have sought out a couple of years ago...sex with no strings or expectations. But Nina ruined me for other women. She was all I wanted.

I made it up the stairs and into the living room where I collapsed onto the couch while the room spun. I turned on the television and became fascinated by a Zumba infomercial. The dancers seemed to be jumping out of the screen and trying to merengue with me.

A few minutes later, there was a knock at the door. I pushed myself up off the couch and opened it.

Lexie.

She lifted up an iPhone. "Forget something?"

"Shit. Thanks," I said, taking the phone. "How did you get up here?"

"You left the front door open. I knocked on the floor below, but the lady told me to 'fuck off,' so I figured door number three up here was the winner."

Before I could bid her goodnight and send her on her merry way, she pushed her way past me onto the couch and crossed her legs as she sat down. With the thigh high black leather boots she was wearing, she looked like a whore.

"What are you watching?"

"Zumba."

She started to laugh. "You're funny, Jake."

I lifted my index finger. "And drunk. Don't forget drunk," I said, joining her on the couch. I laid my head back. "Ditch the workout, join the party," I mumbled.

"What?"

"Never mind."

If I squinted my eyes, with her long blonde hair, Lexie almost looked liked Nina for a second. This girl was definitely sexy, but Nina was much prettier and classier.

A fucking angel.

Sexy alone just didn't do it for me anymore. Actually, nothing except Nina did it for me.

Some time passed, but I was too out of it to know how many minutes. I must have fallen asleep, because the next thing I knew, Lexie was topless and straddling me over my jeans.

She whispered in my ear as she moved over me. "You're so fucking hot, Jake. I want to go down on you."

Fuck.

My dick was hard. I was out of it but not enough to ever make me want this. I couldn't imagine giving myself in that way to someone else. I loved Nina. Even if she didn't want to be with me right now, my body was hers.

I pushed her off me. "Lexie, get off."

"I *was* getting off."

"I meant get off of me. You should have never come in here. I really need to take a leak. When I come back out, I want you to be gone, okay?"

"I thought you wanted it. You were staring at my tits all night and look at you...you're hard."

"Lexie, with all due respect, you were sitting on my cock when I was asleep. It has a mind of its own. And as for your tits, maybe if you put them away, I wouldn't have been staring at them. Now, please. You're a very nice girl (...*for a whore),* but I told you earlier, I am involved with someone."

I said nothing else before walking to the bathroom and taking the longest piss of my life. I must have been in there for ten minutes just sitting on the toilet while my head was spinning. A massive hangover awaited me to-morrow morning.

When I walked back out to the living area, Lexie was gone.

She was gone, but I wasn't alone.

My heart. This couldn't be happening.

Nina stood in the middle of the room with tears in her eyes.

Blood rushed to my head. "Nina? Nina...baby, what just happened? What do you think you just saw?"

She just continued to stand in front of me but said nothing as she licked the tears that were falling and held her eyes closed. She looked like she was about to hyper-ventilate.

God help me. This was so bad.

I tried to compose myself but was panicking inside. "That girl you saw...she drove me home from a bar. I had gone there because I was so sad over you. You weren't an-swering my calls. I had too much to drink. She dropped me off and came back here when I left my phone in her car. Nothing happened, Nina. Nothing happened!"

She wasn't saying anything. My heart was breaking. She didn't believe me.

Fuck, I wouldn't have believed me either.

"I didn't sleep with her. I didn't even kiss her. Nina, I swear on my father's grave!"

She looked up at me.

I walked toward her, but she backed away. She was still speechless.

"Did she say anything to you?" I asked.

Nina nodded slowly with angry eyes. She let out a deep breath. "As a matter of fact, she did." She spoke through her tears. "She asked me if I was Nina."

I shook my head. "What?"

"And when I told her I was...she thanked me for abandoning my boyfriend long enough for her to fuck the shit of him."

No.

This couldn't be happening.

I was stunned and then shook my head vigorously. "No. *No!* Nina...nothing happened. I fell asleep. She came on to me. She...She tri—"

"Did you at least wear a condom?" she spewed at the top of her lungs, her face red and her lips twitching.

I became like a raging madman as I screamed again through clenched teeth, shaking my fists in the air. "Nothing...fucking...happened!"

She screamed back at me. "She was putting on her bra when I walked in. You expect me to believe that? What kind of fool do you think I am?"

One who loved me enough to believe in me.

Just then, Ryan emerged from the hallway. I wasn't sure if he had been there the whole time or if he had arrived with Nina.

"Come on, Nina. Let's get out of here," he said, pushing her toward the door.

My voice was hoarse from screaming. "She's not going anywhere."

"The hell she isn't," he said glaring at me. "Haven't you done enough damage in her life? Just let her go, Jake." He pushed her toward the door as she continued to wipe her eyes. "Just fucking let her go."

That unwanted voice in my head, the one that had been telling me all along to do just that because she was too good for me suddenly emerged in Ryan's corner. If she didn't believe me about Lexie then it might as well have been true. I would never be able to prove otherwise.

Ryan had her by the arm and led her out to the hallway. She looked back at me one last time with sadness in her eyes that shot through my heart like a dagger. Feeling her pain radiating through me along with my own, I was frozen, helpless and broken. That voice had won out. I let her go without a fight then she disappeared from sight. I wasn't sure if I would ever see her again. The girl who had brought me so much joy, who had given me a reason to live, who penetrated my soul...was gone. It was the worst moment of my life.

Just when I thought things couldn't get any worse, I looked down and noticed that I had missed a voicemail from Nina. She must have called earlier when my phone was in Lexie's car. My chest tightened as I played it.

> *"Hey, it's me. I know I have been distant this past week. I needed some time apart from you to understand what that really felt like...to see if living without you was even an option for me. And you know what? It's not, Jake. It's really not. I know that I need to sacrifice some things,*

namely my time with you, if we're going to make this work. As you told me once, sometimes you have to withstand a little pain in life to experience a pleasure you otherwise wouldn't have known existed. You're my only pleasure, and I am telling you that you're worth all the pain and sacrifice in the world. Distance makes the heart grow fonder, right? I need to see you tonight. There is a lot more I need to say. I am heading over there now. I hope you're up. I'm sorry if I worried you. I love you so much."

TWENTY-EIGHT

Eighty-five: the number of times I played that voicemail. Thirty: the number of days that passed before I would see Nina's face again.

One: the number of major mistakes I would almost make after losing it when I finally saw her.

I spent the weeks after Nina left, trying to convince myself that it was for the best even though I was miserable. Not one night went by when I didn't agonize over whether to go to her apartment and plead with her. I would always decide against it because I couldn't handle causing her any more pain. If she didn't believe me that night, she wasn't going to believe me now. The way she looked at me when she walked away would forever be etched in my brain. It was a look of utter sorrow and disappointment. The memory haunted me. Even though I didn't do anything wrong besides getting inebriated, I punished myself by sketching that look on her face repeatedly, so that I never forgot the bad decision that ruined me.

Ryan, Tarah and I didn't talk at all. We avoided each other like the plague and I had started looking for another apartment.

Ironically, in a moment of clarity, Ivy had agreed to cooperate with the divorce and allowed me to continue as her conservator. It was the only thing going my way, but I wasn't sure it mattered anymore now that I had lost the love of my life.

Aside from the paperwork, nothing had changed with Ivy. I was still going to Boston every weekend and actually spent more time at the home, even when she was at her worst. It helped get my mind off of Nina and to reassure Ivy that the pending divorce wouldn't change my being there for her. I had all the time in the world now that I had nothing to rush back to in New York.

I didn't care one way or the other about the divorce anymore. My family convinced me to go through with it, though, since there was now a post-marriage plan in place.

Back in Brooklyn one night, there was a knock at the door, and I opened it without checking the peephole.

Something hit me in the face and nearly broke my nose.

"What the fuck!?"

My hands covered my face, and I was about to punch the lights out of the person until I looked down at the weapon: a bag. It had a cheesy picture of a boy band on it. The assailant was a petite girl with no hair. The realization of who this was set in.

"Jerk!" she yelled.

I dabbed my nose again checking for blood. "Skylar?"

"That's what you get for hurting my friend, ass nuts," she said, brushing past me into the apartment.

Sarcastically, I said, "It's nice to meet you too, finally. Come in."

She dumped her bag and plopped down on the couch. She looked pale and weak. Fuck...this girl shouldn't be here.

"Do you have any water?" she asked.

"Yeah...sure." I rushed to the kitchen to pour her a glass and tapped my nose, which was tingling as I looked over at her. She clearly wasn't feeling well. It amazed me that she would come all the way over here, sick and all, to stand up for her friend.

I handed her the water, and she took it, drinking it down.

I sat on the opposite side of the couch. "How are you feeling?"

"I feel like I look," she said abruptly.

"How did you get here?"

"I took a cab."

"Did you leave the hospital?"

She leaned back and kicked her feet up on the couch. "Look, I'm not here for small talk."

"Okay."

"Did you or did you not screw that tramp?"

I looked her keenly in the eye. "I swear to you that I didn't. I swear. I know that Nina doesn't believe me because of what she thinks she saw."

She stared into my eyes then said, "I kind of figured that."

"Figured what?"

"That maybe you didn't."

"Why's that?"

"Because you would have to be an idiot to cheat on Nina. She has a heart like Mother Theresa and a body like Barbie. Well, maybe more like Badonkadonk Skipper. Anyway, she's hot. She's everything."

Ain't that the truth.

"You believe me?"

"To be honest, I wasn't sure until I looked into your eyes just now. I have this intuition, and I think you're telling the truth."

Relieved, I let out a deep breath. "Thank you. Thank you, Skylar."

She started coughing, and I immediately got up to get her more water before placing it on the coffee table and sitting back down.

"Anyway, she's miserable. She is depressing the shit out of me and that's pretty hard to do to someone who already has cancer."

I chuckled even though I probably shouldn't have. "What do you think I should do? Tell me. I'll do anything."

Was I really asking a 15-year-old for advice? Desperate times call for desperate measures. This girl did seem wise beyond her years, though.

"You need to grow some balls, man. Stand up for yourself until she sees nothing but the truth in your eyes. Take back what's yours! It might take a hundred tries, but you can't just give up."

Shaking my head in agreement I was silent until it clicked. "Fight for her..."

She sat up and smacked my arm. "You're a genius, Tommy Lee."

Skylar stayed for about a half hour. She went on and on about some guy named Mitch and I just listened. It was the least I could do because the inspiration she just gave me was priceless.

I insisted on giving her money for the cab ride home. Before she walked out the door, she turned to me and said, "Life is short, Jake. You're going to regret it for the rest of your life if you let her go."

She was right.

"Skylar, I can't thank you enough for believing in me."

"Oh, wait...before I forget." She took out her phone and put it on camera mode. "Stand up straight and push your muscles out."

"What?"

"Just do it. Roll up your sleeves, so I can see your tattoos...and smile."

I did what she asked, and she snapped a photo.

She winked. "Eye candy for the road."

I shook my head in amusement as she walked away. She was a courageous soul. Did I know an angel on Earth when I saw one? I was pretty sure I wouldn't know one if it punched me in the face.

Skylar's visit had given me the courage I needed. The fact that even one person close to Nina had my back meant the world.

The following day marked exactly a month since Nina walked out of my life. I decided to take that Tuesday afternoon off to go to her apartment and try to talk to her. I hadn't known what I was going to say but wanted her to look into my eyes and see that I was telling the truth.

It was a windy spring day as I walked from the subway station to her neighborhood in Park Slope. My stomach was churning, and my heart was beating rapidly as I recited what I wanted to say to her. I hadn't smoked in months, but today, I really felt like I needed a cigarette. People walking by looked at me strangely because I was talking to myself and gesturing with my hands.

As I approached the brownstone where she lived, my heart sank. I immediately hid behind a large tree.

Nina was walking toward her steps, and she wasn't alone. Some guy with brown hair and glasses had his arm around her. I couldn't exactly make out his face, but what I did know was that he was wearing a Mister Rogers button down sweater and that I wanted to knock him out.

They sat down together on the stoop, and he took the sweater off, placing it on her shoulders. She bent her head back in laughter at something he said, and my chest constricted. It was like heaven for a split second seeing the joy on her face. She had my heart for Christ's sake. How could it not feel good to see your heart happy? On the other hand, it was pure hell because it wasn't me who put it there; it was all because of another man. I had never been more envious of another human being in my entire life.

Watching their every move, I stood frozen behind the tree. She looked so beautiful in a yellow dress that brought out her golden hair that was shining in the sunlight. I wanted so badly to run my fingers through it, to smell her, to hold her. Seeing her made me realize just how badly I had missed her.

He touched her knee, and my fists tightened in response. My heart was beating like crazy and I was sweating profusely.

Fuck, this was killing me.

He seemed to be telling her a story, waving his hands around, and every time she laughed, it felt like I was losing her a little bit more. I just stood there like a stalker, taking it all in. After several torturous minutes, they both stood up. Her back was facing me and my body began to shake when he leaned in to kiss her. I think I may have finally understood what Nina felt like when she was hyperventilating because I couldn't seem to catch my breath.

I was really losing her.

I was numb. It shouldn't have surprised me that someone came along to scoop her up so soon. She was a catch, and I was the fool who caught her and let her go. She loved me, and I managed to fuck it all up.

Mister Rogers hugged her goodbye and she was alone for a moment, watching him leave. Everything inside me wanted to run to her in that moment, but my body wouldn't move. Then, she turned around, walked up the stairs and disappeared from sight.

All of the confidence that had built up in me earlier was depleted by what I had just witnessed. Skylar had said Nina was depressed and sad over me. The Nina I just saw seemed...happier without me. I wasn't about to take that away. No fucking way. I loved her too much.

I wanted to numb the pain and almost went to a bar on the way home to drink myself into oblivion but then remembered that was how I got myself into this mess in the first place. Instead, I vowed never to drink again, so angry that alcohol destroyed my life.

Instead, I went straight home. Depressed could not even begin to describe my feelings.

Devastated.

The house phone rang the next afternoon. I normally wouldn't have picked it up, but if there was a chance it was Nina, I wanted to hear her voice, even though I had vowed to stay away.

"Hello?"

"Is Nina there?"

It was a male and my body immediately went into attack mode.

"Who is this?"

"Spencer."

"Spencer..."

"Yes. Is she there?"

Spencer: Nina's prick ex-boyfriend.

My hands formed into fists and I tried my best to fake a cordial voice. "What's this in regards to?"

"I'm her...old friend. I'm visiting a client in Brooklyn today and was hoping to stop by and catch up with her. I don't have her new cell. I know she moved in with Ryan Haggerty. I had this number for him. This is his home phone, right?"

"Yeah. You have the right place."

"So, is she there?"

"Actually...you just missed her. She walked down to the corner store and should be coming home in a few minutes." I lied. "You're welcome to come by and wait, man. It's 1185 Lincoln."

"Okay, I'll do that. Thanks."

This dude picked the wrong day to come into town.

Fifteen minutes later, he rang the front door and I buzzed him in. When he knocked on the apartment door, I opened it with a grin the size of Texas. I must have looked like I had just swallowed a container of happy pills. "Spencer!" I said loudly, patting him so hard on the back you would have thought he was choking on something. "Come on in."

He was about the same height as me, wearing a gray suit and looked liked a typical yuppie. He was looking me up and down, clearly judging me. It made me sick that this guy had been with Nina. I gritted my teeth and cringed at the thought.

"Who are you?" he asked.

"I'm Jake. We spoke on the phone."

"You live here...with Nina?"

"Yup. Make yourself comfortable."

He walked over to the couch and sat down hesitantly. "You said she would be back in a few minutes?"

"Something like that..." I walked over to the kitchen, grabbed a banana then sat down across from him.

"So..." he said, smacking his hands together, looking uncomfortable.

Good. I was making him nervous.

I mocked him. "So..." Peeling back the banana, I took a huge bite and spoke with my mouth full. "Nina's told me a lot about you."

He looked shocked. "She has?"

"You still getting off on calling people down?"

"I am not following you."

"You know, making people feel like shit to make yourself feel better...to make up for the fact that you have a small dick."

He stood up. "What the fuck..."

"Don't worry. Nina forgives you. See, after I got inside of her, she realized it wasn't your fault at all that you never made her come. I mean, you can only do so much with what you have. The poor thing had nothing to compare it to." I was laughing, shaking my head and said, "She thought that was normal!"

He stood up and pointed his finger at me. "You're out of line."

"You know what's out of line? Cheating on a perfect

angel of a woman who gave you her trust and her fucking virginity. Did you feel like more of a man? Because you look like a big pussy to me. You know, sticking it in more than one woman at a time won't make it grow, Spence."

He walked toward the door and turned around before leaving. "I don't know who the fuck you think you are, but if Nina's been with trash like you, she deserves every bit of pain I ever caused her."

As he escaped, practically running down the hall, I yelled, "Leaving so soon? I was just about to put on a pot of arsenic!"

The front door slammed.

Yeah...I was losing it. But damn, that felt good.

A week and another trip to Boston later, I was still a mess.

One night after work, on my way in the front door, Desiree came out of the restaurant, wearing a black mini dress and stilettos. She looked more like a go-go dancer than a waitress.

"Hey, Jake."

"Hey," I said without making eye contact and continued to walk past her.

Her heels scraped the pavement. "Wait up."

I turned around. "What?" Still depressed and angry, I was being short with her.

I hadn't actually run into Desiree since she accosted Nina in the bathroom on our birthday. That turned out to be the best night of my life. Even now, a week after seeing Nina with another man, my love for her was still as strong as ever. Being apart wasn't going to mean falling out of love with her. It would be about learning to live without her, despite loving her more than life.

Desiree interrupted my internal dialog. "I wanted to apologize for what I said to Nina in the bathroom that night. It was uncalled for. I was just kind of bitter because things didn't work out between you and me, but I never meant to cause such a scene."

"Yeah, whatever. It's old news." I put the key into the front door.

"Wait."

I turned around again. "What?"

"How are things…with Nina?"

It hurt just hearing her name. I gave the only honest answer. "It's over."

She looked apologetic, but I couldn't tell if it was genuine. "I'm sorry. Was it because of what I said to her?"

"No."

"Well, I *am* sorry. I mean that. You're a good guy. And you were always up front with me; you never promised me anything. We were having fun and I had no right to be pissed at you or jealous of her."

"It's okay, Des."

"What are you doing right now?"

"I was going to go upstairs and try to eat something," I said.

"You seem down. Why don't you come back inside to the restaurant? I'll have the chef whip you up your favorite things."

I knew if I went upstairs, images of Nina and that guy kissing would just be replaying in my head and the thought of that made me nauseous. Even though a part of me wanted to be alone to wallow in my pain, it made sense to try to get my mind off it.

I sighed and followed her in the door. "Alright. Thanks."

She sat me down at a table in the corner and went into the kitchen, returning with a huge tray of my favorite Greek foods. She sat across from me as I ate. Even though I didn't have much of an appetite, I devoured about half of each plate.

With her long black hair and big brown eyes, Desiree really was a beautiful girl, just not equally on the inside. We had definitely been compatible in bed, but that was where it ended. Even still, with her, the sex was all about the end result. You couldn't even compare it to what I experienced with Nina.

Not only was Nina physically the most beautiful woman in the world to me, but loving her with all my heart and soul made sex with her all-consuming, something I never wanted to end. My food started to come up on me as I imagined her having sex with the guy in glasses. It hurt so badly that I literally shook my head to erase the image from my mind.

"How about we take dessert upstairs?" Desiree asked.

I let out a deep breath. I should have read between the lines but was so terrified of being alone, so I went with it. "Yeah...sure. Why not?"

Once upstairs, it started out innocently enough at first. We made some coffee, and Desiree set the plates out on the counter. On my suggestion, we brought everything back to my room because I hadn't wanted Ryan and Tarah to walk in and see her with me. We sat on my bed eating the cinnamon and honey fritters in silence. Not a moment went by when I wasn't thinking about Nina. At one point, my throat closed up, and I put the pastry aside.

"Jake, what's going on with you?" she asked.

I forged a fake smile. "I don't think you really want to know."

"Why would you say that?"

"Because it has to do with Nina."

"What about her?"

Was I really about to go into this with her?

"I told you we broke up. Well, last week, I saw her with another guy. It's made me a little crazy."

Understatement of the year.

Opening up to Desiree, of all people, about Nina made no sense, but it hurt so damn much, I needed to get it off my chest.

"I don't know what happened between you two, but she's a fool for letting you go."

I didn't have the energy to rehash everything. So, I just said, "Thanks."

Then, Desiree stopped talking; she never really was one for words anyway. She came around behind me and started to massage my shoulders. I closed my eyes and just focused on the feeling, trying to relax and meditate away the pain.

I wasn't stupid. I knew why she wanted to come up here, and a part of me wanted to let it happen, anything to numb the longing and sadness.

She lifted off my shirt and began to rub her hands harder into my back as I kept my eyes closed. As she continued to massage me, my emotions transformed from sadness to anger over the fact that Nina left me over a lie. The reason for my pain was so senseless. The angrier I got, the more I wanted to erase my thoughts. So, when Desiree took off her shirt pressing her breasts up against my back as she rubbed me, I did nothing to stop her.

Nothing mattered anymore.

Rage continued to build inside me. Desiree stopped massaging and climbed on top of me, wrapping her legs around my waist. I closed my eyes and lowered my mouth, flicking my tongue over her breast. It was mechanical at best, as I continued to obsess over Nina. I sucked on her hard, frustrated at my inability to become lost in Desiree.

She licked my lips, pushing my mouth open with her tongue. We were kissing, and suddenly, anger turned to guilt, because this felt more intimate and despite all that had happened, my body still thought it belonged to Nina. Fighting that feeling, I kissed her harder, moving my tongue roughly against hers. I nearly took her mouth off.

Then, she tugged at my lip ring with her teeth, what Nina used to love to do. I pulled back, panting. It wasn't working. This wasn't doing anything to erase the pain. It was making it worse.

I needed to either tell her to leave or get this over with. An image of Nina smiling at her new boyfriend flashed in my head. Guilt turned to anger again. Desiree was oblivious to the internal battle I was fighting.

She took off her panties and began grinding over my jeans. I was somewhat hard, half-mast at best, the mediocre result of my mind and body being out of synch.

"I can't wait to feel you inside of me again," she said. "Fuck me...now."

Her eyes were closed as she moved over me. I looked up at her face. She was in ecstasy; I was in despair.

Fuck it.

I'd close my eyes, give her what she wanted, and maybe being inside of another woman would help me get these thoughts out of my head.

I moved her off of me and stood up, opening the bedside table for a condom. My stomach was upset, and my hand was shaky as I ripped one off of the strip and it fell to the ground.

What was I doing?

When I bent over to pick up the condom, I noticed a piece of metal glistening on my rug.

My hand shook even more as I picked it up.

It was Nina's charm bracelet.

I froze with it in my palm and sat down on the edge of the bed, staring at it, like it were a live piece of her. I moved my fingers over the charms, as an immense sadness came over me, surpassing all the other emotions. Over the guilt, over the anger...sadness had won out. It was all that was left.

Desiree was breathing heavily and looked frustrated when I glanced over at her naked body. "Desiree...I can't do this. I am sorry. This was a mistake. I'm just not...ready, I guess."

I don't think I'll ever be ready.

She sighed. "Are you sure?"

I nodded silently my eyes still fixed on the bracelet.

I am so sure.

"Okay, suit yourself," she said putting her shirt back on.

I didn't even look at her when I said, "Thank you for understanding and for the food."

"Anytime, Jake. You know where to find me when you *are* ready. I'll be here for you, unlike someone else."

Desiree put on her clothes and quietly left my room, leaving me alone in the same spot where I stayed for the next half hour. As I rubbed my finger over the charms again, something dawned on me. I specifically remem-bered Nina wearing this the night she walked in and saw Lexie. The charms jingled as she shook her hand in anger at me. It was a miserable memory but an awesome revelation. If this bracelet were in my room now...that meant... Nina had been here since that night.

She had been sleeping in my bed again.

It wasn't over.

I didn't know when she had been here, and it didn't matter. This was what I needed—proof from her—that maybe she still loved me, that there was hope. I knew now without a shadow of a doubt, that Mister Rogers had a fight on his hands.

My mind was racing as I paced the room with the bracelet—hope in the palm of my hand. Suddenly, my earlier rage had turned into vast amounts of invigorating energy...clarity. How could I have been so weak to give up that easily? I came to the conclusion that the ups and downs and guilt I experienced over the past year had broken me down, somehow making me feel undeserving of the happiness she brought to me, undeserving of her innocence. Despite the roller coaster of emotions, the one constant had always been my love for her.

It was getting late. I couldn't go to her tonight, because what I had planned was going to take time. Tomorrow would be a new day, one that wouldn't end until I had tried with everything I had to get her back.

Nights like this, I wished my father were around to give me advice. He'd probably smack me in the head for doubting my worthiness and for not realizing sooner that love was something to fight for.

A brisk wind blew into my window, and as I got up to close it, chills ran down my body when I recognized the melody that was coming from a Jeep parked at the traffic light outside. It was *Crimson and Clover*—my father's favorite song. I looked up at the dark night sky and there was also a full moon.

I decided to keep the window open...let Dad in a little. Closing my eyes, I relished the breeze with the confidence that he had my back tomorrow.

I had fallen asleep and woke up covered in sweat about midnight. My heart was beating fast, and a strange feeling came over me. It wasn't physically painful, but it hurt in a different way. It was just a bad feeling that something was wrong.

I tried to go back to sleep but couldn't shake it. About an hour later, my phone rang. It was Ryan.

Why wasn't he here sleeping and why was he calling me at this hour?

I answered. "What do you want Ryan?"

"Jake?"

"Yeah...who else...what's up?"

"I'm at New York Methodist Hospital. You need to get here as soon as you can. It's Nina."

TWENTY-NINE

Ryan wouldn't tell me much about Nina's condition. He said he had just gotten there himself after her roommate called him and that he didn't know details yet but that she was alive and stable. I let out the longest sigh of relief of my entire life.

Thank God.

He just told me to hurry and then hung up.

My entire body was shaking and I scrambled to find a shirt. As I flew out the door, I didn't even know if I shut it behind me. I just started running and dialed a cab company on my phone in case I couldn't hail one.

Thankfully, a red cab came around the corner a few minutes later and took me to the hospital. Nina's eyes were all I could see as I rested my head back on the seat and prayed for her to be okay. I wouldn't be able to live with myself if anything ever happened to her, especially since there was so much left unsaid.

When we arrived, I threw a fifty-dollar bill at the cabbie and told him to keep the change as I ran across the street and nearly got hit by a departing ambulance. I blew through the front doors of the emergency entrance. The room was spinning with the sounds of intercoms, kids whining and stretchers being wheeled in. Dammit, I just needed to get to her.

Out of breath, I told the woman at the front desk, "I'm looking for Nina Kennedy. She was brought here about an hour ago."

"And you are?"

I couldn't even think straight and hesitated, not sure how to answer. "I'm her...friend...Jake Green."

She lifted her phone and dialed it. "Where did they take Nina Kennedy?" she asked someone on the other end.

My chest pounded in nervous anticipation as panic set in.

She hung up the phone. "She's in a room now on the ninth floor. Go down that hallway and take a right. You'll see the elevators. The nurses will be able to direct you."

I started running before she even finished her sentence and nearly knocked over an old man behind me.

When I got to the floor Nina was on, my heart sank when I noticed Mister Rogers getting out of another elevator.

What the fuck was he doing here?

I was too scared to be pissed. We walked side by side over to where Tarah, Ryan and Daria were standing.

"Where's Nina?"

"A doctor is examining her right now. We were asked to wait out here," Tarah said.

"What happened?"

Ryan looked at Tarah. Tarah looked at Daria. Daria looked at Mister Rogers. Mister Rogers looked at me.

What the hell was he looking at? And why weren't they telling me what was going on?

The look on Ryan's face was especially suspicious.

Daria's voice was shaky as she put her hand on my shoulder. "She was losing blood. We don't know what's happening, but she's been conscious the whole time. She's going to be okay. I am sure of it. The doctor is just examining her."

"I guess we'll know something soon," Ryan said looking over at me.

Something wasn't right. I didn't buy that they knew nothing.

I glared at Mister Rogers. "Who are you?"

"I'm her friend, Roger. Daria called me."

Roger. You have got to be kidding me...

"Friend, huh? That's bullshit. I saw you two last week holding hands and kissing outside of her apartment. You didn't look like friends to me."

He shook his head. "We're just friends, Jake."

"How do you know my name?" I seethed.

"She talks about you all the time. How could I not know who you were?"

"What are you talking about?"

"That's how we bonded actually, over our break ups. I am a friend of Daria's. I am at their house a lot. Nina and I have become close over the past month."

"Let me get this straight. She's been talking about me while she's *kissing* you?"

Daria and Roger looked at each other smiling, when he said, "I don't know what you think you saw...but that was no kiss, maybe a peck on the cheek. Jake...I'd rather kiss *you*...okay? I'm gay."

"I know what I—" I stopped talking realizing what he just confessed. "Did you just say you're gay?"

"Yes."

"Gay..."

"Last time I checked."

My body relaxed. I felt stupid but relieved. *Euphoric.* She hadn't moved on from me. I was so happy I could have kissed him...and he would have loved it.

Roger was gay. It was a beautiful fucking day in the neighborhood.

Now, I just needed Nina to be okay. God, please make everything be okay. The doctor was taking forever. I paced the hallway, stopping at one point to look over at Roger. "I'm sorry for overreacting, man."

"No problem. We're all just here because we care about Nina, and believe me when I say she still cares about you...a lot." My chest tightened when he said it.

She still cared about me.

Ten agonizing minutes later, the door finally opened. My heart was beating out of my chest because I could now see her through the crack of the door. She was sitting up in bed wearing a hospital gown, her hair tied into a messy side ponytail. She looked scared. It was overwhelming, and I almost rushed the room when the doctor said, "Who's Jake?"

Practically leaping forward, I raised my hand and said, "I am."

"Nina would like to see you."

I pushed past him in a split second, my eyes glued to her as I entered the room closing the door behind me.

My angel. She asked for me.

She started crying immediately upon seeing me and then opened her arms, an invitation to hold her. I knocked over the plastic water jug at her bedside in my rush to get to her. She held my head to her chest, and I wrapped my arms around her, grateful that she was okay. But she was upset, so the news couldn't be all good. I was terrified.

"What's going on? Tell me what happened to you," I whispered into her.

She gasped for breath through her tears.

I held her tighter. "Shh...take it easy, baby. It's okay. I'm here now."

"It's not okay, Jake," she said, pulling away from me.

I lifted my head to look at her and sat down at her bedside. "What do you mean?"

She closed her eyes and struggled for the words. "I failed you."

"What? What are you talking about?"

She gave me her hand to hold for support, and a tear fell down her cheek. "Can you ever forgive me?"

"Forgive what? You didn't do anything wrong."

"I stopped believing in you. I believed that horrible bitch over your word, and I threw you away."

"No. You didn't throw anything away, baby." I touched her heart. "Don't you know that you have my heart? It's always right there with you. You never really lost me, not for a second, and you never will."

"I love you so much."

"Nina, look me in the eyes. "I love you too. I will always love you. There isn't anything you could ever do or say to change that."

"Do you remember when you asked me to make you a blind promise? That I wouldn't leave you...before you told me about Ivy?"

"Yeah, of course."

"Well, I'm asking you to do the same for me right now. Because there is something I need to tell you."

"Okay. Yes. I promise you. I won't ever leave you...not for anything."

She cried harder. "I can't."

I wiped her tears with my thumb, holding her beautiful face in my hands. "Baby, please tell me what's going on. You're scaring the shit out of me."

She closed her eyes and let out a long breath. "Ryan was there...the night that you were drunk and that whore was at the apartment. He saw everything. He knew that nothing really happened between you two, but he never told me."

My jaw tightened. "What?"

"He was in his room. When he heard her come to the door, he watched you from the hallway without you knowing. He saw that she came onto you while you were sleeping and that you were telling her to leave."

I looked up at the ceiling in disbelief and then back at Nina. "I told you."

"I know. I am so ashamed. He's lied to me all this time, even seeing how devastated I was. He only told me the truth last night."

I would deal with him later.

"What changed?"

"Here is the part I am afraid to tell you."

I clutched both of her hands together and kissed them softly. "Baby, come on. After all the shit I've put you through? I'm not going anywhere."

"I confided in Ryan about something, and he had no choice but to come clean."

"I'm not following you."

"When I came home from spring break, I got sick. Do you remember that?"

"Yeah."

"And then I disappeared for a while..."

"Yes...how could I forget? You explained that in your voicemail, that you were just weighing the decision of being with me long term because of my responsibilities with Ivy, and I understand."

"No...you don't. It wasn't just about Ivy. That factored into it, but—"

I was sweating. "Just tell me."

"I started feeling sick the last few days of spring break. I was vomiting at my parents' house. I had no appetite."

"Alright..."

"So, I took a pregnancy test." She breathed in and out deeply. "It was positive, Jake."

My body jolted backward in a sharp intake of breath as she said those words. My hands began to shake as it started to dawn on me why she was here.

Why there was blood.

Why everyone was looking at each other suspiciously in the waiting room.

Everyone but me knew that my baby may have died tonight.

"Is the baby..." I couldn't even say it, couldn't even fathom it.

She began to cry harder, squeezed her eyes shut and was barely audible. "I don't know."

"What do you mean?"

"He just did a pelvic exam, and now they're running a blood test and coming in to do an ultrasound. We'll know something soon."

I covered my mouth, talking into my hand. "No."

Once the initial shock faded, I closed my eyes and immediately started praying.

Dear God, please let our baby be okay.

My hand moved gently over her stomach as if it were covered in shards of broken glass. "You've been going through this all alone. Why didn't you tell me?"

"When I first found out, I was so scared. You were going through so much. How could I possibly tell you that you were about to be a father on top of that? So, I put it off. I lied to you that first night back from my parents'. I told you I had my period and that I just wasn't feeling well, but it was really morning sickness. Then, I started to freak out, wondering how I was going to continue school and take care of a baby when you were leaving every weekend to visit Ivy. That's why I woke up in a sweat that night. After that, I knew I had to stay away from you, because I couldn't look into your eyes and keep it from you, but I wasn't ready to tell you, because that would have made it real."

My tone bordered on angry. "Jesus...were you ever going to tell me?"

"Yes...of course. The more days that passed, the more I realized how much I missed you, that I couldn't ever live without you or with the thought of not going through with having our baby. I'm too young, and the timing is wrong, but each day, I became more certain that this was just meant to be. I had a part of you growing inside of me. I knew I loved my baby...our baby. So, I knew it was time to tell you. That's when I left you that voicemail and headed straight for the apartment."

"The night you saw Lexie there," I said under my breath, shaking my head in understanding.

"I was still going to tell you if this hadn't happened. I just didn't know how to approach it since we weren't together anymore. I had been waiting for the three-month mark next week to be sure the pregnancy was definitely going to be viable, before turning your world upside down."

"Tell me what happened last night."

"I came clean to Ryan about the pregnancy. I needed to tell someone. Even though I knew how he felt about you, he really is like a brother to me. I wasn't ready to tell my parents. Of course, he knew the baby was yours. He broke down in guilt and told me the truth about the night I walked in on you. He wasn't going to ever tell me because he wanted you out of my life. He's never thought you were good for me."

I wanted to kill him.

She continued. "I got so upset at him for keeping it from me that I hit him. I truly hated him for what he did. But I was more upset at myself for not believing in you. I cried the entire night. I was so overcome with sadness and felt like I was going to die from it. Then, that song that Jimmy and your Dad loved, *Crimson and Clover*, came on the radio, and I totally lost it. I tried to get some sleep, but all I could think about was how I had kept something so important from you for so long." She was starting to break down again.

"Please don't cry. I love you so much. Come here." I held her in my arms for minutes until the tears stopped, and then she continued the story.

"After Ryan left, I was in bed and started feeling some wetness. When I looked down, there was blood all over my sheets. I was so scared because it felt like I was losing the baby. It was my fault for getting so upset. I—"

"No way. No. Nina...you will *not* blame yourself for this."

"It is my fault."

"If you want to blame someone, blame me. I was the one who never used a condom that day I practically attacked you when I found you in my bed. None of this would have happened if I had been responsible and protected you. To be honest, though, I wouldn't go back and change anything, if this baby turns out to be okay. The only thing I would regret is causing you pain, but a child with you would be a blessing." I buried my face in her neck and breathed in her delicate scent.

There may not be a baby anymore.

I suddenly remembered the strange feeling I got in the middle of the night...about an hour after hearing the same song come on the radio. I knew now that I had somehow sensed on a cellular level that my baby was in trouble.

My baby.

Our child.

A part of me and a part of Nina.

I had only known of its existence for a matter of minutes. Suddenly, there was nothing more important. I had given up my dream of ever becoming a father a long time ago, but secretly, I pined for it. I wanted nothing more than to be able to give a child the same kind of love my father gave me in the short time we had together and to be able do the things we never had a chance to.

I was a father.

Even if God forbid, this baby didn't make it, from this day forward, I will always have been someone's father...an angel in heaven. No one could ever take that away.

Fear and pain built up inside me as the reality set in. This situation did not look good. I tried not to get my hopes up. How it was possible to be elated and devastated at the same time, was beyond me, but that was the only way to describe this fucked up confusion.

The sound of a passing baby crying in the hallway startled me. Nina and I looked at each other. It was obvious that we were thinking the same thing. I could see in her eyes how much she wanted our baby too. It pained me that she had been going through all of this alone. Not anymore. No matter what happens, I was more certain than ever that this was the path laid out for me: a future with Nina and our child...our future children, hopefully lots of them.

Her eyes were closed, and I leaned in to kiss her face. "We're gonna get through this. No matter what happens, we are going to get through this together."

The sound of the door squeaking open caused both of us to sit up suddenly. I grabbed her hand and held onto it like our lives depended on it.

The doctor walked in with a technician who brought in an ultrasound machine. The rolling sound of the wheels seemed unusually loud and alarming, like thunder. I wondered if Nina could tell how scared I was, because I was trying to put on strong face.

"Okay, Nina...we're just going to open up your gown. You're going to feel a cool gel on your stomach. This is going to allow us to take a look and see what's going on." The tube of whatever crap they were putting on her made a loud squirting sound.

As I moved out of the way, Nina reached for the return of my hand, and I squeezed hers tightly as they were setting up the machine and rubbing that stuff on her belly, which was still almost perfectly flat. It was hard to imagine a human growing inside of there. She became fixated on the dragon tattoo on my left arm, something she always seemed to focus in on when she was really nervous. I was grateful for anything that could be of comfort to her right now, because I was nothing but a useless ball of nerves.

My hand began to shake. *Fuck.*

She looked at me and said through tears, "It's okay. It's okay to be scared."

She was comforting *me* now. I wasn't even going to feign strength anymore because I was scared shitless.

345

I mouthed silently, "I love you."

Next, they dimmed the lights, which spooked me. It was like they were about to show a horror movie, except instead of popcorn, the room smelled like antiseptic. The woman turned on a monitor, and they put this nozzle on Nina's stomach, rubbing it around over the gel. After about a minute, there was a really strange sound.

Swoosh.

Swoosh.

Swoosh.

Swoosh.

It was freaking me out. "What is that sound?"

The doctor looked at me with a slight smile.

He was smiling.

"Jake, that's your baby's heartbeat."

He turned the monitor towards us, and I became completely mesmerized by the sight of the grayish silhouette on the screen that looked like an alien with a gigantic head and a tiny body. The doctor pointed to the heart beating, which looked like a tiny pulsating bean. My eyes couldn't move from the monitor because I had never seen anything so beautiful as my child's heart beating, arms and legs moving around in Nina's belly. I was in awe, overcome with emotion, as I cried for the second time in my adult life. This time, they were tears of joy.

The only time I tore my eyes away from that screen was to look at Nina, whose expression of wonder matched my own.

It was unbelievable how life could change in an instant. Suddenly, all of my other priorities took a backseat. Nothing mattered more than that heart beating inside of Nina.

"Is everything okay?" Nina asked.

"I'm afraid we've discovered a possible cause for your complications, although bleeding doesn't normally occur as early as it has in your case. You have a condition called placenta previa. It's not typically discovered until the second trimester, when the first ultrasound is normally performed."

Nina's face was turning white.

I shook my head. "What does that mean?"

"It means that the placenta is covering the cervix. The majority of these cases correct themselves in time. However, if it does not, it becomes very serious and can cause excessive bleeding during delivery, putting the mother and baby at risk. In your case, I'm a little concerned because of the amount of bleeding you've already experienced so early on in conjunction with this condition. I think the best course of action is going to be bed rest until we can see an improvement."

Once again, life as I knew it changed in an instant. The doctor continued talking to Nina about the precautions she would need to take. It felt like my heart was pounding through my head. The conversation was muffled because I couldn't focus on anything but the image of our baby still on the screen, unable to take my eyes off of it. Everything else faded into the distance. When the monitor went to black, I wasn't able to let it go.

"Can I listen to the heartbeat one more time?"

The technician repositioned the instrument, and the swooshing sound returned. It was pure music to my ears. There was no doubt that I would give my own life if it meant this baby would survive. I never understood how people could say stuff like that and honestly mean it...until this very moment. It was instant, unbridled love, along with a helpless fear that shook me to my core, because I had absolutely no control.

I can't lose you.

I closed my eyes and listened to the heartbeat one last time before they took the machine away. I never wanted to forget the sound that would replay in my mind over and over, from this day forward, becoming the soundtrack of my life.

THIRTY

NINA
ONE YEAR LATER

I dreaded Saturday because that was the day he always went to see her. I tried really hard not to feel bitter and always smiled when he left, but some days were harder than others. He was only doing what was right, and he shouldn't have had to feel bad about it. I knew what I was getting into when I made the decision to be with him; she was always going to be part of the deal.

It helped a little that I knew in my heart that he would have much rather stayed home. It was written all over his face and I could feel it in the intensity of the last kiss he'd give me before he'd walk out the door. But it was impossible to love him like crazy and not feel some jealousy over his spending time with his ex-wife. It wasn't like he was visiting a sister. This was someone he had loved and made love to, even if it was a long time ago. She had experienced some of the same things I had with him and that made me uneasy.

At the same time, I felt sorry for her, because I couldn't imagine being in her shoes, having to see Jake week after

349

week, knowing that his heart belonged to someone else. She couldn't have possibly loved him as much as I did, because I could never handle that. Maybe her mind was so far gone sometimes, that it didn't bother her as much as it should have. I had never met her, probably never would... but I did feel for her.

This arrangement was a little easier, now that we lived in Boston. We have been temporarily staying in the guest room at his sister's house until we could find an apartment. Jake was finally able to find a job worth leaving New York for. Being here certainly made Saturdays less painful because it meant I would never have to go twenty-four hours without him again. I knew that when he went to see her, he would be back with me by early evening and in my bed at night.

The ironic thing was, as much as his going to her bothered me...it made me love him even more. It showed me how deeply devoted he was to the people he cared about, and it was proof he would treat me the same. Some of the stories he had told me—what Ivy had said and done to him over the years when she wasn't in her right mind—were horrifying, which made his unwavering dedication even more remarkable.

Lately, the routine was the same every Saturday. He would get up, shower, we'd have breakfast together, and then he would leave for the day to go see her. Today, that pattern was going to be broken, because I wasn't ready to share him.

Jake was sitting up at the edge of our bed, about to get up. His hair was getting longer and was sticking out in all directions. He hadn't shaved in a few days and was sporting a five o'clock shadow. Some might call it messy, but to me, he looked hot as hell, better than ever. I had the perfect view of the tribal tattoo on the side of his torso, the one that always teased me. His skin was more tan than usual from working out in the yard, payment to his sister for letting us live here for the time being. My attraction to him had only grown stronger over time, but lately I had been depressed, stuck inside my own head, self-conscious and had stopped giving him what he needed. Right now, though, I was seeing things very clearly, almost too much so, feeling possessive and wanting him to make love to me more than anything. It felt like my mind was coming out of a fog. It had been a while since I had really showed him how much I wanted him. I was not going to let him leave here with any shred of doubt about that.

"Hey," I nudged his back with my foot.

He turned to me and put his hand on my leg, rubbing it gently. His voice was groggy. "Hey...I thought you were sleeping."

"Don't leave just yet. Stay."

He saw the look on my face, and his eyes bugged out of his head. "Are you sure?"

I pulled the sheets off of myself revealing my fully naked body. He hadn't seen me like that, in the light of day, in months. "Yes. Get over here."

He let out a long unsteady breath, and within seconds, he was on top of me. His skin was warm, and he was fully hard as he covered me with soft kisses from my neck down to my stomach. "I have been dying, baby. I missed this. I missed you. God...I love...your body," he whispered in between breaths, kissing his way back up to my mouth.

I wanted to tell him how badly I missed this too but couldn't speak, having become completely absorbed in him once his lips covered mine. The kiss started out slow, then he nudged my mouth open greedily, and it became desperate as if we were competing with each other to prove who wanted the other more.

He broke away just long enough to say, "I need to be inside of you...right now...please..."

I nodded through our kiss, and he spread my legs open, entering me without further permission. I gasped at the feeling, made more intense by weeks of absence. I had been cruel, undeserving of this reward...of him. It felt better than I ever remembered it.

It had been too damn long.

He moved inside of me fast and hard; there was no option to be gentle after the long torturous wait I had put him through. He groaned deeply from the back of his throat, and it was loud. He bit my shoulder to stifle the sounds of his pleasure, defeating the purpose, because the feel of his teeth biting into me made me moan even louder than he had.

Then, as if on cue, came the cries from across the room.

No.

No.

No.

Not yet.

Jake spoke into my neck and pushed deeper into me in retaliation. "Fuck...not now. I can't stop."

The crying became louder.

"Shit. Jake...I have to get him. He never woke up for his four-am feeding. He's hungry."

"So am I," he said hoarsely in my ear. Still inside of me, his movements slowed as he conceded defeat, eventually pulling out.

"I know...I'm sorry."

I searched for my robe as Jake got up, threw his pants on and walked over to the corner of the room, lifting our son out of the crib. A.J.'s dark hair was sticking up, wild and crazy, just like his daddy's. Jake kissed him on the head. "I love you, you little cockblocker."

I laughed as I sat up against the headboard and grabbed the Boppy pillow, as he handed me the baby and placed him on my breast. A.J. immediately started suckling, and I was glad at least one of my guys was happy for the moment.

He sat next to me, and we both looked down at our son in awe, then up at each other. Jake's unsatisfied desire for me still shown all over his eyes when they met mine. He caressed my other breast gently with the back of his index finger. "You have never looked more beautiful to me as you do right now," he said before laying his head on my shoulder.

I wanted so badly to pick up in the shower where we left off, once A.J had been fed, but Jake was already running late. On top of that, I had asked him to come home early, because we would be leaving for a visit to New York this afternoon. It would be our first time back since A.J was born.

"I need to go," he said.

"I know." I nodded, offering a slight smile, determined not to show my sadness.

He got up from the bed and walked toward the bathroom, turning around and gesturing down to his pants. He was still hard. "I have to take care of this in the shower real quick." He snarled. "I'd rather be taking care of it inside of you."

I smiled. "Rain check?"

He walked back over to the bed and kneeled over me, kissing my forehead. "I am so glad you're feeling better."

"Me too."

His eyes smoldered, and his expression turned serious. "I'm using that rain check tonight. I want you...all to myself. Promise me."

I want you now. I want you to stay. I hate it when you leave me to go see her.

"I promise."

He shook his head, and his eyes looked watery. "I love you so much, Nina."

I knew that my behavior lately had scared him. Really scared him. He thought he was losing me. Hell, I thought I was losing *myself.*

"I love you, too."

With no time for breakfast, he showered and left but not before stopping to kiss A.J. and me goodbye, lingering longer than usual this time.

I looked down at our son, who was now falling asleep on my breast, his mouth moving slowly but no longer drinking. "It's just you and me, Bubs. What do you want to do today?" I bent down to kiss his head as his breathing slowed. "I think you're doing it right now."

Alan James was named after Jake's father and my brother Jimmy. He was born six months ago after a difficult pregnancy that forced me to drop out of nursing school. The majority of it was spent on bed rest, and it ended in a planned c-section, due to the placenta previa, which hadn't ever corrected itself. The recovery from surgery was tough. We had just moved to Boston right before A.J arrived, because Jake had to start his new job. Even though my mother had come to stay with us for the first two weeks, after she left, it was a really tough adjustment. Jake's sister, Allison, has been great and tries to help give me a break when she's not working, but living here, as big as their house is, was not the ideal situation. We really needed our own space, but it's been difficult to find some-thing affordable close to Jake's family, which is what we want. Six months later, we were still living in his sister's house, but it's helped us work towards saving up for our own home.

My parents hadn't even met Jake yet when I had to tell them I was pregnant. They were extremely upset at first, but eventually, they accepted everything. After getting to know him, they have warmed up to him somewhat. My re-lationship with Ryan is still rocky, although he and Jake talked everything out one night but not before Jake decked him in the heat of the moment. Ryan and Tarah have since broken up, and she moved out of the apartment. She and I still talk on the phone but have grown apart somewhat since A.J. was born. Ryan is now living with three brand new roommates.

Basically, my entire life was turned upside down in the course of a year. Looking down at my son, peaceful-ly sleeping in my arms, he was the spitting image of his father. I knew everything ended up the way it was meant to. As difficult as all of these transitions have been, they've helped me grow as a person.

My only real regret was how I've treated Jake over the past couple of months as a result of what my doctor diag-nosed as postpartum depression. Even though I seemed to be coming out of it now, when it was at its worst, I wouldn't even let him touch me. I was convinced my body was ru-ined from the baby, even though he assured me that he had never wanted me more and that I was more beautiful than ever to him.

I had also felt really inadequate as a mother and be-gan worrying that I couldn't properly take care of my son. I would have nightmares about harming him that would keep me up at night. I was left alone a lot during the day and had too much time to think. It felt like I was going crazy. But with a light dose of medication that the doctor says is safe to use while breastfeeding, along with a weekly therapy session, I've felt a lot better lately. Apparently, with my history of anxiety issues and the hormonal changes I was going through, it was the perfect storm.

Jake had really wanted to get married before our son was born, but his divorce wasn't finalized until two months after. Even then, I told him it was too early to get married, so soon after his divorce. He and I fought about it, because he felt that I doubted his love for me or that there might have been something else holding me back because of the way I had been acting. I realize now that my feelings at the time were a direct result of the postpartum depression. Lately, he's backed off completely from the marriage issue. The last fight we had, he vowed never to bring it up again for as long as he lived. I almost wished he would, because now I worry that he's moved past it. And I do want to be his wife...badly. When he walked out that door today, I wished so much that I was.

That ship may have sailed, though. My strong reluctance to make it legal as soon as we were able to, really upset him. During one argument, I had accused him of only wanting to marry me because of the baby. I knew that was a low blow and never really believed that. This was around the same time I stopped letting him touch me, at the height of the depression. One night, he came home late from work. I had just put the baby down to sleep, when he walked in and backed me up against the wall into a passionate kiss. Then, he held up his hand. He had tattooed my name around his ring finger and said with tears in his eyes, "You won't make it permanent...well, I just did." That had killed me inside, but my head still wasn't in a good enough place then to make it right.

Thank God, I was coming out of it now and could see so clearly how lucky I was.

I needed to make it right.

Jake made it home right on time and A.J. and I were waiting at the window.

When he walked in the door, I forced my usual question. "How was she?"

"She was okay today...in a good mood," he said. "She didn't kick me out." He always searched my eyes to make sure he wasn't upsetting me.

"Good."

He hugged me tightly, and I felt his muscles relax in my arms. "Still feeling okay, baby?"

"Yeah...I am." I smiled. "Really."

"That makes me so happy." He kissed me, moaning under his breath. "Let's hit the road. I can't get you in that hotel room tonight fast enough."

"You better pray he sleeps then."

"I'll be spending the entire four hour drive praying for that, believe me."

Since it was a Saturday, there was no rush hour traffic, and we made it to New York in under four hours. Jake held my hand the entire car ride, sneaking side glances more than usual, apparently waiting for the ball to drop, for my mood to change. It amazed me how his mood often depended on mine. If I was happy, so was he. It was just another testament to how strongly he loved me. At one point, he smiled and said, "Please tell me my baby is back."

Looking down at his hand squeezing mine reminded me of our plane ride home from Chicago over a year ago. It was hard to believe how much had changed between then and now. One thing that was exactly the same though, was how it felt when he touched me. It gave me the same goosebumps right now, as it did then. I was really looking forward to our long-awaited "reunion" later tonight.

Before we could get to that hotel room in the city, we had a very important stop to make just over the George Washington Bridge in Jersey; it was the main reason for our New York trip.

I couldn't believe how beautiful the strapless white dress was, as I pulled it up...absolutely breathtaking.

It wasn't so much the dress but the person inside of it.

"Skylar...you look so beautiful."

"Thanks, Sissy."

I loved her nickname for me. She deemed me her honorary sister, since neither of us had one. We promised to fill that role for each other during all of the big moments in our lives. She was too sick to come to Boston when A.J. was born but was feeling a lot better now that her treatments were over for the time being. It once dawned on me that cancer had taken away my brother, but in a strange way, it had given me a sister. If she hadn't been in the hospital that day, I would have never met the person who's inspired me more than anyone ever had.

So, as her big sister, I was here to perform my sisterly duties.

"Grab the duct tape. You're gonna bind my boobies together," she said.

"What? Why would you want to do that?"

"Instant cleavage. Come on...it's over there."

I pulled a long piece of tape out as she held her medium sized breasts together. "I can't believe I am doing this," I said as she twirled around.

"Well, not all of us are lucky enough to be as boobiferous as you. Although, I have to say, that situation is getting a little out of control."

"It's because I'm breastfeeding A.J."

"A.J. and a small third world country, apparently."

"Shut up." I laughed. "Jake likes them."

"Well, if he ever goes missing, I'll make sure to send the authorities straight to your boobie trap."

We were both cracking up now. She always put me in the best mood with her sense of humor. I lifted the white dress back up over her new cleavage as she looked in the full-length mirror.

"Much better," she said. "Can you grab my wig? It's on the top shelf of the closet."

Even though her hair was starting to grow back, it was still very short, so she opted to wear the long auburn wig I had gotten her. When I placed it on her head as we looked in the mirror, her expression brightened.

I was smiling so wide, my mouth hurt. She looked like a supermodel. "Mitch is going to die."

My phone vibrated, and then I heard *Love in an Elevator* by Aerosmith, which Jake programmed in as the ringtone for his calls. Classic Jake. I picked up. "Hey, babe...yeah, she's just about ready. You guys can come over in like five minutes, okay?"

Jake had A.J. with him across the street at Mitch's house. They were hanging out there while I helped Skylar get ready. Mitch and she were still best friends, but Skylar had it bad for him. They hadn't crossed that line yet, and I was hoping things wouldn't get out of control tonight, because she was still too young. But I knew how strong her feelings for him were, so we had a talk about being careful in the event that something were to happen.

Mitch had asked her to accompany him to his junior prom several months ago when she was still sick in the hospital. For a while, we weren't sure if she was going to be able to go. He told her if she couldn't go with him, he wasn't going either. Thank goodness, she is feeling better and was able to make it, because this was one of her dreams come true.

We heard the doorbell ring and let Skylar's mother answer it while I touched up her makeup. From the top of the staircase, I could see that Mitch was standing there next to Jake, who had A.J. on his chest in the Baby Bjorn.

Mitch looked extremely handsome in a black suit, his unruly brown hair sculpted to perfection. He had matured a lot since the pictures I had seen of him when I first met Skylar and now had a decent amount of chin hair. He was turning into a man.

When Skylar walked down the stairs, the look on Mitch's face showed a love that had been bottled up, finally set free. If there was any doubt about his true feelings for her, it was wiped away in that moment when I looked at his bright blue eyes upon seeing her.

"Skylar...I..." He was speechless.

In typical Skylar fashion, she broke the ice. "Yeah, yeah...you look hot, too. Let's get out of here."

After stopping to take pictures, Mitch and Skylar walked toward the waiting white Hummer limousine that would be headed to pick some of their friends.

Jake stopped Mitch before he got in. "Hey, *Bitch*. Don't forget what I said."

Mitch looked back at Jake and smiled. "Alright, man."

I wondered what that was all about, as I walked over to the other side of the limo to give Skylar a final hug good-bye.

"Thank you, Sissy," she said and I couldn't help letting the teardrop that formed in my eye loose.

"I love you," I said, now fully engulfed in tears.

Jake, A.J. and I stood in the middle of the empty suburban street as the sun was starting to set, watching the limo until it was completely out of sight.

I turned to Jake. "What did you say to Mitch anyway?"

"I told him not to waste time with bullshit...to tell her exactly how he feels. Did you know that dude started to tear up when he was talking to me about how he feared she wouldn't even be alive when his prom came around, let alone be able to go with him? He has some deep-rooted feelings for her, and it's just stupid to hold them in, you know?"

"Wow."

He looked at me. "I know how scary it can be to love someone that strongly, but you can't live in fear."

I loved him so much.

Ask me to marry you now. I swear, I'll say yes.

"And I also gave him some condoms," Jake said.

"You did what?"

"Come on, don't be naïve. It might not happen, but he damn well better cover it up if it does."

"I suppose you're right, especially with the way he was looking at her. I had a talk with her too." I kissed A.J. on the head as he sat quietly in Jake's arms in the carrier and said in a baby voice, "We know all about the surprises that unprotected sex can bring."

"Speaking of unprotected sex...I plan to have a lot of it tonight," he whispered in my ear.

I couldn't wait to get to our room either. "Let's get going then."

THIRTY-ONE

When we arrived at our hotel in the city, Jake had surprised me with a two-bedroom suite, so that we could have some privacy when the baby was asleep. It must have cost him a fortune. The front desk clerk handed us two key cards. "This one is for you, and you can give this one to your wife," she said.

Jake stared right through me when he took them and corrected her. "My *girlfriend*. Thanks."

Ouch.

We hadn't said anything to each other on our way up to the room. Normally, whenever we were in an elevator, Jake would start cracking jokes about our first experience together in one. But tonight, he didn't say a word. Something was upsetting him.

The suite was small but nice, decorated in cozy warm colors. It had a smaller bedroom off of the main room and a kitchenette. The hotel had set up a crib in the second bedroom for A.J.

I had to feed him before putting him down, so I warmed a small jar of pureed carrots in the microwave.

"Let me do that," Jake said curtly, grabbing the carrots. "Go take a shower."

He seemed tense.

"Okay."

As the water beat down on me, I kept thinking about how his mood seemed to have dampened compared to earlier in the day and how the word "girlfriend" had rolled off of his tongue with disdain down in the lobby. I hoped that tonight I could undo some of the damage my actions had caused these past couple of months.

When I exited the bathroom, the steam poured into the bedroom as I held the small towel tightly over my chest, barely able to wrap it around me. My breasts were full, needing to be emptied since A.J. was overdue for his nighttime feeding.

Jake had finished giving him the carrots and had laid a now sleeping A.J. back down in the car seat carrier, so I'd have to wake him up at some point to nurse before putting him in the crib.

Jake sat on the edge of the bed watching me as I struggled to hold the small white hotel towel closed while I walked over to the overnight bag to grab my pajamas. I could feel him following my every move. I started making my way over to the bathroom to change. As I was entering the doorway, he came up from behind and put his hand on my arm, stopping me.

His voice was gruff. "Where are you going?"

I leaned my back against the sink. "I was going to change in here."

"Away from me? Why don't you want me looking at you anymore? You never used to hide from me like that."

I swallowed nervously, not knowing how to answer. I wasn't intentionally trying to hurt him. "I...guess it's just a habit."

That wasn't an answer, and I knew it. There was no good excuse. I had just become used to hiding myself from him lately because I was still self-conscious about my body. He thought it was more than that. I looked into his eyes and saw that the fear I had instilled in him was very much alive and well. One day of my acting normal, telling him things were getting better—even if I meant it—could not suddenly undo weeks of denying him, shutting him away, not even letting him touch me. For the first time, I really saw how deeply I had fucked him up...fucked *us* up.

"It wasn't a conscious thing, Jake. I didn't mean to hurt you."

He lowered his head onto my breasts and let out a long deep breath through the towel over my skin, holding me against the sink. "Well, I didn't mean to let it show... how badly you hurt me. I'm sorry. It's just that you hid yourself from me just now and I thought...that meant...it was back again."

"You have every right to be angry."

He didn't respond.

He wouldn't look at me. His head was still buried in my chest. His breathing was rapid and my legs began to quiver because I wanted him badly. "I want you," I said. "If you're mad...take it out on me...make love to me."

He spoke against my skin. "I don't know if you can handle me...the way I'm feeling right now."

I tore the towel from in between us, throwing it on the ground. That triggered a visceral reaction in him, and he began to suck on my neck hard as he pulled my hair back roughly. My full breasts tingled, a reminder that I needed to wake A.J., but I couldn't move from this spot. My nipples hardened, and when milk began to trickle out, Jake sucked the excess out of each breast. It was the first time he had ever done that. The sensation of his hot mouth sucking the milk out of me while he moaned, drove me mad. I almost came and could feel liquid pooling between my legs. I couldn't ever remember being that turned on by anything in my life and felt like I couldn't see straight.

His mouth then moved down to my abdomen as he dropped to his knees. He knew I was most self-conscious about my stomach. When he felt me tense up, he kissed it harder, grazing it with his teeth, unwavering in his determination to stake his claim on that part of my body, despite my insecurities.

He looked up at me with both palms on my belly, then gently brushed his finger lower over my c-section scar. "Don't ever hide this from me again. This is where my baby was, where my other babies will come from. It's precious to me, and it's beautiful." He kissed it one last time softly. "You're beautiful."

For the first time, I believed him when he said it.

He stood up, towering over me. His hair was disheveled, and a stray piece fell over his darkened green eyes. His erection was straining through his beige cargo shorts, and he was looking at me like he was about to attack. He then took my bottom lip into his mouth and sucked it hard, slowly releasing it. I was growing impatient with need and tugged at his black *Nine Inch Nails* t-shirt trying to pull it over his head. I jumped when he abruptly moved my hands off of him.

Then, he walked away.

"Go feed your son. I'm going to take a shower."

THIRTY-TWO

JAKE

I turned the lever to make the water colder. I needed to calm the fuck down. I didn't know what came over me out there, but it wasn't good. Even though she was encouraging it, if I had taken another step forward, it would have been like a tornado touching down. I felt incapable of being gentle and knew the end result of the possessive urges flowing through me would have scared the shit out of her.

I had snapped tonight, and it was about more than just her shielding her body from me. It was the fact that from the beginning, I never felt like I deserved her. Aside from the past couple of months, she had always wiped away that doubt with her love and her strong physical need for me. When the postpartum stuff happened, almost out of the blue, she started to push me away, and all of my insecurities moved to the forefront, growing like a cancer I couldn't stop.

Every single day of those two months, I felt like I was losing her more. We were supposed to be happy because we finally had everything we wanted, right? The baby was

healthy. The divorce was final. But that was when everything started to crumble. I wanted the old Nina back, and
these past few days were the first in weeks that I started to
believe she was slowly returning to me.

On the car ride from Jersey to the hotel, I started
thinking about maybe proposing to her again tonight. I
knew she could tell something was off with me from the
way she was looking at me in the hotel elevator. My doubts
had gotten the best of me. I had myself convinced she'd
only say no again and couldn't bear to hear it one more
time. Not to mention, I vowed never to ask her again. So,
I made a decision to hold off, and that put me in a shitty
mood because I wanted nothing more than to hear Nina
say she'd be my wife. I wanted it for A.J., but mostly on a
selfish level, I needed to know that she belonged to me in
every way.

Just when my mind had calmed down a bit from over-
thinking everything, she came out of that shower gripping
her towel closed so tightly you would have thought I was a
grizzly bear. That was when I cracked because it felt like a
major step back, like any minute she was going to be telling me not to touch her again.

That would have killed me.

When I saw how badly she seemed to want me, I knew
I had overreacted. But by that time, my desperation for her
was so strong, I had to just take a step backwards and cool
down. If I gave in to that kind of sexual energy, fueled by
anger and frustration, I knew I would have been too ag-
gressive. Given how vulnerable she was lately, I needed to
get a grip before I scared her away for good.

When I got out of the shower, she was still in the other
room feeding A.J., and I was sitting on the bed, staring at
the closed door, thinking that I wouldn't have blamed her

if she never came back out. I could only imagine what she was thinking now that she had time to ponder my fucked up behavior.

When the door opened about ten minutes later, it had felt like I had been waiting forever. I sat up straighter on the bed as she walked toward me, and without hesitation, she unbuttoned her pajama top throwing it on the ground. She then slipped out of her underwear and threw them behind her. She was now standing before me completely naked. It took all of my willpower not to touch her, but something told me to wait, that she was in the driver's seat.

Her chest was rising, and I could tell she was still uncomfortable with her body being exposed, but she was going with it...for me.

I caressed her milky skin with the back of my hand. "I just got scared, baby. I'm sorry."

"Don't apologize for something I created. I did that to you, Jake. I lost my way because of my crazy hormones, and in the midst of it, I forgot the most important thing: that I belong to you and that nothing is more important than making sure you know you're loved by me. I will never treat you that way again."

"I was being insecure and impatient. You couldn't help it. You were sick. I—"

"I handled it wrong. I ran away from you instead of toward you. I *made* you insecure about us. Your reaction to my covering myself tonight...it didn't upset me; it's proof of how much you love me." She looked away almost hesitant to continue, then said, "You know what? I have insecurities, too. Since, we're being honest...I *hate* that I have to give you up to Ivy on Saturdays. I get jealous. I never tell you that, because you're doing the right thing, and it's hard enough for you. Even though I know you don't love her the same way, it still makes me uneasy because I don't want to share you. I know how desperate my love for you can make me feel sometimes. So, that's how I know that your reaction today was just because of how much you love me."

I couldn't take it anymore. I was bursting at the seams in more ways than one. She was still standing over me when I pulled her naked body toward me. She straddled me as I continued to sit up on the edge of the bed. I had already been hard from just looking at her, but now that she was on top of me, I was about to explode.

My head was down, buried in her golden hair that smelled like the coconut hotel shampoo. I spoke over her skin. "Of all the times I thought I had lost you, nothing has been scarier than the past couple of months. I am still fucking terrified you're gonna tell me any minute not to touch you again."

"That wasn't really me, Jake. Look at me." She put both of her hands on my head and lifted my face to hers. Her eyes were watery. "I am feeling better. This...is me. Coming out of a depression in some ways is like being born again into a better life. If you can make it through the worst, you appreciate everything you hold dear, so much more. It's like the sun after a rainstorm. I can't promise that the darkness won't ever strike again, but I know how to identify it now and learned how to handle it. One thing I am sure of, is that I will never push you away like that again...ever. You and A.J. are my world. I am sorry if I made you suffer along with me."

"Don't you get it, Nina? I can handle suffering with you, baby. Isn't that how we started...my holding your hand through everything? I want to spend the rest of my life doing that. I'd go through hell and back over and over for you. It's losing you I can't bear. When you hide from me, when you tell me not to touch you, it scares me. I'll suffer with you any day, as long as you let me love you."

A tear fell down her cheek, and I ran my tongue over it, licking it away. "Don't cry," I whispered. "It hurts me when you cry. I love you so much."

"I'm not going anywhere. I need you to believe that," she said.

There were no further words necessary. I could feel her heart beating through her chest, and with every ounce of my being, I knew she meant everything she said. In the same way I could always feel her pain, I felt her love for me pouring through her soul at that moment.

I wanted to show her in the way I knew best, how much I loved her, too.

THIRTY-THREE

NINA

Jake kissed away the last of my tears then looked up at me. The hunger in his eyes from earlier had returned. "I don't want to talk anymore," he said.

Good. Neither did I.

Between our getting interrupted this morning, to my longing for him while he visited his ex-wife and then his leaving me in the bathroom tonight...I was overstimulated.

It didn't help that he looked beyond incredible with his chin scruff and tousled grown out hair. I looked down at the contrast between my white skin and his tanned tattooed arms wrapped around my waist. They were three shades darker due to his working out in the sun lately.

And this beautiful man belonged to me.

He lifted my hand to his mouth and kissed it. It was always bittersweet to see my name inked around his finger, a symbol of an unreturned commitment born out of a nasty fight. How could I have turned him down when he had asked me to marry him? The life I had before he came along was empty, consumed by fear of the future and past regrets. *Meaningless.* Being with Jake was always about living in the present. Our lives weren't perfect, but he was perfect...for me.

I was still straddling him when he flipped me over onto the bed so that I was lying on my back. He hovered over me and his smile faded when he realized I had tears in my eyes again.

I was crying because of how much I loved him, plain and simple. Before he said anything, I ran my fingers through his hair and said. "They're happy tears."

"Okay." He smiled. "I want you to relax now, baby. I am going to make you forget all of the pain of the past couple of months. It's just you and me and this moment. I want you to get lost in me. Can you do that?"

I bit my bottom lip in anticipation, as he lowered his head and devoured my mouth with his. I teasingly nipped at his tongue ring, and he groaned playfully.

"Do that again. Bite my tongue like that, but do it harder, pull on the barbell. It fucking turns me on when you bite me," he said.

I kept locking his tongue in with my teeth, and he growled each time I did it. We couldn't get enough of each other, smiling, laughing, teasing. It was heaven.

When he began sucking my nipples, the sensation was overwhelming. We would laugh every time milk would come pouring out, and then he would lick it away. "Mmm... so sweet, just like you are," he said.

He kissed his way down my body and if the need I harbored for him all day was like a controlled burn between my legs, then his hot wet mouth coming down on my clit was the gasoline. The cold metal of his ring sent a shockwave through me. He circled his tongue slowly around my folds while his fingers moved in and out of me. He moaned in ecstasy, enjoying giving me pleasure as much as I loved receiving it. I had my hands on his head, guiding his mouth over me.

"Pull my hair harder," he said, and I complied. "Harder," he repeated.

He was driving me mad.

After a few minutes, he kissed his way back up to my mouth and I pushed his boxers down. "I want you inside of me...now."

He continued kissing me, ignoring my pleas, his slick cock rubbing against my stomach. My need for him was immense. I lowered my hand and started to jerk him off, but he took my hand away. "Uh-uh," he said, smiling over my mouth as we kissed.

He then kneeled above me and stuck his fingers back inside of me, closing his eyes and breathing out slowly. His wet hair was falling over his forehead as he looked down at me and let out a long breath that I felt on my stomach.

"Fuck...you're so wet." With his eyes fixed on me, he kept moving his fingers in and out before withdrawing them and licking each one and I almost came from watching him.

"I can never get enough of how you taste." He licked his lips. "Turn over."

I rolled over onto my knees, expecting him to finally give in. Instead, he continued to finger me. "Jake... please...I want you so badly."

"Believe me. You'll get me." He slowed down the movements of his fingers, and the level of need was getting almost painful.

He took his other hand and moved my head to the side, pulling my hair back to kiss me, groaning into my mouth.

He removed his fingers. I was throbbing as he rubbed my ass gently with both hands. "I used to fantasize about this spectacular ass...the things I would do to it. I never imagined it would belong to me someday." He slapped it once playfully, then squeezed my cheeks together. "You're a dream. Turn back around."

"You're killing me," I said pulling him down onto me and kissing him.

"How do you want me, baby?" he asked.

I knew what he wanted, and if there was any night I wanted to give it to him, it was tonight. "I want to ride you."

He nodded, out of breath, and I could see from the look in his eyes, that he was pleased with my answer. He moved onto his back and held his cock in his hand, stroking it.

I wanted to give him some of his own medicine, so I lightly brushed my opening over his tip. His mouth trembled as he watched my every move and when I abruptly sat down on him, he let out a loud grunt that I was sure would wake the baby. He was now deep inside me and I began to grind my hips over him.

He grabbed my sides. "Shit...you're gonna make me come...slow down." Our eyes locked, and my hair had fallen over my chest. "Move your hair back, I want see your beautiful tits move while you ride me."

After a few minutes, I felt his body start to quake, and I knew he was losing control. "I need to come, baby. Come for me...so I can let go," he said.

He looked into my eyes the moment my muscles tightened around him. He always knew exactly when I was coming. At that moment, his mouth opened to a silent cry as he pushed me down harder over his hot release.

Yeah. He was definitely worth the wait.

THIRTY-FOUR

The next morning, I woke up to two boys with messy dark bed head lying next to me. A.J. was on his Daddy's chest, sucking on Jake's pinky finger.

Jake handed him over to me. "He was hungry, so I gave him some oatmeal. It's not quite cutting it, but I wanted to let you sleep a little more."

A.J immediately latched on. "Ow...easy, buddy."

Jake laughed. "Daddy was a little rough on those last night."

"Mommy likes it rough."

Jake lifted his brow. "Does she, now?"

We smiled at each other, both still sleepy but sated after last night.

Jake kissed my forehead. "What are our plans for today?"

"I told Daria and Tarah I'd meet up with them for coffee before we head back tonight."

"Okay. Why don't you pump me a bottle for him, and I'll take A.J this afternoon, so you can have some alone time with your friends.

"Really? Are you sure?"

"Yeah...but just a couple of hours. There's somewhere I want to take you before we leave the city."

After my alone time, Jake asked me to meet him on 32nd Street because we planned to have dinner at one of the Korean restaurants there.

He hadn't noticed me yet as I was approaching them. He looked so handsome leaning against a brick wall, his disheveled hair under a Red Sox cap. He had A.J. in the carrier on his chest and my heart melted when he kissed our son on the head, not realizing I was watching them.

"Hey, guys."

A.J. started flailing his little arms and feet excitedly at the sight of me.

"Hey, Momma. We missed you," Jake said before kissing me passionately in the middle of the busy sidewalk.

"I missed you guys, too."

After a stop in a department store so that I could nurse A.J. in a dressing room, we enjoyed a delicious dinner of Kimchi Fried Rice and Noodle Soup.

As we exited the restaurant, I turned to Jake. "Where are we going now?"

"You'll see." He flashed me a devious smile, and the way he said it reminded me of our old fear expeditions.

We kept walking until he stopped...right in front of the Empire State Building.

"Jake...what are we doing?" I asked nervously. "I don't want to go up there right now."

"Come on, Nina. I thought you were over that."

"I thought I was too...but...I am just not in the mood."

"Can you do this for me? I want to enjoy the view of the city with my family. It's something I've always wanted to do with you."

I looked into his hopeful eyes and just couldn't say no.

I took a deep breath in. "Alright...okay, let's do it."

He was beaming and led the way through the front doors. We paid for tickets so that we didn't have to wait in the long lines.

I closed my eyes the entire elevator ride up and breathed through it. Even though I was able to get inside one now, it still made me uncomfortable. With everything I had been through in the past year, my old phobias had pretty much dissipated, having taken a back seat to everything else. That didn't mean I was ever going to love elevators or heights or planes. The important thing was that I could now face those things if I needed to.

When we finally got onto the main observation deck, the view was spectacular since it was a clear day. Of course, being up so high still made me uneasy, but when I looked at Jake's expression as he stared out over the city, it was all worth it.

We were on the east side facing Brooklyn. Jake spoke softly to A.J. "See over there...that's where Mommy and Daddy lived when we met. I thank God everyday that He brought her to me."

Then, it hit me: why he had brought me up here. He was going to propose to me.

This was it.

My pulse was going ballistic as I looked over at Jake who was looking straight ahead taking in the view. He would point things out to me, and I would nod along, wondering when he was going to do it and how he was going to transition all of this into a proposal. After about fifteen minutes, he put his arm around me and said, "You ready to head back to the hotel, babe? It's almost time to check out."

I bit my lip and nodded silently, suddenly feeling stupid and realizing that I should have known better. It would take a lot more than one night of normalcy to get him to trust me enough to propose again. Or maybe, he would stick to his word and never ask me for as long as he lived.

Either way, this wasn't going to change the surprise I had in store for him tonight.

We had about an hour before we had to check out of the hotel, and that would give me just enough time to feed the baby and pack up our stuff before we left to go home.

Jake still had A.J. strapped to his chest as he held the hotel elevator open for me.

I closed my eyes and yawned as the elevator began rising, and then it came.

A jolt.

I grabbed onto his shirt. "Jake...what just happened?"

A wide smile spread across his face, and I soon realized his finger was on the stop button. This was an apparent reenactment of our "first time."

"Where's the champagne?" I joked.

"No champagne today, baby."

"What are you doing, Jake?"

"Remember that day? You know, I was starting to fall in love with you, even then. That mellow song I played...I was trying to tell you my feelings, even though I thought I could never have you."

"I loved that song," I whispered, tears starting to form in my eyes.

"You and A.J. are my entire world. The past year and a half with you has given me back every last piece of innocence I lost in the years before and then some. At this point in my life, I would do anything for you. If you told me today, that you couldn't accept my continuing to be there for Ivy, then I would have no choice but to let that part of my life go, no matter how guilty I felt. You love me enough to make sure that I don't ever have to choose, that I don't ever have live with guilt or regret. I know it's not easy for you when I leave you sitting on the couch breastfeeding him to go see my ex-wife. I've always seen the sadness in your eyes. You've dealt with it...for me. There is not one time I walk out the door on those days where my heart doesn't ache with love for you. You are strong enough to know deep down that my looking out for her doesn't change how much I love you. You have given me a life that I could have never imagined...a dream I gave up on years ago, because I never thought it would ever be possible to meet someone who loved me enough to accept everything that came along with me. I wouldn't change one painful thing about my life, if it meant not ending up right here in this stuck elevator with my family."

I closed my eyes for a brief moment, overcome with emotion. When I opened them, I noticed that Jake had slipped something into our son's hand. It was a paper bird. He hadn't made one of those for me since before A.J. was born. This one wasn't black...it was white: a dove.

"I told you I wasn't going to propose to you again. I meant it," he said.

He must have sensed the disappointed look on my face, because he rubbed my cheek and smiled.

"But I didn't say *he* wouldn't do it."

My eyes were welling up.

Oh my God.

"You have something for me, little man?" My heart was pounding as I took the dove that was now crinkled, from A.J.'s tiny fingers and opened it.

See this guy....Jake?
I want you to cut him a break.
Not just cuz he's my dad...
But because he loves you like mad.
He said he was done asking you to be his bride.
Well, Mommy...he lied.
After everything we've been through...
He still really wants to marry you.
Look at him...he's a mess.
Please tell him you'll say yes.

He *was* a mess, a beautiful one, with tears in his eyes, as I pulled him into me, careful not to crush A.J.

"Yes...yes...a million times...yes," I said through my own tears.

He pressed his forehead to mine. "I know you said we should wait. Seeing Skylar and Mitch yesterday reminded me that life is short, and I don't want to wait one second longer to marry the love of my life."

I wiped his eyes. "I wouldn't change anything either, Jake...the good or the bad. What would moments as perfect as this mean with nothing to compare them to? Every bit of pain it took to get here was worth it."

"I didn't have time to get a ring. I actually went looking while you were out with your friends but couldn't find the right one in time. I'll take you shopping in Boston."

Perfect timing.

"No need," I said unable to contain my joy.

"What do you mean...no need?"

I had been hiding my left hand in my sleeve for the past couple of hours. I lifted it to show his name tattooed on my ring finger in the same font as the ink of my name on his own.

His eyes lit up in pure shock. "What the...when did you do that?"

"I cancelled the coffee today. This was something I needed to do, and you gave me the perfect opportunity." I smiled. "It's permanent, you know."

"Yeah." He lifted my hand to his mouth. "So are we, baby. So are we."

"I love you so much," I said.

"And I love you." He kissed me then turned to A.J. who was cooing. "And you, my little wingman...I love you to the moon."

OTHER BOOKS BY
PENELOPE WARD

Moody
The Assignment
The Aristocrat
The Crush
The Anti-Boyfriend
The Day He Came Back
Neighbor Dearest
Just One Year
When August Ends
Love Online
Gentleman Nine
Drunk Dial
Mack Daddy
Stepbrother Dearest
RoomHate
Sins of Sevin
Jake Undone (Jake #1)
My Skylar (Jake #2)
Jake Understood (Jake #3)
Gemini

OTHER BOOKS BY
PENELOPE WARD & VI KEELAND

Well Played
Park Avenue Player

Stuck-Up Suit

Cocky Bastard

Not Pretending Anymore

Happily Letter After

My Favorite Souvenir

Dirty Letters

Hate Notes

Rebel Heir

Rebel Heart

Mister Moneybags

British Bedmate

Playboy Pilot

Acknowledgements

First and foremost, thank you to my loving parents for continuing to support me every day in every way.

To Vi, for EVERYTHING.

To my husband, who puts up with a lot of crap so I can live out this new dream ...thank you for your love and patience.

To Allison, who always believed in me back when all of this was simply about telling stories and to Harpo, my agent in heaven: love you both.

To my editor, Kim York, thank you for your undivided attention chapter by chapter and for your invaluable face-book chats.

To my besties: Angela, Tarah and Sonia...love you all so much!

To all the bloggers who help and support me: you are the reason for my success. I'm afraid to list everyone here because I will undoubtedly forget someone unintention-ally. You know who you are and do not hesitate to contact me if I can return the favor.

To Penelope's Peeps, my Facebook fan group: I adore you!

To Donna Soluri of Soluri Public Relations who or-ganized my book blitz and who always dishes out sound advice: Thank you!

To Elaine of Allusion Book Formatting and Publish-ing – Thank you for being the best proofreader and for-matter a girl could ask for.

To Hetty Rasmussen: for your support and for being my awesome Book Bash assistant!

To my readers: nothing makes me happier than knowing I've provided you with an escape from the daily stresses of life. That same escape was why I started writing. There is no greater joy in this business than to hear from you directly and to know that something I wrote touched you in some way.

To the autism moms (and dads): you rock!

Last but not least, to my daughter and son: Mommy loves you. You are my motivation and inspiration!

ABOUT THE AUTHOR

PENELOPE WARD is a New York Times, USA Today, and #1 Wall Street Journal Bestselling author. With over two-million books sold, she's a 21-time New York Times bestseller. Her novels are published in over a dozen languages and can be found in bookstores around the world. Having grown up in Boston with five older brothers, she spent most of her twenties as a television news anchor, before switching to a more family-friendly career. She is the proud mother of a beautiful 16-year-old girl with autism and a 14-year-old boy. Penelope and her family reside in Rhode Island.

Facebook Private Fan Group
https://www.facebook.com/groups/PenelopesPeeps/_
Facebook: https://www.facebook.com/penelopewardauthor
TikTok: https://www.tiktok.com/@penelopewardofficial
Website: www.penelopewardauthor.com
Twitter: https://twitter.com/PenelopeAuthor
Instagram: https://instagram.com/PenelopeWardAuthor

Printed in the USA
CPSIA information can be obtained
at www.ICGtesting.com
LVHW091830191123
764372LV00002B/197